Who They Was

4th Estate
An imprint of HarperCollins*Publishers*
1 London Bridge Street
London SE1 9GF

www.4thEstate.co.uk

First published in Great Britain in 2020 by 4th Estate

2

A catalogue record for this book is available from the British Library

ISBN 978-0-00-837499-0 (hardback)
ISBN 978-0-00-837500-3 (trade paperback)

This novel is a work of fiction.

Typeset in Bembo Std by Palimpsest Book Production Ltd, Falkirk, Stirlingshire

Printed and bound in Great Britain by CPI Group (UK) Ltd, Croydon CR0 4YY

MIX
Paper from
responsible sources
FSC® C007454

This book is produced from independently certified FSC™ paper to ensure responsible forest management.

For more information visit: www.harpercollins.co.uk/green

Who They Was

Gabriel Krauze

4th ESTATE • London

DON'T WATCH FACE

AND JUMP OUT the whip and I'm hitting the pavement and it's this moment – when you jump out of the car and it's too late to go back – when you know that you're definitely gonna do it, even though the way the adrenaline bursts through your body makes you wish for a second that you weren't here. And now we're creeping up the street, she's too far ahead of us, we got the timing wrong but we can't run to catch up because that will alert her and she'll turn around, so we're creeping fast. The bally is hugging my face tight and I've also pulled my hood over it and I feel the adrenaline explode in the pit of my chest like a dying star and it's like my entire body has turned into the pumping of my heart.

And I'm creeping up fast to get behind her and Gotti is right there beside me and she hasn't heard us, not the way we're moving, low to the ground, black cotton Nike tracksuits on so there's no sound of clothes rustling, Nike trainers silent on the pavement. And for a few heartbeats I notice how everything on the street seems like someone's idea of a peaceful life, sun

1

floating overhead, bulging in the sky's belly, washing the street below in a brightness that breaks over everything; neat rows of perfect houses, polished green bushes lining the pavement, the cool metal smell of morning, and now the woman pushes a gate open and turns off the street and she's walking up a small path to her front door.

And we've fucked up the timing but we can still get her on her doorstep so we start running, still tryna be stealthy but now we really have to be quick before we lose her and we turn through the little gate – she's almost at the door, digging into her handbag for the house key – and we run up the path and then we're right there behind her, I can reach out and touch her hair, I can smell shampoo and softness and then expensive perfume which almost makes me feel sick, and in this moment everything I've ever known falls away, memory, past, future, and then the street, the morning and everything else around us disappears as if I'm forgetting the world and there is only Now, crystal sharp, on the doorstep. And before I can get my arms locked around her neck to put her to sleep, she turns around.

And she screams. She sees me – or just my eyes and a bit of mouth through three holes in the black bally I'm wearing – as if realising a nightmare she didn't know she was in and we know it's all scatty now, fuck it, no chance of this being silent and unnoticed so I grab her anyway, my arm pushing into her throat as I turn her around and hold her tight against my chest and Gotti is trying to pop the Cartier off her wrist but he can't for some reason, he's proper straining and the metal is biting into her wrist and she's screaming just take it just take it and now the pounding in my heart and belly is fully gone because we're actually doing it, nothing else exists in this moment, everything is still and calm inside me and I say stop fucking

2

struggling in her ear but Gotti can't rip the watch off even though it's like she's giving him her wrist and I can see he's like whatdafuck because it's never happened before that he couldn't pop someone's watch off – and this one has diamonds going all round the bezel so we really want it, like it's easily worth ten fifteen bags.

And I think fuck it because she's already screaming, no point tryna put her to sleep now, might as well help Gotti. The front door – solid white with a brass knocker – opens and there's a boy standing there, about seventeen eighteen years old and he just stares at us like frozen and says Mum and I look at him, our eyes meet and in his eyes and also over his shoulder behind him I can see a different life to my own, something better maybe, something without so many sharp edges and broken things. And we're still tryna tear the watch off and suddenly Gotti turns round and bangs the woman's son in the face onetime and the boy drops and Gotti slams the door shut and we're alone with her again. And I clock she's got a big diamond ring on her wedding finger and I try to pull it off but it's not moving, the skin all bunches up and it hurts her and I can't twist it off because she has a wedding band on the same finger in front of the diamond ring, basically blocking it. So I snap her finger back, it folds straight over so the tip touches her wrist in one go and it's strange because I always thought that if you break someone's finger you'll actually feel the bones break, hear it even, but I don't feel anything at all, it's like folding paper, as if the finger was naturally supposed to bend back like that and she's screaming to me take it just take it but I can't, in fact within seconds I can see the break begin to swell up the base of her finger and now I know I'm definitely not getting the ring off. And the door opens again and there's a man standing there in a red sweater and we know it's all fucked now, we have to get away but we're still hoping we can at least cut out with something to show for our efforts and the man grabs his wife around her waist and pulls her towards him, drags her into the doorway while Gotti's like Snoopz come, fuck this, we need to cut blood and he's turning away from the door ready to duss back to the whip which is waiting in the middle of the road and in my head I'm like fuck dat I'm not leaving with nothing. And the man drags his wife into the house and as he does this he's pulling the door shut and I can see their entrance hall is carpeted beige all thick and soft like the kind of carpet that holds the heat of a resting sunbeam so you actually wanna lie down and fall asleep on it and mad quick I reach through the door as it's closing and manage to grab the woman by her wrist and I pull her arm out just as the door is slamming shut and the man slams the front door hard on his wife's arm and I hear her scream. Gotti turns and runs down the path to the gate and I see through the slightly open door that the woman's dropped her handbag so I bend down and grab it quicktime and the door opens fully again and the man has a cricket bat which he swings at me but I'm already ducking down so it misses my head even though I feel the rush of air against my bally as it swipes past. I turn and run with the handbag, down the path, out the gate, but the getaway whip isn't there, it's already moving slow down the road, one of the back doors is wide open and Gotti is shouting for me to get in and the man is running after me waving the cricket bat above his head roaring mad rage – no words just pure noise – and I'm running after the whip, inhaling the morning, glass needles of sunlight piercing through the sky and falling all around me and I'm not sure I'm gonna make it, like I can't get level with the open passenger

4

door, like nah this is so peak, it can't end like this, it can't—
But then I do and I dive in head first onto the backseat and
Gotti grabs onto me and – with my legs still sticking out – the
car bursts forward down the road, Gotti pulls me in, reaches
over me, slams the door shut and now Tyrell is driving us away.

We turn out of the street onto the main road and we're
talking to Tyrell like whatdafuck, man couldn't get the belly
fam, that was a mad ting, and I pull off my balaclava and Gotti
pulls off his bally and it's like coming up for air after diving
into some deep ocean and staying down there for so long that
you hadn't realised you were drowning and Gotti says blood I
don't know whatdafuck happened but I couldn't rip her watch
off, I just couldn't, I kept trying but it wouldn't pop, and Tyrell
says swear down fam? but he says it all flat and distant coz he's
focusing mad hard on getting us out of the area quicktime,
tension creasing his face and turning it ashy yellow, but on a
real he's moving smart; not driving overly fast like it's some bate
getaway, just driving like he's got somewhere he needs to be
that morning. Plus the car looks right; nothing flashy, but at the
same time not too battered or fucked up looking like it's obviously some second-hand ting that's gonna get burned out later.

As he drives back down the high road, past shops and the
type of normal morning life that could be anywhere, a fed car
comes screaming up the road on the other side, blue lights
spinning off onto buildings and windows in pale slices that
disintegrate in the morning brightness and me and Gotti slide
off the backseat and lie down in the footwell because we know
that police car was called for us. We lie there cramped up on
the floor of the car, our legs pressing against each other, making
sure it looks like there's no one on the backseat, heads down
next to dirt and dust and I can see the detail of the rubber foot

mat, which suddenly becomes something significant, its shape, texture, colour, its—

And the fed car flies past us in the opposite direction on its way to the street we left just a minute ago and I'm surprised as well, because you always hear how police response times aren't good enough and all that shit, but this was fast, I mean like the whole move itself couldn't have lasted more than three minutes really, I guess the son or the husband called the feds straight away while we were still clamping up the woman tryna rip her shit off, and true it's about ten in the morning, there's no traffic round here and what we've done is kinda fucking – well, no wonder they came for us so fast. But they never even notice Tyrell, never even look in the direction of our car and we're well down the high road now. We sit back up. We're on our way back to the spot, we can be easy now, we've gotten away with it, they won't get us now.

And now Gotti is saying you're sick fam you're sick, proper bigging me up to Tyrell – Snoopz is sick you know, he just wouldn't leave he says and his eyes are wide and he smiles white white white. And I'm like fuck dat fam I wasn't gonna cut without nuttin and Tyrell says what did you get fam? And I show him the handbag – it's Prada, probably worth a bag on its own – and Tyrell says is there any p's in there? So I start going through it.

It's just the trinkets of a rich woman; perfume and expensive hand cream and some business cards and next random shit that I don't register because it's not like we can sell any of it. And then I get her wallet and Gotti's talking to Tyrell saying man's gotta phone the others coz we don't know where they are blood, and I'm going through her wallet making sure Tyrell doesn't clock it and I've just seen £700 all in £50 notes in there, so I quickly pull it out and slip it deep into my pocket because I know Tyrell and the others will want a cut but I'm thinking fuck dat, it's mine and Gotti's, no one risked their freedom and did any next-level madness the way me and Gotti just did – even if it did go wrong – and since it's such a petty amount for what we're tryna get I'm taking it and no one's gonna know any better. Usually it's Big D, Gotti and me who get the biggest cut like 30 per cent each of the lick. Big D for scoping the ting and putting us onto it, me and Gotti for doing the eat and taking the biggest risk, and the rest goes to Tyrell since all he really has to do is drive us to wherever the move is gonna pop off and then get us out of there. And now Tyrell says what's in the wallet fam, any p's? and I'm like nah g, just bare cards and I pull out a black American Express card and we're all like shiiit, that's how you know the watch and ring woulda been some mad p's still, those were definitely some next-level rich people says Gotti. I mean we already knew she was mad rich from the way she dressed, the jewellery, the fact it's a normal weekday and she was just having some casual morning not really doing anything – probably coming back from a coffee shop or maybe she'd just had her hair done because her hair really did smell good – and the yard she walked up to with the big white door, the kinda house that none of us will ever be able to afford, although we'd like to think we might get there someday. But the black American Express card is something else, it indicates another level of wealth; I'd only heard about it in certain lyrics, rappers like Jay-Z and Lil Wayne, Kanye as well, stunting about how they're balling coz they've got black cards – the ultimate symbol of wealth, of being part of a true social elite, of being above the majority.

I put the card in my pocket, a souvenir of today, something

I'm probably never gonna have with my own name embossed on it anyway, might as well have somebody else's, not that I'll be able to use it, it's probably cancelled already says Tyrell, and everything is feeling normal again; the sun is irrelevant, weather is just weather, people in the street are just people doing whatever people do on a Monday morning, there are shops and cars and noise. Whatever.

We pass through Golders Green; children are at school by now, people are having breakfast in caffs, shops are open, buses are picking up and dropping off people, all following the different and unconnected threads of their lives. Gotti is on the phone to D telling him how the move fucked up so now we're going back to the spot in Willesden where we linked up in the morning and at a certain point I see the other whip ahead of us – I'm not even sure when they joined us, somewhere after Golders Green – and now I'm just chatting to Gotti and we're still mad surprised about how he couldn't pop the watch coz I've seen him do it on like four other occasions, always on his first go, no problem, but for some reason this time it fucked up. And we're going through it all, what happened on the doorstep and the sound of the door slamming on her arm and laughing, like myman blatantly slammed the door on his own wife's arm coz I managed to reach in and pull her arm out I say. And this is the thing, there's no remorse, I don't feel any remorse, Gotti doesn't feel any remorse, and it's not because we're evil or any basic moral bullshit like that. The thing is I don't actually feel anything about it at all. She defo doesn't spend a second thinking about individuals like me, about what it's like to be me. She doesn't care about me and I don't care about her. And it's not that she doesn't care about me because of what I just did. She already didn't care about me before she encountered me and

8

it's all because we're locked away in our own little worlds. So fuck remorse. No point wasting time trying to feel anything if it doesn't come naturally to you. Anyway, so—

So we pull up in the car park in front of the little block in Willesden where we all met up earlier this morning. I stuff my bally into the pocket with the money just so there's a reason for that pocket to look a bit full. We get out of the whip and Tyrell and Gotti are lighting up cigarettes as the other whip pulls in, the gunmetal grey Porsche, which is what Big D always rolls in with his nephew Ghost driving so he can spot the people worth eating. It's an ideal car because it's too balling – too expensive – to be associated with a scatty eat, so D can proper clock people from inside it and calculate who we should jump out on. Plus, when we drive in convoy – usually them ahead of us since they're scoping and we're the ones who actually do the madness – it looks as if there's no way we could be together since their car looks cris and I mean come on, them man in a Porsche, us in some deadout second-hand ting. No one's drawing any chicks in our whip, you get me.

It's a good spot here, away from the ends but at the same time not too far from the blocks, none of us live anywhere on this road or have connections to it, and the car-park area is surrounded by a fence and tall bushes so no one can see us from the road. Big D gets out the whip with his forehead all knotted up. Ghost gets out as well, asking questions, but he gets ignored as me and Gotti start chatting to Big D, going through it all over again, showing him the handbag and dash dat man, fuck dat he says, maybe we'll come back for it later coz dem kinda bags go for p's still, and I go and stash the bag under one of the tall bushes next to the fence and cover it in dead leaves. Gotti and Big D are talking away from everyone else, voices low, D is the big man who's putting us onto this shit but he knows wagwan, especially with Gotti. Tyrell and Ghost are just sideman really, they're only drivers, they're not the ones who make shit pop off, them man ain't got the heart for it like me and Gotti do. It's funny how they both proper care about their appearances even when they go on a move. Ghost is always rocking his white gold tooth with the big diamond in it and Tyrell's rocking some fresh white Moschino trousers like he's going raving. It's not like man's gonna chirpse some peng tings and get their digits on the way to doing a move. But forreal it makes sense not to look greazy when you're the driver since you don't wanna draw attention or look like you can't afford the whip you're driving.

So Big D and Gotti are talking, frowns cutting up their foreheads and as I walk over I hear D saying nah Gotti we have to get a next whip right now. Big D hunches over, leaning in, Gotti sticking his hands down the front of his tracksuit bottoms, turning away whenever Big D leans in as if he doesn't want the words coming out of D's mouth to get too close to him and I can't catch what's being said. Gotti goes fuck dat blood I'm not doing that kinda bateness after what just happened, no way, and he starts talking about how the only thing he trusts is his own instinct and it just don't feel right to go out there again. And D is rushing to get words out his mouth but Gotti turns away like nah I ain't doing that, that's mad bate. He draws his cigarette hard and dashes it. I say wagwan D? And he starts breaking it down; that we need to buy a next whip if we're gonna do more moves, so he wants one of us to run up in a clothes shop in Golders Green where there's one saleswoman who's always rocking a Daytona Rolex and pop the watch off her wrist so that we can use the p's from shotting it to buy a new getaway whip. Obviously we're all gonna eat a lickle p off it for ourselves as well, he adds quickly and then looks away to spit into a bush. And Gotti's turning to me like nah Snoopz, fuck dat, I just have this feeling like I know suttin's gonna go wrong – and I can hear cars passing on the road beyond the bushes but it's all distant as if the world is drifting away from me.

It's never been a problem before. Big D always cops our getaway whips just like he bought the one we were driving in this morning; I mean he's the one who put this team together in the first place so it shouldn't be an issue. He knows me and Gotti are certified eaters, knows we're on this ting, if anything this is the first move that's proper gone wrong, he should know that we'll make back the loss and more next time. But now he wants us to go and do a proper madness – I mean going back to Golders Green which is basically where we just came from – and all just to get money for a next whip. Gotti's right as well, it's gonna be bate round there now, feds are definitely gonna be looking for man. And then running up in a shop in broad daylight? Robbing a sales assistant inside a shop? No creep up, no stealth, no nothing. Just straight in there, rago, clamping her up all scatty n shit, and I won't be able to rock my bally coz I'll probably get noticed before I even get in the shop and I don't know where the cameras are and alladat.

I look at Gotti and Big D puts his arm around me and walks with me to the side, away from the others, but his arm feels too tight around my neck and the sleeve of his leather jacket creaks like a snake shedding its skin and he smells of stale cigarettes and aftershave, and he goes Snoopz I know you're on it, it's nuttin, all you have to do is go in the shop; when you see

11

the woman, walk up to her on a calm ting and then quickly pop the watch off her wrist.

I'm always hungry, even though I've got p's stacked, but I always want more so I let him walk me to the side, although his arm across my shoulders feels heavier and heavier. So I ask D how do I do it exactly? He starts showing me on his Rolly how I have to grab the watch face and jerk it at an angle, explaining how the sudden pressure will break the bit where the strap is attached to the face. I'm trying out the way he's shown me to do it on his wrist but then I think fuck dat, if Gotti's not doing it, nah, this is how I'm gonna end up getting shift for all the madness I've been doing. I let go of his watch and say nah man this shit seems too bate to me, too many tings that could go wrong, I'm not doing it.

I turn around so I don't have to see Big D's face and walk over to Gotti. For a moment, behind me is only silence and then the world drifts back in, noisy, rushing, constant. I get close to Gotti and he already knows I've said no and his face is all calm now and the blackness of his eyes has melted and he says trust me Snoopz, it's better to listen to your instinct and don't watch face. Don't watch face. Who gives a fuck what them man think, you ain't got nuttin to prove brudda, man already know you're on this ting. It's a bad idea to do that shit brudda, I just know it's gonna go wrong.

I don't really notice how we leave them. Big D says something about how he'll phone us later and we spud Ghost and Tyrell. Tyrell walks off towards Cricklewood, Big D and his nephew drive off in the Porsche and me and Gotti make our way back to South Kilburn. I tell him what I was thinking, that Big D shoulda just bought a next whip so we could go out there again and wagwan with dat fam? I thought my man's supposed to be on some boss shit organising the whole ting and instead he's moving like he ain't got p's, fuck dat I say. And Gotti's nodding his head going forreal forreal, and I think we both know – although we don't say it – that we won't be doing moves with Big D ever again.

Grey clouds like heavy sponges tug on the sky's skin and the sun hides its face from the city as we get close to South Kilburn. I give Gotti his half of the seven hundred that I slipped out of the wallet, which raises his spirits a bit, and he tells me to dash the black American Express card as we walk down Kilburn Lane. I crouch next to a drain and pretend to drop the card down it, tucking it up into my sleeve instead. I want something to remember this day. No way can it be used to trace us unless it gets found and I'm not planning to let that happen. We carry on back towards South Kilburn, back to the blocks, to go and cotch in Bimz's yard. We can buy a draw or two now, or maybe we'll get a q, get proper faded, and then jump on the tube all high and numb and go back to east London. As I told Gotti this morning when we set out to do the mad ting, I have to make sure I'm up nice and early tomorrow, full of energy for my 9 a.m. uni lecture.

SOUTH KILBURN

THERE'S LIKE TWO or three shops in the estate and whenever I go to get a juice or Rizla or whatever, there are white posters stuck in the shop window with MURDER in big red capitals running across the top and underneath a grainy photo of one brer called Bloogz and something about a reward, £20,000 for any information, you will remain anonymous, whatever.

What happened was that Bloogz owed his best friend Creeper some money – a bag or suttin. The mandem were all out in the sun, cotching by D-block and Bloogz was there, fresh out of pen after a year and a half on a possession with intent to supply charge, and the thing is he owed Creeper the p's because Creeper had looked after his girl while he was locked up – gave her p's for shopping, bought the baby a new buggy, took her on prison visits – so now the way Creeper saw it, Bloogz owed him. So that day, when everyone was out in the sun by D-block, Creeper comes over and asks Bloogz when am I gonna get my money? And Bloogz says you ain't getting no money pussy, do what you gotta do, so Creeper, who had his gun on him, shoots

Bloogz and walks off. It was a hot day in July, everyone was out on the block – just by the park that stretches out in front of Wordsworth House – and Gotti was there too and he tells me how Bloogz clutched his chest right over his heart where he'd been shot and walked around in a circle for like ten seconds without making a sound before dropping. Nuttin like the movies fam says Gotti. Maybe Creeper wouldn't have done it if all the mandem hadn't been out on the block, soaking up the sun. But they were and Bloogz talked greaze, he didn't show man the slightest bit of respect, so Creeper had to do suttin. Now murder posters are stuck up in the shop windows because there were no witnesses, no one gave evidence to the police, everyone who was there that day wouldn't talk to the feds, but everyone knows who did it. Even Bloogz's mother and sister.

Later, I heard something about how Creeper went on the run to Jamaica, but then he got into one mad car accident and he was all fucked up from it and had to come back for treatment, like if he'd stayed in hospital out there he'd have ended up fully paralysed. So he flew back to London and the feds were waiting for him, they arrested him right as he got off the plane at Heathrow. But still, in the end there was no case. No witnesses ever came forward and I'm guessing he didn't end up paralysed or anything, because I seen him in Queens Ice Bowl last week with some chick, although my boy who saw him too said that one side of his face is fucked up like Two-Face. It's not like anyone outside South Kilburn could have witnessed it. I mean imagine: you come out of your block one morning, walk over to the opposite building where everyone is jamming out in front, smoking and talking and whatever, and you see an enemy and you argue, so you kill him on the spot and then you go home, which is a minute's walk, twenty seconds if you run, and that just tells you how shut off and enclosed this place is.

It's between Maida Vale, which is all red-brick Victorian mansions and houses with columns on tree-lined avenues, and Queen's Park train station where streets bleed off into areas full of lifestyles that contradict each other. Coming from the Maida Vale side, walk straight up Malvern Road, past the bookie and a chicken shop and two Chinese takeaways and the green corner shop on your left and small dirty houses with satellite dishes stuttering all over them and the post office in the little square on the right that always has its shutters down, tagged up with black spray paint, and you're basically right there at the beginning of South Kilburn Estate. You kind of know you're there before you're there, because you see these rows of low-rise flats that you walk past and beyond them the high brown blocks looking like they crashed down from the sky, solid enough to break into the Earth. You know you're in a different kind of place because just ten seconds of walking up Malvern Road and you see a camera right in the middle of the pavement on top of a pole covered in anti-climb paint and under the camera a Jesus crown of sharp metal spikes just in case. And the camera actually moves, it swivels around and looks up and down the road and I've seen it watching me before, following slowly as I walked by.

Further up Malvern Road there's another camera on top of a pole and then you get to the blocks, starting with Blake Court and next to it Dickens House, which is eighteen floors high. They tower above, pouring blue shadow all over you if you get too close and you can feel the coldness breathing off the rusty concrete and the silence straining to burst from all the windows. Carry on past the blocks and you come to a little park, just an open stretch of grass really, with the brown towers staring across from the right and another one of these surveillance cameras on top of a pole connected to some invisible control centre somewhere. Cross the park and you get to Carlton Vale, which is this long road that cuts the estate in two with a stream of cars going up and down, everyone on their way to somewhere else, since no one ever stops here. Back in the day there was a concrete walkway, like a bridge that connected one side of the estate to the other, as if to give people the chance to spend their lives without having to set foot outside of it, so you could always be within the estate, even when crossing a long road full of traffic and other lives passing by.

On the other side of Carlton Vale is Peel Precinct, a little concrete square surrounded by blocks covered in blue and grey cladding with white balconies, and in the centre of the precinct, in front of a next row of dusty shops and low-rise blocks, another camera with metal spikes beneath it and a sign saying 'CCTV in operation. This camera is active.' I always see this camera moving, following mandem as they walk across the precinct, and this side of South Kilburn we call Precinct and the other side – with the rusty colour blocks down by Malvern Road – we call D-block.

When I first came to South Kilburn I was seventeen. I lived at Uncle T's on the D-block side in Blake Court, a five-storey block next to Dickens House, and there were always nittys waiting at the entrance to Blake Court, damp and sticky-skinned with rotten black mouths and yellow eyes and clothes smelling sour, catting to get some b and work, and a lot of the South Kilburn mandem would jam on the open landing of one block called Wordsworth House next to Dickens House which looked out across the stretch of park, and no one really walked past that bit, even though there's a path cutting through the park that goes right past Wordsworth to save you time when crossing from one side of the estate to the other. But most of the time there were mandem on the balconies all hooded up, on the lookout for nittys and feds and enemies, and you wouldn't want their focus to turn on you. It's mad because only when I started doing my English degree did I realise that all the concrete towers on the D-block side of South Kilburn are named after great English authors: Blake Court after William Blake, Austen House after Jane Austen, Bronte House after the Brontë sisters, Dickens House after Charles Dickens and Wordsworth House after William Wordsworth, the block where all the mandem jam and the actual building they call D-block.

Whenever you enter one of the blocks you're already under surveillance. Like apart from all the cameras on poles that watch anyone who walks up and down the roads near the estate, and the big camera in the middle of Precinct and in the children's playground in the centre of the estate – apart from all that, say when you're going into Blake Court, there's a camera just above the entrance. Then once you're through the door, there's another camera watching from a corner, stuck up in the grimy ceiling and a yellow plastic sign on the wall says These premises are under CCTV surveillance, and under it BRENT HOUSING PARTNERSHIP HELPING TO PREVENT CRIME AND PROMOTING PUBLIC SAFETY. When you get into the lift there's a camera in there as well and a mirror, scratched up all over with names so that when you look in it your reflection gets cut to pieces.

There was this brer called Chicken who had a house party one summer night in his flat in Dickens House. Chicken wasn't on stuff, wasn't involved in any of the wickedness, he was just

18

some next brer from South Kilburn, but his cousin and couple next man robbed some top brers from South Kilburn for their jewels and ghosted. No one could find them in northwest London but the problem was that these man they'd robbed were Bugz Bunny's people. So at about two in the morning, in the middle of Chicken's house party, Bugz Bunny runs into the flat masked up, blacked out, with a Glock 9 and shoots Chicken in the chest. Chicken tries to get away, high on adrenaline, runs out onto his balcony and jumps off. But the flat is on the second floor of Dickens House so he breaks his legs when he lands. Someone turns the music off in the party and they can hear Chicken crying for help. People come running out the block, everything is screams and voices and the loud silence of shock shivering through the warm night air. Then Bunny comes out the block, walks over to where Chicken is lying and shoots him three times in the head before disappearing into the night. Chicken dies in the shadow of the block, holding on to his broken legs, not knowing anything about Charles Dickens, no moon or stars looking down on him because light pollution from the city at night burns the underbelly of the sky into an oily haze.

No one ever got arrested for it. No witnesses. And now, if you try and find anything out about it, it's like Chicken himself never existed. If you Google his name you won't find shit. When feds release their lists of unsolved murders in the capital, Chicken's name is never on there. It's almost like it never happened. But it was one of the first things I heard about when I moved here; I heard Uncle T say you mean dat block deya where the boy did get shot and jumped off the balcony – he was just making sure that whoever he was talking to meant Dickens House, it's the standard reference point to that building for people like

19

Uncle T who've lived here for most of their lives. And mandem in SK know what happened, plenty of people who live here remember; I mean most of the residents only had to go to their windows after getting woken up by the gunshots and they'd have seen Chicken, watched the drama of ambulances and fed cars arriving, the quicker ones might even have watched his last moments before Bunny ran off and got swallowed up by the night.

It's kinda fucked up but then again to the mandem round here it's really not, it's actually totally accepted, if anything it sets a standard for the young g's to live up to and you can see it in how the violence becomes the inspiration for everyone's lyrics when they spit rap and grime bars about bussin guns and murking man. Because round here, for certain man it's all about securing a reputation, you absolutely can't show weakness, you can't be seen as a pussy who lets shit slide. If you're nothing without your reputation then violent revenge can be like salvation and deliverance. Even though Bunny didn't actually duppy any of the brers who robbed his people, he knew that Chicken's cousin – and them man who Bunny was really after – would get the message and probably never show their faces round Northwest again. If you can't hit the enemy directly, you hit a relative or a friend because the thing is you're making a point, you're not doing something that is necessarily final and decisive, something that ends a cycle of violence or a feud. You're sending a message that you're ruthless and nothing is safe and don't even start to fool yourself that there are any rules to this shit.

When you leave the ends, say you're going to central London or anywhere else that's more normal, you find that no one's heard about those unsolved murders – grainy photos in shops that sit in the shadow of blocks – you take a bus ride or a trip on the tube and suddenly you're out of one reality and into another, but you still carry all this knowledge with you. And the mad ting is how these murder posters are located in the one place where people won't cooperate with the feds. Here it's all fuck the law, get paper by any means, rob, shoot, trap, spend the profit on some diamond grillz for your teeth or an iced-out Rolex or whatever, fuck gyaldem, bun cro till you zone out, ignore the nittys lurking on the concrete staircases looking half mummified, live life at a hundred miles an hour and just don't stop to think because you never know which day could be your last.

Man like Bunny and next man who are just straight on wickedness raise up the youngers and show them how to live, how to be ruthless, how only money and status matters and they learn quick how in this kind of environment any act of violence, exploitation, whatever, can't be unfair because that's how life works.

Life is violent, things happen suddenly. The law is just another force of power that descends on this place. And not just in raids that happen every so often, but like this one time some brer got run over by a police car as he was crossing a road in the estate, it was just a stupid accident, but the first thing to arrive on the scene was a CO19 unit, armed police jumping out of a silver Mercedes-Benz in bulletproof vests, fingers on triggers of their MP5 submachine guns and then later the ambulance came.

And the amount of things that never get reported – especially beatings and kidnappings and robberies – like if you're a shotter selling crack and heroin around the ends and couple man run up in your yard and rob you, gunbuck you, maybe even torture you a bit with a hot iron or a kettle of boiling water, you're

21

not calling the police. They won't give a shit when they realise who you are, what you do, because in their eyes you've put yourself outside of society's protection by doing crime. Not only that but you have to ride out, you have to take revenge, like if you can't get any of your p's or your food back you can at least get back some of your reputation. And anyway, fuck snitching. None of us trust the feds and if you talk to them you're a snitch and if you're a snitch you become a target, you automatically line yourself up to become a victim. The amount of scuffs and shankings I've seen in the ends where man get picked up off the floor by their boys after getting knocked out and getting their face kicked in, or just jump in their bredrin's whip and go hospital, or if it's not too bad just go to someone's yard to clean up, stop the bleeding with a T-shirt, get some plasters and antiseptic if you got poked up but no vital organs or arteries got hit, and then numb yourself with some cro and some juice and nurse your anger. And since no one goes to the feds, man are getting wrapped up and ransomed to their older brothers who are usually the targets anyway; top shotters who make p's but move too d-low for the eaters to rob them, so they kidnap a younger brother and then the brer they're really after has to pay the ransom or whatever, and I know several people who've done this and it never gets reported, ever.

The bus stops near South Kilburn Estate used to have posters on them advertising Operation Trident with messages about how to contact the police anonymously. There was even one poster that showed a picture of some brer in a pool of blood with a gun next to his outstretched hand and above him big white letters that said Young, Gifted and Dead. You never see any adverts like that in rich areas or in central London, only in the ends. Imagine. Seeing that shit every morning as you wait for the bus to school. Before I lived in the towers, I used to go past them on the 31 bus from my parents' near Westbourne Park. I used to wonder about the lives in there, all those windows in the massive blocks, so many different lives. What were they all going through? You'd think a place like that would be noisy and brimming with life, but it wasn't. From the outside it was just concrete everywhere like a low heartbeat pounding in the silence, and window after dirty blank-eye window.

THE MASK

Perhaps home is not a place but simply an irrevocable condition.
James Baldwin, *Giovanni's Room*

I WAS SEVENTEEN and I had this African mask which a family friend gave me. It was from the Congo, made of some dark wood with shredded palm-leaf hair, a mouth and narrow eyes cut into it; I couldn't tell if they were sleepy or sad or something else. I put it on a bookshelf in my bedroom but whenever my mother came into my room she would say I don't like it, what do you want it for, it's probably cursed.

My mother's fingers are always stained with oil paints. She bites the skin around her nails until it's raw and tries to tidy the damage by picking away more skin but then it bleeds.

I grew up in a flat full of paintings and drawings. Not just paintings on the wall, but canvases leaning against doors, stacked behind the sofa, taking up space in my mother's bedroom and in her imagination. My father slept on the sofa for as long as I can remember, because their bedroom was a tiny box room and although once there'd been a double bed, one day there wasn't and there was just a single bed that my mother slept in and finally a wardrobe and chest of drawers which they shared, and then my mother took the space over with books and papers and me and my twin brother's baby clothes, which she couldn't bear to get rid of. I never hugged or cuddled her as a child, even before our problems started, and so she called me her *sassolino*, which means little stone in Italian, like I was the one pebble she'd decided to pick up from the seashore and keep in her pocket wherever she went. My mother sometimes tells people this story about how she took me to the National Gallery when I was six. We were there for hours; in fact we only left in the end because the gallery was closing. She says that I went from painting to painting with a growing number of people following me, listening as I commented on each picture. I think the last part of the story is her exaggerating things because she was so happy to have a child who was into art. I remember I mostly liked those big battle scenes full of knights in the middle of killing and being killed.

So I was seventeen. I came home from college and I couldn't find the mask. I looked for it everywhere and eventually found it jammed into the broken air vent in my bedroom. It was all scratched up n shit, bits of white paint scraped onto the wood and the palm-leaf hair full of dirt and brick dust. I went into my mother's room and said did you jam my mask into the air vent? And she said yes and I said why would you do that? And she said because I wanted to and I don't like it and I said you can't do destructive things to other people's objects and she said yes I can and I said arright cool and I punched the air vent in

25

the wall of her bedroom and smashed the entire thing so you could see the bricks behind it and then I said now we're even. My mother started wiling out at me so I said fuck it and told her I was moving to South Kilburn that same day. Uncle T had recently let me know there was a spare room in his flat if I wanted to rent it, so I knew where to go.

It was the right moment to leave anyway. I'd been arrested quite a few times before then, including one time for assaulting police right outside our flat after getting stopped and tryna run because I had a shank and a draw on me. And, although I'd always been far closer to him than my mother, I now resented my father for taking my butterfly knife away from me – just when I'd gotten good at backing it out and doing the whole fancy flick ting with it as well. At this point the flat only felt like a home to me in terms of memories and familiar spaces. My bed was my bed and the little wooden stool next to it and the books on my shelves and the CDs and garms in the wardrobe; those were all mine. But the flat wasn't a place I felt comfortable in, with the living room always occupied by my twin brother Danny, practising his violin in there, seven eight hours a day coz he'd stopped going to school after GCSEs to pursue his career as a violinist and my mother said he must have the living room to himself, and even when the living room was free in the evenings, Danny and I weren't allowed to jam and watch TV because if we tried to our mother would switch it off and stand in front of it telling us that we should be in bed, even though it was only like 9 p.m. or whatever. And all through the flat were piles of books and old newspapers and unopened envelopes and broken chairs and old toys which my mother collected for who knows what – her artworks she would say, but the piles of objects only ever got bigger – and I swear she had like three desks in the flat, all piled up with papers so she couldn't even use them. And I couldn't play music in my room, could only listen to it with headphones in because they hated hearing rap or grime or whatever else I was into. One time, after one of our arguments she went into my room, took all my rap CDs, snapped them in half and dashed them in the bin. When I left for school the next day she ripped all the posters of Mobb Deep and Foxy Brown and next rappers off my bedroom wall, which is when it really started to feel less like *my* bedroom and more just the room that I slept in. Also the door to my room was broken – the upper panel was all smashed out – so even if I closed it it made zero difference. But it was me who done that.

I had one of them mini basketball nets in my room, it was a Charlotte Hornets one which my mother bought me on holiday in Italy and one day, after an argument, she stretched up to reach the hoop and snapped off the entire rim with the net and then she picked up the little rubber basketball that came with it and stabbed it with a penknife that I had in my room so it sighed and collapsed, deflated, and she said now you see, now you see what happens when you disobey your mother. I was so frustrated with the whole thing that I started crying burning angry tears like some moist yout and she made a face of fake pity at me, going yes, cry, cry you poor victim, you should be ashamed of yourself, and then I punched my door bang bang bang and smashed a whole panel out of it, which only made me feel worse because my father had spent a lot of his hard-earned money doing up the flat, getting wooden doors fitted onto everyone's bedrooms. And he really did work mad hard, practically seven days a week doing drawings for various newspapers and publications, and when I was younger I'd often

27

never see him on a weekday unless I woke up around one in the morning or suttin and then I'd go downstairs to get a drink and find him at the kitchen table with a glass of sparkling water by his hand, popping away in the silence along with the scratch of pen on paper as he worked on some next drawing to hit a deadline in the morning. He'd stop and smile at me and say *nocny marek* which means night owl or night walker in Polish and then I'd hug him, smelling his sweat and tiredness, before going back to bed. In the morning he'd be up at six with all the windows downstairs wide open, even in the winter, and often he'd be gone before I'd started getting up for the day. I never got the door fixed though. On the day I packed my bag and moved out, I slammed it shut, but I could still see into my room and I hurried downstairs to get away from it.

There was never enough hot water to wash in at Uncle T's. It was always bucket baths, crouching in the tub and sometimes only cold water that made me flinch and gasp as I poured it down my back. But afterwards there was always a zoot packed with highgrade waiting for me and a plate of fried plantain and scrambled eggs and hard dough bread for breakfast, and dinners of curry goat and rice n peas and saltfish fritters, filling the yard with these warm salty frying smells that fought with the sweet stink of cro, smelling like sweet mouldy earth, a smell that won over everything else and brushed softly over the bridge of your nose and eyelids. Not gonna lie I slept good after them meals. Uncle T had a sound system which he was always playing, roots and reggae and lover's rock, and his oldschool bredrins would come and drop dubplates and the whole yard would vibrate with baseline while they smoked and zoned out to tunes. When p's were tight, lunch and dinner would be corned beef, fried with onions and white rice, but he always made sure I got fed. Full up your belly my son Uncle T would say and when his bredrins were in the kitchen while I was eating he'd say watch the boy eat deh, him nah ramp wid his food and they'd all laugh because no matter how much I ate I never put on any weight, I was always marga.

Wagwan Snoopz, Uncle T would shout every time I came into the yard. If I walked into the kitchen while he was bagging up cro he'd give me some buds, saying go on son, something to smoke and then he'd ask have you eaten today? He used to be a dread and one day when I was living with him, he showed me his locks which he kept in a plastic bag after cutting them off when he'd stopped being a Rasta, because there's too much bullshit in it that don't make sense like in most religions he said. He had a cat called Scratch who was probably always high and Uncle T would pick him up while we were all bunning, drenched in punk smoke, and he'd run his hand down Scratch's spine and the cat would push its bony back against Uncle T's rough hand and he was missing the little finger on his right hand which he'd lost as a young man in some factory accident. He rocked glasses and he had a huge belly but it was that kind of fatness where you could tell he used to be mad built when he was younger. But life happens and things change. I'll still box a man down to bloodclart he said as he sat downstairs with a knuckleduster in his pocket – waiting for a customer to come and buy a draw from him – coz there'd been some drama on the block recently and he was on his guard in case someone tried to rob him.

Uncle T was Taz and Reuben's dad, two bredrins I'd made through the music ting. I'd met them at a clash called Battle of the Mics, which I won in the Marian Centre, a brown-brick

29

community centre in the middle of South Kilburn. It was when T-Mobile were doing these contracts where if you bought a month's worth of credit you'd get free calls to any number after 6 p.m., and I murked this brer in the final by dropping '*Blood, your mum's like T-Mobile – free after six any day of the week*'. It was a wrap after that, the crowd went crazy for man, I couldn't even spit the rest of my bars and afterwards Taz approached me and said you're sick fam, lissen man's putting together a crew on this music ting are you interested in joining? and I was like I'm on dat. That was the first time I'd proper been in SK and before I started living at Uncle T's, I used to go and buy draws off him and jam in his yard in Blake Court and bun it up.

So a week after I'd won the battle we were standing outside the Marian Centre, sun pouring warm yellow over the bricks and spilling onto us, chatting about how one next MC called Bashy got chased out of SK when he'd come to do a performance the night I'd won the clash. Taz rolled up his T-shirt sleeve and showed me a cartoon Tasmanian Devil holding two smoking pistols tattooed on his right bicep, saying that's why they call me Taz blood, I live up to my name innit, and the words came cutting their way out of his mouth with his face all stiffened up as we waited for the others to join us. He'd started organising MCing sessions at the Marian Centre. For the whole of that summer we would link up for couple hours every other day and just spit pure bars back to back over the latest grime beats – there was Malice, Predator, Mazey, Bimz, Rayla, Smoothy, Gunja and me – and Taz called the crew Secret Service. He was basically our older since most of us were still teenagers and we just wanted to spit bars while Taz had some vision of us making it in the music ting.

Taz was one of them brers that when you walk through the

ends with him he'd constantly be stopping to say wagwan to someone, olders hailing him up, next man on the block calling out yo Taz wa'um, and he'd raise a fist as he passed by and shout yes g mi deya. Sometimes we'd even be out of ends in like East or North and he'd bump into someone he knew and then he'd tell me I know that brer from pen. He'd been locked up quite a few times. He always had gyal ringing his phone off as well, even when he talked to them like shit they'd be ringing him back, I mean he had suttin about him, it can't just have been his looks although I guess the gyaldem were feeling him like that as well; his skin had this yellow glow to it, but when he'd get vexed about suttin it would start burning as if the blood beneath his skin was literally boiling.

One time I was jamming on the block with Taz, bunning zoots on the balcony outside Uncle T's flat in Blake Court, looking out across the estate and the sun was setting, melting the horizon until it bled into the coming darkness above and I said rah look at that banging view fam, that would be a sick shot in a film ah lie? He barely even looked at it and said to be honest Snoopz I been seeing that view my whole life, I don't see nuttin special, just blocks and windows so I don't really know what you're saying and then he spat over the balcony and went down the stairs and out the block to go shop and get chip n Rizla. But when he'd get crunk with me and we were at a chick's yard or suttin, he'd be grinning teeth with his eyes practically closed – especially if we'd been bunning cro, which on a real we was always doing – and then he'd tell everyone in the room how I'm his brother and no one can chat shit to me. And when I'd tell him suttin interesting he'd be like Don't Lie, as if there was nothing more interesting in the world to him at that moment in time than what I was

31

saying, I mean he could really make you feel like someone special and you wouldn't think about questioning his words or intentions. Then I heard Uncle T calling him Taswan when we went round to his dad's one time to buy a draw and I realised Taz is really just short for Taswan, not Tasmanian Devil.

Reuben was his younger brother. Everyone knew him as Rayla and he always had this crazy smile on his face, eyes full of shine that couldn't stay still, every bit of him just restless energy, but the smile hid the fact that he could switch in a hot sec still. He wasn't shook of no one and although he used to jam with all the D-block mandem, shotting work on the block and all that, he stopped moving with them because one time one of the olders told him to go shop and get some chip so that the older had some cigarette to bill a zoot and Reuben said fuck dat go shop yourself I'm not some sendout and the older switched at him like are you mad?! Reuben said suck your mum and the older went to fight him outside the block, but Reuben picked up an empty beer bottle and dashed it at the older's head and everyone heard the conk and then he ran off laughing. The older didn't chase him because he sensed that Reuben wasn't afraid of getting himself killed, so he shouted watch when I get my strap like he was gonna shoot Reuben. No one else on the block backed it for Reuben so he was like fuck dat these man are snakes and he stopped cotching with them. When Taz started doing the music ting Reuben was instantly part of it, even though he'd always turn up at random for our sets, spit bars with mad energy for like half an hour and then disappear without saying anything.

We'd get on a double-decker bus coming back from doing a set somewhere out of the ends and go to the top deck where Taz would bring out a zoot and spark it right there, passing it around, smoke climbing over seats, making people turn around all nervous before they'd quickly turn back round and then go downstairs, and we all fed off the recklessness and would start billing our own zoots and bunning them until the whole top deck was a hotbox smelling loud, everyone making noise on a mad hype, eyes glowing bloody red out of the shadows of hoods pulled over heads. More times when the bus driver clocked wagwan, he'd stop the bus, push the alarm button and we'd run off, bussin up while a metal voice announced THIS BUS IS UNDER ATTACK, CALL 999, THIS BUS IS UNDER ATTACK, CALL 999.

Reuben stopped living at his dad's when Uncle T found Reuben's strap and a shopping bag full of bullets behind the panels covering the bath in their flat. Taz stopped living there before that happened after coming out of pen and moving in to a hostel for ex-offenders. But they were both still close to their dad and Taz would often bring me there and we'd cotch and bun and listen to tunes and if we were lucky, Uncle T woulda fried some saltfish fritters or cooked some of his famous curry goat. Since his sons had stopped living there he had a spare room available and when I told Taz that I needed a place to stay since my home life was choking me, he told his pops, and Uncle T said to me Snoopz, the room's free when you're ready.

BLAKE COURT

We live in the flicker – may it last as long as the old earth keeps rolling! But darkness was here yesterday.

Joseph Conrad, *Heart of Darkness*

UNCLE T LIVES on the top floor of Blake Court and it's a proper crack block. There are two main entrances on either side of the block and the lifts are often broken, or when they aren't, some nitty's pissed in the lift so you have to take the stairs anyway and you come across bare cats sitting on the dirty concrete stairs, some having just piped up and smoked a rock, all zombied out n shit, others waiting to get served, burnt lips and dirty bodies and you gotta be ready in case they try suttin. So you get to the fourth floor coz it's one of the shorter blocks, and usually there are shotters on the landing next to the lift, waiting to serve the cats with the dark n light which means heroin and crack, or as everyone round here calls it, buj and

34

work or brown and white or brandy and champs or Bobby and Whitney.

I used to feel tense when I first started coming on the block to check Uncle T because these man would stare me in my face without blinking, that look which you know is an instant challenge and I don't just mean a screwface – it's a look that you don't really see on people's faces outside these kinds of environments – and sometimes they'd be standing around the top of the stairs, waiting for nittys, and they wouldn't make the slightest space for me to get past, so I had to try and edge through without bumping into anyone because it was me on my ones, while at the same time tryna show that I'm not shook or anything. I didn't ever want to get looked at like that, stared at until I'd have to look away and then risk getting violated for showing weakness. But if I didn't look away they'd see it as a challenge and the consequences could be even worse. You see, life is ruthless. Sometimes someone would go who's dat? bare loud and aggi and only when I'd say I'm going to check Uncle T would they ignore me and go back to whatever they were doing.

So you get to the fourth floor, you go through a heavy magnetised door that slams shut with a metal clunk, locking you into the balcony, and you walk past rows of doors, some boarded up after police raids, and there are wires hanging down from the ceiling like exposed black arteries and some of the lights are broken and they flicker endlessly. Staring out from the balcony across the estate I can see Dickens House to the left, eighteen floors high, the block where Chicken got shot and killed, and to the right Austen House, another eighteen floors of rusty concrete silence and windows repeating them-selves and all of it holding the sky back from coming down into the estate. And often there's mandem all down the balcony as well and when I first used to come here they'd turn around and clock me the second they heard the balcony door open, but after a while they recognised me and most of them would just ignore me as if I wasn't even there. Some of them are literally Uncle T's neighbours who live a couple doors down from him, like Warlord and Rico – two brothers who were already gunman by the time they were seventeen and eighteen and I've even seen them on the balcony blatantly holding burners down the front of their jeans. Sometimes Warlord says wagwan Snoopz because he recognises me and he'd heard me spit bars at one battle in South Killy, but his brother has these eyes that you don't wanna look into because there's suttin frozen deep inside which you might regret seeing, so I never even try and say wagwan to him because I can tell that the only thing he has for strangers is contempt.

The only time that you don't really see all of this is in the morning when the cats are nodding off on buj and the shotters are catching some sleep after trapping into the early hours. But even then you'll have all the reminders: broken lifts, stairs shiny with piss, sometimes even liquid shit covering a stairwell, broken miniature Martell bottles with scorched black glass scattered about coz that's what the nittys use to bun work, and bits of empty clingfilm like little whispers going down the stairs.

It was like this day in, day out, so I got used to it all very quickly. The screwfaces on the balcony of Blake Court, stony frowns, eyes full of black fire. Mandem shotting crack on the block, diamond grillz shining in black faces like fallen gods chewing stars. Nike hoodies and £500 Louis Vuitton trainers, Gucci belts holding up True Religion jeans and shanks in pockets so they can poke up anyone who tries it, some even with straps on them and you can tell who's holding coz they'll have at least one glove on in case they have to beat it off, knowing that it's only forensic evidence they'll have to deal with coz there'll be no witnesses round here, even if everyone sees it.

I got used to hearing greazy talk echoing loud across the balconies into the night, mandem chatting about how someone knocked out some next brer's teeth, a snatch of conversation which goes he started crying when I shanked him and twisted the blade before pulling it out. I got used to all the cats, the nittys, fiending in the stairwells like the undead lurking in a concrete tomb.

After a few months of living at Uncle T's I got comfortable. I'd walk through the blocks saying wagwan to certain heads I'd got to know and next man who'd got used to seeing me round the ends. I'd come on the balcony of Blake Court and nod to the mandem who'd make space casually as I passed – shank in my pocket at all times coz it's not about slipping and you never know when shit could pop off – and certain times I'd come out of Uncle T's for some fresh air and bun a zoot on the balcony while the mandem were trapping and doing their ting.

But still, there's a constant sense of threat and readiness here, your heart never gets the chance to beat slow for too long because there's always the rush and heavy throb of danger that lingers in your chest long after the sticky cro smell leaves your nostrils. You hear solitary bangs echo across the estate, which you know are not fireworks, and nighttime gets cut up by blue lights and sirens, but you become numb to it all. It's mad how you can live in a city and never see any of this. Or you just see faint smudges of it every now and again around the edges of your existence but even then you don't fully believe in it, because even though we live in the same city, where I'm from and where you're from could be two totally separate worlds. Like say you hear about a shooting on a street you walk down every day on your way to work; it's a shocking one-off occasion, a rarity, something to talk about, and every single violent incident that you hear of or read about becomes a one-off, or at least a surprise or a shock. But to others these incidents are just the punctuation of their reality.

Only a place like this can have mandem putting diamonds in their teeth, needing to flaunt something that looks like it's from another planet. You could say it's like a kingdom of princes and bandits in concrete towers although more times the princes and the bandits are the same thing, and the youngers grow up idolising man like Bugz Bunny, idolising killers and shotters, and my bredrin Gotti was raised by Bunny to be a eater.

I first saw Gotti at Bimz's yard in Precinct. Actually the first time I saw him, was on one DVD that was going round the ends. It was made by some rapper from South Killy, featuring music videos, a twerking contest full of thick chicks in a club in Harlesden called Dreams, and some random footage of mandem on D-block. It was filmed at night, the dim block lights just enough to carve people out of the darkness. Mandem getting gassed on camera, shouting – D-block, Dmotherfuckinblock, free da mandem, fuck da feds – throwing up middle fingers and gunfingers, the camera jerking up to show the word D-block spray-painted in silver above the entrance to the balcony, and as they shouted at the camera the light shivered over diamond-encrusted teeth.

I was jamming at Bimz's after a Secret Service set in the Marian Centre when I saw this DVD. It was something to do while we sat in the yard and bunned zoots. There was a moment in the D-block footage where one brer came up the stairs and passed in front of the camera. He was wearing a black leather Avirex and a black fitted cap and he stared at the camera as if it had caught him out, moon eyes, said wagwan to the cameraman and walked out of the shot, fully uninterested in the hype that was going on around him. Mazey said oh shit, Gotti, I swear he just got out of pen after a five stretch. Gotti? Yeah that's my cousin still. What did he get five for? I think it was some move fam, Gotti's a madman, that guy just don't care bout nuttin, he'll rob anyone anytime. Then Mazey told us how Gotti would go around eating all the nittys for their food and then sell it back to them. He'd rob them as they came out of whichever block they were getting their food from and one by one he'd yack every single cat, bareface, and tell them if you wanna come back to the block you gotta cop from me. Mad ting. One next brer who was jamming with us that day in Bimz's yard said yeah Gotti's active, I remember when him and Bunny went and stuck it on all them Warwick man. Gotti and Bugz Bunny went to Warwick Estate, lined up all the mandem they saw against one wall and took all their p's, phones, food, jewellery – and no one did fuck all. Bunny had mandem on the ropes like that. Of course he was always strapped and everyone knows he won't pet to buss his gun so what could them Warwick man really do?

Later, Gotti heard about me from Mazey and Bimz when I started getting active, but I never imagined we'd end up doing all the madness we did together or how it would all go down.

ANTS

WHEN WE WERE little, my twin brother Danny had a pet hamster
and then it died. We'd always loved animals; nature documentaries
were about the only TV our mother let us to watch – well, that
and *The Simpsons*. When the hamster died, we were on holiday in
Italy with our parents. A family friend was staying in the flat in
London and he called my father to break the news. We were seven
years old and I remember how we cried when we found out.

We were playing in this big garden full of pine trees and our
father came round the corner of the house and as he told us
he was already crouching with his arms outstretched, and he
held us tight against his chest as the tears came. Afterwards, we
went back to playing our game with the ants. We ripped the
bark off a pine tree to make the ants who lived inside come
running out of their nests and as they ran out in shiny black
streams all over the polished red surface of the tree, we torched
them. We made a flame-thrower with a can of deodorant and
a lighter that we teefed from our mother's handbag and the
bodies of the roasted ants curled up and fell away from the tree

in their thousands. When it was done we dropped our trousers and pissed all over the tree, drowning any survivors and washing away the remains of the massacre. I guess that's what they call the innocence of children or some shit.

Then we got older and I stopped going on holiday with my family coz when summer came around I just wanted to stay in London and make sure I went to Notting Hill Carnival. Whereas Danny had decided long time that all he wanted to do was play the violin, I just wanted to jam on road with my bredrins, bunning cro and getting up to madness. In a sense he became my mother's favourite because he never caused her any problems; she probably felt he was easier to understand. So while it seemed that they were always talking and getting along, I was always getting shouted at and slapped across my face for doing suttin wrong and that really bunned me. It hurt me somewhere deep inside like a splinter and the more I picked at it, the further I pushed it in, deeper and deeper until I couldn't get it out. So when I argued with Danny it was bad, I mean real bad, like this one time he was pissing me off and I was pissing him off and then he started talking about how I wasn't doing anything with my life, which felt like an echo of my mother and I couldn't shut him up so I drew for this Moroccan dagger that my mother had inherited from her mother and held it to Daniel's throat. But he didn't react. He just stared back at me and said go on then, stab me, see, you're not gonna do it, so I punched him in the head, put the dagger back on the shelf where I'd taken it from and stormed out of the flat to go and bun it up with some bredrins on road, waiting until after midnight when I eventually came back to the flat, crept upstairs and got into bed while everyone slept.

But I wasn't doing nothing with my life like Danny said. Apart from all my efforts to make sure I wouldn't live a Normal Life

– because the idea of that scared the shit out of me – I was determined to go uni. It was like the thing I had to do for the sake of my brain. I knew I'd go mad if I couldn't read books. As a child I quickly worked out how to turn my bedside lamp on without making the switch click so that my parents would think I was asleep coz all I wanted to do was read. Books took me to other places. And I looked after them. Books don't deserve to have their spines broken, I mean I could read a book and afterwards it would still look brand new. In school I was always sick at English so it felt natural that eventually I'd go to uni and study it. When I did my A levels I got an A in English, but all my mother could talk about was that I got a U in Biology. The U meant Ungraded because I didn't even get the minimum number of marks to get an F. I mean it was pretty fucking shit forreal, I'm not even sure if I got more than two or three questions right in the whole exam but fuck it, I wasn't tryna be a doctor, I didn't need to know how plants photosynthesise to ensure I had a promising future, like as long as you know how to fuck, that's all the biology you need and I knew how to do that. Anyway my mother could never stop clawing away at me with her relentless expectations and criticisms, and she never once said well done for getting an A in English and a B in History, she just banged on about the U like that was what defined me. It just confirmed that I was right to move out and go live at Uncle T's when I did, because I couldn't be me around my mother without having to constantly fight for it.

At Uncle T's I could be myself and no one questioned it. Here I brought my girl, Yinka – short for Olayinka, which means 'wealth surrounds me' in Yoruba she said – to stay with me and it helped her to escape her family and anyway, she didn't even have her real dad around, her mum had remarried. We'd met in

42

one evangelical Nigerian church called Jesus House. A friend of mine had invited me — one Christian girl I knew from youth club who wanted Jesus to save me or some shit — and a friend of hers had done the same. When I clocked her I was like nah, who's this peng ting with amber skin and eyes that look as if they've always got the sun in them, and we spent the whole service snatching looks from each other. Afterwards we swapped numbers, jumped on the tube together back to west London and as I got off at my stop, she kicked me in the back and I almost fell over on the platform as she buss up laughing. We never went back to that church but we kept seeing each other. We used to play-fight and she was always tryna wrestle me and true she didn't bun so she always had more breath in her lungs and I'd try act like I wasn't making too much effort when really I'd be thinking nah this girl is strong I need to have her up, but once I pinned her down we'd start lipsing and two twos I'd be pulling her trousers and her panties down and pushing myself into her wetness. She liked rocking fitted caps and Nike tracksuits but when they came off, her body was full of curves that I couldn't stop gripsing up and she'd laugh and say you make me feel so sexy and I'd say that's because you are Boo.

One day after we'd been fucking in my room at Uncle T's and her hair was all over the place and she was laughing, mouth wide open so I noticed the tiny chip on her front tooth for the first time, she suddenly went serious, her eyes got wet, she looked down at the duvet and said I need to tell you something baby. She told me how her stepdad kept trying to rape her all through her childhood, troubling her at night, coming to her bed up until she was twelve years old, beating her up whenever she fought back and her mum had refused to believe her, had

43

basically left her to her fate, even putting makeup on her bruised arms and legs before school, had allowed her to lose her childhood before she'd ever had a chance to enjoy it because then she ran away from home and lost her virginity – or what was left of it – when she was thirteen to some brer who was almost twenty, and her secrets tumbled out into the room and crashed into my chest while I held her close. From that day on I had to carry it all within me and accept I couldn't change one bit of it, the knowledge of it scraping back and forth from my heart to my guts, and I knew that I could never unknow what she'd told me and even worse, I couldn't take it away from her. You see, no matter what shit you come up with about the past being the past or whatever, you can't fix someone who's already broken. I mean, lemme tell you—

One time this girl who lived like eight doors down from Uncle T, one young ting, pretty and full of unseriousness and curiosity and whatever else you're meant to have in you when you're fourteen or whatever, she got into the lift on her own and three of the mandem who were waiting for sells followed her in. When she got out at the bottom it was a while later and she was a different person, older and not so full of the things young girls are full of when they're fourteen. She screamed one long scream at no one in particular, a scream that ran up the block and then she chased it up the grimy concrete stairs, back to her mum's flat. I was bunning a zoot on the balcony at the time and I remember how I saw her mother open the door and she pulled her daughter in by the hair without saying anything, then looked out of the doorway and the mandem came out of the lift which had just returned to the top floor, and they laughed and one of them said fuck dat sket anyway and the mother closed her door.

Some chicks fall in love with the badness, like some even start rolling with shanks, punching up and robbing next gyal, or the peng tings end up attaching themselves to the baddest brer they can find. Maybe it's protection, a sense of security, or at least some looking after, some garms, some ice, since it's all about image here, I mean the pressures of this environment have no mercy on them, so if you've got your Gucci belt and a fresh pair of creps and hair n nails done up, then at least you can feel like you're not a total nobody. I mean a lot of these chicks come like they only rate ballers, they only wanna roll with man who are trapping and making p's and rocking Gucci and Louis and Balmain. And most importantly, if your man's got some status – maybe his name rings bells on road like he's feared or he's on the gang ting or his older brothers are doing bits and their reputation extends to him or he's a rapper and people know him from YouTube videos or whatever – then no one in the ends will trouble you. Unlike them girls that get beaten out in the stairwells of those massive blocks where most people always take the lift; knees getting scraped on concrete steps, hair getting pulled, panting into the stony silence or giving neckback in some dutty stairwell — and don't even get me started about how much of that shit gets filmed on mandem's phones and sent around. And in those situations it's never usually one brer. He always wants his bredrins to get a bring-in and once she's up in those blocks on her ones she doesn't really have a choice, because it's not like she knows what the fuck she's even doing there in the first place and she starts to wish she never came up here, even though the brer she actually likes tells her it's cool b, don't watch nuttin, they're my bredrins. But afterwards she'll get singled out, mandem will spread the word talking about yeah I hit dat, every man in da block run through dat. She'll practically get dragged into the block by next man who clock her and really, once it gets like that, the only way for her to escape it all is to leave the ends.

Then again there's bare good tings who don't get sucked into it, who don't allow themselves to get impressed by ice and Gucci belts, who resist the pressure, who learn the signs to watch out for, learn how to ignore mandem hollering at them from the balconies as they walk home, learn to avoid getting trapped in situations they can't run from, learn that there's more to life than this place and these reputations.

Yinka was a good ting forreal, but the worst bit about what fucked up her life before she could even say she'd lived it, was that it didn't come from the roads. It came from the place she called home.

Sometimes I lie in bed at night, fantasising about how one day I'll pull up outside her yard on a superbike, all blacked out with a burner, and when her stepdad comes out I'll burst his head open with three shots and ride off. I plan how to get away with it, what cameras to watch out for, where to dump the motorbike and burn it. When the thoughts start tearing at my heart and my insides and I can't sleep because of it, I imagine myself running into her yard on a rago tip, bareface with a borer, and start shanking her stepdad in the face and head before he's even had a chance to get off the sofa and then I'll bang her mum in the face and shout that's what you get for letting a man abuse your child. I'm serious about doing it, but I haven't told any of my bredrins because it's just too much, too much for me to say, too much for anyone to think of and if I do tell anyone I know it'll be the first thing they think of whenever they meet Yinka and I don't want people to see that when they look at her, and I don't want them to know I haven't taken revenge for that shit. So I just keep it to myself and hold her tight whenever she cries.

I told my mother about it one time when I went home to pick up some garms. I was hoping she might offer to let Yinka live in my old room or suttin, especially since I didn't really want her living with me in that greazy block in South Killy, but her only response was to start asking hardface questions about Yinka's mother like why had that woman not done anything about it, as if she hadn't even listened to what I'd said in the first place – as if I could even answer such questions. I said she needs your help and my mother was sitting up in bed reading a book and she just laughed all bitter and said why doesn't she get her own family to help her and I said whatdafuck is wrong with you have you not been listening to anything I've told you? And she said don't talk to me like that I'm your mother, I don't want that girl in my house, she's beneath you, she's primitive and I said I hate you you bitch. My father was in the kitchen and he heard it all and came upstairs quicktime bang bang bang which made my heart start going boom boom boom and he grabbed my head and lifted me off the floor, pressing his thumbs into my eyes and I wrestled myself free and he came after me as I ran into my bedroom and dashed me across the room and shouted THIS IS THAT'S IT, because his English is especially bad when he's angry. Then he went back into my mother's bedroom and they started talking about me in Polish, about how I couldn't come here any more. I grabbed some p's from the shoebox under my bed and ran out of the yard.

But at Uncle T's me and Yinka could be together. We could do whatever we wanted and the pain was a bit easier to bear in this environment because really it can be quite a fucked-up place, South Kilburn I mean, but once you accept that life is brutal – and there are plenty of reminders of that in South Killy – you can cope with whatever madness you might encounter, because you already know life has plenty of that to offer.

NINA

I PHONE MY boy Capo who'll be going to uni with me in September to do aeronautical engineering coz he wants to be a pilot and when he picks up I say yo brudda I need you to hook me up with that girl. He says what Nina yeah?

Nah I want the twenty-two-year-old, even if she's not the silent type.

What about the thirty-eight-year-old? She's there.

Well I was feeling her, but on a real ting she's mad loud and she can't be silenced so I'm not really interested in her.

Ha. She's got a big mouth. I hear dat. I could hook you up with Nina though.

Yeah Nina's cool, I like her, although it's the twenty-two-year-old I really wanna go out with. And the forty-five-year-old is way too old for me.

Yeah and she's got a big nose.

Yeah fuck dat.

I'll see what I can do fam. Anyway, I'm feeling hungry so I'm gonna see if I can get the mac n cheese.

Rah, the mac n cheese. You can get that yeah?

Yeah fam. Well I'm looking into it anyway.

Say nuttin. Just shout me when you know wagwan, but obviously try hook me up with the twenty-two-year-old cah she's the one for me. If not her, I'll go with Nina.

Say no more fam, he says.

I say safe brudda, and end the call.

It is the beginning of summer before my first year of uni and I am trying to get a gun. Everyone I know says they can get that, or they know someone who can get it, but when I start making phone calls, the excuses start coming. It's harder to sort out than you'd think. Plus I want a proper ting, not a rebore, which is basically a replica or a deactivated burner with the barrel drilled through to fire real bullets. That shit can blow up in your hand forreal. I know of one brer who's missing his index finger because he put a strap to someone's head and pulled the trigger but the barrel hadn't been drilled properly; it was too narrow for the shell. The bullet backfired and the ting basically exploded, blowing his index finger to pieces, with no effect on the brer he was tryna shoot apart from possibly making him believe in God or suttin.

So I'm in the kitchen at Uncle T's, billing a zoot, when Taz bells me and says Snoopz there's a ting there one chick's holding for me in Cricklewood.

Is it a proper ting fam? Not a rebore? I go.

Nah it's not a rebore. I'll take you to see it if you want, he goes.

I bun my zoot while waiting for Taz to get to South Killy. I'd recently bought some coke and started trapping so before leaving the flat, I make sure I've got the soft cheeksed properly.

49

I'd wrapped up about ten grams in little envelopes made out of lottery tickets which Taz showed me how to do – coz that's the way the sells like it – and clingfilmed them into a ball which I stuck in between my arse cheeks, just in case I get stopped and searched, which is a daily hazard I gotta be prepared for. It ain't comfortable but like a lot of other things I've gotten used to it.

What really made me want to get a burner was this thing that happened at the end of April. There was a rave organised by Taz in a community centre on Harrow Road and me and my boys were all MCing there. My bredrin Malice, Taz's cousin, was on the door and he didn't let certain South Kilburn man into the rave. It was the way he spoke to them though, like they were some any guys. The rave had just got locked off because one MC let off pepper spray, leaving everyone coughing, choking, heading for the exit, all because someone had tried to shank him up onstage. Every rave in the ends that I've been to gets locked off early coz someone gets poked up or bottled or shot. It's expected though. You'll have mandem from Harrow Road and Grove and Kensal Green and South Kilburn and next ends all suddenly cramped into one space and bare of them have beef with each other, so— Anyway, the next thing I know, I see Malice staggering back into the Yaa Asantewaa Centre while everyone's spilling out into the road, and he's holding his face and it's dripping blood. He'd held some vicious bangs while a next man had him in a headlock. The brer who was giving him the bangs had some chunky diamond rings on that split Malice's face. I was vexed when I saw it like nah, them man violated forreal. True I got mad love for Malice, ever since we got beaten up by some feds in the back of a bully van after getting stopped and searched in Harlesden. So I couldn't let

50

that shit slide. I said to Taz fuck dat, them man buss your cousin's face open, we need to go where they live right now and do them suttin. Taz was moving mad uncertain but true I was nineteen at the time and Taz was twenty-five so he had to set pace as my older.

We went to South Kilburn. The brers who'd done it lived only a few doors down from Uncle T: the two brothers, Warlord and Rico. As we walked down the balcony Taz said how shall I do it? He had an empty bottle so I said jus knock the door and when myman opens it fuck the talking ting, smash the bottle across his face straight away. When Taz knocked the door, a girl answered and said they weren't in. Taz looked kinda relieved. Later, when I really understood who they were – how these were some of the main D-block mandem who had the balconies on lock, strapped up and alladat – I realised we'd had a lucky escape. Them man wouldn't pet to shoot us. After that we went to see Malice in St Mary's Hospital and although one side of his face was all swollen up and he had a deep purple cut under his eye, he was calm. Funny thing as well is there were two next MCs in hospital beds in the A&E, who got poked up outside the same rave. It was in the hospital when I decided I needed to get a strap.

It's a hot summer day when Taz picks me up to get the ting and flies are mating on the air. I'm not wearing tracksuit bottoms under my trousers – which I usually do to make cheeksing the food a bit easier – coz it's baking outside. As I walk down the balcony to the lift, I can see flies chasing each other and I think how nothing about their frantic dance tells you that in a few days they'll all be dead. Tryna get the most out of life while they can. A sour smell slides through the air from the greasy pile of rubbish which sits beneath a sign that says STRICTLY

NO REFUSE TO BE LEFT IN THIS AREA. I press the button for the lift but when the metal door clangs open, I see that the floor is covered in a curving mirror of piss. I take the stairs even though I know there'll probably be couple nittys sitting in the stairwells, piping up or just waiting to get some work n buj.

I jump in the whip with Taz and we drive to Cricklewood. I ask Taz what type of burner it is but he doesn't know, it's not a rebore it's a real ting truss me he says. We park up outside one big block, behind some trees so that we're partly hidden from view. Taz phones the girl and says I'm coming now babes, have it ready for me. He turns to me and says just wait for me Snoopz, I'll be like five minutes, then gets out of the car and goes into the building.

He returns fifteen minutes later with a JD Sports bag and when he gets in the whip he puts it in the footwell between my legs and goes open it and check the ting fam.

I pull my gloves on – always roll with gloves just in case – and open the bag. The strap is wrapped in an old shirt. When I unravel it, the first thing I notice is rust. All over the barrel. All over the handle. Yellow brown swarming the dull blue metal. Whatdafuck is this Taz? It's all rusty to rahtid.

Check it fam, check it, he says, wrinkling his forehead and looking out of the window.

I try to cock it but the barrel is so rusted, the top won't slide. Then I notice part of the trigger is snapped off.

Fuck dat, this ting ain't even gonna buss fam I say, and start wrapping it up in the shirt before dropping it into the JD Sports bag and handing it back to Taz. Taz says nothing, gets out the car and goes back to the block while I get to thinking about how olders chat shit to their youngers, especially when they're tryna act like they know it all, like they have all the connecs, like you can't work shit out for yourself. It's a fake dynamic though. Olders are just shook of the young bucks taking over. Because all it really takes is a bit of wickedness; you just have to be more savage, more badmind, more on it and then bang – you've got your own reputation without needing any olders to certify you. Make your own name and they become mean-ingless. You can always make your own connecs, especially once you prove what you're about and mandem start noticing that you're a problem.

Taz gets back in the whip and starts talking about the chick, going she's dumb innit, she got that ting off her brother but she never even checked it, said she didn't know it was rusty. Obviously man hotted her up for wasting our time.

Who is she anyway? I say.

Just some ting I been linking, says Taz.

Before we drive off, Taz's wifey bells him and I can't hear what she's saying but Taz starts shouting shutdafuckup man, why d'you always do this? Don't worry about where I am, I done told you I'm with Snoopz, we're busy with suttin. She's obvi-ously tryna say something else but Taz just goes bare aggi with no pausing bye bye bye and puts the phone down. I fucking hate when she starts buggin me he says.

Me, I can't do all that fuckery where I'm linking next gyal and lotioning them, calling them babe while I've also got my wifey who's down for me. I mean yeah I link other gyal all the time, but Yinka is the only one who gets to fall asleep beside me and gets in my feelings. On a real though, I don't know what I actually want in terms of a woman. Sometimes it really gets to me how Yinka's always surprised by shit I'm telling her when just once I want her to tell me something about the world that I don't know. It's a terrible thing tryna love someone who can't teach you anything. Sometimes I just want a bad bitch who'll sleep with my gun under her pillow. Other times I want a girl who reads mad books and knows about interesting shit like magic, or Aztec sacrifice, and doesn't get impressed by the badman ting. I know Yinka doesn't want me stuck on the roads but the way she sees it, any nine to five would be better. Fuck dat. I'm not gonna become a version of me that doesn't exist.

Taz gets a call from his bredrin Kane who says he's got some coke sells for me, so Taz says we're going Willesden.

I send Yinka a text saying *Thinking of you* and put my phone on silent.

When we get to Willesden, Kane jumps in the whip, says wagwan and tells Taz to pick up his bredrin Daffy from the barber's, talking about how Daffy's wiling out about suttin, ready to do a madness. Kane is a proper madman, one of them brers with no fear who loves to scuff and he's got the size and muscle that makes him extra dangerous. Mixed-race don with a lisp and eyes like splinters of broken mirror. Always on his way to getting waved off a can or bottle of suttin strong. Next man always begfriend with him like they really want his ratings. The amount of times I've seen him make a man go and cop a bottle – and I mean suttin big like Courvoisier or Henny – and then he takes it and drinks the whole ting to himself. But the brer who bought it stays silent, just looking at the bottle in Kane's hand, shook to say anything in case Kane switches and starts badding man up. When Kane heard that I was tryna get a burner after Malice got rushed and he realised I was serious, he showed me mad love.

We pull up at the barber's. Daffy jumps in the back next to

Kane with his face screwed up. Doesn't even say wagwan to us as he pulls off his sunglasses and starts talking to Kane.

I was in the chair getting my trim he says, and some black yout who's like Brazilian or suttin comes in tryna shot some boog Rolexes n dat. They wasn't even good fakes so I tell him bounce so my barber can carry on with my trim and the yout try tell me to shut up. So I tell him we can swing it out right now, but he starts backing out the shop and as he's leaving he looks at me and says anytime g. True life I'm gonna fuck man up, tryna gwan like he's bad for man.

Daffy has a funny way of talking certain times, saying true life whenever he's being serious about suttin.

Yo Taz, he says, drive up to Church Road.

When we get to Church Road, Daffy says yo that's the yout and jumps out of the whip as it slows down. Kane jumps out as well and they run up to this tall lanky black brer holding a sports bag and Kane bangs him in the face and the brer's knees buckle for a second but he plants one hand on the kerb and pushes himself back upright. He dodges Daffy's swing and Kane rips the sports bag out of his hands and he starts running up the road, back to Willesden. There's a bunch of heads standing around – couple older yardie man and some Somali brers – and Kane starts handing out the boog Rolexes, still in their packaging, to the little crowd. No one's gonna call feds anyway. It's Church Road. Then Kane and Daffy jump back in the whip and Daffy says drive back past the barber's. Taz spins the car round.

As we pass the barber's, Daffy says there he is and pops the door open as Taz slows down. I get out and start running after Daffy coz I don't wanna miss anything and since I'm rolling with these man I'm gonna back it. Kane comes running just behind me.

The Brazilian brer is on the other side of Willesden High Road when he sees Daffy coming for him. Daffy pulls off his T-shirt in the middle of the street and shouts true life true life, and runs across the road. The Brazilian brer looks around for something to grab, picks up an empty beer bottle from the gutter and just as Daffy reaches him, in one swift move he smashes it on the kerb and shanks Daffy with it. Daffy twists round at the last second and the brer crunches the jagged bottle neck into Daffy's back and starts dussing.

I catch up to Daffy, pull my sweatshirt off and stick it against the bloody tear in his back. It's bleeding heavy and thick, so I press the sweatshirt against his back, hard, and go hold dat fam.

Daffy's like I'm cool, I'm cool. Kane runs down the street tryna catch the brer. I run with him and we clock some loose bricks that crumbled off a wall, so we pick them up but the Brazilian brer's cut round the corner and is too far to catch. Taz pulls up in the whip and I jump in the back with Kane. Daffy ties my sweatshirt around his back and gets in the front.

Where was you Taz? says Kane and Taz stares ahead, wrinkling his forehead like he did earlier when I told him the mash was rusty and goes, I was right there in the whip, I was right there.

Shut up man, about you was right there, says Kane. You wasn't anywhere. Snoopz was right there with man, you wasn't doing jack shit.

Daffy turns round in his seat, spuds me and says love for dat g.

Dun know fam, I say.

Fucking drive past the mini park Taz, dafuck are you doing? says Kane.

Taz chews his lip and the car lurches down the back roads of Willesden High Road.

Kane slides his brick under Daffy's seat. I push mine under Taz's and Kane unzips the sports bag. There's a remote-control car, still in its packaging, and three fake Rolexes in cardboard boxes with the Rolex logo printed in silver on the top.

Myman's not even moving anyting serious, says Kane with his face scrunched up like suttin smells bad, and he zips the bag shut.

We drive past shabby little red-brick houses with broken fences and dirty windows full of white curtains looking like you can't tell which is more grimy, the windows or the curtains behind them. We go past the underpass that leads to Griffin Close and the mini park, and then Taz slams on the brakes as a fed car with blue lights flashing almost drives right into the front of the whip. At the same time a bully van pulls up right behind us, boxing us in, and six jakes jump out of the van with their batons in hand, shouting STAYINTHEFUCKINGCAR DONOTGET OUT PUTYOURHANDSONTHEWINDOWS HANDS ONTHEFUCKINGWINDOWS.

They surround the whip and as we put our hands on the windows they pop the doors open. One by one we get dragged out. I get dashed against a low brick wall with my face shoved into a bush, my eyes full of green dots and dust, and a fed pulls my arms up behind me hard and handcuffs my wrists quicktime. I look to my left and see Taz standing right next to me against the bush with his wrists cuffed. The fed behind me says spread your legs, so I plant my feet wider and he says spread your fucking legs, and kicks the inside of my left leg, forcing my feet to spread mad wide apart. I almost buckle and then my heart drops right into a pit of snakes deep in my belly as I feel the ball of coke I cheeksed earlier slip out and drop down my left trouser leg. Fuckssake, I'm gonna get shift I'm gonna get shift and I swear I can smell the bush in front of me, all little green leaves, but they ain't soft on my face and they smell like petrol. It's like suddenly I can see how everything is ugly and dirty all around me – even the sky looks stained and the sun looks swollen – and I just wish I wasn't here. The officer starts patting me down, dragging his hand along the seams of my jeans, pulling at my crotch, feeling up my chest and sides – shit he hasn't felt it he hasn't felt it just don't go patting down my trouser leg again. I clock another fed car next to the bully van with two feds in it and sitting right there, on the backseat, is the Brazilian brer. He points at me and Taz, says something to one of the feds and the fed goes those two weren't involved in the robbery, pointing at me and Taz. The Brazilian brer points at Daffy and Kane and says something else.

At this point I realise that the ball of white has slipped down my trouser leg and stopped on the rim of my trainer, literally balancing there, and the fed who searched me missed it coz he'd started from my ankles and gone upwards as the food slipped down. I need to move from here, I need to move move move, but I need to do it casual like, no big steps, otherwise the food's gonna drop out and I'll definitely get shift.

The fed who kicked my legs apart uncuffs me and I watch as Daffy and Kane get placed under arrest – the whole you do not have to say anything but it may harm your defence speech – Kane looking at Taz in some type of way that I want to understand but I can't work out. The fed starts uncuffing Taz and Taz, who's been quiet the whole time, starts hyping up, turning to screwface the officer – fucking feds, always harrassing man, it's coz I'm black innit, every time you pricks see man you – and the fed says do you want to get arrested?

I say Taz, stop man, they're letting us go, come we cut.

But Taz is on a mad hype, going I know, but every fucking time they see man they wanna harass man, always the same ting with these fucking boydem.

Oi! I'm warning you, says the police officer. One more word and you're nicked.

Kane says just seckle Taz, as he peers out from the open police van door.

Taz says fucking eedyat ting, looking at the pavement as he turns around and starts rubbing his wrists.

We walk back to the whip, me walking extra slow so that I won't dislodge the soft, balanced between my ankle and the rim of my left trainer. As soon as I get in the whip I can breathe properly again and my heartbeat goes away. I take the ball of coke out and it smells kinda mad and then I cheeks it again.

Couple days later, I'm sitting in a room in the Holiday Inn on Kilburn High Road. I'm with one brer from South called Sniper who's linking Grim's cousin. Grim is my bredrin who's literally one of the baddest MCs in Northwest and probably the whole of London. But like a lot of MCs he doesn't really live the life he spits about, lyrics about wetting up man and bussin straps. Still, I got mad love for him. I wish I could write bars like that. Anyway. When he introduced me to Sniper, he was cotching at his cousin's yard in Kilburn and he belled me and said come thru I'm here with my cousin and her man. Real recognise real and that's how me and Sniper connected. It's like he could see suttin in my eyes, hear suttin in my words that made him know I was about dat life. Sniper is one of them typical bang bang South man. He's in PDC which these times is one of the greaziest teams in South and one of the greaziest in London full stop. So after we met through Grim, bunned couple zoots and whatnot, we swapped numbers and the next time Sniper came to Kilburn, he phoned me and said yo cuz, come check me at the Holiday Inn if you're free.

Sniper is bagging up champs and brandy on the table in the hotel room. While we bun zoots with blue halos of smoke curling around our heads, I tell him the whole story of the madness with Daffy and Kane and Taz.

Myman's not even about it like dat, I say. Couldn't even hook me up with a proper burner.

Sniper says I can get you that cuz.

Swear down?

Mum's life cuz. You want a 9 mill yeah?

Yeah fam. Or a .22 if that's about.

Gimme couple days and I'll shout you.

A few days later, Sniper calls me.

Yo my g, what's good? I say.

Yeah cuz, mi deya. Listen, I can't hook you up with the twenty-two-year-old but I got a next ting there for you.

Swear down? What is it?

It's Nina cuz. Two and a half bags. And she's silent. Comes with like ten sweets in the clip still.

Say nuttin my g. Bring that down with you and I'll have the p's waiting, I say.

And so I finally get my burner, my strap, my mash. A Star 9mm with a screw-on silencer and ten bullets in the clip. Now I'm ready to take revenge if I have to, I can do the beef ting on my ones if I need to, I can protect myself differently. And anyway, not gonna lie, one of the main reasons I wanted a gun is because I just wanna know what it would be like to shoot a man. Onetime. Real talk.

AT TAMEEKA'S YARD

Best draw my sword; and if mine enemy but fear the sword like
me, he'll scarcely look on't.

William Shakespeare, *Cymbeline*

AT TAMEEKA'S YARD, I fall asleep sitting in the armchair and although I got my jeans fresh from the dry cleaner's just the other day, they're already smelling frowzy from all the punk getting bunned in the yard.

After I got my strap, Kane introduced me to his bredrin Not Nice. Not Nice heard me spitting bars over a beat that was pumping out of the whip when we parked up in the courtyard of some blocks on Church Road.

Surrounded by the haters, claiming who's the badder man,
I should scar the faces of these Tony Montana fans,
Greazy, from North Weezy where the hammers bang,
My Muslim boys will eat you, even when it's Ramadan.

61

You're sick still, he said. Why you rolling with that pussy Taz?

Not Nice. Hair brushed out into black fire and face like he's straight outta Kemet. Eyes that don't laugh. Thick scar on his left bicep where someone poked him. Tells me, when the blade went in I was like what you tryna do blood? Don't you know you can't kill a man like dat? Then I pulled the shank out of my arm and showed the yout how it's meant to be used.

The first time we jammed together, there was a boxing match on TV. It was a white boxer and a black boxer and when the black brer started rocking his opponent, Not Nice said milk of magnesia can never beat melanin. Then he looked at me and said Snoopz, are you sure you're not mixed?

He's one of them olders in Northwest doing his ting, always scheming, and he's got couple youngers who he sends out to do shit. If there's a drought, he'll bell the one person who's got food and ask them to bring a big bit and then he'll send his youngers to go rob the brer so that Not Nice don't have to pay for it. He could tell I was on stuff, was gassed about my bars and he rated the way I didn't pet to speak my mind. Still, I refused to diss Taz just because Not Nice was dissing him, although he clocked that I didn't really rate Taz no more after that bullshit with the burner and Kane told him how Taz hadn't done fuck all when Daffy got shanked. So all through summer Not Nice would holla at me and I'd come Willesden and jam with him and bun zoots, and more times Kane would be with us as well.

So we end up jamming in this yard between Dollis Hill and Willesden High Road where these three yardie chicks live. Tameeka, Marcia and their seventeen-year-old sister Stephanie.

Half the time I have to proper concentrate to understand what they're saying. Tameeka's got bare piercings; tongue, lips, nose, eyebrow, left cheek, and she has this bright platinum-blonde weave that looks like it wants to get off her head and die somewhere quietly. Not Nice, Kane and me end up jamming there for like a week, staying the night and just bunning zoots and drinking Henny during the day. On certain nights, Not Nice and Kane go upstairs with Marcia and Tameeka. On other nights, everyone gets too mashup and they start arguing, Tameeka and Not Nice always the loudest, badding each other up until Kane and Marcia stop arguing and go to calm the other two down. Eventually Not Nice and Kane come downstairs and just frass out on one of the spare sofas while I sit in the armchair, and the youngest sister, Stephanie, sits on the staircase, busy on her phone.

The real reason we came to this yard is because we needed a traphouse. We've started shotting big bits of cro together. I've got the p's and Not Nice has the connec for big bits of food and he knows everyone round the ends who's shotting punk and wants to pick up from man. So we set up a line. We get a couple boxes – two kilos of amnesia – and break them down into smaller bits. Shotters park up round the corner from Tameeka's yard and Not Nice or I go and drop off the food and come back with the p's. We split the profits fifty-fifty.

Tameeka and Marcia start tryna hook me up with their younger sister.

Ya like she, don't it? says Tameeka. You nuh wan deal wid dat Snoop? Cah me see how unu badboy fi true so wa'um, you nah wan deal wid my lickle sister? I laugh and say yeah I'll deal with her but only if she's on it, and truth is I could tell from the beginning Stephanie ain't feeling me like that. It's not like she's on some shy tip, although compared to her sisters she's mad quiet, always cooking or playing on her phone and bunning zoots in silence. Everything done alone, uninterested. Then Tameeka starts talking all this shit about cah unu av money fi spend, it nuh tek nuttin fi look after mi lickle sister, you cyan buy her one two trainer dem and a Gucci belt nuh true? And I'm thinking allow these ratchet chicks tryna hustle man. I say I ain't spending my p's on no one. Even if we go McD's I ain't buying none of you a meal, not even a cheeseburger, real talk. She says not even a cheeseburger? I say not even a cheeseburger. She stares at me cold and I can see she's wearing bright green contact lenses, and then she says me nah like you Snoop. She picks up the empty bottles of Hennessy off the table and dashes them in the bin proper hard so it makes noise and then she actually stomps across the room to the kitchen and starts billing a zoot. Marcia comes into the room like wa'um to you sis? Tameeka starts chatting bare quick with her voice all scratched up and all I manage to catch is him say him wouldn't even buy we McDonald's to bloodclart and then she looks at me again, kisses her teeth and goes upstairs.

Later that night a big argument kicks off between her and Not Nice. He comes downstairs and says fuck this Snoopz, we're gonna do this ting somewhere else and he starts making phone calls while I drift into uneasy sleep full of things I can't hold on to.

In the morning, we take all the food that's left in a Nike sports bag, jump into Not Nice's whip with Kane and drive off. We end up in the kitchen of one flat in Church Road – the white flats as Not Nice calls them – and I'm cotching with him and Kane and a box of cro all split into four-and-a-halfs, wrapped up in clingfilm, waiting for the line to ring. We know the food is gonna move quick coz there's no dust, barely any sticks and the buds are bright green fat, covered in orange hairs and feathery white crystals that ping when the light catches them. We've put aside couple buds to sample. When Not Nice sparks his zoot I'm like rah that smells mad loud and even Kane, who doesn't smoke, says fuckinell that smells piff, and opens a window.

The yard belongs to one chick who Not Nice is linking and he tells us she's gone to stay with her auntie for couple days, but the kitchen looks like no one's lived there for a hot minute. Stovetop thick with brown grease and oil stains going up the wall behind it. Kane opens the fridge and says rah what's this gyal on though? because there's only two wrinkled peppers and a half-opened pack of that orange plastic-looking cheese that's like 99p in the corner shop. The fridge door has a souvenir magnet from Amsterdam with a big weed leaf on a canal and the magnet is stuck over a Chinese takeaway menu. Beneath it, there's a see-through magnet with a photo of a little boy in school uniform, grinning gappy teeth, although the magnet is upside down and it looks like no one's moved it for time coz it's all dusty n shit.

When we came into the yard, I'd clocked the front room because the door was open and just before Not Nice closed it, I noticed bare garms all over the floor and Nike creps and high-heeled shoes and fake Gucci belts and a hairdryer and bits of Lego and empty takeaway boxes and I was like seen, I know what kinda gyal this is. This is one of them excuse my yard type chicks. One of them there's nothing in the fridge, frowsy bedsheets, Facebook profile works at fulltime mummy to a king hashtag boss bitch chicks. One of them my son goes to sleep when he feels like it but he's got a TV in his room so he won't disturb us type chicks. Allow dat.

Kane opens a bottle of Henny, pours some out on the kitchen

floor and says this one's for the fallen soldiers, and I know that we've all imagined what could be written on our gravestones one day.

Not Nice gets off the phone and says Snoopz go and drop one of these four-and-a-halfs to my don who's waiting outside. You'll see him parked up in front of the playground in a white Benz. I grab one of the packs, stuff it into the front pocket of my hoodie and step outside.

Every time I've come round these flats with Not Nice, I've never seen any youts playing in the playground. It's just empty swings getting pushed by the wind and silent tarmac. Now that it's summer, it feels like the sun has drained the life out of the air. I make the drop, get the p's and walk back into the block.

As I'm going up the stairs, one brer in a red leather AV, white gold chain round his neck with an iced-out Donald Duck pendant swinging off it, comes down. As we pass each other in the stairwell he goes yo who you here to see blood? I stop, look at him and go fuck d'you mean who am I here to see? He's looking at me mad hard face, no blinking, as if whatever once made those eyes alive musta withered long time into nuttin, and he says this is my block blood. I say so fucking what? I don't know you blood. I start going up the stairs. He comes right after me like oi come ere rudeboy, I've had man tryna run up on me in this block before. I get to the top of the stairs, kiss my teeth and say about come ere man. As I walk down the balcony to the flat, I hear the brer reach the landing behind me. He says dafuck are you walking away for? Moving like you're some op. I turn around and he goes who da fuck are you blood? I'm like why da fuck are you asking me who I am? You don't know me blood I don't need to tell you nuttin. But as I say this, his right hand, black Nike glove on, digs into the front of his trousers and pulls out black metal, 9 mill looking kinda scratched up n dat. What's mad is that right then I can feel he's used it before. I can feel some next power that's making my heart kick against my chest like it's tryna get out. When you see a gun in a film it's entertainment, it's just an object, a prop that everyone knows about. And if you start tryna imagine what you'd do if someone pulled a strap on you, there's always this one vital bit missing from your imagination. It's the feeling of being face to face with a power that can end your life in one blink. Of all the days not to have my burner on me, it had to be today. But where is it? Safely tucked away inside a shoebox under my old bed at my mum's yard. Fuckssake.

Now what you saying g?

I hear the door of the flat open behind me and Not Nice and Kane come out. Not Nice comes past me, smell of ammi following him as he goes oi Smek allow it, he's with me, it's my young g, he's bless and he puts his arm on my shoulder and kinda nudges me away. I start heading back towards the flat, looking over my shoulder to see the brer tucking the burner into his waistline as he goes I don't like how this yout's moving you kna. I stop at the door, turn back and go dafuck do you mean you don't like how I'm moving blood? Not Nice goes allow it Snoopz, just go into the yard. Kane puts his hand on my back, says come on g and edges me through the door.

I sit down at the kitchen table. Kane grabs the bottle of Henny and pours some more into his cup and then the front door slams and Not Nice comes into the kitchen. You can't be moving like dat Snoopz he says, that's Smekman, myman's fully on this ting, he coulda bun you right then and I say I don't give a fuck who he is and Not Nice goes shhh all sharp like he's tryna blow the dust of my words away and says blood, you best be careful he don't hear you. Kane stands up, goes to the window and closes it. Not Nice says you don't know what that yout's on Snoopz, my don's only nineteen and already he's known for terrorising the olders, running up in yards on his ones, tying up mandem's babymums and raping them n all sorts and then waiting for man to come home so he can take all their p's and food. Truss me, he don't give a fuck forreal. I look at the bud which I've started crumbling with my fingers so I can bill a next zoot and say how was I supposed to know that though? Anyway, myman's not bulletproof ah lie? I'll go and get my Star 9 right now fam, it's not a ting. Not Nice says come on Snoopz, I know you're smarter than dat, just lissen to man so you don't have no problems round here. Kane laughs and says Snoopz is on it still.

The next day we don't go back to the white flats.

A week later, Not Nice gets his own flat in some block in Wembley and he's got his little son and daughter with him. Tells me he won custody of them but doesn't tell me why or how. I help them move, carrying chairs and cardboard boxes from his mother's yard, unloading the car. The heat of summer sticks to my skin like something you wanna rip off but don't know how bad it might hurt if you do. Not Nice says you can stay the night whenever you want Snoopz.

One evening we're jamming in the living room, billing zoots and spitting bars over instrumentals. We've just been talking about 2Pac and next rappers who died when they were young and Not Nice is saying how it's always a car crash or an over-dose or some gang killing, but really it's some Illuminati shit. They killed him, says Not Nice, fucking sacrifices innit, they wanna hold us down whenever we get power. Then he tells me that black people are gods who fell to Earth and the water in the Earth's atmosphere caused their green skin to rust and turn brown and everything started in Kemet, in Ancient Egypt where the New Beings, or Nubians as history books call them, built the pyramids. Then the white man came out of his caves in the Caucus mountains and stole all our shit, he says. I say I know this one, I've heard it before.

He says I got suttin to show you. He leaves the room and comes back in with gloves on, holding a blue plastic bag with something heavy in it. Put your gloves on, he says. He pulls out a black MAC-10 and hands it to me. The MAC is so heavy that it bends my wrist down with its weight, like I can't even hold it straight with one hand. It's not like the movies where it looks like some light piece of equipment, I mean a MAC-10 is a proper submachine gun, all solid metal and it's got a long clip full of shells coming out of the handle. Not gonna lie, as soon as I grip the ting I can feel the energy, like I just wanna let it off and lick a man down just to feel the power. Not Nice smiles while I point it around the room and then he says he's gonna tell me how to get away with doing a booting.

I hand him the MAC and he wraps it back up in the plastic bag. Just then his daughter knocks on the door and says Daddy, so Not Nice drops the bag under the table and walks over to the door while pulling his gloves off. He goes wa'um princess as he opens the door and bends down to pick her up. She rubs her eyes, looks at me, frowns and turns her head away quicktime as she wraps her arms round Not Nice's neck, and the pink plastic butterflies on the end of her braids bounce against his teeth as he says you want some water princess? The little girl shakes her head and buries herself into him. He starts bouncing her gently against his chest while he looks at me and says never go and do a booting in a vehicle that's registered to you or connected to you in any way. Me, I prefer motorbikes coz you can duck out mad quick through London traffic, down alleyways, over the pavement and alladat, but if you're in a whip there's always the risk you'll end up stuck behind traffic and whatnot. Always burn the getaway vehicle somewhere deserted where it won't get clocked while it burns. I'm just gonna put her back to bed he says and steps out of the room. I look out of the window and a white slice of moon falls slowly into the drifting darkness.

Not Nice comes back into the room, pulling his gloves on. He picks up the plastic bag. Once you've dumped the getaway vehicle, go somewhere d-low where you've stashed a next set of garms and some petrol. Burn everyting you was wearing when you did the booting. It don't matter to bloodclart if you're rocking your favourite creps. You can cop them again. Burn everyting, including your socks and boxers. Nah serious blood, lissen to what I'm telling you. Before you put on the new set of garms, wash yourself with petrol, make sure you use your fingers to wash in all the curves of your ears, up your nostrils and in your hair. It gets rid of all the gunpowder residue. Once you get home, put your change of clothes in the wash and have a long shower, scrub your whole body several times over and don't tell no one what you done. Then he leaves the room and the loneliness of the night holds me in its arms. I drift off on the sofa, sweating in the heat, memory of the MAC-10 weight like a ghost in my hand.

A week before I go to start uni, Not Nice and I fall out because he still owes me nine bills from when we were shotting cro. He hasn't dropped me any p for almost two weeks. When I phone him, I get pissed off and say what kinda wasteman can't pay a lickle nine bills when you got two youts to feed and clothe, like how are you even looking after them? He switches and goes you know what, forget your money, you're not getting anything, watch when I see you, I got the big mac ready for you. True he knows I've got a strap as well, knows he can't just punch me up. I say you got the big mac for me yeah? Don't forget I know where you live blood and I hear the moment of hesitation on his end like the loudest silence. Then he says are you mad Snoopz, I will bun your skin.

So you got the big mac for me yeah? Say nuttin and I lock off the phone.

I've got the strap on me right there and then. It's one of those days when I decided to bring it out with me, tucked into a pair of tight jeans I'd put on that morning under some baggy tracksuit bottoms so you can't see a bulge. Got my balls sweating forreal. Not the right weather for this shit. I've left the silencer at my mum's yard, rolled up in a T-shirt in the shoebox where I keep my p's. I bell my don Stitch who's been my bredrin since we were thirteen going to Stowe youth club on Harrow Road and he's always on crud, but bare d-low with it like his girl and his family would never guess. Stitch picks up and I say fam I wanna lick this pagan down, and I tell him what happened and he says come we ride out on this brer then, you got the strap? I say yeah and he says come link me in Paddington in fifteen minutes. When I get to the spot he's there with the motorbike and two helmets and we start chatting about how to do it.

But there's something stopping me from going to kill Not Nice. I start remembering what he'd told me about doing a booting and getting away with it. I start going through all the rules he taught me, step by step, and I realise I'm going about it all wrong. Stitch holds out the spare motorbike helmet to me but my mind starts racing like shit I can't do it, it's too bate, what if this and what if that and maybe I'm just not ready today and just for a flash another thought pokes in and says maybe you're not ready for killing and I remember Not Nice's daughter with her plastic butterfly hair clips, but I shake it out and it's like my eyes are wide open but I can't see anything, and then I hear Stitch saying oi Snoopz what you on, you wanna do this or what? But then I think nah, not like this, not today. I'm not ready to catch a M-charge over nine bills, even though I badly wanna duppy Not Nice, especially since we'd been rolling so tight and then in one conversation we'd become enemies. Fucking pagan.

FIRST YEARS

UNI IS A fashion show. Especially for the first years. Capo has a Daffy Duck Iceberg jacket. I've got a brand new black leather Avirex jacket. Brers with fresh trims. Chicks who smell of shampoo and moisturiser. Everyone seems to have bought their creps a week before uni started, walking slow and measured so their toes don't crease. Especially when they're rocking Air Force 1s. Muslim tings in fresh headscarves with peng eye makeup that makes you look. White people from out of London, excited about eating their first Perfect Fried Chicken meal deal in Mile End. There's some nitty who teefs books from the uni bookshop, slipping them under a long overcoat that swallows his whole body and then he shots the books for mad cheap to students outside. Capo's cousin, Blix, is a second year so we already have a group of heads to jam with. He shows us where we can go and bun zoots by the canal, behind one of the student accommodation buildings. Introductions to the course, to lecturers, to students. Capo gets a flat with Blix up the road from uni. Sometimes I go and stay the night there. I'm serious about my degree. No way am I ducking any lectures or flopping assignments. Everyone on my course buys the complete works of Shakespeare. It's like a bible.

For one module I have to write a 3,000-word essay on 'Art and truth in the works of Aristotle and Plato'. I long it out and end up writing my essay at Capo's the night before I have to hand it in, bunning bare zoots of ammi and drinking can after can of Boost until the sky goes back to blue and I can hear birds. I don't manage to catch any sleep. In the morning my eyes are redup from all the cro and I swear my hands are trembling from all the caffeine. My body is cold. I go and hand in the essay. A week later my professor hands our assignments back to us and I've got a First – not only that but it's the top mark in my class. And that's how my first year of uni goes by: chirpsing chicks in the library, linking Yinka, writing essays, reading books, discussing literature and all sorts in seminars . . . and doing moves.

After the first big move, I go and get myself some iced-out grillz: two white gold teeth set with diamonds on either side of my upper front teeth. Something to remember that morning, running up in some top badman's yard in a block in Grove and – actually the way it happened was a mad ting, lemme tell you.

I stopped living at Uncle T's when I started uni, because I needed to be able to stay in East to get to classes and to move from place to place without the pressure of rent. In my first term though, whenever I had days without seminars and lectures, which were plenty, I'd go back to West and more times I'd stay the night at my mum's so I could link up with Dario early in the morning and look for yards we could run up in once the owners had gone to work or whatever. We'd pick them at random. Gut instinct, make sure no one's watching on road and then fuck it; run up and kick off the door while adrenaline bursts in the guts.

My brudda Dario. Short, sharp and careless, like a stone. Often rocking a du-rag, big cubic zirconia studs in each ear that he's always losing and replacing, even though with all the p's we've made from moves, he could blatantly buy himself some real diamond ones. Swear down I'd just lose them as well, he says. When he talks, the words rush out of his lips like they're escaping from inside him and you only really hear them inside your head, moments after they've been said. Always linking chicks who are taller than him and mad thick and when they hug him, they press his head into their breasts like he's their baby forreal.

These times Dario was beating some ting who lived in one block in Grove and apparently her dad was some proper badman. The girl was always telling Dario about stacks of paper in the yard and how early one morning she'd come into the kitchen and found her dad cleaning his burner. When she told Dario that her dad would be going on holiday, he phoned me and told me to get ready.

I was fully gassed the morning that we linked up, adrenaline trembling through my muscles as we walked to the block, ballys rolled up on our heads like beanie hats and gloves already on. Once we got into the building – waited for someone to be leaving and caught the door before it closed – we took the lift to the twenty-second floor. Mad high up. You could see the whole area of Ladbroke Grove spreading out into the city and losing itself from there. Dario couldn't remember which door it was but he knew it was two doors away from flat 152. Two doors to the right or two doors to the left he said. We chose two doors to the right. The flats were down a narrow corridor so there wasn't much space for the run-up. We rolled the ballys down over our faces. Dario opened the letterbox, listened and said there's no one in. We did our usual ting: counted one two three, ran up and booted the door hard, aiming for the middle and close to the lock. When I'm telling you this door just wouldn't break out of its frame – trust me it was mad. We were booting the door over and over, I mean we fully stopped giving a fuck if anyone heard us, until the doorframe started breaking out of the concrete. Still, the door itself stayed firmly closed. The concrete at the top of the frame crumbled, little bits of it falling down in a cloud of dust. One more run up and kick, and then slow motion, like some huge animal full of spears, it groaned, separating from the concrete and the whole ting crashed inwards, onto the floor of the flat. The moment we ran up in there we realised we'd got the wrong yard.

There was a dirty little kitchen, a bathroom with black mould growing on the ceiling and a room that doubled as a bedroom and living room. There was a sofa bed with a white sheet on it and on the floor, a little Buddhist shrine with Chinese char-acters carved into white plastic and some blackened stumps of incense sticks. Nothing else in the room.

Then voices, people coming down the corridor, shit shit shit, so I went into the kitchen, grabbed two big kitchen knives, gave one to Dario and we pressed ourselves against the wall, waiting to see if anyone would be dumb enough to come into the flat.

I was ready for it to turn real scatty, I told Dario later. Man woulda had to start poking up whoever came in and he said I know, I saw how you was moving Snoopz, you just went straight into autopilot and I laughed and said dun know my brudda. Whoever was in the corridor walked past the flat. I know they noticed the door and everything because the voices stopped at the doorway and one said rah that door got lick off and another voice said that's peak, and then they moved on and disappeared.

So we stepped out, looking up and down the corridor, dashed the kitchen knives into the flat, went back to door number 152 and counted two doors in the other direction. It was a black door with 150 in brass above a door knocker. I could tell straight away this door would get licked off easy. Dario was certain the chick was at college and her mum had gone on holiday with the dad so it would be empty for us to do our ting. Worst case scenario we'd have to wrap up the girl if she was in there, but that would be nuttin still.

The door burst open on the first kick. It was a much bigger flat. No one was in. We went from room to room. It was in the parents' bedroom that we found the belly in a shoebox: stacks and stacks of £50 notes tied up with orange bands. We jumped onto the bed and threw the money into the air and hugged each other, shouting and laughing. We musta looked mad; black tracksuits with patches of concrete dust on our legs, gloves on, black ballys covering our faces, jumping on this thick white duvet in a white bedroom with pink stacks of fifties falling all around us. When we counted the money it came to thirty bags. Thirty grand between the two of us. I wasn't even twenty years old.

After that move, Dario bought a ticket to Canada and went to stay with some family he had out there for a month because we needed to lie low. The chick's dad would definitely be on duppying us – I mean he woulda killed us forreal if he found out who done it – so I went back to living in South Killy at Bimz's yard, or staying up in East with Capo.

Things were never the same after that.

Now, anytime a van slows down next to me or passes by, my whole body tightens, I'll half open my shank in my pocket and grip it tight, ready for someone to jump out and try wrap me up. Sometimes I wonder if I'll feel the shots when they hit me, or I prepare myself to dive behind parked cars. Lots of other things aren't the same now. I mean this is a whole next level from when I was fifteen, yacking next youts for their phones and wallets. Now that I've had a taste of real paper, I want more.

All this is why one Friday afternoon, after my last seminar of the day – a discussion of poetry and why poets make the choices they do – I go to Hatton Garden with my boy Capo to see a jeweller called Christmas. He's the only one in Hatton who makes grillz these times, and I get him to make me two single teeth in white gold set with white diamonds and Capo gets a single tooth as well, all paid for in fifties. Then I go and cop an Aqua Master watch with diamond chips around the bezel coz everyone in the ends is into them and I also get a gold chain.

So there I am in my first year of uni, sitting in a Shakespeare seminar in a black Nike tracksuit with my iced-out grillz in, after a one-hour lecture on *Romeo and Juliet*, talking about how revenge is the purest instinct whether you like it or not. Revenge is a demonstration of love, real pure love, like when Romeo went to murk Tybalt coz Tybalt murked his boy Mercutio I say to the class, just how you'd feel the absolute need and desire to kill if someone raped your mother, the most natural urge to take revenge, even if it's just for a split second before your moral training kicks in, before the way society has numbed your instincts starts working – and the light in the room breaks into thousands of pieces as it hits the diamonds in my teeth.

THE WEDDING

I'M NINETEEN, IT'S April and I'm done with uni shit for a while since it's the Easter holidays, so I'm cotching at Bimz's yard and I wanna get a draw. Bimz's mum moved out and left him the flat so his boys basically jam there all day long and all night, anyone who wants to can practically k.o. there whenever, there's always at least four five man in the yard, spitting bars over grime or rap beats, bunning cro and playing *Soulcalibur* or *GTA* on the Xbox, watching happy slap videos and footage of mandem chasing down their ops on their phones, getting juiced on Alizé or Henny, chatting shit into the early hours. So whenever I'm not linking Yinka, who's back at her mum's yard, I come to Bimz's and get mad faded and sleep on a sofa or the floor.

So anyway, I want a draw, Bimz wants a draw and so does Ki and Sly, so we come out the yard and start walking from Precinct to Uncle T's. Bimz says Uncle T's got the bang bang. It's one of those warm spring nights that makes you forget things and we cross Carlton Vale under the CCTV camera by the entrance to the park, and start walking to Malvern Road.

There's the quicker route, which is to cut left through the park, going past the front of D-block and then you're basically right next to Blake Court. But true we don't really ever take this route, especially not late at night because all the D-block mandem will be patrolling the balcony and we'll have to walk right in front of them, everyone clocking us, and these are the mandem that hold straps on them twenty-four seven, everyone with iced-out grillz, shotting food all night to the nittys and if they see us, someone might wanna make an example, might try suttin or just talk shit about us in loud voices, boying man off, showing us who's running tings, and that's a stress we all wanna avoid coz no one wants to be aware they're below anyone else. No one wants to feel powerless.

We take the path through the top of the park. Darkness ripples around us, and coming from Malvern Road we see three white brers and a woman, the men in polo shirts, the woman in heels and a miniskirt. They're talking loud, probably a bit crunk. Maybe they thought this was a good shortcut coming from wherever they've been, but it's like they don't realise where they are forreal. There's me, Bimz, Spooks, Mazey, Ki and Sly, and we're just spread out, bopping towards Malvern Road. As I'm walking down the path, one of the white brers doesn't step off. He walks straight forward like it's nuttin, so I brace my shoulder and he bounces off as he goes past. I carry on walking but two twos I hear him from behind as he says fucking prick. Spooks turns around straight away like what? with his face screwed up and I turn and run up to the brer and back out my shank, open it all in one smooth movement as it comes out of my pocket and I wet him deep in his arm which he's raising towards me – I meant to shank him in his chest but he put his arm in the way – and the blade goes in and slices up the length

80

of his arm and I see a thick black line open up on his forearm and the woman starts screaming and I grab her by her jacket and dash her to the ground where she slumps against a fence that surrounds a little playground area for children with swings in it and a climbing frame. Her legs are pale white as if the moon's been poured onto them and one of her high heels is broken and she grips her bag and the man is holding his cut arm with his other hand, looking at it as if the arm isn't his own and he just picked it up or suttin, and the other two white brers are frozen silent, pulling their phones out, so we turn around and walk up to Malvern Road.

We're laughing and Mazey says Snoopz is on a mad ting and I'm like fuck dat is he mad? Walking into man like some dickhead, and Spooks says how can a man turn round and start chatting shit after he blatantly barged you? Fuck dat eedyat ting and I say exactly fam, I seen how you turned round quicktime and we laugh. Bimz says ah it's all gonna be peak now, this is long this is long – we know they're gonna phone jakes on man and when the feds come, if we're still around, everyone's getting shift.

It's the first time them man seen me do a madness. Mazey says you should link up with my cousin Gotti, truss me, you two would be unstoppable, and Bimz says that would be a mad ting still. I've seen Gotti couple times at Bimz's yard, although we've never exchanged more than a few words and I've heard how he's been doing eats around the ends since he got out of pen, robbing mandem for their food n shit. While I've been at uni, he's been coming round Bimz's, tryna get them man to come and do eats with him, but we always seem to miss each other for whatever reason. Anyway.

I'm like I need to cut out the ends right now, so I bell Capo

81

since he knows South Killy and he's usually driving. He picks up and I'm like yo brudda I just poked up some brer in the park in SK, beg you come get me, I need to cut, and he says yeah fam, me and Blix will come scoop you still, we're just at Mo's brother's wedding. I get off the phone and tell the mandem I'm cutting. Safe Snoopz. They head off to Uncle T's and I walk back to Precinct.

Five minutes later, Capo calls and tells me he's parked up round the back of Bimz's block. Capo and Blix are rocking suits coz they've come straight from this Moroccan wedding they were at and they're with some next Sudanese brer they know called Omar. I jump in the whip and Capo says come to the reception, they're still eating n dat and I'm like safe my brudda. This Omar brer starts asking me why did you shank that brer though, like what's the point, that's dumb and I say it's not fucking dumb, don't ask what's the point if you don't get it, you're just not about dat life g and I stare into his eyes and he looks away and goes quiet like he wants to say something but he knows not to chat shit. I can tell he's one of those brers who'll criticise when someone does a madness but it's not because he disapproves morally, it's because the violence in other people scares him, because he's not on them kinda tings, he's not a shooter or an eater and he ain't never wetted man up. He's tryna close the gap between me and him, because what I just done is gonna earn me stripes whereas he's just a nobody when it comes to this road ting.

Later I ask Capo wagwan for your boy Omar though? Man was asking me some bate questions in the whip and Blix laughs and says I saw how quick he shut up when you told him he's not about dat life and Capo says don't watch dat, he's just moist Snoopz, he's not on nuttin.

We go to the wedding reception which is in the hall of a community centre in Maida Vale. Them man go to join the party but I tell Capo I'm not inna dat fam. I feel awkward coz I'm wearing my black Raiders tracksuit and Air Maxes, I'm blatantly not dressed for a wedding and I've still got my shank in my pocket. Capo takes me to the kitchen area at the back of the centre, says something in Arabic to one man who shakes my hand and says *salaam alaikum*, pointing to a chair at an empty table. Capo goes back to the party. I can hear singing, clapping and women doing this high-pitched howling noise, almost like some war cry; it's as if there's joy and pain in it all at the same time. Two twos one Moroccan woman in a headscarf brings me a plate of rice and lamb and I say thank you *alhamdulillah*, because Capo told me that's the right thing to say when you give thanks, and I eat at the table alone, the women in this backstage area sorting out food and taking care of wailing and hyperactive children who are all dressed in smart little outfits with shiny shoes.

When I finish eating my food, I wait for Capo so that he can drive me back to my mum's yard. I reckon it's better not to show up again in SK tonight, just in case feds are looking for man, and anyway, I'm itching to get indoors because I wanna check if my shank still has any blood on it.

ON TAG

It's alright, Ma (I'm only bleeding).
Bob Dylan

I'VE GOT 220 hours of community service to do but I'm gonna ignore that shit. My probation officer doesn't even spell my name right in the letters she sends me.

Being on tag is a real long ting. Imagine. I get into bed at my parents' yard – one of the curfew conditions is that I have to sleep there every night – and there's this grey rubber bracelet holding on to my ankle, tight enough that it can't ever come off; not under any circumstances, with a big round plastic bit holding the sensor that sticks out. If I sleep on my side it rubs against my free leg. Every night. Wake up under the duvet, sunk into the softness of my bed, the same bed I've had for years, dented by childhood memories, but my right ankle feels heavy from the tag.

I've got to do three months on tag at my mum's yard and then I'm gone. It's running from June up to mid-September; basically the entire summer holiday before I start my second year of uni. On a real though, I coulda got a custodial sentence so I guess I'm lucky to have ducked that. I used the fact I'm doing a degree in English Literature in court – like please don't ruin my prospects for the future by locking me up, your honour – but true I've already had too many arrests and previous cases for them to just fine me and give me community service, so now I'm on tag. It was an assaulting police charge times two, but I managed to buss case for one of them so I only got convicted of one in the end.

When I moved back in to my parents' yard, even though the last time I saw them I was at war with my mother, I found my bed ready made with fresh bedsheets and my favourite duvet and pillow set – the one covered in light green spirals on a dark green background because green is my favourite colour – and I lay down on the bed for a minute and inhaled the light powdery smell of my mother's detergent.

If I step out of the flat after 7 p.m., or before 9 a.m., a box in my bedroom sends an alert to someone at Serco, one of them private security companies that make mad p's trans-porting mandem to prison and monitoring people like me. They call you on the box – it's got a phone attached to it – to check what you're doing and where you are. If you trigger the alarm too many times they can say you're breaching your probation and send boydem to come arrest you all over again. I know couple man who used a hairdryer to heat up the rubber strap around the ankle, allowing them to stretch it just enough to slip the tag off. But if it goes wrong, or they clock what you did when they come to remove it, you're definitely going back to court and probably going bin. Bun dat. Like I said, it's a long ting.

I get in the shower and I'm all naked, hot water washing away the remains of dreams as I wake up under the water, and round my ankle I've got this plastic tag. My arms are free; I touch my ribs. My dick is free; it touches the inside of my thigh. My right ankle is tagged; I'm not free.

I go to link Yinka. Her mum is away on holiday with the stepdad and their children so she knows what time it is. Answers the door in a pink thong and bra that highlights the glow in her skin, dripping with softness and I jus wanna bite dat I tell her as I step through the door and grab her backoff. I see melting caramel in her curves and blood oranges and sunset. She is short, with little feet that I wanna chew and her hair is dark ginger, which is a mad ting because her mum is dark-skinned with black hair and so is her dad apparently, although I've never seen him. She tells me that one woman in every three generations on her mother's side has ginger hair. The last woman before her to have it was her great-grandmother back in Nigeria, in Ibadan; the ancient seat of Yoruba warrior kings who made bronze heads that looked as if they could breathe and speak. I lips her up as the door closes behind me and it's all heartbeats like thunder through my legs and up up up and my hands grabbing, squeezing her backoff like I could die squeezing it, and my hands still can't get enough, and then she breaks away giggling, and runs up the stairs. I chase her and catch her at the top and she gets down on hands and knees and pushes her juicy backoff out like a ripe apricot full of sap and I bite it and I wanna open it now and—

Later, all my clothes are off and her pink thong got dashed long time and it's all intense and burning and deep smells of life and wetness that no one else knows, and our bodies are all sticky as they mould into each other and there's that banging feeling like falling through space, endlessly falling past comets and constellations, but there's this one thing that's breaking it all up: hard plastic around my ankle, unnatural, reminding me. It feels like it's getting heavier and heavier the more I try not to think of it, the more our knees rub together on the carpet.

Afterwards she says come we watch *Flavour of Love* and I say noooo like the world is about to end and I fall on my back fake dying and then I sit up and tell her I'm only putting up with this bullshit coz I love you you know and she says shut up Boo you're blatantly into it as well, you've probably got a favourite chick already, you just won't admit it and I say laaater star allow dat, my favourite chick is you and then I bite her shoulder.

Yinka's room is the smallest room in the house; a box room, pretty much just a single bed with a small space next to it and a wardrobe. Always neat and tidy, with the only sign of mess being a pile of hair products and brushes full of tight orange curls and creams and lotions and packets of sanitary towels and hair clips, on top of a white chest of drawers at the foot of the bed. The first time I came over, which was after she told me her secret, I clocked all these posters of Usher and Ja Rule stuck on the wall and it made me kinda sad and jealous when I saw them, as if she had some secret hope in her heart that one day Usher himself would come down from a cloud full of flashing lights, singing a love song to her, bussin out the dance moves, and then he'd take her away with him to a new life somewhere, rescuing her from this place, this very room in which she'd been abused as a child, this bed where she told me she'd sat one day with a kitchen knife and tried to summon up the courage to kill herself.

There is a Me to You calendar on the wall with baby blue borders and blue teddy bears all around the edge, and she's written little notes about meeting up with friends in black biro, bubble writing, smiley faces on days she's looking forward to, and I see my name in one square and black biro bubble hearts and black biro butterflies all around it, because one day out of nowhere she started calling me Butterfly. One time Mazey heard her call me that and he laughed and said Butterfly you know, and I said it's coz man rolls with the butterfly knife innit and Yinka laughed with the light pinging off her chipped front tooth and said shut up Gabriel, stop tryna front for your boys like you're some badman, and then she said to Mazey it's coz he's my butterfly. There is a giant stuffed toy elephant in the corner of the bedroom next to her wardrobe and one time she told me how when she was younger she practised having sex with the elephant, which had me bending up laughing.

We lie against piles of pillows on her bed with her laptop propped up in front of us and she leans her head against my chest like she's trying to hear my heart as we watch chicks on *Flavour of Love* competing for fleeting moments of fame on reality TV. But then I can't even stay the night coz I have to be back at my mum's yard before 7 p.m.

I link up with Dario one morning. He's back from Canada. We go looking for a yard to run up in. If it's a tiny bathroom window, he'll go in first because of how short and agile he is and then open the door for me. It's how we became bredrins in the first place, doing these kinda licks. Before that we used to see each other at pirate radio sets on Laylow FM with Secret Service and a next crew called Hot Off Da Block. One day I saw him on road, he was on his ones, I was on my ones, and he said what you deh pon fam and I told him about this yard

I'd seen with the back window open and he said come we lick it. He went home and came back to meet me by the yard in a navy-blue boiler suit with Nike baseball gloves in his pocket and a bandanna tied over his nose and mouth. We never had to talk about it, just understood it naturally, instinctively; this is what we wanna do.

Since that move for thirty bags, we've become like brothers forreal and his family treats me sameway since I'm always coming over, although more times it's because I'm linking up with Dario before going to lick it. His younger brother Travis and little sister Chynique often see us folding ballys into our pockets and putting empty rucksacks on our backs while they're getting ready for school. Big Bajan family. Last time I went to their yard for a family barbecue I said where can I get a plate and his uncle Kelvin grinned gold teeth and said that's how I know you ain't been around for a while Snoopz, don't you know it's every man for himself in this family and then he clapped me on the back. Dario loves his burgers, or as he calls it, his grease. Whenever he's in a photo, he squints and rolls his lips into his mouth as if he's trying to hide them. Dario was the first to show me about the whole Anunnaki ting after he read *The Epic of Gilgamesh* and whenever we jam at his mum's yard, bunning zoots in the attic, we end up talking about Sumerian gods who came from Nibiru in spaceships and created humans to mine for gold so they could take it back to their planet.

Last time we ran up in a yard, we got laptops, a Playstation 2, Versace colognes and even a few bills that we found in a drawer. I carved Westside 2 Gunz Up into the living-room wall with my shank. We both know we're chasing another big move like the mad one that made us rich. They talk about you should get an honest job. But the way I see it, the way Dario sees it, they mean they want you to submit. Grind hard to fill someone else's pockets more than your own, come home with just about enough to keep you alive for another month so you can repeat the whole ting over and over again. Drains your spirit. Turns you into a shell. If you press your ear to a shell like that you can hear the sound of dreams in the distance. But it's just an illusion. Bun dat.

This time we go for a basement flat. Do the usual one, two, three, run up and kick off the door. It flies open too easy and smashes into the wall. I see four Moroccan brers staring at us, standing in a corridor full of low grey light. I've got a hammer in my hand but Dario's already cutting back up the stairs. Right choice. I cut as well. Running down the road past white-columned houses and hedges with morning burning in our chests. The tag round my ankle slides up and down a bit as I run, I can feel it getting heavy like, rubbing against my skin. But no, only for a moment because I'm thinking about it. I'm still doing what I always do. It's become part of my ankle. I'm used to it now. Imagine.

The most jarring ting is that it had to be during my summer holidays that I'm on tag. Actually, the most jarring ting is simply being at my mum's yard. I can't bun it up in my room so that means I have to get mad charged at Bimz's or Uncle T's before I come home and then she's always asking me if I'm high and next stupid shit because my garms are booting of cro and my eyes are redup and she gets all obsessive and can't just allow me.

One morning she asks where are you going, what do you do with your day? I just carry on eating my fried eggs and she keeps repeating Gabriel where are you going? Then she says are you a drug dealer? But the way she says drug with her immigrant-trying-hard-to-sound-proper-English accent sounds like drag, so she's asking are you a drag dealer? I crack up laughing and then I get tired of it so I say stop chatting rubbish I'm going to see my friends in South Kilburn and she says your criminal friends who do nothing with their lives. I've heard this bullshit too many times so I say shut up man and she says don't talk to your mother like this and I say whatever man and she says I'm not man I'm your mother and I forbid you to talk to me like this. But she doesn't even realise I'm galaxies away from her, I'm on another planet, I'm with the space gods and the fallen angels. I'm not even who she thinks I am. I am the bite of a wolverine and the tongue of a lizard. I am the agony of a thousand outlaws. Tell me where you're going, she says. I say or what? I'm a grown man, I can do what the fuck I want and anyway, you never allow me to have Yinka round here or any of my bredrins so why da fuck should I stay indoors all day? She says I don't let that girl come here because I don't like her. I say how can you not like her? You don't even know her, and my mother says because she's beneath you. The blood in my head explodes and I lose all the words that were waiting to come out of my mouth. I get up and go to her desk in the living room where she has some photos of me and my brother. I tear up all the photos of me into tiny pieces and scatter them on the floor. As I put my Nike creps on in the hallway, I look up and see my mother's latest artwork hanging on the wall above me: a wooden board painted with lumpy streaks of oil paint and stuck onto the board is a pair of white baby shoes – my baby shoes from when I was like two years old or something – and beneath them the dried-out seed pod of some plant. The whole piece is set into a flaking white window frame which my mother found in a skip. I cut out of the yard.

91

Last time we had one of these arguments I went for a walk and threw a brick through the kitchen window of a house down the road while the people inside were sitting at the table eating dinner.

This time I phone Uncle T who says he's got some purple haze. I say I want two draws, I'm coming for that now T. He says no problem my son, listen to this – and then he puts the phone down.

Walking up Harrow Road, I breathe in deep. Hot sugar smell of exhaust fumes. But the feeling my mother sparked inside me hasn't gone away, it's still there clutching my heart.

At the junction with the red Costcutter, on the corner where all the fiends come out at night, I cross the road. Traffic is standing still. Red light. I walk between two whips. The whip to my left rolls forward and bumps into the side of my leg making me buckle. I turn to face the driver like whatdafuck are you on? He stares at me and frowns. Sour eyes. Looks like he's chewing his own mouth. Sticks his middle finger up. I walk back round to his side of the car, open his door and give him three sharp bangs to the face until I see blood come in a quick trickle around his eye, more real than any colour I've seen today, and I can see dark wet patches on the knuckles of my black glove. My hearing comes back. The bus that's waiting behind him is slamming on its horn. The man accelerates out of the line of traffic into the oncoming lane, drives across it, onto the pavement and crashes into a lamp post. I walk away. Need to go and bun that purple haze at Uncle T's and drown this thing that's dancing in my chest even though it feels kinda good right now.

Later, after I've billed a big zoot in Uncle T's living room and the clouds are wrapping themselves around me, mouldy sweet smell taking over the flat so it's in my eyes and brain, I tell Uncle T what happened. I look up at the wall as I talk and between framed portraits of Martin Luther King and Marcus Garvey there are two black-and-white photos of a naked black man and a naked black woman, frozen in graceful strong poses like marble statues, and printed in bold at the bottom of the photos are the words THE ORIGINAL MAN and THE ORIGINAL WOMAN. Further down the wall is a certificate in a golden frame, which says FATHER OF THE YEAR AWARD in raised gold letters, and underneath a printed text reads: *This is to certify that the bearer of this certificate has been named Father of the Year because he is warm, wise, generous, loveable and a very important person in his family. Signed with love,* and on the dotted line in biro is written Taz, Reuben and Yassmin. Uncle T's stepdaughter Ayesha is sitting on the sofa bunning a zoot from a draw which some brer gave her. She's always getting tings for free from different man who probably dream of her but never get to dream next to her. Her slim frame settles into the sofa. We're mad close, basically family since I'm so tight with her brothers Malice and Gunja and her sisters too, and whenever her older sister Yassmin has a party, the two of them wind on me, sandwiching me between their backoffs, and shout bun n cheese and crack up laughing. Ayesha's deep though. She has the vision. Like she can see tings that ain't there. But it's not all good coz I remember her telling me about this one time when she woke up and bare hands were pinning her down to the bed, and she couldn't scream because something was hovering over her and it put its hand over her mouth.

Ayesha shakes her head as Uncle T says well you got a knockout punch Snoopz. They'll soon find out when they cross you. She clears her throat and starts humming.

93

I say I can't wait to get off tag so I can move back outta my mum's yard.

Uncle T says you're a big man now Snoopz, she can't be telling you how to live. No true dat?

I say sometimes I swear I hate her you know.

Ayesha draws her zoot, blows smoke out, stares at the TV and says is love ah breed me, so I and I nah deal wid hate.

MEETING GOTTI

WHEN I STEP out of the tube at Kilburn Park I have only two
things on my mind: cro and eats.

The cro I can get from somewhere in South Killy. Uncle T's
got the ammi and Jermaine, who is living in Bimz's yard, just
got some banging lemon haze the other day. As for doing eats,
the urge is always there within me, hidden and waiting, like
tears and heartbeats and forgetfulness. These times I've always
got my bally in my backpack along with books and notes from
uni. Just in case.

I've started my second year. It's September and I've been off
tag for like two weeks. I come out of the station and night is
closing its jaws around the day. I just got back from East and
all I wanna do is get faded. I don't even remember what it's
like to fall asleep without bunning cro, without being mad high
till my head spins and my eyes sink into darkness. If I don't get
blackup, my mind will just run away from me all night and I'll
stay awake chasing it. When I bun I can't remember my dreams.
Screaming bloody dreams.

95

So I walk down to Peel Precinct. It's not cold yet, summer's still clinging on, I'm rocking my black Nike hoodie and some jeans and it's good enough. But I've also got this unnameable energy keeping me warm, this feeling of finally being back together with the night, like going to link a special girlfriend – your first love who you ain't seen for too long – since for the past three months of being on tag I've always been indoors by seven.

It's just gone ten when I get into the precinct and it's looking deserted; just the camera on top of the spiked pole in the middle watching over everything and all the shops with their shutters down. Warm yellow lights keep secrets behind curtained windows in the three-storey blocks that sit in the precinct. Street lights fight with shadows and lose. Nightfall. In the distance, rectangles of yellow float in unshakeable loneliness: windows in the concrete towers of South Kilburn.

And then I see Gotti coming up to Bimz's block. He's with some white ting who's like half his size, rocking a white coat with fur trimming round the collar. Yo Gotti I say and he says wagwan Snoopz, what you on?

Gotti. Black like a bee's tongue with eyes like some far corner of space where even stars get lost. I can see acne scars on his cheeks and the girl next to him smells of shampoo and cigarettes. I've jammed with Gotti a couple times at Bimz's yard, mostly just sharing a zoot while we all squeezed into the bedroom, finding a place on the bed as everyone took turns to play *Soulcalibur* on the Xbox or whatever. Mazey recently moved in to one of the spare rooms in Bimz's yard and he keeps saying how if I link up with Gotti it's gonna be a mad ting, and I'm always like forreal, I need someone to do eats with. But I'm not a begfriend so I wasn't suddenly gonna ask him to bring me in on a move.

This is Chelsea, says Gotti and the white girl does a little wave and I say wagwan. Then to Gotti, I'm looking to get a draw fam.

He says Bimz ain't even in. I was knocking earlier.

Someone must have dat, I say.

Where you coming from? he goes.

I say uni still, but I'm done for the week so I'm back in the ends for now.

Say nuttin, he goes. I'm gonna see who's got dat, and he takes out his phone.

We sit on the concrete staircase leading up to the first level of Bimz's block. The white girl stands by the bottom, chewing gum, looking at us.

I hear you been tryna get them man to do eats with you I say.

Yeah but them man ain't on it like dat still, says Gotti. I heard you're on this ting though.

Yeah g I'm always ready, I say and stand up, slide my backpack off, zip it open and pull out my bally. It's one of those thick woollen black ones with two holes for eyes and a little hole for the mouth.

Don't lie, he says, smile opening across his face and he takes it from me. I swear down I see a spark in his eyes like embers stirred by something unspeakable, or maybe I've been reading too many books and my imagination's being extra.

I love this shit, says Gotti, holding the bally almost gentle and looking at it like it's his lover's face. The silence of the precinct rolls over us and the white girl spits her chewing gum out and puts a fresh one in her mouth. Then voices.

We see Ryder – one of the younger SK mandem – and his bredrin with two little lighties in vest tops, swaying and laughing, bumping into each other, the chicks almost supporting the brers who lean over them holding half-empty bottles of Hennessy.

Wagwan we all say to each other and Ryder says it's my birthday and we say happy birthday g and the chicks are laughing at something, their tops pulled down tight with little gold chains nestling between breasts, tangled up with baby blue and pink plastic prison rosary beads, tattoos on wrists, babyhairs gelled into little curls that stick perfectly to their foreheads. Ryder's boy says I'm so mashup and his ting says pass the yak then b and every one of them is mad wavy, but still the silence of the precinct flows all around us like a lonely river while we splash in it. Then, walking across the precinct by the shops, we clock one Asian brer and Gotti turns to me and says come we eat him and I say I'm down.

Gotti pulls my bally over his face and I pull my hood over my head, tightening the drawstrings so that it closes around my face and we run across the precinct. Panther feet. The man stops, freezes as if the shadows around him just came to life, and it's all blatantly under the CCTV camera in the middle of Precinct. I grab the man's sweatshirt collar and pull him back like nah you're staying here blood and at the same time Gotti pops the man's watch off his wrist onetime and the man says allow it please no please no and I tap his pockets and pull out his wallet and Gotti grabs him by the front of his sweatshirt and I swear I can see Gotti smiling but it's like the bally's become one with his face and I open the man's wallet and pull the money out – only sixty pounds – and Gotti pushes the man away and I throw his wallet at him. The man stops, picks up the wallet, looks at us and says allow it man. He's fully slipping though; walking through Precinct at night like he don't know it's dangerous out here, probably taking a shortcut to Queen's Park station or suttin. That's what you get for lacking. I say duck out man and move towards him like I'm gonna do him suttin and he starts running away and I stop and Gotti laughs and I laugh and then we turn around and walk back to Bimz's block.

Chelsea is standing there waiting and Ryder and them lot are swaying all waved off, taking sips of Henny while they watch us. Then Ryder says you man safe yeah, and they walk off to wherever they're going because the night's not over for them, not even close to being done.

See that's how I know you're on it, says Gotti, pulling off the bally and giving it to me. You didn't even hesitate, and he spuds me hard like he's punching my knuckles and I'm feeling gassed up, mad energy like power running through my arms and legs. I think about how I've just become a part of what makes these ends dangerous. Part of the landscape; the most unpredictable part of the landscape, more like its own weather system than the sky itself.

What watch is dat? I say and he shows me. It's a stainless steel TAG Heuer. He says you can have it brudda, passing the watch to me like he's not even interested in it. Don't lie, I say. Yeah brudda that's you, he says. Come we get a draw, I say.

He grabs Chelsea around her waist from behind, puts his face into her hair and says you can come and stay at mine if you want Snoopz. I say swear down brudda? And he says mum's life.

I tell him I wanna go to my mum's yard quickly to grab some p's and a couple tings and he says cool fam I'll come with you.

One rule I have is that I don't let anyone know where my parents live so that no matter what I get myself into, it's never gonna come to their doorstep, and more importantly no one can ever hurt my family or try do them suttin to get at me.

So when we walk down to Harrow Road, I tell Gotti that

my mother lives just behind the blocks on the opposite side to Warwick Estate. He tells me that Chelsea lives in Warwick so he's gonna drop her off there. I walk through the blocks on the opposite side and as soon as I'm out of sight I sprint down to the bridge crossing over the railway tracks, through the alleyway on the other side and come out near my parents' road.

At my parents' yard I repack my bag. The house sleeps. The digital clock on the stove glows midnight. I reach under my bed for the Nike shoebox and take 3,000 out of my stack. That should last me for a while and anyway, I'm sure I'm gonna do some serious moves soon which will add to it. I grab my strap. It's in the same shoebox under all the fifties: my Star 9mm with a silencer, unscrewed for now, wrapped in an oily T-shirt and tied up in two blue plastic grocery bags. The clip has eight shells in it and there are two loose ones rolling around at the bottom of the shoebox. I have a feeling I'll be needing it at some point. I put the three bags in the front pocket of my backpack along with my textbook on literary theory, sheets of lined paper, a copy of *Das Kapital*, and my pens. Then I pack some clothes which I wrap around the strap before putting it into the main bit of the backpack. I leave without waking my father and mother up. I've become a ghost.

I run back the way I came, through the alley, over the bridge, catch my breath and phone Gotti saying I'm just leaving my mum's yard now g, where you at? He tells me to link him on Harrow Road by the petrol station. We walk back to South Kilburn.

Nighttime smothers South Killy, orange block lights and black shadows sucking the colour out of the place. Gotti's mum lives in a flat in D-block, in Wordsworth House. Four floors, with a permanent darkness oozing over the balconies. A notorious place. I almost feel like I need to take a breath before I follow Gotti in, but since it's well after two in the morning now, the block is drenched in a heavy silence. Gotti tells me about how once two undercover feds pretending to be nittys, a man and a woman, went onto the balcony of D-block. The mandem banged them out, says Gotti, kicked their faces in when they was ko'd, stripped all their clothes off, took their handcuffs and radios and next shit. You shoulda seen the way boydem come for the whole block fam. Two vans full of riot police kicking off every single door on a madness, says Gotti and then he laughs, gravel in his voice.

Did you get through to anyone? I ask because I wanna get high right now. Nah, but I know one yout who'll have that. Man will just knock his door and make him wake up, says Gotti.

When we go in, I notice that the cameras inside the block have been spray-painted over with black paint. We get to the first floor, walking up stairs that smell of stale skunk and piss. It's like Blake Court up here; a long balcony that looks out across the park towards Precinct and rows of doors. One of the landing lights stutters, dies, comes back to life and repeats its struggle. I'm thinking how this is where all the D-block mandem jam, watching out for feds, ops, nittys, talking smack in loud voices with guns tucked in the melting shadows of the balconies, dirty rain-beaten concrete all around, looking like they've pulled the stars out of the sky and stuck them in their mouths. Gotti walks up to a door and claps the letterbox a couple times. No one answers so he does it again.

Rah, ain't my man gonna be conked out nah? I say. Even if he is, fuck it he can wake up, says Gotti. He pulls his hood off and turns round to stare across the night-filled park, dim electric light holding the roundness of his head. Then he leans over

101

the balcony, spits at the park, turns around, walks up to the door and clatters the letterbox again.

The door opens and there's this tall lightskin brer frowning. Says wagwan and rubs his eyes. Gotti says get me a draw and make sure it's nice. The brer doesn't say anything about the fact that Gotti's knocking his door near two in the morning.

He goes what did you want? Gotti goes what did you want Snoopz? A score. Gotti goes make sure it's buff yeah, I don't want no small tings when I know you got that lemon.

The brer steps back inside and comes out after a minute, handing me the cro wrapped up in clingfilm. I say safe and give him a twenty from my pocket and Gotti says cool and the brer goes back indoors and I hear the lock turning.

I follow Gotti to the stairs and we climb to the fourth floor. One of the plastic-covered lights on the stairs is pink for some reason. The others are all yellow. Part of the plastic casing is smashed and on the jagged edges I notice a spiderweb. A fat brown spider hangs from its thread as I pass, but I don't kill it because Capo once told me that spiders saved the Prophet when he was running from his enemies.

We get to the top and as we walk down the landing, I see something wrapped in white plastic, looking like rubbish, tucked right next to the balcony wall in a dip which is there to drain rainwater. Gotti picks it up, puts it in the front pocket of his hoodie and says them man stash their food here all pebbled up so it's ready for the cats and he laughs but his eyes stay like outer space. Banging, I say, not bad for one night, and we both laugh. We get to his mum's door. He opens it and we creep in, locking the door quietly. I follow him to his bedroom.

He's got a single camp bed set up with a thin mattress and quilt on it, and he pulls out a sleeping bag from underneath, spreads it out on the floor and says you can have the bed fam and I'm like safe brudda. I sit on the bed and start billing a zoot with the cro I just copped and Gotti turns on his stereo and puts on an Uncle Murda mixtape. He sits on the sleeping bag and opens the plastic bag he found on the balcony and it's full of buj and work, all chopped up and wrapped in clingfilm, all in £10 pebbles. Gotti says yeah we're gonna make a nice p off this, probably shot it all in a couple days still, and I say seen, that's a touch still.

On the radiator, written in black marker pen I see 'Kilburn Banditz' and I say was that you yeah? He says yeah and starts telling me how him and couple next man used to do mad eats, how they called themselves Kilburn Banditz and how mandem in the ends were shook of them because of how ruthless they used to move – holding man's mum for ransom when we couldn't get to the brer we wanted he says. And I say we should bring that back fam. It was all because of Bunny, he says. Bugz Bunny. Myman had us doing mad moves Snoopz. I swear onetime he even set a car on fire on one road, pulled out his strap and beat it off into the air for extra impact, and then we all went and licked one jewellery shop only three streets away, but all the feds in the ends were attending the car that was on fire and responding to all the phone calls about shots going off on that other road. It's Bunny who gave me my first strap. Swear down Snoopz, myman's different. I say yeah, Mazey and them man told me about him still. Gotti says when I was a yout, I'd see him coming back from a move with bin bags full of money and he'd tell us to stick our hands in and pull out whatever we grabbed. Swear down? On my mum's life Snoopz. When we got older, Bunny trained us up by sending us to stick up the petrol station next to Precinct. That's why it got shut down coz it got robbed too many times.

103

We go out onto the balcony to bun the zoot I billed and Gotti says the way you was just on it the second I said come we eat that brer, that's how I know you're on this ting Snoopz, and my heart swells and fills my veins with sunset glow.

Later, I'm on the camp bed, billing another zoot as Gotti lies back on the floor and stretches his arms out.

Nuff of these man ain't got heart like you Snoopz, but they try fronting like they're about dat life, and he laughs. Like this brer Yellow, he says and I'm like oh yeah I know Yellow and he says Yellow ain't about dat life fam. But I seen him all iced out, I say, rocking mad chains n shit, doesn't he shot or suttin? He's a eedyat Snoopz, says Gotti. His grandma died and left him bare p's so myman went and copped couple iced-out chains and like three straps or suttin mad like he's some gunman, but really he's always been a dickhead tryna beg it with the mandem. And I say how's man buying guns and ice with p's he inherited from his dead grandma? That's some wasteman ting. Gotti says I know. Yellow might have straps but he definitely ain't clapped nuttin. The joke ting as well is myman's broke now, he spent all that p's tryna stunt and now he's got nuttin except for the iced-out chains. I say fam the only way I'm spending p's like that is if I get it from a move, otherwise what's even the point ah lie? And Gotti says true dat. Then I sit up and open my backpack. I dig around in my clothes and pull out the Star 9, still wrapped up in plastic bags, and pass it to Gotti saying, check this my brudda.

Gotti sits up and says don't lie, and I can hear the excitement like a wave crashing inside his voice and he holds it, feels its shape through the plastic, grips the handle and points it at the window. He's switched the light off in his room but the street lights outside melt orange all over the muscle of his arm and catch the side of his face. Black and orange. Prison-gym body like he's made of sharp wires with muscles bunched all over them.

We're gonna do some serious moves Snoopz, he says and hands it back to me. I stuff it into the rucksack, between my T-shirts and socks and boxers, and go back to billing a zoot. Gotti lies down and buries his eyes.

I feel something come over me like the lemon I'm crumbling is the sweetest smell and the bed I'm lying on is the softest mattress and the words of the Uncle Murda track we're listening to is pure shit from the soul and the darkness embraces me, fills my heart and holds it, squeezes it. I'm tapping the zoot to pack the weed and baccy down tap tap tap so it's nice and tight, and it hits me how I don't want an easy and boring life. I want to run from the law and feel my heartbeat making me sick. I want to fuck gyal like it could be my last night on Earth. I want to see fear in people's eyes and eat my own fear. I want to live dangerously, on the edge of existence.

I tap tap tap the zoot and the tap tap tap becomes bang bang bang in time with my heartbeat, which is going boom boom boom in time to the music, and everything around me has a pulse, like this this this is real life. I clock that Gotti has drifted off and for the first time in ages, a massive sense of calm floods my body and I fall asleep listening to Uncle Murda.

DIARY OF AN EATER

LAST NIGHT, THIS brer from SK called Daniel Ross got slumped in the middle of a rave in Scala in King's Cross.

In fact it was early this Sunday morning, Gotti tells me, around 4 a.m., right in the middle of everyone shacking out, one of the D-block brers walks up to Daniel, pulls out a strap and bursts him in the head. Then the gunman joins the screaming crowd and cuts out with the tide. It's literally the first thing I hear when I wake up on the camp bed in Gotti's mum's yard – yo Snoopz you awake yeah? Lissen to this . . .

Gotti's already been up for a while and he tells me all about it while rain taps away on the window. It only happened like five hours ago. He tells me who done it as well coz he knows them man and it ain't a secret. The way he goes on about it, it's like he's excited the way you would be over a football score, or some celebrity gossip.

Everyone is talking about it in the ends today. Uncle T keeps chatting about it when I go to cop a draw off him, phoning people up as I bill a zoot in the kitchen, repeating exactly what he said to me when I walked into the yard – did you hear what dem bwoy deh from the balcony did to one yout inna rave last night? I tell you the yout dem are getting worse rasta, he keeps saying. Maybe he talks about it like that because if he doesn't it'll become normal and he doesn't want to let that happen, even though this isn't the first murder of someone from the ends, someone who was basically a neighbour, a brer I used to see around the ends when I lived at Uncle T's. But all that shocked talk about mandem are getting worse? Bullshit. To me that's like the ultimate sign of getting old, when you start getting left behind by how things go and you start to feel shocked like you can't keep up or suttin. Nothing's getting worse. This is just how it is. It's South Killy. It was and it is and it will be. The mandem are in its veins and this place is in theirs.

I phone Gotti. He says I'm at Bimz's, you coming through? and I'm like yeah and then I squash the rest of my zoot into the ashtray even though there's a good few tokes left and leave.

When I get to the yard it's stopped raining and Bimz says he wants to go and get some DVDs. Puddles capture pieces of the sky, treetops and blocks, and flip them upside down as we walk up to Kilburn High Road. Bimz, Spooks, Gotti, Mazey and me. Garms radiating smell of cro. Streets marinate in city dirt and rainwater. Mazey says rah I can't believe they slumped that Daniel yout in the middle of the rave you know and Bimz says them man ain't ramping. Head *gone*, says Spooks and everyone starts bussin up laughing and Bimz says you man ain't serious and kisses his teeth.

Kilburn High Road is chicken shops, barbers, banks, nittys like Shakes and his son sitting outside the corner shop begging change. Two generations of nittys, both looking as old as each other with that haunted look that you can spot from across the road, and as we pass Shakes he says yo Gotti you got that light? Gotti says I'll get at you later still. £1 bowls of fruit outside the shop absorbing fumes from passing traffic. Undercover feds in New Balance trainers, tight jeans and Superdry hoodies suddenly clamp someone and pull out handcuffs and radios. Chinese DVD shotters hide their DVDs and act as if they're waiting for a bus. JD Sports and Foot Locker where all the mandem cop Air Maxes and tracksuits, Western Union money transfer shop with Jamaican and Polish flags in the window. Nail shops. Mazey and Bimz stop by the window and stare at some chick who's getting her nails done and Mazey's like rah she's fire still and Bimz says she needs to finish them nails and come outside blood, she's got them DSLs and then he laughs that cartoon character laugh of his. I say what's DSLs? Dick Sucking Lips fam, wa'um to you? Argos, McD's, the big Primark where people look at £2 T-shirts, then drop them on the floor and no one picks them up. Market stalls selling string vests and sunglasses and bandannas even though summer's done and it's wet and grey with the start of a new rain stinging everyone's faces. Weed crushers and fake Ralph Lauren tracksuits and incense sticks and fake chains that'll turn your skin green if you wear them for a week or more.

We clock the Chinese DVD shotters going DVD, DVD, just in front of Argos. We start ripping packs of DVDs out of their hands, ripping the bags off their shoulders and I see Bimz has already got two bags and when one of the brers tries to grab his bag back, Bimz towers over him and the brer shrinks back and Bimz starts bopping off, doing his lean walk. I chase one brer and a chick into WHSmith and right there next to all the pens and stationery I rip the bag off the brer's shoulder. The chick tries to fight back and the shop's security guard comes up to us and goes please take it outside. I take the bag and walk out. Outside, all the DVD shotters are huddled in a group by the bus stop, hugging their bags and looking at us while they talk out of the side of their mouths in a language none of us understands. Everyone's got a stack of DVDs or a bag so we head back to the blocks.

At Bimz's yard, Bimz and Spooks go into the bedroom and start sorting out DVDs. Me and Gotti do these licks just to break the boredom, I mean it's fucking DVDs, it's not a serious move or anything. But Bimz has got this hustle on smash, sorting them into piles, says he's got enough pornos to buy at least ten draws from Chris or Uncle T, since them man will take three pornos for a £10 draw. Next mandem in the ends will buy DVDs for three nugs each as well, especially when they're the latest films and they're not those shaky cam jobs where you see people's heads blocking the screen n shit. At least we'll have some movies to watch.

In one of the packs we find *Paid in Full*, so me, Mazey and Gotti go and watch it in Mazey's room. It's based on a true story about these three Harlem dons called Alpo, Rich Porter and Azie, who got rich shotting work in the 80s. There's this scene where the three friends are jamming together after Azie just survived being shot in the head. Azie says he's decided to get out of the crack game for good and Alpo tells him ayo, niggaz get shot every day b. Gotti cracks up and starts repeating it, turning to Mazey – yo Mazey, niggaz get shot every day b, and we all buss up laughing and Mazey goes this guy, while he passes me a zoot.

The next day is Monday so I have to go uni for a lecture and two seminars. Mazey and Gotti are still ko'd when I leave. When I get on campus, I buck Capo and we talk about how that Daniel yout got duppied and then later I'm in a seminar with people who know nothing about South Killy, nothing about their neighbours getting murdered and all that madness, and the class is talking about *The Birth of Tragedy*. Butterfly knife in my pocket. All I wanna talk about is how a man got slumped in the middle of a rave and how his killers are probably gonna get away with it, as if talking about it here, in uni, in the classroom, might make it normal, because since I touched uni, being around everyone catching jokes and studying and whatever has made me start to doubt that it's normal. But in the end I don't say anything because really and truly it feels abnormal that no one at uni talks about things like that when it's going on in other blocks, in other ends like Pecknarm and Bricky and Hackney, and I barely take part in the seminar which is unusual for me, but all I wanna do is go back to SK and jam with the mandem.

In the last ten minutes I snap back into the discussion – hand up – yes Gabriel? and I start breaking down the concept of the Dionysian and the Apolline, art as a beautiful end product that hides the dark and disturbing origins of its inspiration. Our seminar leader Dr Jerry Brotton says that's good that's good, says did everyone write down what Gabriel said? I say if anyone wants private tuition come holla at me. Everyone laughs and one girl says Sara would like some private tuition with you and the Iranian girl sitting next to her blushes deep pink burn and holds her book up in front of her face.

The second Renay starts whispering to me during our Critical Thinking lecture, I know I'm gonna smash. Pretty gyal who studies English literature – what more could I want? After the lecture we swap numbers. Says she lives in Kensal Green and I say rah that's up the road from me, I live in South Kilburn. We jump on the tube together after our seminar. She invites me to her mum's to continue the conversation we've been having on the tube, although really she says nothing and just listens to me filling the silence. Afterwards I go Precinct and tell Mazey yo I got this little peng ting from Kensal who goes to my uni and she's on man and Mazey says gwan Snoopz.

The next day I don't have any lectures or seminars so I go straight from Bimz's yard round to Renay's and again I do most of the talking for us and it feels like I'm not learning anything about her and if this continues soon I'll actually have to start opening up to her. Fuck dat. Whenever I stop talking, tryna think of suttin else to say, she goes why you being so quiet for? until it gets jarring and I have nothing left so we start lipsing, rushing it, as if we mustn't stop to think, and then we end up banging on the sofa and she's mad petite so I pick her up and beat her out against the wall and her pussy's so tight I can't fully push myself in and she wraps her legs around my back like she's holding on for dear life or suttin and I look at her face and her eyes are shut like she's forcing them to stay closed and then I pull out and buss all over her mum's living-room floor.

Later, when it's evening times I get waved with Gotti and Mazey, drinking Rémy Martin cognac on the block. We go Kilburn High Road and I put one brer in a headlock and Gotti goes through the man's pockets and takes his phone, takes his wallet, takes his watch – some dead Seiko ting – and as soon as I let go of him the brer runs across the busy road like he wants a car to come and lick him down. Then we go back to D-block and we don't even need to bun any zoots coz we're so mashup from the juice. I crash onto the camp bed without even taking my creps off. Gotti lies on the floor, playing with the watch we just licked, winding the dial round and round as if it might make tomorrow come sooner. Ragged night flutters outside the window and as I drift off Gotti says yo Snoopz, niggaz get shot every day b, and his laughter scatters into the darkness that fills my eyes.

THE SEEKERS AFTER SMOOTH THINGS

This saying, referring to the last days, concerns the congregation of those who seek smooth things . . . who despise the Law and do not trust in God . . . As robbers lie in wait for a man . . . they have despised the words of the Law.

Fragment from the Dead Sea Scrolls

IT WAS THE morning that I told my lecturer to shutdafuckup. Gotti phoned me and said I got a serious move for us fam, come buck me when you finish uni. Then I went to my lecture feeling gassed up and told the lecturer to shutdafuckup. The whole year, everyone doing an English degree, packed into the lecture theatre to listen to someone talking about Nietzsche and *The Birth of Tragedy*.

The lecture starts. I'm sitting high up towards the back in my Nike tracksuit and Avirex jacket – all black – and I've got my pad out, taking notes. Three chicks who are sitting in the row just in front of me whisper to each other and laugh. The lecturer stops, looks up and says you don't have to be here if you want to talk. She is staring in my direction and several rows of students in front turn round and look at me. The lecturer continues talking about Nietzsche, I continue taking notes, the three girls continue to whisper. The lecturer stops again and says look if you're going to keep talking just get out, there's no need for you to be here, and her eyes pin themselves to mine. Students turning round. The lecturer goes back to Nietzsche while my face gets hot. I stand up and say are you talking to me? She looks up from her notes and says yes, if you want to keep talking you can just leave and I say shutdafuckup and the entire lecture theatre turns into one voice which gasps and hangs, suspended above everyone's heads. I say I wasn't even talking, don't make random accusations that you can't substantiate otherwise you'll get embarrassed like you just did, and she says can you leave? I say no I can't, fuck dat and then I sit down and she stands under the loneliness of the spotlight onstage, shuffles her papers like she's trying to make all the edges line up neatly and then continues with the lecture.

When it's done, I leave the lecture theatre screwfacing anyone who tries watching me and they look away quicktime and no one says nothing. I phone Gotti and tell him what happened and he says swear down? You're too rago Snoopz, and he laughs and I say I swear down I wasn't even talking fam, and then he says I got a serious move for us tonight brudda, make sure you come link me soon as you're done, and I say course fam, and then I go to the seminar.

In the seminar I can tell bare people haven't really read *The Birth of Tragedy* or *Beyond Good and Evil* or any of the extra Nietzsche shit they gave us to read, because no one's really saying shit, or whoever *has* read it is keeping quiet like they don't wanna share. I love seminars. You can really get into the meat of an idea, pull it apart and crunch it all up. Then again,

The Birth of Tragedy is some heavy shit, a swamp of words and ideas, I had to read it using a raasclart dictionary I say to the teacher and some of the girls in the class laugh and look at my mouth coz I've got my iced-out grillz in. Still, I'm looking forward to the end of this seminar because I'm itching to go and link Gotti. The professor talks about human suffering being a confirmation of our existence and I start rubbing my finger over the sharpness of the diamonds in one of my teeth, looking at faces in the room, attentive, uninterested, thinking you don't know what I know about myself and then I raise my arm. The professor says Gabriel. I say one of the points that Nietzsche makes is that morality is just a rule of behaviour relative to the level of danger in which individuals live. If you're living in dangerous times, you can't afford to live according to moral structures the way someone who lives in safety and peace can. So it's not actually some universal natural ting, you get me, and the professor says did everyone just get that?

After the seminar is done, I grab a munch and eat it as I walk to Mile End tube station beneath a metal November sky. Wind cannibalises the air around me. I take my grillz out to eat. Fried chicken wings turning my fingers shiny and chips slathered in orange burger sauce. I close the chicken box, now full of greasy bones, catch sight of a smiling cartoon rooster on the front of the box next to the words Delicious Favourite Chicken and beneath it Tasting is Believing, the rooster radiating sunbeams from behind him, looking all excited at the prospect of people eating his relatives. I dash it away and enter the tube station.

When I come out of Kilburn Park station I phone Gotti and say I'm going to Bimz's to drop my bag off and he says where are you brudda? I say I just got to Kilburn. Have you got dro? Gotti says nah not even, I just bunned my last zoot but Jermaine's got blue cheese. Cool, I'm gonna get a draw from Jermaine and he says phone me when you're there and I'll come link you in Precinct.

Later, Gotti takes me to the flats behind the shops in Precinct to meet Little Man. Dirty cream blocks, balconies piled up with bikes and clothing lines and all sorts of shit and everywhere the same white-framed windows repeating themselves, too small to look into, too small to look out of.

Little Man is bunning a big zoot, bloody half-moon eyes, when we spud each other outside his block and Gotti goes this is Snoopz and Little Man says Snoopz yeah? I hear you're on this moves ting and I say dun know. We go into his block and sit on the stairs in the half-light and I spark my zoot and draw Gotti on it. Gotti says we're gonna do a proper move tonight but we need to wait for Big D who's gonna break it down for man.

Little Man is short, Haribo cola-bottle skin and his earlobes are weighed down by white gold studs crammed with canary yellow diamonds. He's kinda typical of SK mandem. Dropped out of school at thirteen, started trapping, first hitting sells as a worker for one of the olders, eventually saving enough p's to start his own line shotting work and buj. Living in some cruddy block, stacking paper, spending it on ice and designer garms, just doing his ting without stopping to work out where he's tryna get to. His whole family is deep in it anyway. Uncles, cousins, nephews, even his mother. Nothing to hide, just don't chop up crack on the kitchen table because people eat there or whatever.

Later, Little Man tells me how he had this peng lighty, mad pretty forreal, every man was feeling her on a different tip he says, and she loved off Little Man. Little Man got her to smoke the hard food and once she was hooked, he pimped her out to the mandem. Pimped her out so she never had to buy any work and occasionally he'd fuck her too, which is what she'd really wanted in the first place. Like all nittys though, eventually she started looking all fucked up and dead-eyed, bones sticking out at sharp angles like her hips could cut you and no one wanted to hit it any more so she had to start buying the white off Little Man, although sometimes he'd give her couple rocks in exchange for some neckback.

While Little Man is on the phone I clock the Rolex on his wrist. Soon as he ends the call and says Big D's on his way, I'm like yo g that watch is hard. Gotti says ah lie? Little Man holds out his arm to me so I can look at it. It's an 18-carat yellow gold women's Rolex, the face completely flooded with white diamonds and instead of numbers there are twelve pink rubies like drops of frozen blood. Where did you cop dat I say and he says one of the mandem yakked it on some move, only cost me six bags n dat, and I'm like I need to yak myself some shit like dat forreal.

We leave the block. A grey Porsche pulls up and one brer in a leather jacket jumps out and says wagwan mandem and Gotti says that's Ghost and passes me the zoot. Little Man goes over to Ghost while Gotti and I carry on bunning, getting closer and closer to the roach. Gotti says he's a dickhead really, he's not on moves or nuttin, just wants to feel like he's a part of it – it's as if his image collapses under the weight of Gotti's eyes – and I say seen, staring at Ghost's Porsche, blue snake of smoke sliding out of my mouth into the air.

Ghost comes over to us and Gotti says this is Snoopz. Ghost says so you're gonna be doing the lick today yeah? Where d'you get your grillz from? I say Hattons innit. He has one white gold tooth with a single big diamond set in it but it looks kinda stupid still. He turns to Gotti and says Big D should be here in a minute, I jus dropped him off at the shop to get a lickle juice.

I end up in the back of the Porsche. It's a two-seater so I'm squashed up with my knees almost touching my chest and Big D and Ghost are in the front. Big D is late thirties, pushing forty, little lightning bolts of grey running through the evening of his hair. A couple small scars on his cheek and forehead are the only things that tell the story of some kind of life, the rest of his face like dead and cold, eyes with nothing behind them. He turns round slightly and says, for the second time, you don't have to do it if you're not on it. Real talk, no fronting ting, just say if you're not on it.

I wouldn't be sitting here chatting to you if I wasn't on it, I say.

Ghost looks straight ahead and says it's cool if you're not though, just say and we'll find someone else innit.

I go I don't do this talking ting. I let my actions speak for themselves, looking at D as he cranes his neck round to watch me.

Big D laughs and says nah he's on it, he's on it to rahtid.

Now that I've committed to it there's no backing out. Better to take risks, better to plunge into the fire and feel alive, if only for a moment, than not to have really lived at all. Some people spend their lives dying. Fuck dat. Anyway, no way am I letting these man think I'm a pussy, that I'm not on it, that I don't back my talk. Then I'd lose my name before I even make it.

Big D says look, this is the move: we're going to Central, to Knightsbridge or Chelsea or one ah dem rich areas. I'm gonna roll with you man, you're gonna have your driver in a separate whip and I'm gonna scope the belly. More times it'll be a diamond ring or a kettle, but sometimes them rich women rock diamond ear-studs or a necklace. If it's a man, more times it'll be a big kettle like a Rolex or a Cartier. Once I've clocked it, I'm gonna phone you man and tell you who to jump out on. It's a clamping ting you get me.

Yeah so how do I do it? I ask.

So you're gonna run up on the eat, make sure they don't notice you creeping up behind them, clamp them, don't do it too tight, but you wanna hold them tight enough so they know what time it is and then Gotti's gonna rip off the belly. He knows exactly how to pop kettles coz he's done this shit before. All you have to do is hold them until Gotti gets it. If they try a ting, just clamp them tighter and truss me, dem fi know what time it is.

He stares at me and goes so what, you still on it yeah?

Yeah big man, I'm on it.

We get out of the Porsche. Dusk drains the day away. I'm in the wilderness.

Big D bends down to brush something that only he can see off his Louis V monogram trainers, then pulls a copy of *Loot* out of his jacket and starts flicking through the car section, looking for a getaway whip. Ghost is on the phone to our getaway driver, Little Man is bunning another zoot and Gotti is showing me how to clamp people properly.

I practise a few times on Gotti and he laughs as I pull him back against me with my left forearm tight across his throat – left hand gripping my right bicep so the hold can't get broken – and says yeah brudda you've got it on point.

A boy and girl in school uniform walk up to the block and

stare at us and Little Man says spud me my lickle g and the boy bumps fists with Little Man without any expression itching his face. The boy opens the block door with his electric key fob and goes in with the girl, followed by a cloud of dank that Little Man blows after them.

D walks over and says it's on, I got a whip for you man waiting for us right now in Maida Vale. Where's Quincy?

He's on his way now, says Ghost.

I know he's still smoking hard food so man won't even need to give him more than a few bills, says D.

The brer who's gonna be our driver is a nitty. One of those half-functioning nittys who isn't totally fucked but is also possessed by that constant hunger for the light and dark, which means he'll move reckless and do anything to get us away if the move turns into a police chase. At the end of the day a nitty is still a nitty – you can't trust the way they think – but like Big D says, he'll be happy with a few hundred pounds just to feed his habit. More p's for us that way.

I turn to Gotti and tell him about Nietzsche and how we're following our purest instincts, and Gotti says forreal, that's sick you know Snoopz, you're different fam, I swear you're one of the realest people I know. Something bright flickers for a moment in his eyes and goes out; a star swallowed up by a black hole. I say morality is a luxury that man can't afford, you get me. And if you live dangerously then it's just a restriction, it don't count for shit ah lie? And I can see that Gotti fully gets it. He's not afraid of his own downfall. Like right here, on the edge, is where he'd already found that truth. Except it's more than that. It's like revealing a vital ingredient of the cement holding our world together.

I go and drop off my Avirex jacket at Bimz's since I don't

want the heavy leather restricting my movements. I get my bally and surgical gloves out of my backpack. Gotti's already got his tucked into the front pocket of his hoodie. Quincy, our driver, shows up at Little Man's block. Tall, walking skeleton, shrinking into oversized clothes that once coulda fit, front teeth dying in yellow and black from piping all that hard food, and Big D says come you man, we're gonna get the whip.

We drive to Maida Vale where Big D buys our car from some white man, cash in hand, no need to sign any papers, nothing traceable. The plan is to dump it after the move anyway, so no need to bother with documents and all that shit. We drive back to South Kilburn and park up in front of Little Man's block. The team is ready.

Six in the evening and a chill November night spreads itself all over South Kilburn, concrete turning blue as darkness glazes everything in shadow. Lights turn on in windows. Stars drown. Gotti and I jump into the getaway whip and head off to Central.

I'm sitting in the back listening to Gotti talking to our driver. Quincy tells Gotti how on the last move he did, they didn't have a two-man team. It was just one crazy brer called Icer, with Quincy as the getaway driver. Icer clamped up this woman but he couldn't get her ring off, says Quincy. Her finger was too fat. She started screaming, so Icer tried to bite the big diamond out of her ring and his front teeth snapped clean off. Came running back to the whip, screaming, and all the blood he left on her ring, pure DNA. Wasn't long before they nicked him for it. Got a straight six for it. Six years in the bin, two broken front teeth, no diamonds.

Oh my days, I say and Gotti says nah that's fucked still.

Gotti looks out of the window, waiting for the call from Big D and I notice how detached this whole moment is from ordinary life, as if time don't exist for us right now, cars full of ordinary people leading ordinary lives passing us, oblivious to the fact that we're about to change the rhythm of someone's existence. We're in a computer game. Fuck it, we're in *GTA*. Nothing is true. Everything is permitted.

Gotti's phone rings.

Which one? he says and looks out the window.

I can see Little Man's whip two cars ahead of us. I pull on my gloves and put my bally on my head, ready to pull it down.

I see her, I see her, says Gotti staring out of the side window and then he puts the phone on the dashboard and tells Quincy to slow down. I feel my heart in my belly, my chest hollow and empty now, feeling almost like I wanna be somewhere else as I watch Gotti pull on the surgical gloves snap snap and then he puts his bally on and the blackness becomes one with his eyes and I roll mine down over my face and he says come Snoopz and opens his door as the car pulls to a stop in the middle of the road.

Across the road is a mews, the entrance through a high stone archway, white stone now muted by the evening, and walking up to the archway a woman: long blonde hair, a bit fat under a green padded jacket with fur round the collar – you know them ones that rich people wear, like they just stepped out of the countryside from hunting foxes or some shit – and I'm out of the whip and the road and passing cars and teardrops of light merge into a blur around me and now there's just this moment. Every moment devours the previous one. Every birth is a death. Right now someone is being born and someone is dying. Fucking, living and dying are all one and yet none of it lasts, because it all gets erased by the next moment, never to exist again.

The moon sinks into a pit of clouds and we are running – black bally tight on my face – running across the street as the eat walks into the mews. And now we're in the mews and I feel like I'm ready to rob the night itself. As we get closer we slow down, creep low like shadows and the bally feels like it's become a part of my face and I don't think I've breathed once since I started running, but before I can think any more I am behind the eat and time stops.

Everything behind us has turned invisible. I notice the red painted wooden door with a brass 35 nailed to it and the windows next to the door glowing orange behind a thin white blind and it looks warm inside and there are flowerpots on the window ledge with pink flowers, green leaves looking blue in the dim light and all this in a split second before I realise the eat is about to enter her house. The automatic light outside the door blinks on and everything is bright and I know she's gonna turn around coz she can feel our energy dimming the light, even as her hand rises with a bunch of keys to the door and I straighten up and then I'm a shadow wrapping myself around her.

At the moment of clamping her I feel immortal. I can feel her chin tuck over my arm, I know I've got it right – just how Gotti showed me – and I pull my right hand over her mouth and shutdafuckup and you won't get hurt comes out of my mouth and her scream crawls back down her throat and I wonder what her face looks like as I pull her tight against me and I hope she won't try biting my hand so I press against her mouth hard like I want to crush it. Gotti pops the watch off her wrist and I hear the metal snap. Gotti is a spirit, a ghost, his instincts can't hide themselves any more, and the eat's arms stretch towards him as if she wants to grab the air around her, fingers glittering, arms flapping slightly and I pull her back again and feel her lean heavy against me. Gotti rips a gold chain from her neck and twists a diamond ring off one of her fingers, but he can't twist the ring with the biggest belly off her finger, it's stuck or suttin, and he looks at me and starts dussing, leaving the moment, reality rushing back in a flood of sounds and colours pouring in and the eat slumps to the ground as I let go of her. I realise I musta clamped her too tight and I've put her to sleep, she's actually snoring in front of her door and I'm no longer high on my own blood and heartbeat and I can hear and see properly and I lean over her and carefully twist the sparkling belly from her middle finger but I still don't see her face – even though I look right at it – and then I turn and follow Gotti out of the mews.

Jammed right into the entrance of the mews, so there's no space for me and Gotti to run through, is a car. At first it's like someone's parked it there, but as we get close we clock it's some man who's seen what happened and is trying to block our escape. No long ting. Gotti jumps onto the bonnet, I follow him and we duss right over the front windscreen, catching sight of the man at the wheel on his phone – probably on a 999 call that very second – run onto the roof of the car and I look up and for the first time that night I can see stars stinging the petrol black sky and then we jump off the roof and back to the getaway whip which is waiting for us in the middle of the road, engine running, open the doors and throw ourselves in. The whip speeds away.

We pull our ballys off and Gotti turns around and says you're sick fam, I seen how you managed to get that ring which I couldn't pull off her finger, I love you for dat and I say dun know my brudda, I wasn't gonna leave without dat, I had to take suttin and he says you got mad heart Snoopz, mad heart. Then the phone rings and he tells Big D how we got the belly and we're heading back now.

Driving through the city, the world blurs. City lights like scattered jewels, glow and splash into the night around us. I wonder what my mother is doing at this point in time, what my father is doing. It's after seven in the evening, more like eight, so they're probably sitting down to eat – maybe it's boiled rice and chicken thighs dripping in gravy or cold Russian salad and red wine for him and white wine for her and Daniel my twin brother is probably practising his violin somewhere and – and I've done what I had to. I feel good. Really good. No. I feel amazing. If we get caught, we're getting six years each for this shit at least. What a way to feel alive; the possibility of that downfall. But I've embraced it now. I'm feeling a stillness within me that I can't even describe. Whatever. Pulling up at a red traffic light on Edgware Road, Quincy says yeah you man are shower still. You did dat nicely, what kettle did you get? It's a stainless steel Carti with a gold bezel, says Gotti. Then he says show me that ring Snoopz and I give him the ring and he says rah this is like three carats at least, we're gonna get a nice p for this. You got the belly Snoopz, he says and I just sit on the backseat and nod like it's nuttin.

Later, Big D gives me and Gotti three bags as our cut from the Cartier watch, so we get a grand and a half each, and he says he'll go with Gotti to sell the rings in Hatton Garden the next day. I've got uni tomorrow afternoon. Don't watch dat brudda, I'll deal with it, says Gotti. Anyway, I'm holding these rings for now he says to Big D. Say no more, say no more; tomorrow we link up and take it to the Jewish man in Hatton, says Big D.

I tell Big D I wanna do this again, but I wanna do this to get rich, like I wanna make at least thirty bags off this ting in the next few months, and he's like truss me Snoopz, if you're on this ting, we'll do more of these eats and by February next year, three four months and you'll have your thirty bags to rahtid. Ghost says bloodclart my man's on this ting forreal.

I go to Bimz's yard, pick up my backpack with my uni books and my Avirex jacket and follow Gotti to his mum's yard in D-block. As we walk through the groaning darkness of the park, I remember a book that my father used to read to me and my brother in Polish before bedtime when we were little. It's a story about these two brothers who decided to steal the moon. People said they wouldn't ever amount to anything and they refused to submit to a life of back-breaking work and respon-sibilities, so they made up their minds to steal the moon and sell it to get rich quick. They ran away from home and had loads of adventures, eventually realising that they're never gonna be able to steal the moon and how their greed is empty and meaningless or some shit like that, so they decided to return home. But when they got home they found their mother had died because she worked and worked and waited and waited for her sons to return and in the end she worked herself to death. So in the end, all they could do was bury their mother.

OUTLAW TATTOOS

WE DECIDE TO get Outlaw tattoos so one morning, Gotti and I go up to Harlesden to a tattoo shop called Krazy Needles. We get mad high beforehand, bun like two zoots of ammi back to back until our eyes are redup and quickly yam a chicken patty each before leaving. When Gotti starts getting Outlaw tattooed on his neck, he frasses out in the chair and the tattooist has to wake him up. He must've passed out a second time as well, coz when he opens his eyes again he says once the 'O' is done that's the worst bit over, but the tattoo is basically finished by then, the tattooist filling in the last curve of the 'w'. I get Outlaw tattooed on my left arm in one gothic type script which I sketch out for the tattooist and then watch my blood, turned black by the ink, dribbling down my arm as the needle buzzes away. Afterwards we go back to Bimz's yard and Gotti says he needs to go to his mum's to pick something up, so I say cool, lickle more brudda.

Blood you need to slow down you know, says Bimz. He is drizzling Maggi Spicy Liquid Seasoning onto a bowl of rice with chopped tomatoes and onions. Bimz is that guy who can turn a packet of ramen noodles and an onion into a banging meal that will fill your belly for the rest of the day. As long as he's got some Maggi Spicy Liquid Seasoning.

What d'you mean? I say, putting a bud of amnesia into the plastic red crusher.

He's right you know, says Ki, staring at the TV screen and he laughs in that way people laugh when they think they know something's gonna happen regardless of what anyone tries to do. He says it out of the side of his mouth because he's bunning a zoot at the same time as playing *Soulcalibur* on the Xbox with Mazey. We're all sitting around the edge of Bimz's bed and the air is hazy thick with smoke from all the cro; a living cloud contracting and expanding around us like a pulse.

You pussy. Pussy. PUSSY, says Mazey as Ki's character does a nine-hit combo on Mazey's character and ko's him.

I told you Mazey, you ain't gonna stand a chance against myman with that spear, says Ki as he puts the control pad to one side and sparks his zoot. We're always doing *Soulcalibur* tournaments and everyone's got their favourite character, mine being Raphael with the rapier. I swear I got that swordplay shit on smash. But my favourite game without a doubt is *GTA: San Andreas* since you can just roam the city and beat the fuck outta people, blow cars up, have shootouts with feds and gang members and whoever. It's like real life – real g shit – on steroids, living out some badman fantasy on screen where forreal there's no limits to what you do, and when you die you just pass the control pad and wait for your next turn.

I ain't tryna preach, man's just tryna look out for you. Remember you're not Gotti bro, says Bimz, raising his eyebrows, slices shaved into them on some pretty boy shit.

I laugh while I'm emptying the crusher onto the *Soulcalibur* case and go what d'you mean fam?

Blood do you know how many enemies Gotti has? says Bimz. How many man are looking to do him suttin? Don't get it twisted Snoopz, mandem ain't forgot how Gotti robbed them you know. He shovels a forkful of rice into his mouth.

I go yeah, so what? Oi who's got the blue slims?

Ki passes me the packet of Rizla and I take out a sheet and rip a bit of card off the packet to make a roach.

Bimz chews and goes so if one day someone rolls up on Gotti to lick him down, they're gonna see you rolling with him and they ain't gonna leave you out of it you know.

Fuck it, man will just deal with it when it happens, I say.

Ah this guy, says Bimz, laughing bitter as he puts his empty bowl on the floor. Then he turns to Ki whose eyes are glued to the screen, fingers clicking away on the Xbox pad and says big man ting, I'm tryna save him from himself and he says man will just deal with it.

Yeah fam, I say, licking the edge of the sheet before rolling it. Them man ain't ready for me and Gotti anyway. Ride or die.

Straight up, says Mazey.

You're not listening to me though, says Bimz. I know you man are moving raw and alladat but if next man roll up on you to beat shots at you, you ain't gonna suddenly be bulletproof blood, you get me. Do your ting innit, man's just tryna help you, like you don't need to be taking them risks just coz he's your bredrin.

It is what it is fam, I say as I spark my zoot and feel the burning ammi heat up the back of my throat and fill my eyes.

Oi that smells piff fam, pass me the crusher, says Bimz, taking out his draw and spreading a sheet of Rizla on his knee.

An hour later I'm in Mazey's room. We've just come back from the shop in Precinct. Mazey is eating Skittles, I've got a can of KA Black Grape and I've started billing another zoot when Gotti comes back.

Timmy just put a strap to my head on the block you know, he says as he walks into the room and drops himself onto the sofa next to me.

Mazey and I go whatdafuck?

Gotti tells us how he'd gone to his mum's yard to pick up some things. When he got onto the landing he saw Timmy and couple next man jamming there, probably waiting for nittys. Timmy saw Gotti and said I know you teefed my food blood. At first Gotti tried to play dumb like he didn't know Timmy was talking about the b and work that we'd found wrapped up in the gutter on the landing the first time I'd come to stay the night at Gotti's mum's. Gotti made around a bag, a bag and a half, shotting that food, so it wasn't even some minor loss for Timmy to ignore. The way Gotti played it, he knew them man were shook to try and swing on him for that p so he stood there acting like he didn't know what Timmy was on about. Timmy said you need to run me my p's blood. So Gotti told Timmy to suck his mum. But he didn't expect what Timmy did next. It was pressure for Timmy, getting boyed off in front of the mandem who were there on the balcony, and reputation – well it's like your face around here and if you lose it you can't show yourself no more since what's there for people to look at if you ain't got your face? Maybe he didn't really wanna do anything but it musta bunned him inside. Bunned him for Gotti to just stare back and not move, not showing any sign of shookness. Bunned him to see the emptiness in Gotti's eyes that fully knew wagwan about the food. Bunned him – wait this brer just told me to go suck my mum, is he dumb? Timmy pulled a strap out of his waistband, cocked it, walked up to Gotti and put it to Gotti's head; stuck it right between his eyes. I ain't gonna lie, my heart started beating then, like I thought this might be it, says Gotti.

So what did you do? says Mazey.

I turned around.

Gotti turned around and opened the door to his mother's flat because he didn't have time to wait for his own death. I mean at the end of the day, life is only life.

I could feel him right behind me, still pointing the burner at my head, says Gotti. So I opened the door, walked into my mum's yard and thought whatever happens happens, I won't even feel it if he pops me anyway. But nothing happened. I think my sister came downstairs and closed the door while I was upstairs. Then he turns to me all calm and says don't worry Snoopz, your p's are still there.

I guess we'll be staying somewhere else from now on. Lucky I took my strap back to my mum's, I say and spark my zoot.

RITES OF PASSAGE

I MUST NOT have bunned enough cro last night.

These brers in black puffer jackets, solid black woollen masks covering their entire faces, keep tryna soak me up with zombie knives on the top deck of a double-decker bus and I can't throw a single punch. It's like my arms are paralysed while I strain to break through the thickness of the air. But instead I just slowly slooowly stroke my fist over this one brer's head as he goes to shank me and it proper hurts when the blade goes in and then I wake up because my phone is vibrating and I see it's my mother calling.

Hello Mama.

131

Gabriel?

Yes.

Gabriel, detectives from the robbery squad came to the flat this morning looking for you.

Oh swear? What did they want?

They were looking for you, they want to talk to you.

About what?

I don't know, they wouldn't say. But they said you're wanted and there's a warrant out for your arrest.

Did you tell them where I am?

I don't even know where you are. Where are you?

I can't even think why they'd want to chat to me though.

I don't know, but it's the third the time this month that they've come to the flat looking for you. We can't have the police coming to our house at six in the morning trying to find you, going through your old room when we don't even know where you are. You need to hand yourself in at Notting Hill Gate police station. That's what they said.

I'm in east London staying with uni friends in their flat.

Please hand yourself in.

I will. I'm just gonna go to a lecture at nine and a seminar right after and then I'll hand myself in.

Please hand yourself in.

I will, I promise Mama.

Make sure.

Bye Mama.

Bye Gabriel, she says while I'm putting the phone down.

I'm itched up on the sofa at Capo's yard in Mile End. I've been staying here most nights since Timmy put the strap to Gotti's head in D-block. Gotti is asleep on the other sofa. Before leaving to get to my lecture on time, I wake him up and tell him I have to hand myself in for questioning at Notting Hill police station.

After my seminar, I jump on the Central line at Mile End with Gotti, headed for West, but I never even get to Notting Hill Gate. Lemme tell you—

The train stops at Liverpool Street. It is ram up with people who will never remember each other. Travelling on the tube is just brief bits of lives getting shared by strangers who don't even notice. Everyone like the background of each other's dreams. I'm at the end of the carriage with Gotti and everyone is close, close, close together.

The doors open. There's no space to get on but this man in a suit presses himself into the crowd and his backpack clips my face as he pushes past.

I go you could fucking say excuse me.

He turns round, looks at me and says what?

Dafuck is wrong with you, didn't your mother teach you no fucking manners?

He frowns, moves up close to me, sticks his face in front of mine and says don't talk to me like that boy.

I headbutt him. Nothing happens so I headbutt him again. Everyone around us is trapped in the moment. Flies in amber. His left eyebrow swells. He grabs me by my throat and tries to pull me out of the open carriage door. I bang him in the face. A wave crashes through my body and it's like I'm watching myself, banging him in the top of his head as he starts to go down whack whack whack and I can hear voices all distant like oi oi stop stop and his hand lets go of my neck as he staggers onto the platform. Tries to grab me around my waist so I give him a bang to the side of his head and he stumbles against the train and his leg drops into the gap between the train and the platform and he tries to push himself out so I knee him in the face and I see heads poking out of carriage doors all the way down the length of the train.

He pushes himself out of the gap and shouts pull the emergency stop and a voice in the carriage says we already have. Then he moves towards me and I say are you mad? Bang him in the face again and someone jumps onto my back and I bend forward under the weight – almost buckle – and the man in the suit backs away and I hear Gotti behind me shout get dafuck off him and I hear a punch connect with someone's head and then the weight on my back is gone and I turn around and see that Gotti's jumped off the tube and banged some brer in the face who tried to clamp me up. The brer backs away from Gotti and runs down the platform. Gotti gets back onto the packed carriage and then I see bare London Underground staff in orange hi-vis vests and blue caps, running towards us. The man in the suit points at me – he assaulted me he assaulted me. A London Underground worker steps into the space between us and says to me calm down mate calm down and I shout at the man in the suit you fucking pussyole go suck your mum starting shit you can't finish you dickhead – calm down mate calm down – he assaulted me he assaulted me. Then I see police officers in white shirts and black stab-proof vests coming down the platform.

No one listens to me. The feds surround me and the man in the suit says he headbutted me he punched me he assaulted me and two of them grab my arms, pull them behind me and one snaps handcuffs onto my wrists while giving me the usual that I've heard so many times: I am arresting you on suspicion of committing ABH, you do not have to say anything but it may harm your defence – all that bullshit – anything you do say may be given in evidence, do you understand? I look away and say fuckssake and the fed says suspect made no reply and another one writes something in his notebook.

They walk me down the platform and the man I just banged up points at Gotti and says he was with him he was with him and at the same time Gotti and I go I don't even fucking know him and we make eye contact and look away quick coz this would be the wrong moment to start laughing and the feds carry on walking me down the platform. Up the escalator, people staring as if all of a sudden this moment of my life is being shared with them. The feds take me out of the station and walk me across the road to Bishopsgate police station.

Then starts the process. I've been through it so many times already that I'm resigned to it; motions, beats, stages. First: custody suite. Uncuffed in front of the sergeant who sits behind a desk, grey skin, looks at you like you're an empty box on a form he has to fill in. Pockets emptied. Blue rubber gloves go pat pat grab grab from head to toe. Shoes off, shaken out. All property taken, noted down and bagged up. Black doggy-ear cap with grey fleece lining and voodoo skull on the front bagged up. Keys, phone, pen, a list of books I have to get for one of my uni modules – *Things Fall Apart* by Chinua Achebe, *Heart of Darkness* by Joseph Conrad, other titles. Scraps of paper with writing on them – lyrics, ideas, plans, moments I don't wanna forget; isn't that what we're all made of? Avirex jacket bagged up. I don't like the way they fold it up. Shoelaces removed so I can't strangle myself in the cell. Name, address, date of birth typed into a computer – tick. No suicidal thoughts – tick. Says you're a violent offender on here, you're not going to give us any trouble are you says the custody sergeant staring at his computer screen – not a question. Taken to another room where a next fed grabs your hands as if they don't belong to you and rolls finger after finger over a scanner; fingerprints, thumbprints, palm prints, edge of palms. Sit down on a chair in front of a camera. Look this way – flash. Turn to your side and look ahead – flash. Photo done. Back down corridor of plastic white light that feels like it will never go out, even after every man in here is dead. Chemical smell. Taken to cell number whatever. Heavy slam, thick steel door, shutting out the last shreds of time. No answer to when you'll get interviewed or how long you're gonna be held. Echoes of someone banging their cell door down the corridor, echoes of someone shouting, screaming, cursing the feds and God. Echoes of silence.

It's always the same. Four walls. Solid. Steel toilet bowl in one corner. Cemented into the concrete floor on one side is the bed. Blue plastic mattress and a blue plastic pillow. Body heat doesn't ever warm it up. A thin blue blanket made of synthetic fibres that are basically impossible to rip so no one can make a rope to hang themselves with. You're not even allowed to kill yourself. The lights never go out. If you manage to sleep, when you wake up you might think the day's gone by, only to realise it's been half an hour. Imagine. You start to feel the weight of every minute. But once you've been shift ten or more times like I have, you know how it goes. It won't last forever. On the ceiling a question, stencilled in black: *Are you sick and tired of feeling sick and tired? Then ask to see a drugs worker.* Up in the corner a camera, recording. I could do with a zoot right now.

I'm surprised when they come and take me for interview. The madness happened around midday and when the interview starts, one of the feds says time is 17:55 on the 28th of November, so I know I've only been in the cell for a few hours. There's something about light in this place, in all police stations, that

136

is more obliterating than darkness. It hits me as I look around the interview room; the brightness of lights, constant, blank whiteness that eliminates the natural presence of shadows, even your own, and it feels like you've been separated from some immortal part of yourself. The interview lasts about twenty minutes and then I'm taken back to my cell.

Later, I get taken to the desk sergeant. I'm exhausted from the effort of doing nothing.

Right. Krauze. Do you want the good news first or the bad news?

The good news, I say.

Well the good news is that you're getting bail for the ABH, he says, and I think calm, that's the worst of it over now, I can get ready to go.

The bad news is, because there's a warrant out for your arrest we're going to hold you here tonight and then you're going to Feltham Young Offenders Institution tomorrow morning.

Feltham. Fuck. And then I think oh well. Finally. HMP Feltham. Gang city and gladiator games. Everyone knows Feltham is greazy. Gotti told me about mandem getting their faces sliced on the wing when he was in Feltham. I remember he used the word chopped. Said he saw one yout chopping open a next yout's face. Not Nice mentioned suttin about window warriors. Taz told me about the fights in the showers, how he had to cave a man's head in coz if he didn't the same woulda happened to him. Nowhere to run or hide, just face to face with fate. If you're from London, it's mad easy to meet your enemies there, depending on what gang, what ends, what dons you might have beef with. Well now I'm gonna find out what it's really like. Fuck it. Knowledge is to be found on the edge of experience. As long as you don't fall off the edge . . .

I ask for my phone call. I call Yinka and tell her what's happened and then it's like I can't even remember what the desk sergeant says, I can't remember what Yinka says, I can't remember any details of anything, as if my thoughts have deserted me, broken free. Tomorrow I'm going bin and it's something I can't change. A moment of my life that doesn't belong to me.

In the morning they put me on a Serco van. The sweatbox. You get locked in this cubicle which isn't high enough to stand up in and there's only enough room to sit down on the moulded plastic seat. No room to stretch your legs forward, no room to stretch your arms out, no room to move and the windows are so heavily tinted it turns the day into night. No room here for words. No space to describe anything.

The van drives to Willesden Magistrates' Court to pick up some next prisoners. It gets there at midday which means I've spent over two hours in this box. My sweatshirt is stuck to my back. I get taken to a holding cell in the basement of the courthouse. Someone from the court comes and explains that I'm gonna get remanded in Feltham for two weeks and then brought back to Willesden Magistrates' coz the warrant is connected to me not doing community service and not attending probation linked to a case I had for assaulting police. Two weeks. I just wanna get to Feltham now forreal, all this getting taken here, put there; it's disorientating and tiring. Your face dries up and your belly churns but the food they bring to the holding cell is so shit – some microwaved nothing that seems to be one with the plastic container it's in – that I don't even eat it. Anyway, food won't take away this feeling. I can hear next man getting put in the holding cells. More waiting, then taken out, handcuffed and put into cubicles on the Serco van. Early after-noon. The drive to Feltham takes another hour.

One moment I'm in Mile End, thinking about a lecture, zipping up my Avirex coz the wind's tryna wrap me up, thinking about what Nietzsche said, thinking about smashing one peng Somali ting I drew at the bus stop the other day, thinking about doing the next eat with Gotti and Big D, thinking I want some fried chicken or no I want a chicken doner wrap with garlic and chilli sauce on the meat and lots of burger sauce on my chips. And the next moment I'm locked in this box, looking at my hands, making fists, wondering what Feltham's gonna be like, am I gonna have to swing it out with anyone on my first night? As soon as I can tell it's on, fuck a talking ting, I'm straight banging man in the face, even if I get fucked up afterwards. It's like Gotti said, you gotta ride it out, you gotta soldier that shit. Otherwise you'll come out damaged by the inability to be violent.

We are basically all products of each moment in our lives, sometimes becoming things we never knew we could be. When I go pen I'm gonna have to fold up all these other parts of myself and stash them away in the caves of my being. Then again people *say* there are so many parts to you, all these different sides to a person – the side that plays the piano, the side that writes and wants to write more, the side that thinks about ancient aliens creating the human race, the side that wants to shank man up and rob the rich and do this gang ting – but it's not really different sides or parts or pieces. It's all just part of a whole. One thing. It's like imagine a gigantic column; you can't ever see all the way around it in one go, so people only ever get to see the side that's in their immediate view.

Anyway, I'm here.

Her Majesty's Prison Feltham. Dirty red bricks and barred windows that will never open. After the strip-search in reception

– trousers off, boxers off, crouch, hold up your balls, cough – after getting booked in, after they take my clothes and I put on the prison-issue jeans and short-sleeve shirt with thin blue-and-white stripes going down it, after I pull the grey sweatshirt on top, after all that, I become prisoner TF6677 and get put on the induction wing with all the newcomers: a gang of tired faces, cardboard skin, hard stares and haunted eyes, anaesthetised emotions, expectations ripped out.

The wing is called Kingfisher. I have a cell to myself, up the stairs on the landing. They put everyone in cells on their own to avoid any beef on the first few nights. Blue metal doors. Yellow walls. Metal railings. Simple words. Scratches in metal. Scratches in walls. Names, dates, postcodes. 3 the mandem, Kofi Real Killa woz ere '04, Fuck da feds, Pecknarm, Fuck OTF, Yung Steamer On Tour '03, Bridge Mandem, LOM Love Of Money, free Elka, N15, SW9 Real Ridaz: traces of lives lived in vicious moments. The good news and the bad news. Ha. The desk sergeant really fucked me up with that one.

In my cell. A metal bed frame with green sheets on it and a hard pillow. On the wall above the bed someone has written NO LOVE GANG. Toilet in one corner. Sink. Desk. Need paper and pen. Breakfast pack when they wake us up at 7 a.m.: prison cornflakes and carton of long-life milk. Put it on the window-sill next to the metal air vent to try and keep it cool. Screws check on you to make sure you're not sleeping during the day. If they catch you you get put on report. Lunch at 12 p.m. Dinner at 5 p.m. Prison food; I'm not gonna waste words on that shit. Fourteen hours from dinner to breakfast without food. Breakfast is such a minor ting that it's basically nineteen hours without a proper meal. Every day. Twenty-three hours locked up in my cell. There's something strange about this story like I can't even tell it because no amount of words can describe what it's really like. You can try and use evocative and complex words, try and be as detailed as possible but that just leads you further and further away from what it's like, because really it's all basic words, basic sensations that everyone can understand – cold, hard, empty, nothing – it's those words' limitations that sum it all up. And even all of this is a waste of words. Making it sound like more than it is because you're using words to keep describing it when it's all just deadout and there are thousands of other people going through the same process at that very moment.

Chatting to one brer from New Cross called Smiler on association. Live Every Day As Your Last tattooed on his neck. In my cell that night, I find the broken handle of a plastic toothbrush which someone started sharpening. I spend the night scraping it against the concrete floor until the job's finished. Rip a piece of my bedsheet and wrap it tight round the bottom for grip. Next day when I go out on association, I have the shank between my cheeks. I walk a bit slower and don't stretch my legs as much so that it doesn't fall out. We stand in a small tarmac yard with red-brick walls and barbed wire looming over and smoke burn for fifteen minutes. Some of the youts spit bars. I just stand and watch and taste the air. One screw gives us a talk about bullying and how if anyone feels like they're being bullied, they must report it to a screw so it can be investigated. Anyone with a bit of sense knows this would be the dumbest ting to do. If you report being bullied everyone will know you snitched and you'll be getting moved to on the regs, whatever wing you go to. Every night I wash my boxers and socks in the sink in my cell with a bar of soap, then leave them to dry on this one hot pipe that runs through my cell. No one tells us anything about laundry or where to get clean garms.

In the showers during association, some youts from South are bunning a zoot. One tall white brer starts talking to me about some random shit while he dries himself with a towel – I've done trials for Arsenal, he says out of nowhere – and I can see he's fully gone. One of the South youts asks me where you from cuz? He offers me the zoot. Nah I'm cool blood. Twenty minutes later we hear low animal screaming in a cell on the ground-floor level. It's that white brer from the showers. Then banging like furniture getting broken and silence. A screw walks out of the cell and says wants to give it but can't handle it when he gets some back the whiny cunt. I don't see the white yout again.

I get pen and paper. Prison paper. Blue lines like the prison shirts. Number, Name, Wing; you have to fill it in if you're writing a letter. I draw one brer in an AV, holding a 9 mill and a MAC-10, baggy jeans and Nike Air Maxes and a fitted cap pulled down over his face with evil eyes embroidered above the brim. In the background I draw South Killy blocks as I remember them and fed cars with lights flashing and I write *by Snoopz TF6677 HMP Feltham 02/12/06 Loyalty 2 the Hood.* I show Smiler the drawing and he says that's sick cuz, do man a picture like that I beg, I wanna send it to my babymum.

The next morning I get moved off the induction wing with Smiler and couple next man to a wing called Mallard. Getting walked from one wing to the next, we go down brick corridors full of gloomy shadow with bits of light falling through bars, but it's like the gloom blocks the light from coming anywhere near us. See next mandem with couple screws and they're all watching and fuck looking away even though you can feel the tension come into your face, the nerves in your arms and legs beginning to twitch. You can tell who's not shook coz they almost look like they're enjoying themselves. They stare and their teeth show. Gates open. Keys rattle. Metal on metal. Now I'm on Mallard.

In prison talk, doing bird means doing your time. When you get sentenced you get birded off. What a mad ting that every single wing in Feltham is named after a bird. Kingfisher, Mallard, Wren, Raven, Osprey, Kestrel, Heron. Pisstake. I hear that Raven and Osprey are the greaziest wings where it kicks off every day. Bare murderers and lifers. Man are getting shanked up on the regs on dem wings deya says one brer I'm talking to. He wants to go to Raven coz his boys are there and he's moving salty coz he's with the newbies. All around the prison grounds are peacocks. Real talk. You see them through your cell window, showing off their feathers, unreal colours like the eyes of some mythical beast. You see them through the windows when you're out on association. Sometimes you hear them cawing high and loud in the loneliness of night. Mad ting ah lie?

One night, voices shouting from cell to cell.

Oi number 20, come to your window blood.

What?

What d'you mean what? I'll break your fucking face blood, don't get me mad.

Allow it.

Haha myman said allow it you know.

Other voices laughing.

Yo number 20, you still there?

Yeah.

Yo suck your mum.

Blood allow talking about my mum. My mum's dead innit.

Suck your dead mum then.

Oh my days allow me.

Shutup man.

Yo number 20 sing me a song.

What?

I said sing me a fucking song pussyole, otherwise watch what happens when the doors open tomorrow.

What song?

Sing me happy birthday.

He starts singing.

Laughter echoing around the wing. Mandem banging on their cell doors.

Sing it properly blood.

I'm sitting on the stairs during association – forty-five minutes out of our cells every afternoon – chatting to Smiler and some next brer from South. Then I zone out of the conversation coz I start thinking about Gotti. True I'm glad he never got shift with me coz he woulda ended up going bin for way longer than me. I wonder what moves he's doing. He better not hit that super belly without me.

Something happens around the pool table. One tall brer with mini dreads jumps over the table, grabs one next yout's head and smashes it off the concrete edge surrounding a cell door. The brer crumples like a puppet that suddenly got its strings cut. Someone says rah, myman got moved to. Blood smears the cell door as he slides down against it. Some next yout kicks the brer in the face and pulls off his trainers, tucking them under his sweatshirt. The brer on the floor goes stiff and starts shaking. Then the screws are everywhere shouting GET BACK TO YOUR CELLS, siren going off, cell doors slamming and association is cut short.

In my cell I start thinking about uni. I'm meant to be handing in my main pieces of work for the end of the first term today and they don't even know where I am. I think about the fuckery of how I got here. People like me who go from zero to one hundred real quick will always have to face consequences. Now I'm missing out on doing my final essays which I know will damage my chances of getting a First for my degree. Pissed. But more than that I miss the roads. Real talk I don't feel no way about anything I've done so far. It's easier to die than to live with regret. Sometimes I think it would be more painful to feel regret than it would be to get stabbed or shot.

Night presses its cold forehead against my window. I get a letter from Yinka. It's been opened already and stamped HM Young Offenders Institution Remand Centre Received 5 Dec 2006. There's no letter, just a passport photo of us together. It makes me smile and then I catch feelings so I put it away.

The next day, a screw comes to my door and tells me to get ready for a visit. It's Mama and Capo. In the visiting room I don't know what to say so I ask Mama to contact my advisor at uni and to tell her what's happened with me. She looks around, says it's not bad here at all and I say well you don't get to see the bit where I have to watch out for getting stabbed in the showers and Capo says chill Snoopz chill. I'm bare happs to see him and it just makes me wanna get out of here more. Families huddle around their sons, talking in low voices. Girlfriends lean over tables to kiss their boyfriends. They grip each other's hands. Some even have their children there.

As Mama and Capo leave, three screws rush across the room and grips up one brer and his chick, and there's a package all wrapped up in clingfilm like a tube on the floor. Probably had it hidden in her pussy and tried passing it over but flopped. She's screaming her head off as they take her down.

They bend up her man and take him out of the visiting room. Fuckinell. This place has everything. Love, violence, sacrifice, longing, oppression. Everything and nothing. I'll be out in a few days anyway.

When they take me back to Willesden Magistrates' for a hearing, the numbness is there within me, muffling the outside world even as I get brought back into it. I get sent off for a probation review. The probation officer has only one arm and the sleeve of his suit jacket is pinned up around the stump. Eyes like rusty hooks and tea-stained teeth. I say I'm doing an English degree at Queen Mary University and he says so what? I've got two degrees. I consider banging him in the face and trashing the room but I need to go home. The magistrate gives me new curfew conditions, this time without putting me on tag. I have to report to Paddington Green police station every week and do 250 hours of community service. Bun dat. Anyway, I'm free to go. The day feels detached. I'm oil on water. Nah I'm frozen, waiting to melt back into normal life.

Go to my parents' house. Shower, change of clothes. My mother says Gabriel, you got deregistered from uni because you didn't hand in your final essays and they didn't know where you were.

Ah shit I thought they'd do that.

But I spoke to your advisor and they've made a special exception for you so you can retake year two without having to pay extra.

That's banging Mama.

Do you want something to eat?

Nah I'm going out to get suttin.

She looks at me, then looks away. My father's at work. She can tell him I'm back. Time to go SK. Phone calls. Mazey, Gotti –

when did you get out? Come buck me in SK as soon as you can brudda – Uncle T, Capo, Bimz. As I leave, my mother says if you can't be good, just be careful. Yes Mama. Then I go to Uncle T's.

Walking down the balcony of the fourth floor of Blake Court I see some of the lights aren't working and there are blocks of shadow filling the spaces. Shadows. I remember the hard brightness of the police station. I can see shadows and it feels good when I walk through them.

Then I'm at Uncle T's, starting to feel a bit more normal. Welcome home son, I started cooking as soon as I heard you was out. You got something to smoke my son? Wagwan roots says his bredrin Sparky and spuds me. Baseline rises up from the sound room downstairs. The flat is alive. Thaw. Plate of curry goat and rice and peas and coleslaw and fried plantain. I wax it off onetime and then I buy a draw.

Later I go and link Gotti who's jamming with Little Man in front of Little Man's block. He hugs me and says come we get a bottle. How was it? Calm innit, I'm just glad to be out, I say. Any madness? Nah brudda, true I was only there for two weeks. Gotti says it was mad when you started banging that brer on the tube like you was never gonna stop. I can tell you've just come out of pen brudda, you've got that look in your eyes, and I say lemme draw dat zoot. I walk away from him and Little Man and I phone Yinka and say Boo I jus wanna rip your panties off and flip you around and push myself into you and doggy you mad hard, I jus wanna fuck your brains out until you go blind and she says oh my days I've missed you so much, I'm so wet for you Gabriel.

WEEPING BLOOD

JAGGED WINTER. MAKES the bones in my back feel like they're gonna break as I tense up because no matter how many layers I wear, this winter turns me cold. Thank God for Avirex jackets. Shitty snow that never lasts for long and turns the balconies and staircases in SK wet as it melts, slowing everyone's pace down. Too cold to do moves. We stay indoors. The eats probably stay indoors too. Only the nittys don't stay indoors. They come through whatever weather, shrivelled up inside oversized jackets and coats. Determined. Frosty air turning their breaths into rags of steam that hang in front of their mouths. Shotters come quick on bicycles to hit the sells before going back indoors.

New Year's Eve is wavy enough that I don't remember much. Party at Yassmin's in her block in Precinct. Dancing in the front room to Mavado and Vybz Kartel with all the lights turned off and then outside in the stairwell everyone gathers to bun zoots. I throw up all over the stairs and Uncle T shouts go on son, get it all out of ya and everyone laughs. When I've finished, I come back down the stairs and say right I'm ready for another drink, who wants some Henny? Later, I sit on Yassmin's lap in her kitchen and she says you should be a lover not a fighter. Then I pass out in her bed on my ones and when I wake up other people have come and conked out on the bed and the floor – Bimz and Ayesha and others.

I don't need to go uni. I can do what I want until September. Yinka says well at least you can start spending more time with me now, we can actually start planning for the future.

You don't understand, I say. I'm gonna do some serious moves with Gotti and once I get rich off that we'll be able to create whatever future we want.

I don't care about all that, I just want you to make more effort to spend time with me.

I spend bare time with you, just last week I paid for us to go hotel.

That's not what I mean Gabriel.

Well I need to be around the mandem in case suttin pops off.

The mandem the mandem, and she kisses her teeth. Fuckssake Gabriel. Being in love with you isn't easy. Sometimes I think you love your mandem more than me.

Don't be stupid, I say. I love you more than anything. But right as the words come out of my mouth, I know that the effort it took to say them means they're not real. I know that one day it will end, but I can't bring myself to tell her.

I stop going to Paddington Green police station every evening to check in for my curfew. I can't be fucked with it and it seems neither can they, coz my mother doesn't call me at any point to say feds are after me again. While I'm jamming at Bimz's, waiting for the next move to come from Big D or the next whatever to fall out of the sky, the new term of uni starts. Capo phones me and says he's getting himself a flat in Fish Island with his cousin Blix. Says I can come and stay with them whenever I like and Gotti can come too since he knows we're on a mad ting and might need to lie low after doing a eat or suttin. Say nuttin my brudda, I'm gonna come uni anyway, couple gyal I need to draw still, and he laughs and says dun know.

One morning I bell Gotti. He says you're gonna live long you know, I was just about to call you, come buck me asap round the back of Little Man's block.

The sky is clean, the sun is out, the chicken and vegetable patties are hot, the camera in the middle of Precinct is pointing downwards. I see him just outside the entrance to the block. He says wagwan Snoopz without looking at me and his eyes are somewhere else, they've slipped away. The sun trips over him, picks itself up quickly and keeps it moving, and I'm like what you saying broski? He starts telling me how some next shotter came onto the the strip and started taking his and Little Man's sells.

They'd tell the nittys to come onto that little road coz it's secluded and out of range of the big CCTV cameras. They were using that little strip to shot buj and work and this brer – he's actually turning nitty coz he's been smoking hard food innit, he's called Stefano, I think he's from Neasden or suttin says Gotti. But he ain't one ah dem fucked-up cats who's finished, he just started smoking, so he's moving aggi like he's fucking invincible, know like dat? So anyway he's come onto the strip out of nowhere Snoopz, I don't know who he knows in SK to be coming here like dat and he starts taking my cats, shotting his food to them and I've told him he needs to move from the strip and he's gone yeah whatever and the next day this dickhead is there again. I swear down I actually seen the brer hitting a sell who'd just called me for three light and two dark like ten minutes earlier. So I tell him you can't be coming on this strip to shot and he's like whatever blood, what you gonna do about it? Gotti's almost choking on his anger. I say so what did you do? Nuttin brudda, it's like this . . .

The sun creaks across the sky. We walk out of the estate onto Kilburn High Road, start bopping up past the shops and he goes rah that's Stefano and points to some brer in a shiny black Moncler puffer jacket with a fur hood, drinking a bottle of Supermalt. Gotti walks straight up to him and says yo g wagwan, what you after? Stefano says you got dat? And Gotti says yeah yeah. Stefano don't look finished yet forreal. He's about twenty-three and he ain't all skinny and fucked up like most nittys who've been smoking for a while, but I can see the crack in his eyes like it's plucked all the life out of them, leaving behind only something grimy and vicious, waiting to unleash itself. He ain't shook of Gotti, I mean myman's actually looking to cop work off Gotti right here right now. Brazen ting. He must be catting coz he ain't smoked nuttin for a while. Must think that because Gotti didn't do him nuttin it's calm. And since myman's been shotting but now he's asking Gotti for suttin, I'm guessing all his food is done – probably smoked most of it himself anyway. Everyone knows that's like Rule One of the Ten Crack Commandments: don't get high on your own supply. I mean you can't be a nitty and a shotter at the same time ah lie? That's just bad business. I want two light, he says. That's two £20 rocks of work. I know Gotti ain't got food on him, so as soon as he says arright come then and we start walking back into SK, I know what time it is innit.

151

So boom, we're walking down to the blocks and it's this little road coming down off the high road that goes into the estate and there's a long wall to the right with a Royal Mail depot on the other side, and this wall's covered in ivy, the ivy consuming it, digesting it. As we walk down this road, the ivy moves but there's no wind to blow through it or anything like that, but it's moving as if there's a massive snake hidden inside it and I can't stop looking at it like whatdafuck, how is it alive? Just ahead of me a huge rat comes running out of the ivy, scurries up to a bin, climbs into it, then comes back out with something in its mouth and skitters back into the green wall. More rats come running out, making the same journey to the bin before disappearing back into the writhing wall.

We walk up to this block called Alpha House, a big yellow block with dark red balconies going all the way up for eight floors. Gotti says come we go in here and Stefano takes a sip from his bottle of Supermalt and Gotti jerks the door open, breaking the magnetic lock, so we enter the block coz it's too bate with all the cameras to hit a sell on road. We step into the lift.

At this point Stefano's not saying nuttin, he's just looking at us hard, back n forth, from me to Gotti from Gotti to me. I look away like I'm not involved or anything and Gotti starts moving like he's getting the food out, hand down the back of his tracksuit bottoms like forreal he's gonna shot Stefano some work. The lift starts going up. Floating. I look at Stefano who backs the rest of his drink and casually drops the bottle in his hand so he's holding it by its neck. Shit this pussyole's ready, I need to be on point now I need to be on point. The walls of the lift close in.

Ping. The lift stops. Doors open. Stefano goes to bottle Gotti.

Part of the bottle glances off Gotti's head but he's already started dodging out of the way. I boot Stefano in the side and as he staggers out of the lift, I forget my heartbeat and the world shrinks into this moment and I'm lost inside it. Gotti follows straight and sparks him in the face. Myman goes to bottle Gotti again and Gotti dodges it quicktime, high on lightning in his veins, and bangs him in the face again. Stefano drops backwards against the wall. We're in the stairwell just outside the lift, balconies and flat doors to the right of us, and to the left a concrete staircase going all the way down to the bottom of the block.

Stefano tries to get up so I boot him in his chest. He starts kicking upwards like some giant beetle full of poison tryna get up, 10,000 volts of adrenaline. We hesitate. As he gets up, still holding on to that Supermalt bottle, I kick him in the face and his head just goes BONK off the fucking concrete wall behind him, mad hard like I actually hear his skull bounce, but myman's still tryna get up and go for it.

It happens. Springs back up, tries to bottle Gotti again but this time Gotti gets the bottle and it drops and smashes, and it's like Stefano suddenly realises rah these man really wanna do me suttin, he clocks he actually needs to get out of there coz we ain't gonna stop, especially since we know he's got some p's on him innit.

Gotti shouts give us the fucking p's blood. Stefano tries to run and Gotti gets hold of his hood so as he tries to get away he sheds his puffer jacket and his T-shirt underneath rips off so now he's fully bare chest, running past me to get onto the balcony and Gotti's like Snoopz stop him and I grab Stefano's neck from behind, pull out my shank, flicking the blade out in the same moment and just jook jook jook jook jook five times in his back and I never feel the knife go in but I see it slip

153

right in, so smooth, and nothing happens, like my blade goes right in up to the handle, I pull it back out and then these five eyes open up on his back and start weeping blood. Long red streams that run down to his waist.

He gets onto the balcony just a few metres away from me and he holds himself, arms wrapped around his body as if it's about to fall apart, as if he wants to keep it from splintering into pieces that'll scatter all over the balcony. He's breathing in and out, in and out, in and out, rasping, loud breaths, eyes wide, his gouged back dripping onto the balcony and he throws two scrunched-up £50 notes at me and I pick them up and put them in my pocket. Gotti says that's what happens when you come on the strip and try shot food when you're not from round here innit. I turn around and I don't look where I'm putting my feet and I skid on the blood and almost lose my balance and Gotti grabs my arm to steady me and then we run downstairs to the bottom of the block.

We come out and see one older brer, proper OG who's in his forties, coming into the block and he's like wagwan you man? and we're like yeah yeah cool cool. We go back to Bimz's yard.

Mazey's just gotten up. Bimz is making breakfast. Gotti goes into the front room and says Snoopz just wetted up Stefano five times you know. Everyone's like rah mad ting, Snoopz is mad. I go into the bathroom, pull my shank out, open it up and start washing the blood off into the sink, cleaning the blade and handle, and then I fold it back up and put it in my pocket.

I go shop with Gotti to break the fifty-pound note on some chip and munchies, and as we're walking across the precinct we see that OG again, on his way to the shop as well, and as he sees us he goes oi you lot are fucking dangerous man, you lot are dangerous, and we start laughing. I'd started getting bored just jamming at Bimz's but now it's just another normal day, me being me, Gotti being Gotti, whatever. We go back to Bimz's yard and Gotti falls asleep on the bed and I start bunning a zoot with Mazey and the TV is on for once, like no one's playing *Soulcalibur* n shit and there's something on the news about gun crime and knife crime and the mother of some yout who's recently been murdered is saying This Has To Stop and I say see Mazey, this is exactly the kinda bullshit that pisses man off. All this talk don't mean nuttin to mandem who are on soaking people up and alladat. The killers are gonna stay being killers, no one's gonna turn around and say oh shit yeah, we should stop forreal because this dead yout's mum said it has to stop. Mazey laughs, says you're mad broski, nah but forreal, you're right still and he puts his arm around my shoulder.

It gets me thinking what a load of wasted money those anti-knife anti-gun campaigns are, I mean they ain't gonna change the will of the brers who wanna buss guns and hold shanks, them man have already made their decisions, they've already committed themselves to living like that. But the government's always doing this big show where they go preaching around schools and youth centres and they get some washed rapper talking about how there's more to life and all that shit like that's all the youts need; some ex-roadman who ain't got nuttin going for him so now he's tryna do the positive ting. Whatever that is. What a load of empty bullshit. Do you not remember when you was on the roads doing madness? I bet no one could tell you to stop. But now that your career on road is done, no one rates you in the hood, you're not a badman any more, probably ain't got any p's left coz the game flopped for you or whatever, now that it's all done you're tryna reinvent yourself. Half of these rappers ain't even done any serious dirt on the roads anyway, some ain't even shot a £20 rock in their life. But then the government gets them to come talk to the kids about put down the knives save lives and whatever neeky message they have to say, while the eaters and the killers and the trappers watch and think this brer's a dickhead, who does he think he is? He best not come round the ends wearing them jewels coz man will yak that off him onetime.

Later Renay, that girl I've been linking from uni, hollers at me like my mum's away do you wanna come over? and I say yeah yeah see you later. In the evening I go to her yard and when she answers the door she's all dressed up in white stockings and a thong and as soon as I get in it's like bang she knows what time it is. I go upstairs to her bedroom and she climbs onto the bed and turns round for me to fuck her from behind. But as I look down at her naked back I see the five stab wounds on her back as I'm about to put it in and I keep seeing them flash across her back while I'm tryna beat and it proper kills the whole vibe and I make up some excuse. I pretend that I've hurt myself, that I've accidentally bent my dick inside her and it's mad painful, like ah ah shit shit I hurt myself and I quickly end the whole ting coz all I can see are those red eyes weeping blood on her back, and then I tell her I have to go. But after that I sleep easy when I get back to Bimz's yard, everyting is cool, I never really think about it too tough again.

CATCHING CATS IN GHANA

I DON'T KNOW why he done it. I mean he coulda just waited but nah, myman can't ever wait, it's always gotta be now now now.

Last week, Gotti broke into Bimz's yard coz everyone was out and he didn't wanna cotch on the block and wait for someone to come home with the key. Well he didn't really break in. He just pushed open this tiny window next to the front door, which is the bathroom window, pulled himself up, slid through. When Bimz came home, Gotti was chilling on the sofa in Mazey's room, bunning a zoot and Bimz said how did you get in blood? When Gotti told him, Bimz started screwing like fuckssake, this guy. How is man moving like some burglar and not showing any respect for my yard? he said to me when I came through later. That's *your* bredrin Snoopz, remember what I told you. It was like he'd disowned Gotti. After that we went to stay up in East at Capo's.

March. There's nothing to do really and the sofas are mad uncomfortable, man can't ever fully stretch out and more times we get woken up when Capo has to go to a lecture early in the morning. I keep having this mad dream about me and my twin brother stabbing each other up and I swear down it actually hurts in the dream when the blade goes into me and I always wake up with my heart banging like I've just been in a madness forreal and it doesn't feel like I've slept. I'm bored says Gotti. Me too. Time to go back to SK where something's always happening and I can feel real and normal and alive. Gotti says I'm not going Bimz's yard though, bun dat – as if Bimz had done suttin badmind to him. I just laugh. I'll be at Little Man's he says. Calm.

As we step out of Kilburn Park tube station, word comes through that just a couple of hours ago, Rico got shot and killed. Gotti's phone is ringing off. Yo fam. Whaaaat? *Don't lie.* How? My phone starts vibrating. Uncle T. Yo pops wagwan? Snoopy, did you hear that bwoy that rush Malice from the balcony get shot and kill jussa hour ago?

It's the first thing that Mazey starts telling me when he opens the door to Bimz's yard. Everyone inside is talking about it – did you hear? Rico got duppied. Rah. Mad ting ah lie? Rico is – was – one of the top brers in FAC, which is what the D-block mandem call themselves. FAC, Family About Cash. I've seen them filming music videos on the block or in the square inside the estate, opposite Blake Court, everyone dripping in Gucci and Fendi and Louis V, flexing iced-out Rolexes and Cartiers and diamond grillz and white gold chains. One time they were doing a video right in front of the little shop and some of the mandem hung their iced-out chains around the necks of their children who were there with them in the middle of it all, looking mad confused, unsteady on feet that had only just learned to walk. Those video shoots were fucking lit, everyone shouting FAC and SK at the camera and then they'd throw up a middle finger with one hand and gun fingers with the other – the tip of the gun fingers touching the joint of the middle finger – the FAC sign.

I saw Rico with his brother Warlord just last week when I went to cop couple d's from Uncle T. They were on the balcony and Warlord said wagwan Snoopz but Rico never said nuttin coz I've always been a nobody to him. It's not like I'm tight with any of them man anyway. I remember he was laughing at suttin with mandem on the balcony and just for a second as I passed he went quiet and looked at me hard. He was the one who fucked up Malice's face outside that rave. But now he's gone and Malice can actually come down these ends coz after that shit happened to him he stopped coming to Uncle T's, you know—

All I hear over the next few days is that Rico got popped as he sat in his whip in Scrubs Lane near Kensal Green. His window was down and someone pulled up and burst him in his head. Everyone in SK – everyone in Northwest – is talking about it because Rico really was one crazy brer who had a lot of man shook of him. So now everyone's saying there's gonna be a war, like no way can SK not retaliate and drop a body or two. And we know it musta been someone from Kensal Green or someone from Mozart Estate who duppied Rico coz them man have been beefing SK from time. There's gonna be some serious gunplay now, says Mazey.

The story goes that the beef between SK and Mozart started back in the day because one SK brer came out of a corner shop in the ends and some Zart brers who were passing by asked him for Rizla and he wouldn't give them a sheet so they shanked him up and he bled to death before the ambulance got there. He was well loved in his ends and it kicked off a whole cycle of retaliation between South Killy and Zart, inherited by the next generation. If that even *is* how it started, I don't know – no one's really sure. Everyone from these two areas can tell you some story of rivalry and revenge and there's already enough bodies on both sides and survivors of shootings, stabbings, acid attacks, kidnappings – all that fuckery – to keep the cycle going on and on. What's crazier still is that a lot of these mandem went to the same schools and colleges. Mazey went to school with that same brer whose murder supposedly started the whole beef, and he was in school with Daniel Ross and Rico, and quite a few of his old classmates are now dead because of all sorts of shit. It's nuts because the ends are right next to each other. It's only a five ten minute walk from Malvern Road to Mozart and yet for both sides these are no-go zones, everyone knows what roads you can't cross, where the invisible lines are drawn, where to keep an eye out, because you never know when you might get caught slipping by the other side. At the very least you'll get sucked for your jewellery and p's, you'll get punched up, you might even get stripped and filmed and then the footage gets sent around and if you want to live it down you have to take revenge, you have to even the score and on and on and on – ah so it go said Uncle T when he told me about Rico getting murked. But it goes beyond just these two areas. SK is linked up with Stonebridge in NW10 and Zart with Kensal Green, so the Bridge mandem and the KG mandem are also part of the beef and really it's all just one giant trap which I do my best to avoid coz I have bredrins in KG and SK and Zart and I don't wanna get sucked in to all that gang ting, mandem beefing over blocks and postcodes n shit, when I'm already watching my back the second I step out the door coz of all the moves I've been doing with Gotti.

Then one day in April, 500 police storm South Kilburn

Estate. 500 feds, including 65 armed police, dogs barking, battering rams licking off doors at four in the morning, and me and Gotti watch it in Bimz's yard getting replayed on the *BBC Six O'Clock News* that evening – oi I swear that's myman's door getting licked off, yeah forreal, I was always tryna draw his sister still, bloodfyah that's whatshisname getting cuffed innit – and a news reporter says 17 people were arrested, manhunts are underway for at least four fugitives.

Basically, the FAC mandem had been shotting straps to under-cover feds for months in one mad sting operation, until eventually the undercovers decided they'd got enough evidence to fuck the mandem up. So South Kilburn gets raided, bare man get shift and the brers who went on the run get featured on *Crimewatch* a week later. I recognise a couple of faces from when I used to see them on the balcony of Blake Court, trapping or just bunning zoots and whatever.

The blocks quieten down after that. There ain't as many heads about no more. We start seeing the youngers in Precinct more often, coz shotting b and work to the nittys ain't gonna stop. Now that a lot of the olders are getting birded off there'll be a lot more opportunities for hungry youngers to make some bread.

A few weeks after the raid, me and Mazey are walking down Malvern Road from Uncle T's and a bully van drives past slow with the door wide open. One tall white fed leans out of it without his cap on like he's ready to jump out, watching us, actually screwfacing man, and as we stare back he says what the fuck are you looking at? We both have shanks on us and draws of ammi stinking out our pockets so we don't say nuttin, just look away and carry on walking, saying fuck dat pussyole, hoping the van won't stop. When we get to Peel Precinct, we see the same bully van pull up and three feds jump out and rush up

161

to these youts who are jamming on the staircase of one of the little blocks and the first thing they do is grab the youts by their throats and slam them against the wall, pinning them there before searching them and we can hear the youts choking, one of them going I can't breathe man I can't breathe, sounding like bubbles bursting in his throat. I swear down I actually hear the big white fed who'd been watching me and Mazey earlier say there's been reports of you lot shotting on this block, and I say to Mazey nah myman just said shotting you know, and Mazey kisses his teeth and says come we go inside. And I swear those youts are like fourteen, fifteen at the most, I mean they're still in school or at least the age when most youts are in school, but round here it's normal when the boydem stop you like that, violate you, choke you up, pull your trousers down in the middle of Precinct or wherever, pull your boxers down to look at your tings in case you've got food stashed there, although really it's done to embarrass man since they're not actually allowed to search us like that in public places but they know mandem round here ain't gonna file any complaints.

A couple days later, two bully vans full of jakes come round Bimz's block and they cut down all the bushes and flower beds in front of the building. They find a strap and some food, but no one replaces the flowers and bushes.

So I'm jamming in Bimz's yard and we can hear some brer outside saying I fuckin told you, you fuckin prick and we can hear one chick crying. Bimz opens the door and we see one of the youngers sparking some girl in the face. She's crying – why are you doing this? He says I fuckin told you, bangs her in the face, her head smacks against the concrete wall of the block and then he goes oh shit are you all right? She starts crying even more. He says shutupman and sparks her in the face again. Bimz says blood allow doing this shit in front of my yard wa'um to you? The brer says stay da fuck out of it blood. Bimz stares at the brer and the brer looks away coz Bimz has one hardbody screwface that makes him look mad greazy, like he could switch at any moment, even though once you get to know him you'll clock that man has a good heart forreal.

Although he's surrounded by all the greaze that goes on in this place, in reality all Bimz wants to do is draw gyal, spit bars, shoot music videos, make customised garms and fly his remote toy helicopter. Bimz looks at the brer who's now pinning the chick against the wall, kisses his teeth, mutters wa'um for this yout, as if he's talking to himself and says come away from my door g. The yout takes her by her arm and walks out into the precinct, dragging her along with him. We go back inside to play *Soulcalibur*.

Not gonna lie though, I feel kinda sorry for the girl but this is the thing: if you get involved in someone else's mixup, like say we stick it on this yout and punch him up and tell the chick to go home – forget this dickhead, he's a wasteman and all that – it will instantly spark off a next beef ting. Myman will have to come back and prove suttin. He isn't just some any little dickhead; I've seen him in Precinct, hitting shoots, getting his line banging with nittys calling him at all hours and he hits them in Bimz's block because it shields you from the camera in the middle of Precinct. Bimz coulda smacked up the yout but then what? He'll come back with all his mandem and he knows where Bimz lives now, knows where all of us cotch, so— It's like I resented the chick for being part of this drama popping off on Bimz's doorstep since none of us wanted to allow it, but we also didn't wanna get involved in the passa passa. It's happened before; man getting into beef with up n coming youngers who can't win a one-on-one, so they'll come back later and shoot up your yard, beat off a whole clip full of shells into your front door, even pour petrol through the letterbox and burn the yard down while you're sleeping or whatever. It happened to one brer I know called JD. He sliced one brer's face open with a samurai sword because the brer and his team were trying to gatecrash a little shoobz that JD was having in his yard – couple man and couple gyal getting juiced and listening to tunes on some calm tip. JD didn't have it. He opened the door just as the yout was tryna boot it off and sliced his face open with a samurai sword. A few days later, JD came home from doing a shift at the IKEA warehouse and saw his flat gutted out. Just a black shell flayed by fire, surrounded by firemen and police, nothing left for him to return to. So real talk, you can't be inna. If it's not your business just leff it alone, says Mazey because he knows how these tings can gwan.

Later in the evening, we're all sat in the spare room at the front of the flat, which is completely empty now since Jermaine moved out after the raid. The only thing in the room is a rolled-up rug on the floor that everyone leans against – Mazey and Sly and Spooks and Ki and Bimz – and we start billing zoots and chatting shit.

Bimz says listen, do you know how they catch cats in Ghana? and starts laughing with that laugh of his that fills the room and infects everyone, so you start laughing before you even hear any jokes.

Fam the cats out there are proper alley cats, there's bare of them roaming about says Bimz. So what the mandem out there do yeah, they get a rotten fish and one of those big pipes that's used in construction for like sewage or whatever and they put the rotten fish at one end of the pipe and they wait for a stray cat to enter the pipe from the other end to get the fish. Mandem

164

are bussin up now, it's the way he tells it I swear down. When it's inside the pipe they quickly flip the pipe up so that the cat drops to the bottom and gets stuck down there, trapped against the ground with the fish and it can't climb up the pipe coz it's all slippery and curved.

Sly laughs at the same time as he inhales a cloud of ammi and starts coughing up his lungs.

Blood, that's not even it says Bimz. Then the mandem bring a cage and they lower the pipe and put the cage next to the end where the cat is and the cat only wants to get out at this point, so it runs into the cage and bang, man close the cage. And then they cook it.

My side hurts and I press my hand against my ribcage and feel the laughter tightening my bones.

They cook it like that fam, in the cage you know. They put it over a pot of boiling water and the cat goes mad, screeching and going nuts while the steam burns it and then it drops dead and they scrape the skin and fur off and use the meat to make a stew. Swear down, you think it's a joke blood, says Bimz and he's laughing hard now, tears in his eyes along with the rest of the room.

Then BAOWww cracks through everything, practically rocks the room, as if the hand of God slapped the concrete precinct, and we all know what it is because we hear plenty of fireworks round here, mandem love to have firework fights and that definitely wasn't a Roman candle. Another shot goes off outside, so we all rush to the window and pull the curtain open but we see nothing, it's just the stillness of night decaying all over the precinct and everything around it. After a few seconds everyone leaves the window and sits back down and then Sly and Bimz start arguing about whether Nigerian jollof rice is better than Ghanaian.

LINKING MYSTERY

MAZEY'S GIRL IS pregnant, so when Gotti says come we rob this brer carrying the week's takings from the bookie at the bottom of Kilburn High Road, I'm like come we bring in Maze.

Mazey is twenty-six, six years older than me and three years older than Gotti and he's the one brer who never asks me for anything but is always down for man – mad heart, never hesitates to back it – and he loves Skittles. Especially the tropical flavour ones. Always gives me the green ones coz he knows green is my favourite colour. Sometimes we call him Five Foot Five coz he has this grime bar which he always drops when we're spitting that goes, *Don't step to this five foot five coz this five foot five will take your life / Your life span ain't nuttin to me coz that can be changed easily,* even though he's actually five foot six, which he knows from getting measured in police stations. He's got a tattoo on one arm of Mighty Mouse wearing Nike tracksuit bottoms and Huaraches that I drew for him.

At first, he's a bit uncertain about the move coz me and Gotti are moving mad and it's not like he wants to risk getting locked up before the birth of his child. We end up pressuring him into it – you need to do this before your baby is born brudda, one last time, do it for your wifey – like it's his stag do or some shit.

Bimz says Gotti can only be in the yard when Mazey's there. That's *your* cousin he tells Maze. We stay the night, sleeping on the two sofas in Mazey's room in our tracksuits and, early in the morning around six, we get up, ready to go and lurk on one block just off the high road where we can watch people passing by and wait for the brer we're gonna eat. As we head out of Bimz's yard, I watch dawn's pink fingers claw the sky open and sun spills from its guts.

The plan is that when this brer walks to the bank with the week's takings from the bookie, we're gonna run up on him. Gotti says I know the yout, he's a normal guy, once he sees the wetters we're carrying he'll definitely melt and let off with the p. Then we duss back to Precinct and once we're indoors it's cool, no one will ever know wagwan. He'll be going to the bank before the bookie opens, so we just have to watch and wait.

We're jamming on the concrete staircase of this block with a clear view of Kilburn High Road and I can feel the tide coming in. That familiar wave that sinks your chest into your belly before you do a move. We've brought kitchen knives for this one, big wetters to make a man shook. Me and Gotti have ballys rolled up on our heads while Mazey is carefully folding up a bandanna to tie over his nose and mouth. One thing I've always clocked about Maze is that no matter what his situation is, he always looks fresh. He's always got a trim, his garms are always ironed, and his creps are always clean and not scuffed up n shit. Even now, the way he's folding the bandanna is mad neat and precise, and when he ties it round his face he gets me to take a pic of him with his phone, which he then looks at as if he's making sure he looks cris or suttin. Gotti watches the road.

Mazey gets a call from Davina and says babes I'm just doing suttin with Snoopz and Gotti, lemme bell you later. I say lemme chat to her broski and Mazey says Snoopz wants to speak to you babes and passes me the phone. I say yo and she says hey Snoopz what are you doing with my man? She laughs, stops and says no but seriously. I say we're about to do a move and if it pops off, we'll all have a few bags and true you lot are having a baby so he needs it innit. You're mad Snoopz, she says, and then, I swear sometimes I think he's got no motivation you know, we're supposed to be getting ready for the baby and he ain't even working or anything. I say just chill b, he's on dis ting, we're out here, p's for the baby soon come, and she says you better not get him into trouble though, I can't have my man in prison while I'm giving birth to our child. Don't watch dat, no one's getting shift, it's all bless, and then I say bye and she says lemme speak to Jerome again, so I pass the phone back to Mazey and he locks it off without speaking to her.

When Mazey first met Davina, he told her his name was Jerome, even though he's Sierra Leonean and an actual prince – his father being a tribal chieftain – and his real name is Saar. But whenever we draw chicks we give them fake names coz it's usually just a beating ting and you never know when you're chatting to a set-up chick. It's headache though. You end up spending half the time tryna concentrate on not letting your real name slip out, or at least *I* think it's headache, although man like Bimz and Maze draw so much gyal on the regs that they never have any problem with it. Anyway, when Mazey met Davina he told her his name was Jerome and by the time they realised they were in love with each other, it was too late to call him anything else. To her he was Jerome and to her family too: mum, dad, aunties, brother, all of them. Whatajoker.

Davina is a good ting. She ain't one of them dutty hood rats who love danger too much, who'll link a man one day and then let his bredrin smash the next day, who get gassed if a man they're linking rolls with a burner and shots crack or whatever, love the money more than anything, get hype off Gucci belts and thugged-out talk, will give a man brain in the traphouse. That's what you call a badderz. Only good for a quick beat and then bye.

Gyal like Davina might be from the hood, but they just want a better life for themselves even though they've long ago accepted that dreams are only meant to pass the time when you're sleeping. Them kinda chicks are loyal forreal. If you end up in pen, they'll ride it out and wait for you.

Gets me thinking how recently it's all been one fucked-up mess between me and Yinka. We haven't spoken properly on the phone for months. Only time I've linked her it's really just to beat and then we both drift away without looking back. She knew it was my birthday last week on the 5th of May and all she did was send me a text message. It popped up on my phone screen − *Happy Birthday Gabriel, may all your dreams come true. Yinka xxx* − while Bimz was pouring out cups of yak for me and the mandem, everyone toasting me like happy earth strong Snoopz, more life more life, and then I forgot to text Yinka back. She knows that I'm stuck in this life. Maybe she's just waiting for some change. But I ain't gonna change. I wear the same clothes to do a move as I wear to go uni. I kiss my girl soft n slow with the same lips I use to tell a man to go suck his mum. I stroke her hair with the same hand in which I hold my shank when I'm about to wet someone up. Anyway, more times I'm questioning if it really is love or just the ripeness of her body and her lips that draws me to her, makes my heart beat with excitement and my dick hard. When I'm not with her that's when I start thinking I love her. When I am with her I know that I don't. When she chases after my love I know she's going to trip and I can't prevent her falling. Most of our relationship is mad arguments and splitting up n shit. She'll lock me off because I say I can't meet her coz I'm doing suttin with Gotti or whoever. Then it's back to square one, me telling my boys fuck her anyway, I'm done with that chick, while I write eleven text messages in one evening, proclaiming how I'll finally change for her because nothing is more important than us. But really it's because when I can't have her, her body takes on some almost mythical form in my mind that I crave and I start remembering all the good shit. Her crashing into the back of me that time we went go-karting. Nights under her electric blanket. Her getting hyped off my bars at some clash in the ends. I don't know. It's gotten to the point where we split up every few months and then I'm always fucking around with next gyal.

There was this one chick I was going out with in uni for a hot sec called Tiwa. Mad peng. Tall light-skinned ting with curly hair and a body that made any man stop and look twice like oh my days. She loved me off and bare man at uni were mad jealous. This one time, I went to her yard and while I was fingering her on her bed I stared up at a larger-than-life poster of Leonardo DiCaprio in *Titanic*. The whole room was on some little princess shit; fluffy pillows and teddy bears everywhere like she was gonna have a tea party with them after juicing all over my fingers. When I suggested putting on

170

some slow jams, she said I hate that music and then gave me neckback, sucking and tossing me off onto her big olive oil breasts. I was like fuck this shit, this girl's an eedyat. It all ended between us in some house party in uni halls, her chasing after me in tears while I shouted I'm done with you you fucking eedyat, I don't need your stupidness around me and you can't even lips me properly, which was true. She had this way of kissing me with her lips tightened up like she was afraid our teeth might smash into each other. All the mandem in uni thought I was mad for letting her go but I can't just turn fool over some pretty gyal. Later though, I started wishing I was still with her but she wouldn't reply to my messages and then she blocked my number coz I kept calling her. Now who's the eedyat?

Sometimes I wake up in the dead of night and I know I'm waiting for someone who I've always been connected to but who I haven't met yet and the fact I can't find her fills me with a sadness that always takes me by surprise. It goes away when I bun a zoot and go back to sleep and then I wake up in the morning with my dick hard, thinking about robbery. Anyway.

We've been on the block for about two hours now and still no sign of this brer from the bookie's. My belly grumbles and Mazey says I need some breakfast. Gotti spits over the railing of the staircase, says where dafuck is this brer. Mazey folds and re-folds his bandanna and Gotti says he ain't gonna come now, it's too late, the shop will be open by now and they don't carry the p's to the bank once it's open. It's jarring, but the adrenaline left us all longtime and we're hungry, so we head back. Mazey yawns and says I'm tired and I say brudda you just woke up not long ago, what you on about? But I can feel it too, mad drained by all that readiness which came to nothing.

We go to the shop in Precinct and I buy a can of KA Black Grape. Mazey gets a Ribena and a bag of Skittles. Then we go into the little caff next door and buy chicken patties before returning to Bimz's yard.

Gotti is mad restless, like his brain won't stop ticking away as he looks through his phone. Mazey and Bimz are taking turns to play *GTA: San Andreas*, just running around shooting people, blowing up whips, getting as many stars as possible until they get wasted or get arrested and then they pass the controller. I'm bunning my last zoot. The emptiness of the day fills the room and clings to us.

You man come follow me to get a draw, says Gotti, so me and Mazey get up and follow him out of the yard. I say I wanna cop one too and Gotti says yeah that's deya my brudda, I got one yout in Craik Court waiting for us. We walk over to the block. Gotti buzzes some number and the door opens.

As we go up to the first floor, I see two white nittys just ahead of Gotti, climbing the stairs, one of them holding a bottle of White Lightning. Without saying anything, Gotti leaps up the stairs to the landing and bangs one of the nittys in the back of his head. I take my little shank out and stab the second nitty who is closest to me in the top of his head. The blade bounces off his skull and he puts a hand to his head and goes aah what did I do? He drops to his knees like he's checking the stairs for something. Gotti bangs the other nitty in the face and shouts you ain't got my fucking money yeah? I jump up the stairs and get behind the nitty who Gotti just banged and shank him in the back of his neck. Blood starts leaking and the nitty says aah what the fuck and puts both of his hands to the back of his neck, squeezing tight, then he slumps sideways against the wall like he's gonna drop. One of the flat doors on the landing opens and some older African man in glasses peers out of his hallway, says what's going on and we say nothing boss. He looks at the two nittys like he's looking at some mess on the floor and steps back in, closing the door. We go upstairs and Mazey says rah, Snoopz shanked that brer in the head like it was nuttin, and Gotti laughs and says that pussyole owed me money from when I shot him three bits of food, musta thought I'd never see him again or some shit and he laughs his usual AHAHAHA and then he knocks a door to get our draw.

By the time we get downstairs the nittys have disappeared. Drops of blood left behind. I notice that my shank is broken. When I jooked that brer in the head, the blade bounced off his skull and the plastic handle snapped. I show Mazey like fam, I broke my shank on that brer's head and Mazey says don't lie, lemme see that. I'm like fam, that was my favourite little shank you know. Mazey says that's a proper shame Snoopz, I don't think they had any other ones like it in the shop, and then we walk back to Bimz's yard to get charged.

Later, we're in Mazey's room and we've just finished eating. The room smells of Chicken Cottage and punk. I'm on my phone messaging Mystery. Mystery is one chick Taz introduced me to when I was doing the music ting. She's on this MCing ting as well, blatantly a tomboy, always rocking trackies and beanie hats but it can't hide the fact she's peng. The first time I really clocked it was when she messaged me like do you wanna come round and write bars? I went to her yard and she was in a tracky but she wasn't wearing a beanie. Long black hair like a Japanese ghost, satin yellow skin and I noticed her eyes were soft and oily like weed seeds. She's nineteen, although she looks younger coz she's mad petite. She's got a one-year-old son but the dad is some wasteman who's nowhere to be seen.

I went round in the evening after she'd put her son to bed. We wrote lyrics to couple grime beats and then we ended up fucking on her sofa, bareback. Every now and again I holla for the linkage. Every now and again she hollas at me. You know how it goes.

I message Mystery *u wanna link up?*

She texts back *yh cum thru this evening like 6 or something my mums got my son 4 2nite so u can stay.*

I message *have u got a friend 4my boy?*

She replies *yh I mite do still wots he like?*

So I describe Gotti and at the end I write *he's shower still* and she messages back *LOL yh I'll holla at my girl to cum thru this evening x.*

I say yo Gotti, I got one link tonight in Harlesden, she says she's got a friend for you, you on rolling? And he says course my brudda, I'm involved. We say lickle more to Mazey and cut.

Gotti buys a bottle of Rémy Martin cognac, his favourite yak, from the corner shop that has the murder posters in the window. We jump on the tube from Queen's Park and go Harlesden. Mystery actually lives on the road right opposite Krazy Needles where we got our Outlaw tattoos done. She answers the door and gives me a hug, tiptoeing while I bend down because she really is mad short and then she says wagwan to Gotti who says you arright yeah? I say this is Gotti and we go into the living room. Mystery's bredrin is sitting on the sofa billing a zoot. Curvy dark-skinned ting with her hair relaxed, dressed up enough to look good but not enough to make it look like she's trying. Mystery's rocking baggy tracksuit bottoms and a little vest but she don't need to wear nuttin special for me. Gotti and Mystery's friend introduce themselves to each other and we all get comfortable on the two sofas and start chatting. Mystery leans against me. Gotti opens the bottle of Rémy Martin and two twos we're all juicing and bunning, talking shit, listening to tunes and it's a nice little vibe.

It's all dark outside. We've been vibesing together for a couple of hours when Mystery goes to the kitchen like she needs to get something and I follow her. She doesn't turn the light on and there's only the blueness of the night pouring in through the window in patches that hit the floor, the wall, the fridge, her face, eyes soft and oily like weed seeds. I lips her up, taste weed and cognac and that something else which no one can describe, that makes a kiss taste good. She moans and breathes hard and my hands are inside her tracksuit bottoms, grabbing her little backoff, and her hand goes into my tracksuit bottoms and pulls me out and I swear she can feel my heartbeat in her hand and then I turn her around, bend her over the kitchen table, pull down tracksuit bottoms and thong in one go and push myself into the warm, wet and tight and she says fuuuck you're so big. You're hitting it too deep and I say too deep? She says yeah like it's scary, I can feel it in my belly and she laughs and I pull out and she turns around and smiles in the darkness. She kisses me softly, lips lips lips, and pushes me to sit down in a chair. Pulls my tracksuit bottoms and boxers down to my ankles, turns around and eases herself onto me, her pussy all next types of wetness and I think how it makes sense that water is a goddess and iron – like guns and shanks and hard dick – is a god. Then she rides me with her back to me and I am mesmer- ised as I always am with beautiful backoffs, two perfect curves that the universe invented, and I jus wanna bite dat I say. She lets me. Later we creep out into the hallway in case Gotti and his ting are beating and we go into Mystery's bedroom and do it all over again and then I buss all over her back and fall asleep.

175

I wake up mad early in the morning. It's not even gone past eight. The house sighs. Mystery is asleep. I get out of bed. Looking around the room I see pieces of my life scattered about without any sense of order. My black Nike hoodie on the floor. An empty weed bag with green dust at the bottom. Black and white Nike Air Max 90s. The shank with the broken green handle on the bedside table. An empty can of KA Black Grape. My diamond teeth. Mystery's shaved pussy like a polished stone.

I put my tracksuit on and go to the front room, slowly pushing the door open because I don't wanna disturb Gotti and his ting. Gotti is lying on one sofa and the chick on the other. They both look pretty much how they looked last night apart from the creases of sleep. Gotti opens his eyes and says wagwan fam? Wagwan brudda you bless? He sits up and says what time is it? My battery died. I say I'll see if Mystery has a charger and I look at the girl on the sofa who's still fast asleep and say did you beat? Nah not even, says Gotti and then, you got any dro left? Nah it done last night. Gotti goes over to where the chick's handbag is, on the floor by the sofa, looks through it, pulls out a bag of punk which is still half full and takes out a bud. I say brudda. He says she ain't gonna notice that and laughs. I laugh and say nah, you're badmind fam. He sits on the sofa and bills it. We smoke in silence while morning breaks the sky open. Then Gotti says fuck it, goes over to her bag and takes out a next bud so there's only some dusty leaves and a few crumbs of dro left, not even enough for a tiny zoot. He drops the baggie on the floor by her handbag and comes back to the sofa and I say you're moving savage brudda.

Two twos the girl wakes up and says hello. Gotti is sitting there bunning a big zoot, staring at the ceiling. The chick looks down at her handbag, sees the baggy next to it, picks it up

176

between two fingers, looks at it and says are you fucking taking the piss? You smoked my loud, she says to Gotti, raising her voice. Gotti kisses his teeth and says I only took a little bud. A little bud? Are you mad? I still had half my fucking draw left, don't try take me for some dickhead and Gotti says seckle yourself and stop shouting man. The girl says I can't believe this and kisses her teeth mad loud. She gets up and walks out of the room and I can hear her going into Mystery's bedroom where she starts letting off. Gotti carries on smoking and we can proper hear the chick saying whatdafuck is wrong with that brer, he bunned my whole draw while I was sleeping. Gotti finishes the zoot, drops the roach into the empty Rémy Martin bottle – hear the hiss as the ember hits dregs of yak – says fuck it and goes over to the chick's handbag. He pulls out her wallet, opens it and takes all the notes – two tens and a twenty – and stuffs them into his pocket. Come we duck he says and I'm creasing up, nah you're fuckery brudda, and then he starts laughing too. Mystery and her bredrin walk into the living room. Mystery says I'm sorry Snoopz but— and Gotti says it's calm, we're going anyway. I'm like I'll holla at you later to Mystery and Mystery's friend says you're taking the fucking piss. We walk out of the door and the sun spills all over us and we're proper benning up laughing. But it's a shame though, his ting was kinda peng still. I woulda definitely beat it.

THE PRINCE

LEMME TELL YOU about my brother Rex. Rex was in the William Hill on Willesden High Road. One hour before closing time, bare heads tryna find that last win of the night, punching the roulette machines as they lost their money. Two cashiers at the till were busy paying out, checking tickets, whatever. Rex went into the toilet where there was a closet under the sink, opened it, squeezed himself in and shut the door. An hour later, he heard the cashiers telling everyone closing time, the stragglers shuffling out, someone opening the door to the toilets, switching off the lights and then the door to the bookie getting locked from the inside, before the cashiers started preparing to go home. Rex jumped out of the closet under the sink holding a 9 mill,

178

gloves on, bally over his face and ran out of the men's toilet. The two cashiers didn't know what was happening. They were behind the counter, putting jackets on over their William Hill shirts as Rex vaulted over, grabbed one and cracked him over the head with the strap. He told the other one to open the safe but the brer said they didn't have the code. Rex gunbucked the cashier he was holding again and the brer dropped to the floor semi-conscious. Then Rex cocked the strap, grabbed the one who said he didn't know the code, stuck the nozzle of the nine under his chin and told him to open the safe. Eight bags in there. Eight thousand pounds. The key to the shop door was still in the lock. Before leaving, Rex gunbucked the brer who'd finally remembered the code to the safe – I clapped his face off brudda, he told me – and then he walked to the door, tucked the mash into his waistline, put the rucksack of money over one shoulder and stepped out into the night. His getaway driver got shook and ghosted, so Rex had to run down Willesden High Road with his bally on, cold metal rubbing against his dick as he ran, bag full of p's bouncing on his shoulder. Later, when he heard about my move for thirty bags he said that shoulda been me n you brudda, and I said William Hill shoulda been me n you, and he said I know.

He's my brother in a way that no one else is. It's not like me and Gotti where it's all about eats and scatty moves and getting high on adrenaline all the time. We've known each other for way longer. He was always getting gassed off my lyrics when I used to clash next MCs and when I met him I recognised the realness right away. Type of person who'll really show you how effective moral principles are when you're staring down the barrel of a burner. I bumped into him one day on Kilburn High Road and he was going through some real hard times;

179

his mum had kicked him out, he was sixteen, living in some shitty hostel full of nittys and his mum had taken his stack so he had no p's, which meant no food, no weed, no sleep. I was eighteen at the time, I hadn't done any big boy moves yet and I didn't really have any p's myself. But I had a draw and I'd just eaten some chicken n chips. I gave him my last twenty and he never forgot it.

Bare mandem rate Rex. He's known and feared and loved. But when he's low, it's like there's never anyone around, apart from all his loyal chicks who go through phases of loving him and hating him whenever they find out about each other. But they never stay mad for long. You know Rex means king in Latin I said to him one time when we were bunning zoots while listening to Sheek Louch and Styles P mixtapes in his room, and he said yeah obviously brudda but it's not just Rex, it's T-Rex. King of the dinosaurs. Rex was shanking up people way before me. Like this one time, he was sixteen and some olders were watching him from across the street so he said what you watching me for blood? One of them said what, you think you're a badman yeah? Rex crossed the road, no talking ting, plunged his wetter into the brer's chest and walked off while the brer's friends put pressure on the wound, everyone's garms getting soaked in blood, someone screaming for an ambulance.

His mother didn't treat him right. He told me there was something she must have hated about him, because before she kicked him out of the yard in Harlesden she said you know you're only here because your father raped me and Rex punched a glass panel in the living-room door and the broken glass cut his wrist open. The scar from where the doctors stitched it up always reminds him of that moment.

His name alone is power in this one estate by Willesden bus

garage, but the actual ends that he moves with is Kensal Green. There's a lot of shooters and eaters who come from there still. It's kinda mad coz like I said, Kensal Green is beefing South Kilburn, you'll never catch anyone from KG walking through SK and vice versa. But at the end of the day I'm not really one of the SK mandem, I'm just a visitor with a lot of bredrins there and I'm not tryna pretend I rep SK or that I belong to the history of that place innit. And Rex is on this lone wolf shit, going wherever he chooses to go and doing his own ting, you get me.

We've got this bond that nothing can break. I don't know what it is but it's like I don't have to see him for months and then one phone call, yo where you at my brudda? Say nuttin, I'm coming now. His face reminds me of this huge granite head of Osiris, the Egyptian god of the Underworld, which I seen in the British Museum one time.

One day I go to his new yard in Kensal Rise and he's chopping up work in the bedroom. Razor blade – split bang, split bang – getting stuck in the table. I rip little squares of clingfilm and spread them out on the table for him to wrap the pebbles in. When he's done and all the pebbles are ready, he picks up a screwdriver, unscrews the cover of the dimmer switch on the wall and puts all the clingfilmed rocks into the electrical cavity, screws the cover back on and sits down on the sofa with me, waiting for his line to ring. Tells me he might have to war some next mandem. He's always hitting sells in this one block in Willesden and two twos he's seen some next brers from Harlesden moving about his spot like they're tryna do a takeover. Rex don't give a fuck who they are or how many of them there is, fully ready to go to war with them, big shank down his trousers every day, ready to back it out and soak man up.

I don't give a fuck if they kill me fam, he says, raising his pharaoh face to look at me, eyes like Hennessy swimming through the bottom of a bottle at night. I can't die anyway, my ancestors are gods. If they kill me I'm just gonna pass on to another dimension and turn immortal.

I didn't hear from Rex for some weeks after, and then his bredrin Gavin bells me and says he got shanked up by some brers as he was walking into the estate in Willesden. As soon as I see him, about a month later, he shows me the fresh scars, three thick ones around his torso. That was one big knife that went into him and I touch one of the scars and say brudda what happened? He says Snoopz, I was walking into the estate and this whip pulls up beside me and three brers jump out with blue bandannas tied over their faces and this brer says what you think you're a badman yeah? and he's backed out one big shank. Obviously I'm Rex, I'm not running from these dickheads so I banged him in the face and before I know what's happening they're all on me tryna fuck me up. Truss me I got my own shank out and managed to poke one of them, but as I've done that the brer with the shank wets me in my back and then one of the other brers backs out a big fucking borer and wets me in my front and then I feel myself get poked in the back again and then they all duss back to the whip and drive off. It was mad brudda. Everyting in my vision went red, you know like in *GoldenEye* on the N64 when you get shot and the screen goes red; it's like I was looking at the world through some red glasses or suttin, the whole road was red and the sky and trees and yards, all red, and then I dropped. Next ting I know I'm on an ambulance stretcher and Gavin's crying telling me not to die, but brudda, all I could think of was how shook I was that my dick had shrivelled up – no joke Snoopz

182

I swear down, they cut away my trousers and boxers and all my garms was soaked in blood and when I looked down at my crotch I couldn't even see my dick, it's like it had gone inside of itself to rahtid. My Uncle Paul was there and I was like Uncle what's happened to my tings, is it ever gonna be big again? and then the paramedic told me it was only like that coz all the blood in my body had left all the parts of me that it didn't need to be in to try and keep me alive. After that I lay back on the bed and frassed out.

I decide to introduce him to Gotti. It's high time my two bruddas met, innit. Rex phones me, cracking up as soon as I answer the call, saying how Gavin had gone to shot some cro to these yardie chicks in Willesden and when he got there they were like do you know Snoopz? Talking how I was some badman making real p's n dat, and Rex is bussin up saying my brudda, I know you're on this ting but jus cool nuh, how can the yardie ting be saying do you know Snoopz? I tell him about the moves I've been doing with Gotti, clamping rich peeps for their ice in Central and I say you should meet him still and Rex says cool brudda, come tru when you're ready, I'm in my yard all day today.

So Gotti and I are sitting in Rex's bedroom. It's the only decent room and more times it only looks tidy coz Rex's gyal, Alicia, keeps the place neat. We bun zoots and Rex and Gotti chat about next older badman they both know, as if testing each other's knowledge of the roads. I sit on the edge of the bed and bun zoot after zoot after zoot until I don't know if I'm high or what. They're talking about some next showerman called Magic and Gotti's saying yeah I know Magic, and I start thinking how these names hold power, become even more than the people who actually own them when they start to live in people's words. It's mad how I know this world of wickedness and doing mad tings that earn respect, and at the same time I know the world of going uni and trying to write a 3,000-word essay on *The Birth of Tragedy*, and I also know the world that's all about get up, go to work, go on holiday, buy this, buy that, tick this box, tick that box, box tick, box tick, box tick. But people in that uni world and in the box-ticking world, don't know this one I'm in right now. This world where the most ordinary conversation in a room between three people is about one brer called Magic who shoots man and gets away with it and the conversation continues like this while the sun sinks and drowns in the purple distance outside and night comes creeping in.

A few days later, I'm at Rex's on my ones. Just another summer day, sweating with the windows open and the heat from all the cars outside mixing with clouds of cro smoke. Rex has a puppy Staffordshire terrier but it keeps shitting in the hallway and I can see the novelty's already wearing off. He comes into the room and says that dog's pissing me off. He's taken his T-shirt off because it's baking and I can see the scars, like ropes that have buried themselves in him, tied around his bones or suttin. I say I'm restarting my second year of uni in September brudda. Rex says that's good still, I'm proud of you. Then he turns to me and says you know your boy Gotti didn't look me in my eyes once Snoopz. I say really? What makes you say that brudda? He wouldn't look me in my eyes says Rex, I'm telling you Snoopz. Like when I was chatting to him, it's like he kept looking past me. Maybe he was just bare charged I say and Rex says there's suttin about him I don't trust, just be careful brudda I'm telling you and I say nah brudda, Gotti's down for man, we've done a whole lotta madness together and he's never left man to deal with anyting on my ones. Rex says

Snoopz, he wouldn't look me in my eyes. Then he says I need a juice, come we go shop. He tries to take the puppy with him but he wants it to walk down the stairs. The dog doesn't even know what stairs are. It peers over the edge and shrinks back. Fuckssake come on man, says Rex and kicks it down the stairs. The dog breaks its leg and lies on the bottom step yelping. Wa'um to you brudda, I say. Rex says I wanted to train this dog to go for a man's throat you know.

A month later, it's August and Rex is in pen riding a four-year sentence. It happens like this. One brer who knows Rex is getting violated by some next mandem outside a shop in Harlesden. He phones Rex on some begging tip asking man to back it for him. Rex shows up at the shop, clocks the brers outside, says nothing and walks into the shop. He asks the bossman for a large bottle of E&J brandy, grabs it by the neck without paying, walks outside and smashes it over one brer's head. The others cut out quicktime while their bredrin lies on the pavement with blood and brandy in a pool around his head. Bossman in the shop phones boydem and Rex ends up getting shift. The yout who phoned Rex in the first place doesn't say shit. Rex gets bail for GBH since it's his first ever offence on record. While he's on bail, his gyal Alicia finds out that Rex has been beating her best friend for months. He's even fucked her in the same bed that Alicia sleeps in with him. Alicia isn't some moist chick who'll just take it or hate him quietly. She loves him too much for that. So it kicks off bigtime and they end up arguing in the street outside Rex's building. Two twos some man comes along and gets involved like he thinks Rex is abusing Alicia or some shit, so Rex wiles out and knocks the brer out with one vicious bang. But what makes it worse is when Rex boots him afterwards in the face like a football penalty and the brer's teeth fly out all over the pavement and Alicia has to turn him onto his side coz she gets shook that he might just choke to death on his own blood.

Rex tells me all this on a phone call from the prison phone. Four years. If he doesn't get into any more madness while he's locked up, he'll do two. That means he'll be out by the time I graduate from uni. He tells me his credit is running out so I tell him I promise I'll write to you my brudda and he says I beg you send me a pair of Bapes, size 9, and some Soulja Slim CDs, and then the phone cuts out and I almost feel like crying, which is a feeling I'd all but forgotten about.

EASTER EGGS

I START THE second year of uni again. Cans of Boost and all-nighters tryna finish essays before the morning deadline. Quotations. Linking gyal. Texting and arguing with Yinka. One chick gives me brain for fifteen minutes in an empty classroom and only stops because her jaw hurts.

Jamming at Bimz's yard whenever I don't have lectures. Gotti's got bare spots on his face. Always restless. Asks if he can roll with my strap for the day. Course brudda. He screws the silencer on and tucks it down the front of his tracksuit bottoms. In Queen's Park we see one brer rocking a Rolex Daytona. Blatantly a shotter. We go to eat him. He fights back, flips me over his shoulder when I try to clamp him. He's bigger than both of us. Gotti pulls out the strap. The brer looks surprised. He's not sure if it's real. He looks around but it's a quiet street, everyone's at work or whatever. Then BAOW. Oh my days I can't believe what I'm seeing, Gotti actually shot the brer in the chest. The movies lied. A silencer doesn't actually make the shot silent. Nothing like that James Bond shit. Maybe a bit quieter but fuck me, no way could you call that quiet. We don't even try and get the watch after that. The brer slumps against a wall, grabs a bush as he slides down and there's already a dark red flower growing on his shirt. I run like I've never run before. Almost fall over. As Gotti runs he tucks the strap into the front of his hoodie. Mad bate. Luckily SK is round the corner.

Brudda. I gasp for breath as we slow down by the little park next to Precinct. You know we can't tell no one about dat, I say. I know, he ain't gonna die though, says Gotti. I fucking hope not, I say. I swear I can still hear the shot going off in my ear – got me feeling like I need to clean it out. The way the brer grabbed the bush, it's like he was tryna save himself or suttin. Sirens in the distance. We go back to Bimz's yard and close the door to Mazey's room. Unscrew the silencer. Wrap the ting up in an old T-shirt and plastic bag. Stash it under one of the sofas in Mazey's room. Gotti goes out and comes back in with a plastic bag. Put your gloves in here, he says, we need to dash them. You need to burn your garms, I say. I know, I'm gonna do it round the back of Little Man's, he says and leaves. I don't sleep for two days and Mazey says what's wrong with you blood? Your eyes look mad tired and I say I need to go back to East, I got bare uni work to do for next week.

Christmas is the same as the previous year. Quick stop at my mum's to eat, not really talking to anyone while my brother makes my parents laugh. Soon as the main course is done, off to Uncle T's. Big zoot, bottle of Courvoisier and some greasy, over-seasoned leftovers. Then baseline and red eyes, me knocking into the table and Uncle T and his bredrins going him redup to bloodclart, cracking up.

I've been more focused on uni since I restarted and Rex went pen. In January I even miss a couple moves that Gotti tells me about. Not gonna lie I wish I'd gone and done them but I had essays to hand in. When I miss a next one in February because I had to pull an all-nighter in the library he says don't worry brudda, there'll be more. I hope so. Truss me Snoopz, there'll be more.

When I'm working on essays in the library, I plug my headphones in and put on some classical music, some Rachmaninov piano concertos or some Chopin. It helps me zone into my work, but it's also as if I'm tryna preserve something of my mother's memory of me. Reminds me of when I used to play the piano. An hour's practice a day. I start missing something about my parents but I don't know what exactly it is I'm missing. I decide to go home and see them for Easter. Maybe I'll stay for Easter Sunday lunch and do my best to talk about uni. Maybe I can make them laugh like Danny does.

I link up with Gotti in Peel Precinct. We're standing on the balcony of Bimz's block, trying to shield our zoots from the wind which is whipping all around us and I'm telling him how my father loves *The Godfather* films because they're all about family loyalty.

Gotti says the only thing I remember about my dad is when he tried to burn the flat down with me and my mum inside.

Swear down? I say.

It's my earliest memory Snoopz. I can still remember waking up and the yard was on fire.

Rah, you was sleeping?

It was like three in the morning or suttin when I woke up and I could smell burning because my dad had started a fire in the flat. All now I wake up certain times and I swear I can smell burning.

How did you get out?

Well my mum woke up as well and she got me out of my room, but we couldn't get out the front door coz the hallway was on fire. He was gone, so my mum took me into her bedroom, called the fire brigade and broke the window. It was only the first floor so we jumped and then the firemen arrived and put it out, but we couldn't live there no more.

Fuckinell.

That's all I can remember about my pops. I remember I was sleeping under this dark brown bedsheet with a zigzag pattern on it, but I can't even remember what he looked like.

I waiting for you, says my father on the Saturday morning before Easter Sunday. He is in the kitchen as he says this to me and I'm glad my mother isn't there to correct his English. She always does it, especially when he's telling a story and just as he's about to reach the punchline, she'll interrupt him until he repeats the correct form of grammar or pronunciation which she's insisting upon, by which time the story's deflated. I prefer it when he speaks Polish anyway, although my mother refuses to speak it to me since I'm supposed to be proud of being British, of speaking English and living in what I've been told is a better country. Not that I've got anything to compare it to.

My father sits at the kitchen table, fingers moving aimlessly over the patterned tablecloth, his hands tough and pale yellow due to bad circulation. My father has been drawing all his life. He often laughs instead of using words in a conversation. But at the moment his spark is dimmed. Maybe he's worried about me, maybe it's something else; I can never really tell. I haven't been back to the family home since Christmas, but I've come to stay for the weekend since it's the Easter holidays and I don't have uni next week. He looks at me as I stand in the doorway and says tomorrow we will painting eggs.

All my boys who've met my father proper like him and always ask after him. Sometimes I'll be in some far-off corner of London, room floating in blue rivers of smoke, and someone says yo Snoopz how's your pops? And then whata g, whata legend, your pops is mad safe.

Your pops is da truth, said Dario once and I always remembered that. One time Dario told me he'd bumped into his dad, completely by accident, outside a William Hill bookie. It was the first time I'd ever heard Dario mention him. I asked him how it was to see his father after all these years of not having him in his life and Dario said Snoopz, I realise my pops was just one of the mandem and now he's just one of those older brers; always in the bookie's, cracking jokes with his bredrins, catting for chip so he can bill a zoot or whatever. Dario's younger brother Travis said fuck him D, you shouldn't even have chatted to him. But all I'd heard in Dario's voice was pity. I don't think Dario ever saw him again.

Although Mazey's father is a chieftain in Sierra Leone, the chief never comes to London to see his son and every now and then I can see Mazey is vexed about suttin and then he starts talking as if he's continuing a conversation – my pops never makes fuck all effort to check for man, but he's out there in Sierra Leone digging up diamonds n shit, telling people about his son in London when he don't even call me. Every time I try get hold of him on one of his phones, I speak to some fuckin stranger I don't know who tells me to call some bar in Kono where my pops is chilling and by that time I've run out of credit on my calling card.

Anyway.

My father sits at the kitchen table looking at me, while rows of framed pictures and paintings stare down at us from the walls. There's a black-and-white photo of him when he was younger, wearing a mask pulled up on top of his head and he's making a face at the camera.

When are we gonna do it Tata? I ask, putting my black Nike Air Maxes on in the kitchen doorway.

I waiting for you, he repeats, picking up one of the little packets on the table.

Tomorrow is Easter Sunday. There's a tradition, which my father has always maintained from his childhood in Poland, that I take part in every year: the painting of eggs for Easter Sunday. On the day, we sit down for a big meal of Polish food – rye bread and salmon and horseradish sauce and potato salad and pickled cucumbers and *kabanosy*, which are these thin dried sausages with wrinkled red skin, and beetroot soup and poppy-seed cake and Polish cheesecake – and we play this game with hard-boiled eggs. One person holds an egg and another person tries to break it with their egg. They take turns until one of the eggs is broken on both ends and then someone else has a crack at it.

We're not religious in my family but there are certain rituals which are repeated every year, as if to remind us of where we're really from. Before Easter Sunday my father buys these packets of coloured powder. They're not made over here so he usually buys a German or Russian brand that he finds, stashed on some dusty shelf at the back of the Iraqi grocers on Porchester Road. We hard-boil a whole load of eggs, waiting for them to cool down before lining up some empty glasses, shaking out a differ-ent-coloured packet of powder into each one – red, purple, blue, green, yellow and orange – then add boiling water until there is a rainbow sequence of filled glasses. The next step is to take the boiled eggs and place one in each glass, leaving them in there for about three minutes at a time before putting the next egg in, so that the shells absorb the colour. We take out the dyed eggs with a spoon and put them in a dish lined with paper towels, leaving them to dry. The first egg in each glass always retains the strongest shade of colour and the last eggs to be dyed are always pale shades of the glass they sat in. The final thing to do is to polish the eggs. You stick your fingers in some butter and rub it all over the eggs until light shines off the shell's coloured surface. And that's how we do Easter eggs. Me and Tata. That's how we've always done Easter eggs. Every year.

I was supposed to help him yesterday but I was out, cotching on Little Man's block with Gotti and I only got to my parents' yard at four in the morning. I'm only gonna stay for Easter Sunday anyway. I crouch in the doorway of the kitchen, my father and the pictures on the wall looking down at me while I put my creps on, staring at the floor with its chequered pattern; green, grey and red, painstakingly hand-painted by my mother years ago when we first moved in to this flat.

I'll be back in the evening so we can do it then.

Okay, he says as he fingers the packets of dye on the table and a tremor goes through my chest, my back pocket bulging where I've stuffed my bally and I remember that I need gloves.

By the time I link up with the mandem in SK, I've forgotten Easter eggs and family traditions and we spend the afternoon on the staircase of Little Man's block bunning cro, getting blackup, talking to Tyrell, our new getaway driver, making sure he really will do his ting if it gets on top and boydem start chasing us.

Later we're in the whip, hearts beating faster than normal – the usual feeling when we're gonna eat someone – driving into Sloane Square, with Big D in a next whip driven by Little Man. And then it's night outside, dark all over, as if the sky has fallen down and broken all over the pavement. We've been driving around for more than two hours and the day has slipped by without my noticing. Gotti gets a call from Big D and when he gets off the phone he tells Tyrell to park up. We stop on one quiet street just off King's Road and wait.

There's something I don't like about these ends.. Grand red-brick buildings looking down on us, clean pavements and elaborate door knockers and video-intercom systems and shiny black railings and warm lights peering out of high-ceilinged rooms and private gardens full of black trees and black bushes – the night turns them that way – and always a stillness coating everything, too easy to disturb, like if it's so peaceful then the consequences of breaking it must be on a next level. Gotti's voice tears me out of my thoughts, urgent, excited, that one, that one Snoopz, he's got the iced-out Rolex Presidential on.

I clock a man in a suit walking by, headphones in, hair gelled neat from how he musta done it this morning, the bezel of his Rolex watch winking at me in the dark and I know this is it now.

We are out in seconds, the bald white moon watching from above, and all I can hear is my own heartbeat and it feels as though there are hidden faces everywhere, watching every move, while outside of my body everything is as still and calm as a lie.

I clamp him in the middle of the pavement, just as I was taught; forearm pressing into his throat hard, locking the grip round his neck, cutting off the oxygen so that within seconds his body is leaning heavy against me and he's stopped thinking about struggling. I can smell the hair gel. Gotti pops the Rolly and I let go and start dussing back to the whip. The man drops to his knees and holds his throat.

We jump in the getaway whip and now Tyrell is driving us away and I feel totally detached from everything, on a next wave completely, while Gotti chats to Big D on the phone about shotting the Presidential tonight.

The city flashes by, a blur of noise that sinks into the sea of night, gems of light floating through its depths and I'm thinking what if we're karma – that brer musta done suttin really bad in his life for me and Gotti to happen to him – and I want a Rolex like that for myself and it really pisses me off that I've been losing my hair recently and now in the car I'm brushing my right hand over my hair, watching white flakes and little hairs with roots still attached, floating onto my jeans and now I'm wondering – as we pass glowing lines of traffic on Edgware Road and the neon pink lights of shisha cafes – what my mother's doing at this exact moment and in my head I can hear the sound of a knife hitting wood as she cuts the crust off a stale loaf of bread – her favourite part of the loaf – on the chopping board in the kitchen with the painted floor and blue and yellow walls, Mama wearing her round fake tortoiseshell glasses that make her look a bit like an owl and it's mad because usually I don't ever think of her, don't ever think of my family, and now *finally* I manage to pull myself out of my thoughts and I notice that we're nearly back in South Kilburn.

It is around three in the lonely throb of morning when we get paid eight bags for the Rolex. Gotti and I get two and a half bags each and Big D gets two for setting it all up as usual and Tyrell gets one. We say safe, lickle more you man to Big D and Little Man and Tyrell, and head over to D-block to Gotti's mum's yard. Are you sure it's cool to stay at your mum's,

I say and Gotti says most of them man are in pen after the raids, no one's gonna be about. We bun zoot after zoot after zoot on the balcony and when we go indoors and I lie down on the camp bed, I swear I'm so high my eyes fall out and I can't feel my face.

When I wake up, night is sneaking into every corner, down every street, and it is Sunday evening. Nah. Fuckssake. How can I just end up sleeping through the whole fucking day? It takes a while for my mind to adjust, to wake up – fog still pushing against the inside of my forehead – and the only thing I can think of is that I've missed Easter Sunday, I've missed the painting of the eggs with Tata and more than anything else I need to go home. Right now.

It is close to midnight by the time I am stood outside my parents' building, looking up the length of it to the top-floor windows and there are no lights on. Everyone's gone to bed. When I get to the top of the stairs in the building, I pause, keys in hand, staring at the brass letter E nailed to our flat door. I slip the Nikes off my feet, unzip my Avirex jacket and fold it over my left arm. Pick my creps up with my left hand and make sure my phone and the stack of p's are in my pockets. Open the door slowly, holding my breath while I pull the key out gently, barely clicking in the stillness. Once the door is shut, I tiptoe up the stairs in my socks, wrapped in darkness, no need for light since I know from childhood exactly where to tread on the wooden staircase without creaking. It's mad how you can really know your home by its creaks. I reach the top of the stairs, breathing out quiet, putting Nikes down, hanging up my keys and jacket, hoping no one's woken up. As usual when I'm bare charged, my mind starts going into mad thoughts and this time I start imagining I'm a ghost, haunting my parents. I make a floorboard creak. My knee clicks, popping the silence open and I stop and hold my breath again. Noises in the night, noises in the night.

The kitchen is shrouded in moonlight. I don't even bother switching the lights on as I see the bowl in the middle of the table, only four eggs left, already dyed, already polished, and I walk over to the bin knowing what I will find but still wanting to see it. In the bin I see red and green and purple and blue and orange eggshells scattered among empty dye packets, rotting food, plastic and other rubbish, and now I close the bin and I need to sit down. I am at the table, holding one of the uneaten eggs – a green one, my favourite colour – and I rub the egg softly with my hands and I don't know what it is but I feel like somewhere out there I have lost a part of myself.

SLEEPING WITH SPIRITS

There is only cursing, lying and murder, stealing and adultery;
they break all bounds, and bloodshed follows bloodshed.

Hosea 4:2

WHAT I'M TRYNA say is you can never tell what's ahead of you. All you can do is brace yourself. That morning when I broke the woman's finger, I never knew when we set out to do the eat that it was gonna happen. But it did and everything fucked up, we never got the belly and then Big D wanted us to go back and do a next move just so we'd have p's for a new whip. Like I said, whatdafuck was that about?

A few days after we decide to stop doing moves with Big D, I'm jamming on the first floor of Bimz's block with Gotti, mouth burning from hot wings, bunning zoots. The day slithers along on a wet grey stomach, ready to burst. Although we don't say it, I know we're both thinking about that broken finger move and how we shoulda got the belly.

Gotti says we should do this gunman ting you know. We should become hitmen. I look at him but he's not even smiling, just staring into the distance, seeing something that's not there. His thoughts have sharp teeth. How d'you mean become hitmen? Well there's people who will pay you mad p's to go and turn a man ghost, innit. Especially in London. Someone always wants to kill someone. I'm like but how do we even go about dat? How would we even get started? He goes, well there's ways to get your name out there innit. All you gotta do is lick one person down and people will know you're about dat, and once people know you can get away with it, that's when certain heads will approach you, offering you p's to take care of their problems. I'm like rah, but how do you make sure you get away with it though?

Gotti draws his zoot and dashes it off the balcony. I bite into a hot wing. He turns to me and goes, man's gotta do this juju ting and get a spirit. A spirit? Yeah. You go to the juju man who deals in spirits and powers – he'll do certain tings like he'll make you do a ritual, give you some magic powders that you burn or you gotta put in the bath and then bang; you get a spirit. What kinda spirit? A spirit that attaches itself to you and protects you or does certain tings for you. It could make you invisible, or it could make you bulletproof. Swear down brudda? I say. Mother's life Snoopz, I know couple man who went to smoke one yout, they blatantly peppered the brer, let off a full clip at him but they saw the bullets go right through him like he wasn't even there, and the brer just carried on dussing. They couldn't kill him, you get me. Myman had powers. Certain man even have powers that makes them invisible so the feds can't see them when they go to do a madness innit. I'm like rah, that's a real ting? Gotti says yeah fam and looks at me without blinking, without a trace of anything moving in the lakes of his eyes and he says brudda, it's fully real – lemme have a hot wing. I offer him the box and he pulls one out. Then he leans back over the railing and says but you can't fuck up the power, you can't make one mistake. If the juju man says you gotta wear these beads, the day you take them off is the day that the spirit will detach itself from you and you'll fuck up. It'll ruin your whole life. Or he might tell you that if you wear the beads when you fuck gyal you'll lose your powers. I lean against the flaking metal railings. My head starts spinning but it's probably the cro we've been smoking. Gotti dashes his chicken bones over the balcony and licks his fingers.

If a next man said this to me, I'd be like whatever, you're just chatting some mad shit about magic, you don't even know what you're on about, we're in the twenty-first fucking century, we don't deal with them tings. But this is Gotti. This is a very serious individual. We've been through a whole lotta madness and all I've seen is realness. This is an intelligent person. Not someone who believes in bullshit and superstitions that you can't see or prove. Man don't even believe in God. We don't even know if God believes in us, so why bother? But Gotti's talking to me about this juju ting like it's as real as the air we breathe, like it's gravity n shit. He points to one block in the distance and says see that block there, if you come with me I'll take you to the juju man who lives there, myman will put a spirit on you for the right price. Truss me. And then he starts talking about Bugz Bunny.

I'm leaning over the balcony and I look up at the sky, bleached by rain. There's two hot wings left. The day is dying. Gotti says how d'you think Bunny's always gotten away with it?

What, Bunny's duppied bare man?

Gotti laughs like it's something obvious and says course fam, myman's got bodies. And he always gets away with it. Just like the Chicken ting.

Yeah I heard about Chicken still. Didn't he get popped in one house party in D-block and then jump off the balcony?

Yeah, it was me who made that happen.

How you mean?

Gotti tells me:

Chicken wasn't on stuff, wasn't involved in fuck all, just a next yout from SK. Whenever it was summertime he'd bring out this little drinks stand on the block and try shot juice to the mandem n dat. But his cousin and couple next man yacked some of Bunny's peopledem inside one chicken shop. Took their chains and gunbucked them n all dat. I was in the shop getting a burger when it happened. Them man disappeared afterwards, so Bunny couldn't find them. Two twos, Chicken has a house party. Bare man from SK come. So I'm in the party and Chicken's got one chick winding on him right next to me, so I phone Bugz Bunny and tell him one of the brers who robbed the mandem is right here. Bunny says are you sure? I say yes, coz true Chicken is the cousin of the main guy who robbed the mandem, so it'll have to do. I tell Bunny I'll be standing right next to him, just come now. About twenty minutes later, Bunny runs up in the yard blacked out, bally'd up, holding a Glock 9 with a red laser attached to it and he pops Chicken in the chest right in front of me. Chicken tries to get away, so he runs out onto the balcony and jumps off. But the yard was on the second floor of Dickens House, so he breaks his legs when he lands. I swear down everyone could hear his legs snap and then he starts crying for help. Everyone goes running out the block and I remember some woman was screaming help him, help him. Bunny comes out the block and says help him yeah? And then he says move back, move back, and he waves his strap at the crowd like he's swatting flies away. He walks over to Chicken and shoots him couple times in the face. Then he calmly turns Chicken's face over with the toe of his trainer and gives him couple more in the other side of his face before cutting out.

As he tells me this, Gotti's eyes go all distant, almost drowsy, like he's well fed on memories, drunk on the past. That's peak, I say. I'm still eating a hot wing and something shivers inside me and I say standard fam and laugh, but I can smell the dead flesh of the bird through the greasy skin and I put the half-eaten bit of meat and bone into the plastic bag with the box of chicken wings and dash it off the balcony. Everyone knows it was Bunny, says Gotti, but there's no way feds can get him for it. His powers are too strong. I never even liked Chicken anyway, he was a dickhead, and then he laughs.

Then he tells me about how Bunny got paid to go and duppy one brer for some next bosses in Northwest. He's in the back of the whip and it's the brer who's sitting in the front passenger seat that he's gotta kill, says Gotti. They park up somewhere in Maida Vale and Bunny takes out the strap and busses it in the back of myman's head. But the strap was a rebore, the barrel wasn't drilled through properly, so when the bullet hit myman's head, it's like it broke on his skull, it didn't go fully in. Myman's clamped his hand to his head and gone aaah fuck. Then Bunny's clapped it off another seven eight nine times in the brer's head and obviously that killed him. The brer's cousin, who's in the driver's seat, jumps out and runs off, and Bunny's all shouting after him, come back bruv I ain't gonna kill you. So whenever he goes pen, it's never for a M, it's always suttin else, and that's the spirit. That's the power that Bunny got put on him, you get me.

A couple of children in school uniforms walk across the precinct and the camera swivels down to look at them. They walk into the little shop where we're always buying Skittles and cans of KA and chip n Rizla. I look at Gotti and I'm thinking rah, this is forreal, it's true. Certain man are really going around London, dropping bodies and getting away with it. You don't read about it in the papers, you don't read about people not getting convicted of murders. Stories with loose ends that no one wants to tell. That no one knows *how* to tell.

Gotti says but there's a downside to this shit Snoopz. If you get a spirit protecting you, that ting will attach itself to you for life innit. It'll never go away. You'll wake up and the spirit will be there in the room with you. And I don't mean the spirit will be in the room with you like you can feel a presence, I mean you'll wake up and see suttin standing at the foot of your bed. Trust me Snoopz, I know this. Wherever you go, wherever you sleep, this ting will always be there, it'll never leave you alone. I lean over the balcony coz I've got a sick feeling in my stomach. Probably those chicken wings we ate earlier.

I remember when I was a Listener, says Gotti and I'm like what's a Listener? And he says when you're in pen, to try and get privileges and show the parole board that you're reforming or whatever, you can become a Listener. It's where you're basically available for mandem to talk to when they've got problems but don't wanna talk to a screw. You go into a man's cell when he's feeling depressed and you listen to his problems and try reason with him n shit. I became a Listener last time when I was doing five years, says Gotti. I'd go into certain man's cells who was doing life for murder and them man would be telling me how they can't sleep. Like every time they close their eyes, they see the face of the person they duppied. Or they get into bed to sleep, pull the covers over them, and the next ting they know, this person who they bodied is under the covers with them. But real talk Snoopz, it's not the ghost of the person they killed, it's the spirit that they got on them, that's attached itself to them and ain't gonna leave. I'm like rah, whatdafuck, that's some deep shit forreal. And Gotti's like yeah truss me, it's proper mad, people won't tell you about it, most people won't even know about that shit, but it's real, swear down.

He spits over the balcony and says anyway brudda, I think we should do this gunman ting innit. The sky above is drained of light, turning his face blueberry grey as he looks at me, blank eyes. He says if man's gonna do it though, man's gotta be serious about it you get me, coz once we decide to go and lick a man down, there's no going back. I'm like yeah I hear you, lemme think about it still. Water kisses my forehead. It's started raining, so we go downstairs and knock for Bimz. He opens the door and lets us in.

Later, I zone out after a big zoot of amnesia, thinking to myself how this life seems forever, like it's always going to be me and Gotti on the block, scheming on how to get rich and maybe one day we will. But for now it feels like this place is going to be forever, this life is going to be forever. Bimz and Mazey and Precinct and SK and Uncle T and everything all together like a massive whirlwind that can't stop.

WEREWOLVES

It is the meaning of all culture to breed a tame and civilised animal . . . out of the beast-of-prey, man.
Friedrich Nietzsche, *The Genealogy of Morality*

VISIONS OF BACKOFFS in the morning. Visions at night when I'm sleeping alone. Visions of gods and fallen angels and great battles on far-off stars. I wake up and pull the sheet over my face and head as if I'm in a shroud – to get buried like this will hide me from the world. I miss the feeling of Yinka's pussy clenching round my dick. She's got herself a flat in Chiswick but I rarely go and stay there. I sit in her blood like mercury; up down, hot cold. When are you gonna move in, she asks. Soon Boo, soon. You're always saying that. Next week I promise. Next week comes and I don't even go and stay the night with her. I air her calls. Nineteen missed calls. The next day I pick up. Why the fuck are you always playing games with my heart

Gabriel? What fucking games? You know what I've been through, you know how important building a life with you is to me. Well it's not my life is it, I say, it's yours and I'm not your cement. Yinka starts crying and it's this high-pitched noise, chewed up by pain. It's like she's realised I'm gonna ruin her. She says you always fucking do this to me, you make me think you want a life with me but you don't, you're just stuck on the roads with your mandem, and then I just listen to her tears because I don't know what else to say. I've run out of words and I don't feel anything right now even though I want to. My heart has escaped from my chest and it's sitting on my shoulder, dangling its legs, and the world around me is a groan. Yinka says I can't do this no more and the phone goes beep beep beep as she locks me off and I start walking up the road with nothing inside me. Back to South Killy. The love song is over.

Can't believe she split up with me. Feels like it's forreal this time. Funny how now I want her more than I ever wanted her when we were together. Waking up, tortured by visions of her on all fours with her back arched and her backoff pushing up and I— it's as if memory, like history, only exists in torment and sacrifices.

Back at uni. Third term of the second year which I'm redoing, but as usual I'm getting up to plenty fuckery. Last night was a mad ting when Lexi lost her virginity to me. I only realised after as well. It took a whole episode of *The Simpsons* for me to push it in and when I said why is it not going in she said I don't know. Short, dark-skinned ting, with a long weave, always immaculate-looking without a hair out of place. Tongue pierced, red blusher on her cheeks like pink frosting on choc-olate cake, always rocking them thigh-high boots over her jeans.

She's a whole snack. It took me a while to realise she was fully on me and no one else. Her bredrin Keisha told me one day you know Lexi's waiting for you to move to her and I was like bang, next time it's just me and her in her room I'm dealing widdit. She lives on campus, so it wasn't a long ting and I wasn't tryna drag it out when these times I'm desperate to feel alive, as if I could get locked up tomorrow or someone might kill me.

I went to her room just before 6 p.m. I lipsed her up and her tongue piercing clinked on my diamond grillz and then she lay back on her bed and pulled me on top of her. I pulled the cover over us and we scrambled to pull each other's jeans down, trying not to stop lipsing as if that would break the trance we were in. It took me twenty minutes to push myself in and I couldn't understand it. I know exactly how long it took coz *The Simpsons* started as I was tryna push it in and I could feel the wetness but I couldn't get anywhere and only when the end credits started rolling did it finally go in and it was crazy tight. Afterwards she sat in her bed with the duvet all bunched up around her and then I was like yo I gotta bounce coz I'm linking up with Capo and them man on Roman Road. I texted Gotti *where r u* and he messaged back *Im at the yard* and then I left.

I've been staying with Capo and Blix in Fish Island since the third term started. Gotti comes through on the regs and both Blix and Capo said he can stay on the other sofa as well. It's a good change of scenery. Especially since the raids in SK, especially since we stopped doing moves with Big D, especially since Gotti heard that he's wanted after feds came looking for him at his mum's yard. I've brought toiletries and uni books, as well as some garms. Gotti brought some garms but most of his shit is still at his mum's in D-block. I brought my Star 9 as well. After unpacking, I wrapped it up in a fresh towel and stashed it under one of the sections of sofa that I sleep on. I haven't told Capo or Blix about it because only me and Gotti need to know and I don't want them man to feel a way. Capo's shotting cro in uni now, £20 draws here and there, and I guess it helps with the rent. Me and Gotti ain't dropped him no p's for letting us stay here and he ain't asked for nuttin either. Capo is my darg forreal.

I get up and prepare for the day. Lecture at nine, followed by a seminar. After that I'll link up with Gotti and go Northwest since it's a Wednesday and I've got no uni for the rest of the week. Capo and Blix are asleep because they don't have any classes until the afternoon. Gotti is curled into his sofa. I wonder what he dreams about.

We're doing Nietzsche again and after the lecture I'm in my seminar in full flow since I've been reading *The Genealogy of Morality*. We're talking about justice and its origin and I put my hand up and when the professor says yes Gabriel, I say well in *The Genealogy of Morality*, Nietzsche makes the point that justice exists as a social restriction, like not just as a form of control but an actual restriction of human nature. So if I wanna follow my instinct to pillage a next man's city and take it over, or just kill my enemies, I can't do that. Because the law will punish me and justice will take revenge on me for following my instinct and breaking society's rules innit. The teacher says exactly. I say and that's not good coz it's forcing me to suppress what I feel I need to be happy, or at least – in terms of revenge – to get some kinda closure.

One next brer in the class says but based on what you're saying, if we lived in a society where we could all just follow our instincts, paedophiles would be allowed to abuse children because that's them following their instincts. So are we supposed to just say oh they need to do what feels natural to them?

I say, well you're right about that on one level, but then at least I could follow my instinct for revenge and kill all paedophiles, any rapists in fact. And not just kill them but like keep them alive and do it slowly, make them suffer, chop pieces off them n shit, sorry, like not to sound too raw to everyone here but I'm being real.

Some people in the class nod. Some look down at their books and frown. Others stare. Someone breathes out loudly. I continue. People could take proper revenge against these kinda tings and those abusers wouldn't just get a measly five-year sentence on a wing in prison that protects child molesters, then come out into society and live normal while the child they abused remains damaged for the rest of their life, you get me. And then it's mad, coz in this society you've got people who sell drugs to people who already want drugs, getting way longer sentences. Shows you what the lawmakers really care about ah lie? Some of my classmates say it's true it's true and the professor says okay let's all calm down.

After the seminar, I go and link Gotti at Mile End tube station and he says Snoopz come we roll Willesden, I reckon we might be able to set up a move or suttin. I say I'm on whatever. On the platform, he leans close to me and says brudda I got the strap tucked you know. I say swear down? Swear down he says. I've got two boxers on and two tracksuit bottoms. I'm like I was gonna say fam, there's no way anyone can tell you're holding anyting and he says the only thing is I can't sit down properly coz it'll look like my dick's hard, and then he starts laughing. You madman I say, ain't you hot? A little still, he says as the train pulls in. Rah, Gotti's nuts forreal. Just when I think I've seen it all he shows me some next level of no fucks given. Man's strapped up on the tube to rahtid. Here we go. We change at Bond Street and take the Jubilee line to Willesden Green.

We go to these blocks in Willesden, just off the bottom of the high road and jam at the back of them, Gotti introducing me to certain man who come over and say wagwan. Red bricks and narrow windows, grass outside covered in rubbish and the sun above heavy and rotten. Couple young tings with their hair gelled down shiny, babyhairs like little crowns on their foreheads, stare at us from the stairs leading up to the back entrance of the blocks. One of them chews her gold chain as she clocks me. I look at them; puffer jackets with tight jeans rolled up showing ashy ankles and the girl with her chain in her mouth says oi that boy's buff you know and I smile at her and turn back to Gotti. One brer who's rocking yellow-gold grillz top and bottom walks over, says wa'um Gotti and Gotti says this is Snoopz, he's shower, and the brer spuds me, says rah you're that Snoopz brer yeah? Nodding like something's just fallen into place in his mind, then says so what you man dealing wid?

Gotti called me shower. Like I'm a showerman. Manabadman manawickedman manashowerman. But he's way more shower than me. Gotti on the block with a loaded 9 mill down his tracksuit bottoms. That's shower. I guess what makes me shower in his eyes is everything I've done since I started rolling with him. Into the darkness. Man like Bugz Bunny are *real* showerman though. Licking man down with no regrets. Living with demons until you become one yourself. No fear in your eyes while you put fear into a next man's eyes. Being shower is having mad heart, going to mad lengths, never backing down – it's having no heart in fact. Moving so badmind that the wickedness you do come like you got no heart inside you to feel anything. I don't think I'm shower though. I don't know what I am. Not gonna lie though, I felt mad gassed when Gotti said that. It's like he put some kinda power into me.

Later, we're on road and Gotti tells me he can't walk fast coz if he does, the nine is gonna keep poking through his tracksuit bottoms and obviously man can't be getting clocked on road with a strap. We're in NW10 and the undercovers move different round here so we gotta be mad on point. Anyway, I don't mind walking slow coz I'm rocking a fresh pair of Jordans and I don't wanna crease them.

We grab some chicken n chips from Sam's and then we go to check some next mandem who Gotti knows just off Willesden High Road. The yard looks like a traphouse from the outside but it's just one of them random red-brick houses you see in Brent, run down and neglected. We sit on the wall and bun zoots. When Gotti wants a zoot he goes oi lemme get a zoot to one of the brers we're jamming with and when the brer passes his draw over, Gotti pulls out the two biggest buds, and gives the brer back his bag, which basically has one dowy little zoot left in it. But the brer don't say nuttin. I can see defeat in his eyes. Then Gotti says we're looking to pick up a two-and-a-q or even four-and-a-half if the punk is live, you know anyone who's got big bits? These times I'm thinking we ain't even got the p's on us to front like we can cop a big bit, but I trust Gotti to run it however his mind is scheming. The brer Gotti asked gets mad eager, says yeah I'll make couple calls still, I know someone.

Evening blossoms over the street. The brer gives Gotti a number to call and says myman's got blue cheese still, I told him you wanna pick up. Call him when you're near Willesden

Green station and he'll tell you where to come. We walk to the station. Gotti goes into a phone box, calls the number and says yo my boy gave me your number, said you got big bits for man whatyousayin? . . . Where shall I come? Then he puts the phone down. We pull our hoods up and put gloves on. The yard is down a side road, right next to the station. Another terraced house, except this one's better looked after. There's not a lot of street lights and the yard is on the corner as the road bends to the right, the door set into the building under a wooden awning. We nestle into a pool of shadows, press the buzzer and wait.

One yardie brer with his hair in fresh canerow, rocking a white vest, opens the door. He looks at us both and says to Gotti ya Nino bredrin? Gotti says yeah that's me. Man wanna cop a big bit but I wanna see what you're working wid still. Wa ya want? Bring me a two-and-a-q innit. He looks at Gotti, then me and says me ah bring dat, soon come, then steps into the yard and closes the door. Through a pane of frosted glass in the door we see him go upstairs and into his flat on the first floor. I turn to Gotti and say we gotta get at least a ninebar brudda and he says yeah course, let's see how he's moving when he brings man the food. Nine zeds, nine ounces – a quarter of a kilo – is the least we should try and get, since a couple zeds ain't gonna be worth more than four bills at the most. The yardie brer comes back down the stairs, opens the door and gives Gotti the two-and-a-q wrapped up in clingfilm. He says blue cheese bigman, as Gotti peels back a bit of clingfilm to see the cro. He smells it, passes it to me and says what you think brudda? I smell it and say yeah it's banging. You got more of the same food yeah? The yardie brer says how much you ah look fi buy? Gotti says bring man a four-and-a-half of dat. The brer closes the door and about thirty seconds later opens the door again and hands Gotti two clinged-up balls like the first one. Me have everyting wrap up in two-and-a-q, he says to Gotti who passes me the four-and-a-half and says bring me a next one then. The weedman looks at me, then back to Gotti and says look bredrin, how much you ah want cah me nah deal wid— I say I'm not feeling how you're moving like you wanna set man up or suttin. The brer looks at me mad surprised. His eyes are redup from bunning. Set you up? Ah wa di bumbaclart you ah chat bout set up, me nah set up – and I say nah blood you're moving off key, and then to Gotti, brudda I'm not feeling this, come like some set-up ting, and Gotti says yeah forreal.

I stuff the zeds we've already got into the pockets of my Avirex which are just about deep enough to hold the food and at the same time the weedman looks at my hands like he's seeing the gloves for the first time. Gotti pulls out the strap mad quick and I grab the brer by his throat. Gotti sticks the nine right into his belly, hard, and with his other hand grabs the brer's belt, pulling him into the strap. The weedman's eyes open wide, two black moons coming out of clouds, and puts his hands up next to his head. His hands are shaking. Bossman, me ave mi granmudda upstairs. Fuck your grandma, says Gotti, I swear down I'm gonna shoot you if you don't back up right now. The brer steps backwards and we enter the yard. I let go of his throat and close the door behind us. Click.

The hallway and staircase are hushed up in shadows and at the top of the stairs, through a door with a pane of glass in it, I can see a hum of orange light. The grandmother has no clue what's going on downstairs. I can hear a TV programme bubbling. Gotti lets go of the brer's belt, cocks the strap ch-clack and puts it right between the weedman's eyes, pushing hard so that he crouches, shrivels into himself and goes cross-eyed as he looks at the burner. I'm gonna give you one chance, otherwise we're going into your yard and if your grandma's there, no lie I will gunbuck her face off, says Gotti. I say how much food you got upstairs? I only had half a box bossman, his hands together like he's praying. Bring me the rest right now, says Gotti. You got one minute blood, if you're not down in one minute I'm running up in your yard. The brer backs off slowly, still crouching, with Gotti aiming the Star 9 at him. He runs up the stairs, trips just before the top step, drops to his knees and pushes himself back up, wobbling on shaky legs as he gets to the top, opens the door and enters the humming orange light. Half a box. That's half a kilo; eighteen ounces or two nines. Standard trap maths. That'll make us three bags easily.

You reckon he's gonna try a ting fam? I say and Gotti says nah brudda he's not serious, blatantly moving on some eedyat ting, trapping out his grandma's yard like that's gonna keep him d-low. Anyway, if he don't come back in thirty seconds we're running up in there. I say standard and he says you got room in your jacket? Not for half a box I say, but if it's in bits we can put it down our tracksuit bottoms and just walk extra slow innit. Forreal, says Gotti.

The door at the top of the stairs squeaks opens and the weedman comes down with another clinged-up ball and what looks like a loaf wrapped in cling. Issa two-and-a-q and a nine bossman he says handing me the loaf. I stuff the ninebar into the front pocket of my hood. Gotti grabs the brer by his vest and pokes the strap into the top of his head, pushing it into the man's canerow hard. Hair grease shines on the barrel. I turn around and open the front door. Gotti has the brer on his knees now, the man repeating 'low me bossman, 'low me I beg and Gotti says look away. The brer puts his face to the floor and

Gotti turns round, tucks the strap into his tracksuit bottoms and steps out the door. We don't say anything as we start running back up the road to the station. The night snarls around us and halfway up the road we burst out laughing. We jump on the train, breathless, stinking of blue cheese and head back to East.

Back at Capo's we tell him wagwan, although we leave out the bit about the strap and he says you man are moving greazy. We give him the nine zeds and say just give man a bag for that and the rest is payment for having us here. He says ah safe you man, I was looking to reload as well since I just shot my last draw today. I say don't watch that brudda, safe for letting us stay here n dat. We keep the other ninebar for ourselves so we can shot it later at some point and get the p's. When Capo's in his room, Gotti pulls out the burner and gives it to me. I wrap it up in a T-shirt and put it back under the seating section of the sofa I sleep on. Come we bill it. Gotti's already unwrapping the clinged-up loaf, the sweet Mother Earth smell of blue cheese exploding into the room in all its ripeness as he rips out some buds for us.

Later, I'm on my third zoot, mad charged, head spinning out, riding the rollercoaster as my brain travels out of my face and into my belly. I close my eyes and see galaxies of pink and green and then all the stars explode into the blackness of space and my brain flies back into my head. Gotti already ko'd and I'm thinking about the day. Mad how people talk about good and evil and how I know that society as a whole would definitely call us evil. But see the brer we robbed today? He don't think we're evil. Just like we don't see him as evil. Why would we? There's just stronger wolves and weaker wolves. What was it that Nietzsche said about wolves? Suttin about it being absurd – yeah that's the word he used, absurd – for sheep to call wolves evil when all they're doing is following their instinct. The only thing that is bad is powerlessness. Anyway, on another day that shotter might catch man slipping, buss his gun on me and done my dance. And then what? Then it's him who's the showerman and I'm the victim. The thought starts to make me nervous and I start thinking nah, he couldn't have clocked my face, too dark in that hallway. Fuck it, I'm not going Willesden for a while now, them youts that connected us to the whole ting better not chat our names coz I dun know that weedman will wanna come for us and—

My head starts spinning off again, smoke licking the ceiling, and then my phone vibrates. It's a text message from Yinka which reads *I still love u*. I look at the text for a few moments, then delete it and I don't remember falling asleep.

SIGNS

I COME BACK from uni and Gotti is lying on the sofa in Capo's flat bunning a zoot and playing with a Cartier watch.

Where did you get the Carti brudda? I say.

I stuck up some brer with the strap while you was at uni, he says.

Swear down? I say. Where?

Just over the bridge where the shops are, he says. I seen one man with a Carti on his wrist walking towards the bridge, so I run up to him and pointed the strap at his face.

What did he do? I say.

He got mad prang and said I'll give you anything you want just don't shoot, and Gotti starts laughing. I told him to give me his watch so he took it off for me and then he started dussing and I cut back to the yard. Anyway, what was uni saying?

The next day, when I get back from uni it's mad late and Gotti is already asleep, turned into the sofa with one arm reaching around himself.

I'm getting ready to bill a zoot and I clock that Gotti must have been bunning bare cro since there's only about six zeds left of the nine that we got when we done the move on that shotter in Willesden Green. I ain't even had time to smoke that much since I've had bare essays to do for uni. My p's are starting to run low as well coz I'm always getting takeaways and buying fresh pairs of creps. I'm gonna have to shot that cro soon and since Gotti's bunned most of it, he better not try gwan like we're splitting it fifty-fifty. I bill a zoot and try not to think.

I come back from uni and Gotti tells me that Little Man just got rushed. He is sitting on the sofa, rubbing his hand over his head, bunning a zoot and looking at his phone. His acne's gotten a lot worse.

What happened? I say as I put my backpack on the floor and sit down on the sofa opposite him.

Little Man went Harlesden to shot some food and he goes into one block and the sell who belled him ain't there but suddenly bare mandem come into the block with ballys on and bandannas tied round their faces and they surround him and one of them backs out a shank and tries to poke him. One next yout ripped out one of his ear-studs.

What the canary diamond one yeah? I say.

Yeah, them ones still. So Little Man tries to like run through them to get to the door but obviously there's too many man and then one of the brers shanks him in his stomach.

Rah, was it deep?

I don't know. He told me he felt it go in and as he's put his hands to his belly, one of the youts poped his Rolly, says Gotti.

Not the one with all the rubies? I say.

218

Yeah fam, that one, says Gotti.

I love that watch, I say.

Yeah that watch was hard still. And then a next yout rips his other ear-stud out and it tears his earlobe n shit. And then, coz he's bleeding bare from his belly, them man get shook that he's gonna frass out so they cut out the block, but he never frassed out. Some woman seen him and belled an ambulance coz he couldn't stand up no more.

Is he cool though? I say.

Yeah fam, he's just vexed innit, says Gotti.

Mad ting, I say.

He was slipping though, says Gotti. Going Harlesden to hit sells when there's blatantly bare man tryna shot there as well, and them Church Road youts been beefing SK from time, he should know how it goes, especially since Brandzino got popped in the barber's. Anyway, it's not like he was rolling widda strap or anything so what could he do ah lie?

I come back from uni and Gotti isn't there.

He's left his shiny blue Bape trainers, which are practically new, his brown leather jacket and D&G jeans. He's probably gone to do a move. I bell him but his phone rings out. When I sit down to bill a zoot I'm like whatdafuck – there's like three zeds of cro left, if that. He can't have smoked it all. I pull out a bud and start billing a zoot.

Before I fall asleep I bell him again but his phone just rings out.

I come back from uni and Gotti isn't there.

His Bapes and the leather jacket and D&G jeans are still there, which means he hasn't been back since the other day. I try belling him but his phone keeps ringing out. What if he got shift? But if the feds got his phone it would be turned off. Either he left it somewhere or he's still on road. Phoning him like I'm his fucking chick or suttin, what's this brer on? No point in me tryna shot what's left of the cro since I need to bun and anyway, Capo's gonna give me a bag for that nine which me and Gotti dropped him. But I need p's and what's left of my p's from all the moves – about three bags – is still in Gotti's mum's yard in D-block. It's not like I can go there on my ones anytime I want. I bill a zoot and drift.

I come back from uni and there's still no sign of Gotti.

I say to Capo and Blix, I can't get hold of Gotti you know, I swear down suttin musta happened to myman.

Blix says I had 250 that I put away under my T-shirts in the chest of drawers in my room and now it's gone.

Capo says yeah it's bate that Gotti took it.

I'm like whatdafuck though, why would he even do that?

Capo says you know that food you gave me, I checked today when I got back from uni and a whole two-and-a-q is missing. I hadn't even unwrapped any of it yet.

Yeah he blatantly took that, says Blix. Who else could it've been? And he turns the kettle on and says you man want tea?

I bell Gotti eleven times but his phone just rings out.

I come back from uni and Gotti's phone is still ringing out when I call him. I haven't been to SK for a while coz I've been busy with uni, but I'm gonna go the day after tomorrow.

I can't find my stainless steel Aqua Master watch that I copped like three years ago and I realise I don't know where my gold signet ring is. Yinka gave me that ring for my nineteenth birthday. I don't remember when I last had it on. I swear I left it on the bathroom sink and I ask Blix and Capo have you man seen my Aqua and my ring?

Fam, myman must've took it, says Capo straight away.

Yeah, Gotti blatantly took it Snoopz, says Blix and he turns the kettle on. You man want tea?

I come back from uni and I put my bag down and because it's been bugging me the whole day, I lift up the seating sections of the sofa I sleep on. The strap isn't there. I lift up the seating of the sofa Gotti was sleeping on and there's nothing there apart from a pound coin, breadcrumbs and some dust.

I feel sick. I phone Mazey and ask if he's seen or heard from Gotti at all and Mazey says nah broski, not even. Why, wagwan?

I tell him about the last few days and Mazey can't believe it.

Why would he just ghost like that and why would he take man's tings when you man have been looking after him in East? he says.

I know brudda, that's what I'm saying. What you on tomorrow? I ask.

Nuttin brudda, says Mazey. I'll probably go and kick ball in Grange Park at some point, come check me if you're about.

Say nuttin fam, I'll see you tomorrow, I say.

My arms feel like bone and skin. Weak. Empty. I bell Gotti but his phone just rings out.

I bun six zoots back to back until I feel like the sky's underneath me. I wake up with a hot rock burning a hole in my T-shirt, burning my skin. Musta fallen asleep with the zoot still smoking and dropped it on my chest.

I'm at the astroturf football pitch in Grange Park, just off Kilburn High Road, watching Mazey play five-a-side and I'm bunning a zoot with Akin and Biggz. I'm telling them how Gotti ghosted. They listen without saying anything, let me finish the whole story and then Biggz says Gotti was smoking hard food, real talk.

Nah man, no way, I say.

Listen, my man was bunning work, no lie, says Biggz.

Biggz and Akin are two olders from South Killy, couple years older than Gotti and they've known him from when he was a younger. It was in Akin's block that I shanked up Stefano.

Akin passes me a zoot but I don't even want any right now. Everything around me looks artificial and deadout. Like the way life is just being performed by everyone right now – mandem kicking ball, people walking in the park with their kids, sound of traffic rolling in from the high road, the texture of Akin's leather Avirex jacket, Biggz's breath marked out in the air by a cloud of weed smoke – it's as if everyone's playing a part and everything around us is a prop, details in a film, none of it real. I start imagining what would happen if I fell onto my face right now without even trying to break my fall, right in the middle of the conversation. What would happen then? But in the same moment I know that there's nothing to wake up from and I think about how I can't even remember the last time I had a proper dream.

I'm telling you blood. Mandem know he's been on it for the last few months at least, says Biggz.

Biggz turns to Akin. Gotti was in the whip with us couple weeks back. Mellow and them man was hitting sells so they had the brandy and champs on them. Two twos man pull up at one shop and Gotti says you man give me five white to hit one cat I know who works in the shop. So Mellow gives him five pebbles and Gotti goes into the shop. Blood, dem man was waiting for like half an hour for Gotti to come back out. Mandem are belling off his phone but it's ringing out, so one of the mandem goes into the shop to see wagwan. Bossman says your friend came into my shop and asked me where the back door is. Blood, myman's only gone into the shop, run out the back door onto Willesden Lane and cut out with the food. Biggz is laughing, coughing. Akin draws the zoot and nods. Biggz clears his throat and spits. Truss me Snoopz, Gotti's been smoking hard food long time. You can't trust dem man like dat.

I can't believe it, I say and shake my head. Gotti smoking work? But he wasn't all fiended out, looking skinny n shit, I say.

Blood didn't you notice all them dutty spots on his face? says Biggz.

Biggz and Akin spud me – safe g, safe you man – and leave the park. I wait for Mazey to finish football. He doesn't smile when he sees me, just comes off the pitch and we clap hands, bump shoulders and then he kisses his teeth.

Gotti you know, he says.

At Bimz's yard I borrow my next bredrin Stranger's phone and call Gotti, thinking he won't recognise the number so maybe he'll pick up.

Yo, says Gotti.

Blood, it's Snoopz.

Oh wagwan brudda. I been meaning to call you but I jus been dealing widda lickle madness still.

Why? Wagwan?

I'll tell you when I see you fam, don't really wanna chat about it over the phone you get me.

Blood I need to get that three bags from your mum's yard and I need the wap.

I know I know I know. Listen, lemme bell you back coz

I'm just in the middle of suttin with Little Man. Is this your number yeah?

Nah blood you've got my number, I've been ringing you for days.

I know Snoopz, I know. Lissen, I'ma bell you back later one hundred.

Make sure blood, I say and he puts the phone down.

I bell him later that night but his phone is switched off.

I bell Gotti the next day but his phone is still switched off. I decide to phone Alice, the girl who used to go out with him back in the day and who still kinda loves him in some sort of distant and regretful way. Alice is from a proper good family: well spoken with certain words she likes to roll around in her mouth that she's picked up from Gotti, flirting with his world. Rich parents, living in a big house in the nice bit of Willesden. I remember the carpet in their yard was thick and clean like I almost wanted to lie down on it and there were photos of the family everywhere in silver frames. Gotti and I went round there one time and I could tell that whatever once existed between him and Alice hadn't fully disappeared. After we left the yard, Gotti turned to me and told me how she loved it when he used to blindfold her before they fucked. She was into Gotti coz she recognised the unique combination of his brain and his mad heart, and the darkness living inside him sucked her in.

So I phone Alice. When she picks up she sounds happy to hear from me. I go straight into it, telling her how Gotti ghosted, how he took my strap and all them tings from Capo's yard and then I say man are telling me that Gotti's been smoking work but I can't believe that, I mean he's like a brother to me.

She's quiet for a moment and then she says it's true Snoopz. She tells me how it happened before. Before he went pen for five years. They were still in a relationship when he'd started smoking work. She found out when he broke into her parents' yard one day and teefed her mum's jewellery. That's when she finally decided she was done with him. They met on the platform of Willesden Junction train station so she could look him in the eyes while she searched for answers.

He was crying when he admitted it you know, she says. Told me he'd been addicted to crack for like three months and how he couldn't help himself and didn't know what to do.

I say but Alice, it's not like he looked like he was bunning hard food. He was living with me in East and he was still kinda wedge, I mean he had a lot more muscle on him than me, he defo didn't look like a nitty.

Yeah but didn't you notice his spots? The way his face would randomly break out in mad acne? says Alice. He always got it bad when he was smoking crack.

Then she says you know what made me fall in love with Gotti? It was how rago he was. He didn't give a fuck about what anyone thought. On our first date we were walking down the road in Willesden. He said he needed to piss and then he suddenly stopped, pulled out his dick and started pissing in the middle of the street like he didn't care about anything and it made me fancy him even more.

That's how it happens. The betrayal. Not in some dramatic way, not in some complicated way, like there's no story to even tell. The end of the friendship. It's like some poet once said about the end of the world – not with a bang but with a whimper. I feel cold inside and my stomach swims and I go and get a bottle of Courvoisier and a draw. I drink the whole bottle on my ones at Capo's and bun two three zoots and frass out on the sofa.

We're playing *GTA* in Bimz's bedroom and it's my go. We're taking turns to play the gang war mission and we've been chatting about how Gotti snaked me, how he took all my shit, the three bags in his mum's yard, the burner I paid two-and-a-half bags for, and Bimz says blood I told you, them kinda man are different fam.

Mazey says yeah even from the beginning, remember Bimz that time when we was all here and Snoopz had the envelope and—

Bimz cuts in: and my man starts talking about robbing him, oh my days. He stops to draw his zoot.

Mazey says you tellim, I can't tell it as good.

I say what? What you man chatting about? I pause the game.

Mazey says let me draw dat Bimz, and Bimz passes him the zoot.

Blood watch the ting, my man wanted to rob you when he first met you you know, says Bimz and when he says this it sounds like he's got a blocked nose coz he's still holding smoke in his lungs, trying not to breathe it out.

Whatdafuck?

Bimz says remember when you was here and you had dat envelope with the three bags inside it?

A scene in his bedroom creeps into my mind.

Bimz says that was the first time you met Gotti and you was showing us the p's you got from some move you done. When you left, Gotti asked us if he could rob you and we told him blood if you try dat it's gonna be World War Three, myman is not a joke.

I say why didn't you man tell me?

Bimz says coz two twos you man linked up on your own and started eating people n getting up to madness, so I wasn't gonna preach to you. Bro, I can't say that I've seen mandem who were tight like that.

I rock back on the bed and say myman wanted to snake me from the beginning?

Mazey says don't get it twisted Snoopz, he was fully down for you when you lot was doing your ting innit, but the first time he saw you that's what he said coz he didn't know you.

Mazey draws the zoot and says it woulda been World War Three forreal, I swear Snoopz by looking at you, mandem can't really tell you're on soaking people up. But issa good ting still, man are not ready.

Bimz laughs high-pitch joker laugh and says man are not ready forreal. Then he kisses his teeth and his voice goes low, oi pass it back blood, you already hit dat, and Mazey gives him back his zoot. I put the control pad on the bed and say yo I don't even wanna play no more, Maze you can have my go, and I rub my eyes like I'm trying not to fall asleep.

It's like the first week of June when I hear from next mandem in SK that Gotti got shift and is in pen on remand, awaiting trial for robbery. I don't know if it's for one of the moves we did, but even though he snaked me, I dun know he'd never break the code and snitch on man. Little Man got shift for shotting food and he's in Feltham coz he's still young enough to be in Young Offenders. Then I hear that Tyrell went and handed himself in to feds for the moves when he was our driver. He wasn't even wanted. What a neek. Tyrell always wanted to feel like he was a badman even though he didn't have the heart for it. I guess a long prison sentence is gonna make him feel like he finally earned some stripes. Eedyat. The things certain man will do for reputation when it's beyond their actual reach – beyond their capabilities. Whatever. Either way all them man are gonna get years inside. Years.

I take Gotti's garms, the shiny Bapes and the brown leather jacket and the D&G jeans, and go to shot them at one shop in Notting Hill Gate. The brer behind the counter offers me twenty pounds for the whole lot. Twenty fucking pounds. Are you mad? I want to lean over the counter and grab the brer and shake him and say do you fucking realise who used to wear these garms? Do you realise that the person who used to rock these creps isn't just your average human? Would you be capable of doing the things he did? But instead I just look down at the garms spread out on the counter and then I say I'll give you the jeans and Bapes for fifteen. The man says done and I leave with the jacket, although I'm not ready to put it on and I don't know when I will be.

Later I see Kaution, one of the up n coming youngers from SK, in Precinct. He comes over and says wagwan and I tell him about Gotti.

He says you know that time that Gotti shanked up Stefano five times yeah?

I say what? Gotti shanked up Stefano? Gotti?

Yeah you know that brer who was tryna shot food on the strip n dat, he says.

Yeah I know who Stefano is. But wait, you're saying Gotti shanked up Stefano yeah?

Yeah, that's what Gotti told me.

I shake my head and laugh, broken glass in my mouth and I say Gotti never shanked up Stefano. It was me. Then I walk back to Bimz's without saying anything else, while Kaution stands there in the middle of the precinct.

CHICKEN AND CHIPS

*Meditation on inevitable death should be performed daily ...
every day without fail one should consider himself as dead.*
  Yamamoto Tsunetomo, *Hagakure: The Book of the Samurai*

I SWEAR DOWN I'd seen it happen to me before it even happened,
in visions, in dreams, in my imagination.

I'm feeling more and more parro, tryna drown my thoughts
in clouds of loud – bunning amnesia non-stop, morning to
night – and I only want the strongest punk I can get to lick
off my head and send me to sleep. But on a real it doesn't work,
it just makes me lose myself in a maze of thoughts while time
drifts by without me noticing and I have to snap myself back.
Mad ting.

If I'm walking on road alone and people pass me, I'll start
thinking that they're chatting about me, hearing snatches of
conversation that my mind turns into something that relates to me.

Sometimes, I swear I can hear people chatting behind me and when I turn around to see who it is, there's no one there. When people make eye contact with me on the tube or in the street, I put it on them quicktime and say dafuck are you looking at? Or say some next mandem are clocking me, I'll screwface them while I put my hand in my pocket, feel for my borer – I bought a new one couple weeks back, with a metal handle that won't break like the last one – and flick the blade out in my pocket, ready to stab man in the face. Waiting for it to pop off. But it never does.

It's as if I'm preparing for something inevitable and necessary. I'm on road on my ones a lot more now since Gotti snaked me and Rex got locked up, and I feel more alone. I catch myself hoping that suddenly Gotti will call me and it'll turn out to be some massive misunderstanding, but I know I'm lying to myself and then my heart fills with anger, red hot, melting, like the only way to remove it would be to cut my chest open and pull it out. I can't get juiced on Rémy Red no more coz it reminds me of Gotti and without him I'm back to walking the long way from Precinct to Uncle T's, avoiding D-block just in case someone tries calling me out, but even more because I've started thinking about what Bimz said when he warned me about rolling with Gotti – now that he's birded off, what if someone does what Bimz said they might: use me to take whatever revenge they wanna take for getting robbed by Gotti?

During the final term of my second year, I go to a warehouse in east London with Capo and buy a bulletproof vest. But after couple weeks of rocking it every day I stop, coz my T-shirt is always soaked in sweat and the material of the vest starts smelling kinda frowzy, which really isn't a good look, especially if I'm linking gyal.

When the second year of uni is done, I come back to my

parents' flat and I can see my father is itching to say something. One evening, before going to bed, he stops in the doorway of the kitchen while I'm sitting at the table going through my phone and says you know Gabriel, biggest worry of my is that one day someone will come here and try to kill you. Or the police will come to tell me you are dead. Or that you kill someone.

I look up and say Tata no one knows that this is my family home, no one knows. Don't worry, and he stares at me like he's concentrating on an X-ray, looking for the detail that a doctor warned him was there, and then he says goodnight and goes to bed.

I never thought my father worried about me like that. Now I realise that adults are really just grown-up children. When you're a yout, you think your parents are invincible. Like they don't ever feel fear or worry or sadness or any of that shit. Like they never tell lies or want more than they already have. But it's not actually like that. Parents are grown-up children with their own fears and sadness which they carry with them all the time, it's just that as they grew up they learned how to hide it all. In their hearts they're still the same, it's their bodies and faces that look different, and they have just a bit more under-standing of the world that surrounds them. I wonder what my parents were like as children, what combination of fears and hopes they grew up with. If I could go back in time to a moment before the world knew I would exist, before they even knew of each other's existence, I'd tell them be strong, brace yourselves, it's only just started.

Now that I've finished my second year of uni, I've got plenty of time to kill so I go to Grove to buck Dario who's back in London. I've got a tazer on me that I recently copped and I go round to this massive twenty-four-floor block in Latimer

Road where he's cotching with all these Grove olders. I pull out the tazer and one of them offers to buy it from me. I wanna get some chicken n chips coz my belly's rumbling, but I literally have no p's on me so I'm like I'll shot you the tazer for edge note. One Filipino brer gives me the fifty pounds and starts tazing himself with it right there and then in the front room, pressing the tazer to his arm and dropping it as the electricity zaps him. Then everyone else starts having a go at tazing themselves to see if they can hack it.

Me and Dario leave the block and start bopping to the chicken shop next to Ladbroke Grove station. We come onto the main road, which to Grove mandem is frontline – it's where they shot work and buj to the nittys who surface at night, like ghosts passing through from another dimension. These times I'm in my all-black AV with the leather arms and collar, I've got my diamond grillz in my mouth, I'm rocking my new Aqua Master watch that I ain't seen no one else rocking, mad exclusive, with a gold bezel and gold face set with tiny white diamonds. One brer pulls up on his bike and goes yo what watch is that g? I'm like it's a Aqua still, and he's like rah I ain't never seen one like that, it's banging still, and I'm like dun know. We carry on past the tube station and go into the chicken shop.

I go up to the counter – yo bossman lemme get the two pieces deal, I want sidebreast and make sure you put bare burger sauce on my chips and a can of Mirinda yeah – then this brer called Toxic comes into the shop, goes up to Dario and says yo Dario where's my p's you owe me eighty quid. Dario smiles sideways and says blood you'll get your money when you get your money and he pulls out a little stack of £50 notes to pay for his chicken. Toxic starts shaking his head as he looks at Dario, dreads bouncing around his shoulders from under his beanie. He knows Dario from back in the day so it's not gonna kick off, even though it's getting tense right now. Toxic says blood, how you pulling out fifties and you're telling me I'll get my money when I get my money? Don't try boy man off. Dario goes outside with him and I can see them chatting through the shop window while I wait for my food, leaning against the wall in the corner.

I look to my left and see this brer called Charged Vibes coming through the door. Light shivers across spiky yellow-gold grillz on his top row of teeth but his eyes are buried in shadow as he leads bare man into the shop with him and they're all hooded up, ten man deep, coming right at me. I know what time it is. I've been waiting for this day.

Several months back, this Charged Vibes brer saw me and Dario walking up to Westbourne Park tube station. He was on his bike when he pulled up and said wagwan to Dario and then he leaned across his handlebars and whispered suttin in Dario's ear. Dario frowned, stepped back and said nah blood it's not dat, don't get it twisted, you don't wanna try dat, trust me. Then the brer turned his bike around and cycled off. I said Dario whatdafuck did he just say?

Snoopz, you don't wanna know.

Bruv, you need to tell me what he said.

You're not gonna like it Snoopz.

What did he say?

He asked if you're a eat.

Basically, he was asking Dario if he could rob me. Dario knew I was gonna be vexed coz that's a next level of disrespect. I was pissed, locked into my thoughts, not talking, just thinking I need to go and fuck this brer up and handle it before word gets around that this brer asked if I'm a eat – which is standardly

233

a boy off – and that I didn't do anything about it. Later that day, I was in the park with couple Grove man and I mentioned what happened with Charged Vibes and one of them man said boy, when you see him it's gotta be on sight, you gotta move to him straight, no talking ting. But I never did see him.

So fast forward four months later. When I see myman come into the chicken shop followed by a bag of man, it's like it's all fallen into place, as if I've suddenly woken up, coz that brer pulled up earlier on his bike, gassing about my watch and now I'm clocking he blatantly told everyone on the strip yo there's this white yout rocking an iced-out Aqua and diamond grillz in his mouth and Charged Vibes musta remembered me and been like rah come we eat him. I know them man would blatantly think, if he's a white yout maybe he's soft innit, like he'll get shook if we put it on him. So when I see him coming into the chicken shop I know what time it is, I know there's no way to escape my fate.

The chicken shop is brightly lit with all these chicken n chip deals and pictures of burgers looking fresh and juicy, nothing like the real thing, special offers in bright colours, glowing down from above the counter, warm smell of chip fat, and then this fucking storm comes in from outside, thunder in the distance, everyone hooded up as they make their way straight towards me without one look at the chicken deals.

They surround me in the corner so I can't go nowhere. I stay leaning back like I'm relaxed, but in my head I'm waiting to see who makes the first move. Charged Vibes steps up to me and goes that's a banging watch blood, just staring at my wrist. As he says it, one of the youngers in the group goes eat him, eat him, not looking at me but standing right in front of me as he says it. So I'm like eat who blood? Who da fuck are you

234

gonna eat? The yout goes quiet and shuffles back into the crowd that's surrounding me. Again Charged Vibes says that's a banging watch blood and he grabs the watch on my wrist, holding it around the bezel like he wants to look at the face. I rip my hand away and go don't fucking touch my watch blood and straight away he's like what, you don't wanna do this friendly nah? And I'm like friendly what blood? Whatdafuck is friendly about you grabbing my watch like you wanna lick it? I kiss my teeth and he moves bare close to me, the brim of his cap touching my forehead and goes where you from blood?

I know what's gonna happen. I know I'm gonna get rushed. That in a few moments I'll be fighting for my life and my name, and all we're doing right now is delaying the inevitable. Imagine. A real moment where you see into the future and know there's no way of changing it. So I'm like fuck it innit – Grove has beef with South Killy, they don't like SK one bit, so I say I'm from South Kilburn blood, knowing it'll just make the situation worse. The brers surrounding me start going rah, SK yeah? and then Charged Vibes goes where does your mum live? Soon as he says that, in my head I'm like nah, you mentioned my mum, you're getting banged, I'm Snoopz, I do moves and madness that these man ain't got the heart for, manabadman to these lot, fuck dat and BANG, I punch him in his face as hard as I can. He goes flying backwards. The crowd surrounding me draws back. Freezes. Charged Vibes staggers towards the door of the chicken shop like he's tryna stay on his feet. I grab the back of his hood, pull him towards me and start banging him in his head whack whack whack. Then I feel bare hands grab the collar of my jacket, dragging me to the ground. I lose my footing and then I'm lying on the dirty tiled floor of the chicken shop and mandem are running up and doing penalty kicks into my back, booting me in my head and everything. Showers of sparks. Instinctively I tuck into a ball to protect myself and at the same moment I'm like nah, that's how people get knocked out, tucking into a ball while everyone kicks the shit out of you until someone's kick puts you to sleep. Fuck dat. I jump up tryna throw punches and for a second they fall back like waves pulling away from the shore. But then someone runs up and sucker punches me in the side of the head, so I start looking for a way to get my back against the wall, at least that way no one can hit me from behind. Seconds drip into slow motion, each one becoming a separate and important moment. The only thing that exists in the galaxy right now is this chicken shop. Dario runs into the shop, grabs one yout and dashes him away, shouting 'low it you man, 'low it, getting in the way of kicks and punches and I clock how they don't wanna hit him coz most of them know him, so they're tryna get round him to get to me. I'm in the corner, down on one knee, with the wall behind me, making myself a smaller target so no one can kick my legs out from underneath me and I put my fists up to defend myself. Trainers squeak on the floor, mad noise all around, although I can't tell what they're shouting, bangs and kicks hitting my arms as I block and dodge, it's like I'm drowning, like I can't pull myself out of this and then one of the youngers comes from the side and digs his finger into my right eye. I pull this yout's finger out of my eye coz he's jammed it right in, my right eyeball getting pushed back deep into my eye socket and when I pull it out I feel my eye move back into place and it feels wet and everything's gone black. I try to snap his finger, but he wriggles out of my grip and backs away.

And then in the next moment it's like everything just dries up around me. I get off my knee and stand up and they start

236

ducking out the shop and I swear down these man are some pussies coz as they're walking to the door they're going ah he's fucked he's fucked. I'm not fucked I shout, a whole bag of you pussyoles and you can't even knock man out? Still they cut out and I look at the floor of the chicken shop and clock a big streak of blood across the dirty yellow tiles and I'm like fuck, they got me. I start checking myself for stab wounds, touching my back and side where I felt a lot of impact coz I know that getting poked can feel like a very hard punch. I check my arse cheeks coz them man like to shank you in your arse coz they know it won't kill you but it'll cause mad pain innit. But I'm not bleeding anywhere, so it must be my face. There's a little mirror on the wall so I walk over to check my reflection and see that there's not one mark below my forehead line, not even a tiny bruise or a scratch on my face. But just above my forehead there's a fucking shoe print in purple, there's the imprint of a ring, purple constellations of bruising going into my hairline. But no cuts. The blood on the shop floor is from Charged Vibes – when he tried to pop my watch and I banged him in the face – that's all the blood from his mouth.

Just then, he comes back into the shop going why did you bang me blood, why did you bang me? His mouth is bloody, I musta split his lip on that spiky golden grill he's rocking, and I'm like why did I bang you? Are you fucking mad? Why did you try rob me you dickhead? He backs out of the shop going watch blood, watch what happens, and then some next brer comes into the chicken shop, picks up the Wet Surface sign that's by the door – you know them plastic yellow signs that they set up when the floor's slippery – and dashes it at me. But the sign doesn't even come close to me. All them Grove man are crowding into the doorway now, going come outside pussy, watch what happens to you, so I pick up the sign and start walking towards the shop entrance, even though I don't wanna fight them in the street coz they'll be able to get me from behind. Dario says don't go outside Snoopz, but I move towards them like I'm ready to do suttin and they all back out of the shop.

An ambulance shows up. Paramedics walk into the chicken shop and say are you all right, do you want to go hospital? I'm like nah. They're like what happened to you? I'm like I fell over innit, I'm cool, I'm cool. They're like but you've clearly been assaulted, you could have concussion. I'm like nah I don't have concussion, I literally just slipped on the floor and banged my head on the counter, it's nuttin, and they're like so you're not willing to receive medical attention? I go medical attention for what man? Fuck off. They leave the shop, get back in the ambulance and drive off. Literally twenty seconds after that, feds show up. Three officers come into the shop, going we heard someone got assaulted by a gang, are you the person who just got assaulted? I say I don't know what you're chatting about, I'm just tryna buy some chicken n chips. They say, why's your head all bruised up then? I say coz I fell over innit, and they're like why's there blood on the floor then? I'm like I don't fucking know, it's got nuttin to do with me. And they're like so you're not willing to press charges? And I'm like go suck out about press charges. They give up on me and try talking to some of the other people in the chicken shop but no one says anything so they leave.

I check my wrist and see that my watch is gone and as I run my tongue across my front teeth I realise that my grillz must have fallen out of my mouth at some point during the fight and someone's taken them as well so now I'm really pissed.

238

That's the one thing that upsets me the most, losing my grillz. I lean across the counter and say lemme get a next chicken n chips bossman – coz the first one I'd ordered is scattered all over the floor. They make me a fresh portion and give it to me on the house. That kind of shit happens in chicken shops all the time, for them it's just a case of mop the blood off the floor and go back to serving customers.

I leave the shop with Dario and the strip is empty, everyone's ghosted. We walk back to the block in Latimer Road and all I can think about is how I need to get my revenge, no matter what. My desire for it is the darkest part of the night.

Later, we're cotching on the stairs inside the block and I'm bunning a zoot with Dario, zoning out with anger gripping my insides. Dario goes brudda you held it down like a g, you were banging man like crazy, truss me you held it down. I go I swear there was like ten man rushing me and Dario goes there was at least twelve man rushing you, at least twelve. Dario says Snoopz all I know is I was arguing with Toxic outside the chicken shop and suddenly I see Charged Vibes come flying out the door with his mouth buss, spitting blood onto the pavement, legs all wobbly n shit and when I looked in the shop I see all them man rushing you innit, and I say I shouldn't have shot my tazer to that Filipino brer, I shouldn't have shot it but I was hungry and I wanted to get some chicken n chips.

All I can think of is revenge. It's a knot in my chest that keeps getting tighter and tighter, pulled by my thoughts. Gotti woulda been on riding out with me if he hadn't snaked me. Fucking pagan. Nah man that shit hurts my heart forreal. I bell my boy Flipz like yo brudda I just got rushed by a whole bag of man in Grove and he's like rah bruv I'm on this ting, lemme know when you're ready, but he's not around that night and he doesn't have transport. I phone couple next heads but I can't get hold of anyone. Stitch is on holiday in Dominica with his family for the rest of the summer, so I can't even get through to him. Rex, who woulda come down on his ones with the strap on his bike and licked down at least one of them for me, is in prison. Seb is in prison. Couple next man who I know would ride out are in pen as well. I go back to South Killy.

Everyone at Bimz's is feeling it for me like they've got my back n shit, giving me buds to bill, asking me if I want suttin from shop, but none of them say come we go down to Grove right now. I don't want fuck all from the shop. I want mandem to ride out with me on these pussyoles who rushed me. I go and jam in Mazey's room for the rest of the evening because I don't wanna see none of them man's faces, like fuck the buds of cro n shit, although I take them coz it'll help me sleep tonight. I know Mazey will be on it if I sort out a whip and a burner, so once I spark my zoot I start making phone calls to try and get a strap. How I wish I had the Star 9 right now. I'm gonna duppy that Charged Vibes brer, no question in my mind, I'm gonna bun his skin and get away with it, exactly how Not Nice showed me to.

I call Yinka. She picks up my call and straight away I tell her what happened. I can tell she still cares, but her voice has this distance in it, threatening to drift out of reach. She starts asking me questions like she wants to know all the details so I start telling her, but then I stop and say Boo come we go hotel tonight and she says Gabriel – doesn't even call me Boo or anything and the way she says my name makes it sound all hard and unnatural like I don't even like the sound of it in her mouth – we're not even together any more, I'm not going hotel with you. I say whatdafuck, I just got rushed, how can you be so

240

coldhearted? She says I'm not being coldhearted, I'm protecting myself. Silence like a scarf getting carried away on the wind. And then, you can come and see me next week Thursday after I finish work if you want to talk. I put the phone down.

My head starts pounding and I notice I've nearly done my zoot so I start billing a next one but my hands are shaking and I spill the crushed-up cro onto the floor of Mazey's room and I shout fuckssake and Mazey comes in and says wagwan Snoopy and I say brudda I'm so fucking vexed and he says make yourself at home broski, my room is your room and I say love for dat fam. I look down at my chest and I swear I can see my top just over my heart actually jumping a tiny bit, real talk, jumping as my heart pumps boom boom boom and I swear it's not supposed to be beating this fast and I feel like suttin's crawling inside my belly and I wanna get it out.

I wake up mad early on the sofa in Mazey's room and watch the sun rising through the window, peeling away the skin of the previous day. My shoulders hurt and I can't get back to sleep. When I sit up, I pick my AV off the floor and clock that there's bare scuff marks and scratches on the leather sleeves and collar. It's like it went from being fresh to being used in one night. I need to duppy that brer. I need to— yo Maze I'm cutting I say and Mazey mumbles safe Snoopz from his bed on the other side of the room and turns over.

I go to my parents' yard because I need to get some fresh garms. When I get there, Tata has already gone to work, but my mother is in the bathroom, folding clothes into a pile on a wicker chair. I walk into the bathroom and say hello Mama. I don't hug her or anything. I haven't for so long that it just feels unnatural, difficult, easier to maintain the distance between us than to try and cross it. She looks at my forehead. What

241

happened to you? she says. I got rushed by ten people in a chicken shop in Ladbroke Grove I say. She carries on looking at my forehead without saying anything, holding a black T-shirt in her right hand. Her fingers are stained red from dyeing her hair. Then she starts folding the T-shirt in half and says why didn't you run away? I'm about to say something about how you can't run away when someone's tryna put it on you, but instead I tell her the other truth, which is that I was surrounded with no way out and there was too many of them. She finishes folding the T-shirt and adds it to the pile of clothes before picking up another top. I wait for her to say something else – I want her to say something else – but she doesn't, so I say I'm gonna grab some things from my room and she just continues to fold clothes without looking at me. I look in the bathroom mirror and watch my mother's reflection. She looks hunched and small and then I feel the world outside disappearing so I quickly go to my room to get some clothes and what's left of my p's. When I'm ready to leave, I stand in the hallway, washed in shadow coz the lightbulb in the corridor has gone and there are no windows to allow daylight in. I say I'm going now Mama and she says okay bye in a flat voice without coming out of the bathroom and I can hear the snapping creak of wicker as she adds another item of clothing to the pile. I head back to SK.

For days I sit in Bimz's yard, smoking cro with the mandem while my bruises start to fade, checking my phone obsessively in the hope somebody might have hollered at me about the strap so I can go and do the madness. But I don't get any texts or missed calls. I just sit on the sofa in Mazey's room, getting faded, eating chicken patties and Skittles, crushed beneath my thoughts.

Couple days later, some of the brers who rushed me start

ringing off Dario's phone, going yo tell your bredrin sorry, we didn't mean to touch him, because they got shook of repercussions, thinking that I might bring down a whole bag of SK mandem to light up the strip, and this brer Diddy who was one of the main brers who rushed me, kept belling Dario, going tell your bredrin I'm sorry innit, I didn't mean for dat to happen, I didn't know – like he was shook forreal. And the funny thing is two twos, Dario tells me how he's gone to some white brer's yard in Grove to get some dro and as he walks into the yard he sees Charged Vibes there and practically straight away Charged Vibes goes yo tell your bredrin it's done, the beef's squashed, it's over. And the white brer who's chopping up a zed of light to shot to Charged Vibes, goes haaa you got fucked up by that Snoopz brer, I heard myman rocked your jaw, and Charged Vibes just keeps saying to Dario, tell your bredrin it's squashed, tell your bredrin it's squashed. When Dario tells me this I laugh. Of course he's gonna say it's squashed. If I was swinging it out with all them man on my ones, what's it gonna be like when I catch him slipping on his ones? Dario says truss me Snoopz, they don't want this smoke. I say it's squashed when I say it's squashed and he says dun know my brudda.

July. Summer sun strips the sky naked blue and makes the concrete hum. The bruising on my forehead is gone and while all them man wanna go park and draw gyal, I just wanna stay indoors. Man are already talking about going carnival but that's not even suttin I've thought about. It's almost been a month since I got rushed and I can tell I've become someone different since then. The idea of beef with one or two man seems like nuttin to me now. You'd need a whole gang to kill me.

Jamming on the staircase of Bimz's block watching the day

roll by, smell of punk and cocoa-butter sweat mixing with voices all around me, fresh polo shirts, sunlight running up and down mandem's chains, sunglasses covering eyes. Two chicks walk past in vests and little dresses too small for the curves and yo draw dat ting, oh my days that ting's got backoff. Excuse me, hello, says Bimz all sweetboy, gassed up coz he's got his hair done in fresh canerow, can I talk to you for a sec? Mandem laugh when he jogs back without the digits, kisses his teeth and says she's got a man and Mazey says I swear that's Reese's cousin and Spooks says yeah I hit dat last summer still. What about the bredrin someone asks. Nah the bredrin was fully clapped says Bimz, didn't even have a backoff and you know man can't be dealing with a lack of backoff, and he sits down to spark his zoot, cartoon laugh. Mini bottles of Cherry B and Alizé on the dirty concrete steps. Mazey plays a beat off his phone and I start spitting:

> *Me and my co-d blacked-out ninjas,*
> *Made a living kicking doors off hinges,*
> *Inspired me to spit poems about it,*
> *Flowing like heroin out of syringes.*

and man are like yo you're killin that beat. Sly says man like Snoopz. Later I drink a whole bottle of yak, get mad waved, feeling like I can fight the whole ends. I don't even remember frassing out but I wake up on Mazey's sofa with a bad back and my head pounding, blood all metal in my temples, thinking I need to get a proper good night's sleep.

Considering all the shit that I've done to people, I got away pretty lightly; the fact I didn't get shanked, I was really surprised about that. I mean this was a long time coming, it was practically inevitable. Because that's the reality; once you start doing all this fuckery on road, it's not like bad karma will come back to you because of suttin specific, like if you go and shank some yout his brother or his mandem will come and even the score on you – I mean that can happen as well – but what I'm saying is that if you go around shanking up people and eating people and all of that, you create a negative energy that surrounds you and it attracts madness to you. It's happened to everyone I know who lives in this way. Like if you're rolling with a strap on this gunman ting for example, the next time you have an argument with a stranger they'll pull a gun out on you, someone's suddenly gonna try shoot you, someone's gonna try come for you, and it's all coz you've created this power that's stronger than anything, a magnet that pulls all this darkness that reflects your own lifestyle towards you. So at the end of the day I feel like I got away. I got away without anything too serious happening to me. But true what bunned me the most was losing my iced-out grillz.

I can't sleep another night on Mazey's sofa. I need to let my body stretch out instead of sleeping all itched up, so I decide to go to my parents' yard again. I'm sure my mum will let me stay a few nights as long as I talk about how I'm looking forward to going back to uni in September. I make sure I've got my shank on me coz I know that as soon as I start going past Westbourne Park station, I'm gonna be thinking about that first time I encountered Charged Vibes and the thirst for revenge will come rushing through my blood and my stomach's gonna do that clenching ting it's been doing recently when I think about it and I'll be on the lookout for any of them man who rushed me. If I see them it's gotta be On Sight, no talking, no thinking, just straight wickedness. I take couple zoots pre-rolled for bedtime so I don't have to trouble myself tryna bill it on the d-low while I'm at my parents'. Since the bruises have gone I won't have to answer any more awkward questions. Still, I get home after midnight when they're both in bed.

I stay the night in Westbourne, in my old bed, fresh sheets that smell of another time, space to stretch my legs out properly. But I decide to leave the next day, coz in the morning my mother tells me how last night she heard me shouting like mad, saying all sorts of things, swearing. You were saying things I can't even repeat, she says, it sounded like you were fighting someone. And she tells me that when she came running into my room to see what was going on, she found me fast asleep in bed, shouting my head off. And she couldn't even wake me up.

RED GIANT

WHEN YOU KILL a wasp it releases a pheromone, which sends a message to other wasps that one of them has been killed. It's a signal that calls other wasps to come and attack. This is what the screw tells us before he locks us in for the day and that if we kill any wasps in our cell, we should try and throw them out of the window or flush them down the toilet. Otherwise more will come and try to sting you, he says and slams the door.

It is August and I am spending the summer holidays before my final year of uni locked up. Summer is just a glimpse of sunburnt sky through the barred window of my cell. The only real part of summer that we get in here are the wasps and the heat.

In July I finally went to trial for that fight I had on the tube more than a year and a half ago. I met my barrister on the first day at Southwark Crown Court. He was like something from a typical English courtroom drama: middle-aged, posh, pink, a bit fat, sweating under his wig. He asked why I hadn't just pleaded guilty, said the evidence against me was pretty overwhelming and that a jury won't be sympathetic once the prosecution brings up my previous. I was lucky not to have done proper time already he said. We were standing in the corridor outside the courtroom and he said it's a shame they can't just give you ten lashes.

I laughed.

I mean you've seen what it's like, you've been to Feltham, it didn't kill you. You're clearly an intelligent chap, but you might just have to do your porridge. Read some literature, he added.

Crime and Punishment, I said.

Yes, very appropriate, he said and chuckled.

Or *The Trial*, I said – we'd recently read it in one of my modules.

Yes, Kafka. Or perhaps something more penitential, like *The Pilgrim's Progress*.

Or *A Rake's Progress*, I said and he laughed again.

I didn't really know what *A Rake's Progress* was about, but I knew it was some oldschool story which had something to do with a brer who lives the highlife and ends up losing everything and going to prison.

My mother and father were on holiday in Italy so they didn't even know I was on trial. But I did let Yinka know what was happening. You see, feelings are a spiderweb that your heart flies into and gets trapped in. Then something big comes along and starts eating you slowly from the inside out. After a few months and a few texts later, we started linking again. The first time I saw her after all them months apart, we went for a walk in these woods near Hounslow. I gave her a rose and later doggied her out against a tree.

Every day I came to court dressed up smart. See this is how it works, lemme tell you—

You have to make it look like you don't belong in the dock, like suttin must have gone wrong to land you in this place. A suit and tie is the first step. I know bare man who come court in a suit and tie but they'll add things like a fitted cap or sunglasses or they'll pull a gold chain out and have it hanging over their shirt collar. I've even seen mandem rocking iced-out bracelets and Rolexes and silk Versace shirts, when the case is for trapping and they're planning to argue that they don't live that lifestyle at all, don't even have enough p's to pay child support, even claiming they're on benefits. Some of these man have no sense. Think it's a movie or suttin. You have to make sure you never drop slang when you're answering questions in the dock, have to watch how you pronounce words, have to talk like— you know what I'm saying. Don't come like some bad breed, don't come like you're dangerous innit, coz at the end of the day people will see what they wanna see. So I let my hair grow out and I wore a smart blue shirt and black trousers. Not gonna lie though, I was rocking my favourite black and white Air Maxes coz I figured no one's gonna see my creps while I'm standing in the dock.

I go into court with my barrister at about 11 a.m. There's all sorts of discussions going on between him and the prosecution, moving about in their wigs and black gowns while my solicitor stands to the side without saying shit. I swear, getting a good duty solicitor is a myth. Take my first solicitor on this ABH case. She never even bothered to read the case file. When she asked me if there was anything I wanted to discuss I was like didn't you notice the bullshit witness statement where a man described me as light-skinned of West Indian origin with dark Afro hair? For a start I was wearing my doggy-ear cap the whole time so how da fuck could he see my hair? But even

249

more ridiculous was the description of me being light-skinned of West Indian origin. These d-low racists. Soon as they see aggression and hear some road talk they assume it must be a black yout. I've been getting this kind of shit from white people for as long as I've been on the roads; I must be mixed race, I must be half black, feds saying are you half Jamaican? Mocking the way that I chat whenever I get arrested. All just a reflection of their instinctive prejudice towards anything in which they don't recognise themselves, their way of doing, being, thinking. Anyway. How da fuck can my solicitor have all these witness statements for months and she never noticed that bullshit? Pure fuckery. Not long after that meeting I changed solicitors.

So anyway, the judge comes in, everyone stands up and then it turns out that the victim isn't even there to give evidence. The judge says it's ridiculous, this case has dragged on for more than a year and a half without getting anywhere, in the interest of the court's time I won't adjourn the matter any further. Does the Crown Prosecution Service offer any further evidence? The prosecution lawyer says no further evidence and the judge says I direct a formal not guilty verdict to be entered, will the defendant rise. I'm like rah that was quick. Two women in suits with bitter lemon-rind faces stand up and say we're from the Probation Service. Mr Krauze has continuously breached his community order, hasn't attended probation meetings and has failed to do community service. The judge says these are very serious allegations and then he adjourns the court session for lunch.

I could never be fucked with community service. Hours of pointless work with other doughnuts, coz let's face it, if you get caught or you fuck up and get sentenced to community service, you're a bit of a doughnut. I won't go as far as calling myself a wasteman but let's be real; serious criminals get locked up coz they're seen as a danger to society, a threat to the rule of law. Community service is a slap. You're a nuisance, a mosquito. You won't toe the line like everyone else so here is 180 hours of unpaid work that you have to do. That's what I get for never getting caught for any of the serious shit I've been doing. Just minor stupidness like carrying a shank or possession of cannabis or resisting arrest.

There was this one work placement I did with an ex-policeman as our supivisor that was good. He'd let us bun zoots in the morning while he read a newspaper and then he'd take us cinema coz he had a link there who'd let us in for free. The film would finish by lunchtime and then he'd let us go home and mark us down as having done the full seven hours of work. We never had to paint no railings or any of that bullshit.

So I go back into the courtroom after lunch, the probation officers start listing all the breaches and the judge says it is clear that you have committed a serious breach of your probation, especially taking into account that you had a six-month suspended sentence, but it's too late in the day to sentence you, so I'm remanding you in custody to be brought back to court tomorrow.

Two twos I'm in the sweatbox, heading to HMP Wandsworth. The tinted windows turn the summer evening into a burning red gloom, as if the sun has turned into a red giant, which I remember from this picture book I used to read as a child. It's what happens when a star is dying and it expands and engulfs other planets close to it.

HMP Wandsworth – Wanno – is an old Victorian prison, dark, brooding, solid; something cruel and sad about the bricks and blank windows. I get booked in at the reception desk.

They take a photo of me that gets printed onto a label and stuck on a green piece of card; my ID and what I really mean to them now, which is number XF9367. So now XF9367 gets strip-searched behind a little curtain with one big screw wearing purple rubber gloves watching me the whole time. I get naked in front of him and he orders me to turn round, lift my balls, squat and cough, coz if you've got anything plugged a cough will usually make it fall out or part of it will drop down. At least I get to keep my own garms since I'm on remand. One of the screws gives me a bedroll and I get taken with all the other new arrivals to E Wing, which is the first night wing.

All I've had to eat in the last twelve hours is a sandwich. My stomach feels like it's stuck to my back. We are told to go into the servery and get some food. Mashed potato. Corned beef. Cup of water. Everyone sits down at a table in the middle of the wing – chairs all moulded metal attached to the table so no one can fling them about – and we start eating. One nitty with wet eyes and wax skin dripping off a skull face sits opposite me, shoving mashed potato with grimy fingers into his mouth. Couple seats down there's three black akhis – on this Muslim gang ting – rocking grey prison tracksuits, one of them with a massive pink gash down the side of his face, raw, fresh from being gunbucked by armed police. One of his eyes is red with blood. The three of them are starting eight-year sentences for kidnapping. There is a deaf guy who shrinks away from everything, even the few people tryna help him understand wagwan.

Once we finish eating, we get banged up in pairs in one-man cells that have bunk beds in them due to overcrowding. My celly is one white yout from Essex. We spend the evening watching TV and smoking burn. He tells me about his chick

252

who's got two youts for him and how he can't wait to see them. He also has a daughter by his previous chick and he's got her name tattooed on his back and the new girlfriend's name tattooed on his neck.

Night pushes against the window, filling the gaps between the bars. It hits me that I could get the full six months suspended sentence dropped on me tomorrow so I sit down with some prison paper and a pencil, and write a letter to the judge using my most eloquent English, explaining how I'm studying at uni and a custodial sentence will ruin my future chances, I regret all my actions, I'm truly and sincerely sorry, all that shit.

The next day I'm back in court. Before I know it, the judge is about to sentence me. My solicitor hasn't said shit, hasn't even mentioned that I'm starting my third year of uni in less than two months. I ask him to give the judge my letter. The judge reads it and says you are clearly a very articulate young man, but you did not *neglect* to fulfil the terms of your probation, you *wilfully* failed to do so. Then he sentences me to three months. Calm. I'll only have to do a month and a half, I'll be out in time for the third year of uni – the letter worked – and then the judge says take him down. I get handcuffed to a court guard and he takes me downstairs to put me in the sweatbox.

Wandsworth is way over capacity so I spend the first night of my sentence in Catford police station, nothing to do except go to sleep. In the morning I get told I'm going to HMP Bullingdon in Oxfordshire.

Not gonna lie, the journey there is like some prolonged way of dying inside. We get put in the Serco van after chips and beans for breakfast, then driven to Mile End to pick up some people from Bow Magistrates' who just got sentenced. We sit inside our cubicles for an hour, sweating, stiff, waiting for the van to leave. I read all the names scratched into my window. We've been locked in for at least three hours. Then another few hours in London traffic, nothing to eat the whole time, just little tins of water pushed under the door to each cubicle. No space to stretch my legs, the new Dizzee Rascal track, Dance Wiv Me, banging out on the radio non-stop – what a piss-take. Through the tinted windows, the world carries on. Then countryside.

By the time the van gets to HMP Bullingdon, we've been in the sweatbox for like six hours. It is early evening and I swear it's against human rights or some shit but I ain't got time to pity myself. There's nothing I can do to change the situation, I can't go back in time, I can't suddenly decide that it's too much for me, that I wanna go home, that I'm not cut out for this or any of that moist talk. So rather than getting all nervous – like oh my days man's going pen, what am I gonna do, what's gonna happen, what if this and that happens, what if someone tries to rape me in the shower or someone tries to cut my face while I'm getting dinner – rather than all that, just accept the reality. If you can understand that, you can survive anything. Even life.

When I step out of the van I'm so relieved to be out of that box, to stretch my arms and legs and stand upright, that I'm actually glad I've arrived. Bullingdon is a big modern prison in the middle of the Oxfordshire countryside. Sandy concrete with brown corrugated roofs, high walls, barbed wire everywhere. Straight into induction. Clothes taken away apart from boxers and socks. Property bagged up. Strip-search. Naked. Shiver. Squat. Cough. Blue T-shirt and grey tracksuit. Bedroll. Smoker's pack. Breakfast pack with two teabags because tea is a human right in England. Get put into a general holding cell with next mandem sitting on benches.

254

Walking in I'm greeted by one older prisoner who's doing the induction for new arrivals; hench brudda with gold teeth all through his top row, puts out his hand and as we shake we both say I'm Gabriel—

Nah don't lie, he says.

Swear down, I say.

My name's Gabriel, he says.

So is mine, I say and show him my prison ID from Wandsworth.

Jesus fucking Christ. Come sit over here he says, grinning gold as we sit down on one of the benches and start talking. He's doing life for murder. I'm not into superstitions and alladat, but I swear down this must mean suttin. It's a sign, know what I mean? Like how many mandem do you know called Gabriel? I bet you don't even know one, let alone two man banged up in the same pen to rahtid.

In the holding cell. Birmingham brer well over six foot comes in rocking a yellow tracksuit, transferred from another prison. Eyes moving about like they don't trust his own face. Says he's from the Burger Bar Boys, them man that are always doing mad shootings in Brum. Says he's looking for his bredrin who's in here for popping his own sister. Says the brer's sister try snitch on her brother for a shooting and man don't tolerate snitching. Next young brudda opposite me rocking Muslim prayer beads, talking like I swear he's from South London. Calls everyone cuz. I ask him and he says his name's Hollywood. Says he's from Lewisham. I say I'm Snoopz. I'm from Kilburn. We smoke a burn while we wait.

Couple next man come into the holding cell. Some Muslim akhis who know Hollywood. One of them is a white brer who sits down next to us. Hollywood says what you in for akh? The white brer says he robbed one Asian woman in Slough for her

255

kettle and while he was tryna rip off the watch, the woman started reciting the shahada, which is the prayer Muslims recite before they die. I swear down akh, I thought she was Sikh, it was too late to stop, if I'd realised she was a sister I'd never have done it, and Hollywood laughs and says nah that's fuckery akh.

Some next older brer comes in to sweep the holding cell. He has grim reapers tattooed on both arms. Lift your legs up boys, he says as he sweeps under the benches. Fuckinell, I sound like my mum. I'd make a great mother I would, he says and walks out with the broom over his shoulder.

My name gets called – XF9367 Krauze – and I pick up my bedroll and smoker's pack and the Burger Bar brer gets called and we follow two screws out. We get taken onto B Wing. It's near 9 p.m. and the wing is disintegrating in darkness. It is lined with blue steel cell doors all the way down on either side and there are white metal staircases leading up to two more levels of the same thing. Between the balconies on each level, I see wire netting, there in case someone gets dashed over the railings or someone tries to throw themselves off one of the levels. Shit. I'm actually in big man prison now, it's gonna be a whole next experience. Whatever. Man will ride it out either way.

BEHIND THE DOOR

JUST TRYING TO write about prison feels dead, like I'm giving it something it doesn't deserve. You don't realise how much life there is in a blade of grass, in a shop, in a pavement, in the smell of fumes and dirty streets, until you're in pen where it's all just these lifeless surfaces that aren't even worth describing and so many lives on pause, removed from the outside world.

I get taken to the top balcony, known as the threes and the screw unlocks a door and says in here. The door to cell B333 slams behind me.

The room is just a TV screen flickering blue in darkness. It's a proper two-man cell with one bed on the left and another on the right. From the right a voice says turn on the light mate. And that's how I meet Brutus. White brer, shaved head, scar like a crescent moon under his eye, bulldog shoulders. Brutus is facing eight years IPP for armed robbery. He is thirty-two, he's been in bin several times before and he's got bare family on the wing. He tells me stories about ordering three-course meals in expensive restaurants with bottle after bottle of Cristal, then dussing without paying the bill and pulling out a machete on waiters who tried chasing after him. I tell him stories about doing moves in London and I do shit celebrity impressions that crack him up until he's laughing his head off. After a couple days we're getting on like old friends. He sees one of my drawings and says Snoopz do one for me and above it write Brutus, Armed and Dangerous.

Press-ups on the concrete cell floor. I show Brutus a trick with the whitener that they give us for our tea. Open the packet, start shaking it out over the sink, spark the lighter and as the whitener hits the flame it goes whoosh into a little fire-ball and he says fuckinell that's what they're giving us to put in our tea yeah? Wasps fly into the cell. We chase them around and kill them but more come later. The breakfast pack is a tiny portion of prison cornflakes with long-life milk that you can't even keep cool because it's summer and there's a little packet of jam to mix in but that's about it. Lunch comes at 11.30 and it is truly deadout. One time it's just a bowl of soup and two slices of bread. Dinner is at 4.30 p.m.; rice and chicken or some kinda stew, and an apple if you're lucky enough not to be at the end of the queue, by which time they've run out of fruit. Soon as I can, I start trading my burn with next mandem on the wing for crisps and Mars bars and cans of tuna.

I'm on twenty-three-hour bang-up so I only get fifteen minutes in the exercise yard in the morning, walking around with Brutus, then forty-five minutes out of my cell for association in the afternoon when I can have a shower. When I go back into my cell and the screw locks the door behind me there are wasps in the cell again so I kill them.

I'm bare tight with one next white brer on the wing called Solo. He's only twenty-one, the youngest on the wing, sent from a YOI because he shanked his cellmate in the neck with a chicken bone. The screws were doing the whole gladiator ting with the mandem there. One day they put Solo into a cell with some brer who had beef with him. Fam I woke up in the night with the brer on top of me, strangling me with the cord from the kettle, says Solo. Lucky I'd been sharpening this chicken bone from several days before. I cheeksed it when I got moved into the cell with him and put it under my pillow before going to sleep. As he was choking me, I pulled out the chicken bone and shanked him eight times in his face and neck. Fam there was blood all over me, all over the bed, all over the ceiling and walls and they charged me with attempted murder. The brer almost died, but I pressed the buzzer and the screws came and took him to hospital coz I didn't wanna catch a M for that shit. If it hadn't been for that chicken bone I'd be finished, says Solo as we jam on the landing outside our cells during association. Solo isn't allowed to share a cell with anyone.

Solo tells me the Birmingham brer's been asking him if he's got p's on his account for canteen where you can buy extra food and other things once a week. Fam, fuck this brer, I say. He's a big guy, we might just have to rush him in the showers and poke him up or suttin, blatantly tryna come like he can bully man, and Solo says I'm down fam, whenever you're ready.

The next day, Solo comes out of his cell in the morning and pulls his top up to show me he's padded himself all over with newspapers tightly rolled up and packed around him. He says this will at least stop a shank from going deep in man, fuck that Burger Bar yout, if he tries talking shit to man I'm telling him to suck his mum.

Solo's cousin, an Irish traveller, comes on the wing. He's on remand for a double murder and he keeps telling everyone how he'll be out soon. We all know he won't be. He gets put in a cell with the Birmingham brer. The next day, the Birmingham brer doesn't come out of his cell and Solo says to me that problem's sorted still, man ain't gotta do nuttin. He spuds me. He has his dead brother's name tattooed on his hand, killed in a motorbike accident. Fast life.

There's one screw on the wing called S.O. Squirrel. Massive ex-army man who no one likes. One time this brer called Caple is walking back to his cell after making a phone call at the end of association and he's laughing. Squirrel tells him to stop laughing. Caple says shutdafuckup. Squirrel follows him into his cell, grabs Caple by the face and gives him one vicious headbutt. Knocks him out cold. Later, we hear Caple screaming but no one can see what's going on. The next day his celly tells us that when Caple woke up, three screws including Squirrel rushed into the cell and grabbed Caple. Caple's celly says all the screws know Caple's got an abscess in one of his teeth, he's been tryna get an appointment with the prison dentist for months. Two screws held Caple's arms, while Squirrel wrenched Caple's jaw open and shoved his hand into Caple's mouth, grabbing the abscess and pulling him out of the cell like that. It only stopped coz he went unconscious from the pain and the cunts had to carry him out, says his celly as we stand on the landing during association. Caple's been sent down block for two weeks and he ain't even seen the dentist yet. Fuckery.

And on and on. Behind the door. Days without breath. Nights without silence. Dreams without sleep. Scars on faces and heads and knuckles. Knot in the chest that slides into the belly all tight, tension and tension and waiting and waiting, but for what? Who even knows. You wanna phone people and say I'm locked up in pen as if you're tryna remind them you exist. Locked away from the sky. Locked away from the air. Looking through the window just to catch a glimpse of the world, but there's only more walls, barred windows and cameras. The world outside only exists in memories. Voices shouting from one cell to another. Plastic rosary beads. Black, white, baby blue, glow-in-the-dark rosary beads. Two cans of tuna for a drawing. Tinned tuna tastes so fucking good in here. Chicken is raw. Stomach pains. Pot noodle come like some gourmet ting. Don't wear prison-issue trainers, mandem call them fraggle flops and don't rate you if you rock them coz it means you ain't got no one outside sending you shit. Rock hard pillows. Neck pain when you wake up. B addicts on methadone. Murderers addicted to buj. Exercise yard walking around anticlockwise. The sky looks far away, too far away, like if it started raining the rain wouldn't even reach here. Someone gets their face cut on another spur and the wing gets locked down for twenty-four hours. Showers steaming up, burning skin. Back and chest tattoos with names of gangs, girlfriends, sons, daughters, dead friends. Always wear your boxers in the showers coz man ain't no battyman tryna get raped n shit. Screws come searching through your cell, tapping the bars on the windows, going through your shit and leaving you to tidy it all up. If it isn't tidy the next time they do a cell check, you get put on report. Someone hangs himself while his celly is asleep and the body gets discovered in the morning so we don't get let out for our usual fifteen minutes in the exercise yard. Someone on the spur shouts did he piss and shit himself and someone else shouts did he get woods and bare man start laughing and I hear the same voice go I read it in a book, it's what happens when you hang yourself, your tings go hard like it's the best feeling in the world and another voice shouts shut up man, allow dat battyboy talk about man's tings, wa'um to you. The Olympics are on TV. Everyone is behind their doors, stuck on the same channel. Usain Bolt breaks the world record in the hundred metres and the wing explodes in noise, cell doors banging clang clang clang, mandem doing gunshots brap brap brap. Pool and table tennis on association. Squeaking of trainers, ping-pong match, p–tik p–tok p–tik p–tok. Keys rattle. Someone's got his stereo tumping Giggs's album *Walk in da Park*. Books getting passed around like *The 48 Laws of Power* and *The Art of War*. Snitches get moved off the wing for their own protection. Brutus tells me about someone getting kettled when he was here before; it's when you boil your kettle, put bare sugar into the boiling water and then dash it in a man's face. The sugar clings to your skin so that when you touch your face, your skin melts right off, says Brutus. No female screws on our spur. Someone says that the last one got caught giving his co-d brain in their cell. I laugh, swear down? Mum's life g. She even wrote him love letters after she got sacked. Burning incense to mask the smell of the toilet. Taking a shit while your celly watches TV. Man are plugging mobile phones up their arse. Plugging hash. Plugging cro. Plugging work. Plugging b. Plugging razor blades and homemade shanks. Bed bugs. Keys rattle. Doors open. Doors slam shut. Constant sound of metal; a timer. Voices are echoes. Only one present for everyone. Behind the door.

Always time to kill. Nothingness is long. Turns the day long. Makes it drip, but as it drips down, it doesn't separate from its source, like honey or golden syrup, a long sticky string, and you're waiting for the thinnest part of the drip to finally break and separate so the drop can hit the floor. But it doesn't.

One afternoon I get some disposable razors for shaving. Brutus tells me how to do it. I break the blades out of the heads of two razors and throw the broken plastic out of the slit in the window so there's nothing in my cell to make the screws think I've made a weapon. I get an old toothbrush and melt the head with a lighter. As soon as it goes soft – blackened, twisting, yellow bubbles – I stick the two razor blades in side by side and wait

262

for the plastic to re-harden. I rip a small strip of my pillowcase off and tie it around the handle tight, so that if I have to slash someone repeatedly, my hand won't slip and I won't end up cutting myself. You can't poke man up with this but if you slice a man down the cheek, their face will open up. Two or more blades next to each other means they won't be able to stitch up the cut, which will leave a real nasty scar. Mark up a man's face for life.

After two and a half weeks I get moved with Solo to C Wing. We don't want to go. We take all our shit in plastic bags marked HM Prison Service. Follow one short little screw and just before he opens the gate to put us onto the next wing Solo turns to me, makes a fist with his arm down by his side and says shall we go block? If I say yes, Solo's gonna bang the screw in the face. The screw knows it. He looks at me like he's just waiting for me to decide. I say nah brudda, 'low it. Solo says come we go block and I go nah fam, allow him, jus allow him. The screw has soft eyes. Solo doesn't like not knowing what the next wing's gonna be like. Neither do I, but I've only got a few weeks left in this place and I don't wanna spend them down block in solitary confinement, only the bare essentials, concrete slab as a bed, no associating with other prisoners, basically no human contact apart from when the screws take you for a shower. Nah, allow dat labyrinth. Mandem turn into minotaurs down there.

There are wasps in my new cell and they don't know how to get out so I kill them. It's a one-man cell with a bunk bed for two man. There's not enough space for two people to be standing up and doing things at the same time. The toilet is at the foot of the bed with a little curtain around it for privacy. My new celly is a Tamil Tiger, them nuts Sri Lankan brers who beef with axes and samurai swords from Wembley and them sides. He asks me what my sentence is. I say I got three weeks left before I go home, how much you got? He says you will cry if I tell you how much I got left. His name is Ragul.

That evening he tells me how he was involved in some gang war in Wembley. He says that the gang his team was beefing kidnapped one of his boys in east London and cut off his head with a samurai sword. So they did a drive-by on one of the brers they were after. Wembley High Road, broad daylight, early afternoon, but all the shots missed. Later they went to the brer's yard and kicked off his front door. But he wasn't there so Ragul popped the brer's cousin. Afterwards he tried to execute the brer's father, making him kneel in the hallway of the family home, but when he pulled the trigger, the gun jammed. He is six years into a thirty-year sentence. Every night, Ragul sits on his bed on the top bunk, reading Bible verses for half an hour in a steady emotionless drone of Tamil, while I watch TV.

One night, staring up at the ceiling it hits me. This life is like being in an ocean. Some people keep swimming towards the bottom. Some people touch the bottom with one foot, or even both, and then push themselves off it to get back up to the top, where you can breathe. Others get to the bottom and decide they want to stay there. I don't want to get to the bottom because I'm already drowning.

The next day, during association, me and Solo get our heads shaved. Then we go into his cell and write bars together. I get some letters. One is from Yinka and she tells me she misses me like mad and that the rose I gave her months back is now dead. She says she'll be waiting for me when I get out. I read and re-read the last paragraph over and over again:

You've always been in trouble with the police, ever since I've known you. Even when you met me it wasn't enough to deter

*you. It's a shame because I thought I could change that side of
you, really, how stupid. You're a drug which I'm addicted to but
it's an addiction which is no good for me. Even though we can't
be together you'll always be my Butterfly . . . this pussy is
yours xxx*

I feel to throw away the letter afterwards because I don't want
the burden of someone loving me like this. I've started having
dreams again since I got locked up and stopped bunning cro,
but the women in my dreams don't have her face.

My mother and father have written to me as well. The stamps
are Italian. I read the letter from my father while the day fades
and night lingers outside my window, looking in.

Dear Gabriel,

    *It's only short note because I really don't know what to tell
you in this situation. You are in the prison and I'm at luxury
place, like the paradiso from Milton's poem.*

    *From my nature I'm the bird so cages and boxes my enemys.
I need my wings keep straight and moving them all the time.
I need to be free . . . I told you before but I want to repeat.
The life is too beautiful and too short. I see it now every day
when my time is shorter, my energy weaker, my friends and
places which I know passed away. I want to talk to you – I
hope we will find time for this at home.*

    The owl in our garden is crying – time for hunting.

    With hugs and kisses

    Tata

    *P.S. I hope you are alright there and life treat you well, and
soon you will be free . . .*

Underneath this he has drawn a bird flying through clouds but the bird's wings are sticking out of a wire cage which holds the bird within. I put the letter away with all my other papers, sticking it underneath my probation reports as if I'm trying to bury it.

Then suddenly the screws tell me I'm getting early release due to overcrowding. Thursday association is my last time out on the wing. I jam with Solo the whole forty-five minutes and when I go, he hugs me and says brothers for life. I promise I'll write to him.

It's the last day of August when I get released. When I step out the prison gates it's like the sky comes down and touches the earth and I swear everything smells different out here. I can smell atoms moving, vibrating, free. It feels like that moment when your ears pop after a long flight. While mandem are hitting up carnival in London, I'm jumping on a train from Bicester to Marylebone station.

Yinka meets me at the station and she's looking peng, not gonna lie. White jeggings mad tight on her backoff, skin looking fresh and silky, lips all shiny like strawberry glaze on doughnuts. I hug her tight. She has candy-pink nails and she smells of sugar. We go back to my parents' yard because they're not back from Italy till the day after tomorrow. She's acting all stoosh like she don't wanna let off, won't even hold my hand when we walk from the tube station to the yard. We go upstairs and end up play-fighting on my bed and she's saying what Gabriel, you think you're bad just coz you went pen? I get between her legs and she starts breathing heavy, moaning as I pin her arms down and then I lips her up and I pull her jeans off and her thighs are thick like cold honey and she says fuck me daddy and we end

266

up fucking for like an hour until neither of us can see properly. Later she goes yard coz she's got work in the morning. I go to Uncle T's. Welcome home son he says and hugs me hard. A plate of food. Then I buy a draw of ammi. I go and link Mazey.

We bun a zoot outside my mum's yard and my head starts spinning after just five tokes. Everything's moving around me and when Mazey talks it's like he's acting in a movie and I start laughing for no reason at all. I say rah, whatdafuck is in this? I swear I'm gonna frass out and Mazey says swear down fam? Swear down Maze and then I give him the rest of the draw and say that's you fam, have the rest of the zoot as well, I need to sleep. Rah, safe my broski. I go into my parents' building and climb the stairs. I wake up at three in the morning sprawled out on the landing, one floor down from the door to my parents' flat. I never even made it to the front door. The moon is standing over me just watching.

A few days later, I have dinner with my parents. We sit at the kitchen table, the light above holding us in its warm glow while night seeps into the rest of the kitchen. In a frame on the wall is a drawing of a crocodile with its mouth open in a big sharp-toothed smile, approaching a rabbit. Dinner is roasted aubergines in olive oil and garlic, based on a new recipe my father picked up from one of his Italian friends, followed by mushroom tagliatelle. I'm chewing focaccia which is this banging salty white bread from Italy that reminds me of my childhood when I used to go with my parents to Tuscany every summer holiday. It makes me think of the beach in Forte Dei Marmi. The salty taste of the sea. Jumping, somersaulting in the waves, laughing as they knocked me over.

Silence hangs over us. Small talk. How was your holiday? Good flight? I don't really know what to say though. It's like I've become so used to daily conversations about who shot who and who stabbed who and who robbed who and who went pen for whatever, that I can't talk about other shit. I can't deal with talking to my parents about Tuscany and the figs they picked up off the street out there and the lemons and tomatoes and the beach and their Italian friends and the sea and the pine trees and— I swear I almost feel like I don't even know how to talk about things like that any more. Then my mother asks me Gabri how are you? Are you okay? Yeah I'm fine, I'm fine, I say. Distant, strangers almost, we all seem to be searching for something to say. It's like meeting people you once had a great holiday with, but it's been so long since that golden time together that when you see them again, everyone's just forcing the interaction while hiding what they're really thinking.

I get pissed off with the hesitant silence boiling the air around me and say why are you acting like you're not sure how to approach me? I was only locked up for a month, it's not like I went through some deep experience and it's changed the person I am.

Well it has hasn't it? says my mother.

Oh my days, allow it, I say, trying to finish everything on my plate as quickly as possible.

My father doesn't look at me, just pats my mother's hand on the table and says her name gently, like he's telling her to leave it alone.

We carry on eating, the kitchen filled by the sound of cutlery knocking against plates and I'm thinking about Gotti and Rex and Solo and Yinka and Mama and Tata when it hits me: only love can hurt me.

ON THE MORALITY OF MURDER
IN *HAMLET*

Orun ni ilé, Oja ni ilé aye.
(Heaven is home, the Earth is just a marketplace.)

Yoruba proverb

A WEEK BEFORE uni starts I hit one uni rave with Capo where I grab one big-batty Nigerian chick and start daggering her. I smell shea butter and olive oil in her sweat and her skin shimmers silver as she says you're so bad, I've got a boyfriend you know. Then she gives me her number, tells me she's a first-year Biomedical Sciences student and I should holla at her when uni starts. The club night itself is pretty dry. Nothing like the hood raves I'm used to.

A few days later I hit up a rave with Dario. It's in Willesden in one spot called Theorem. Gyaldem looking cris, fresh weaves, tight braids, dancing with their backs arched to show off their backoffs while bare man stand around, chains out, hoods up on some screwfacing ting. Then one brer starts getting bottled with an E&J brandy bottle – you know those thick glass bottles with hard edges – and it doesn't break. Every time it

269

connects you can hear this hollow CONK sound as the glass bounces off his head. The music gets locked off and me and Dario push through the crowd to see if it's anyone we know. Everyone's standing in a circle watching the brer get fucked up, pulling their phones out to film it, going oh shiiiiit myman's getting fucked up. It's not anyone we know so we carry on watching. The brer who's getting bottled tries to get away. The crowd surges into the street. Outside, the brer collapses on the pavement, head all lumped up and bloody. But still, that E&J bottle ain't broken. That's one thick bottle to get licked with ah lie? says Dario. When the bredrins of the guy who got bottled see what happened, they jump in a whip to go and chase down the mandem who done it. As the whip pulls out into the road, the brer who got bottled stands up, staggers into the middle of the road and gets run over by his own boys. The impact of the car flings him into the air like he's doing some kinda front flip. Imagine.

For my final year, I find a room to rent in a big yard in Plaistow, shared with four other students from Queen Mary. Since it's in East, far from the ends, I can just focus on the uni ting and finish my degree. Still, I start shotting coke and MDMA to students, and also to some people on my road just to make a little p's on the side so I can buy whatever I want and be comfortable.

I still have couple cases, which means I have to go to court every now and again, and I end up missing handing in the proposal for my dissertation. My supervisor knows what's been going on with me, so he writes down that I already gave it to him and says we know it'll be of a high standard anyway. People like him give me hope forreal. Incidentally, he was my professor when I first did *The Birth of Tragedy* and got so into Nietzsche.

I get a letter from Rex. We've been writing to each other since he went bin.

Wagwan Snoopz,

Blood it's good to hear from you fam I'm glad you ain't forgot about me still because everyone else has I swear down. Blood niggaz have been living nice making dough forgetting bout Rex like I'm dead fam, it's nothing though coz when I land road I'm moving to man on some greazy ting.

Snoopz even my bitch left man blood can you fucking believe it blood, even you thought she was real ah lie fam, it's nothing though coz now I feel no love my hearts turned cold as Antarctica. Snoopz I will never forget our friendship and never ever ever will I forget what them Grove pagan pussyoles done to you fam man will get them youts trust me.

Blood you give man joke you remember how much ho's I got, do you remember that lighty when man ate that yout at her house for the vouchers that shit was funny.

Fam I want the see-through Bapes or it could be the see-through Air Forces I don't mind as long as they're see-through fam.

Anyway man's just bored in here fam I'm missing the roadz nuff I swear down blood I need some pussy badly. Blood I need to touch road fam coz certain man are trying to play gangster and move like I'm some prick coz I'm locked in here. I can't wait to see them, I'm not saying no names coz I don't want you to do nothing you get me blood.

Anyway you dun know
Gangster for Life
from Rex HMP Gangster #1

It's mad how no one really writes letters any more. It's all phone messages and emails and all that; words made up of the same recognisable digital letters for everyone. But when you go prison, you end up writing letters to people you care about and they write back to you and it reveals a secret part of themselves. It's like handwriting is the most truthful part of a person or some shit. And the maddest ting is how you can know everything about your bredrin – his habits, his life, even his hopes – but you don't know what his handwriting's like until he goes pen and writes you a letter. I'm not sure what exactly it reveals, but it's definitely something. We speak on the phone, since Rex got one smuggled in from early, but it's the effort of letters that keeps us connected in a deeper way.

Rex sends me a V/O – a visiting order – and I take a train to Kent because he's doing his bird in HMP Rochester. When I see him in the visiting room I feel bare happs. He bops over in some shiny multicoloured Bapes and he's looking hella stocky. Brudda, we both say at the same time and then we sit down to chat and I tell him how I finally split up with Yinka. Really and truly she split up with me coz she couldn't take how I didn't want to live with her, I say and he says she wasn't the one Snoopz, she wasn't the one, fuck her anyway, and I say it's well and truly over now. Then he looks at me and says I told you about Gotti didn't I? I told you he couldn't look me in the eye when we was chatting in my yard. I say I know brudda I know, and I pass my hand over my face as if I'm trying to rub the memory away. After an hour the visit is over and he says man's only got five months left Snoopz, soon touch road my brudda and I say I can't wait fam, we're gonna ride out on these fake brers. Rex says course brudda, all we need is couple burners and the bike and it will be Rex and Snoopz on a greazy ting, but make sure you finish your uni first, don't do anyting to anyone until I touch road.

So now it's Friday and I have exactly a week left before I have to hand in my dissertation, my final major piece of work before the end of my degree. I haven't even started it, but then I decide to go country for the weekend to shot work and buj. Bare man go country to shot food coz there's bare nittys down there, feds are less on it than in London and there's less competition. Get yourself a nice spot in cunch, pattern the ting, and eventually you can end up kicking back in London while your boys run the line. Or you can send workers to run it and all you gotta do is pay them a salary. So the food ting in all these seaside towns in England, like Bournemouth and Hastings and wherever, is usually controlled by mandem from the big cities. The south coast of England is all London man and then the further north you go you get mandem from Brum and Manny and Liverpool and so on. When there's a shooting in one of these places that has pebble beaches and a pier with a funfair and arcades and all that shit, it's almost always different teams from London beefing over the lines they're running. Coz if too many teams get the same idea, there's less nittys for each line, less profit and slower turnover. So sometimes a little war breaks out to establish who's really running shit and all the locals are shocked and horrified – this kind of thing never happens round here, they all say.

I've decided that my dissertation is going to be called On the Morality of Murder in *Hamlet*, coz *Hamlet* is all about honour and loyalty and being tormented by the need for revenge. I haven't started it yet but I've made bare notes and I've got bare Nietzsche quotes lined up. I've only got seven days to write

10,000 words but I always do this, I always wait till the last minute when the pressure forces me to act. It's the most important part of my degree and obviously I'm not looking to flop. But then I get a call from Stranger and he tells me his boys in Hackney are looking for someone, preferably a white brer – coz if you're white you'll stand out less in these small places where the most multicultural thing they have is a Chinese takeaway – to go country with two g-packs of b and work, and dot it out over the weekend. We'll get back on Sunday since their line bangs and the food should all be done by Sunday morning, says Stranger. The p they're offering is decent and Stranger says I just want a drink, which means he'll be happy with a little cut of what they pay me. We'll be staying in a hotel room that's already paid for, so why not? I could do with a break from London, sea air and alladat, and anyway I haven't really had much excitement this year so I say I'm on it fam and he says cool, I'll come pick you up and we'll go link them man in Hackney to get the food.

We buck up with Stranger's people in the hallway of one crumbling block in Hackney. Low yellow lights infecting the gloom and Stranger's boy with a couple goons in puffer jackets with hoods up, watching me like they're tryna work suttin out. The brer whose line it is gives me a Nokia 3310 and says I'll be dinging you on this when the sells holla. All you gotta do is hit dem with whatever I tell you they want and I say calm. Skitzo's gonna drive you down there, he says and nods at one of his boys. Then he gives Stranger the two g-packs, which is two grand's worth of heroin and crack all wrapped up in £10 and £20 pebbles. He gives Stranger £250 and says that's for you man's hotel room and then we follow Skitzo to his whip.

It is late afternoon when we get to Folkestone, seagulls crying out as they glide through the air, sounding like a gang of children going me me me. We book the hotel room, Skitzo leaves us and the line starts ringing.

I'm in a nitty's house in Folkestone with Stranger and we are sitting in the living room. The floor is covered in broken toys. There's literally nowhere to step without treading on one. It looks like Father Christmas crashed here a year ago and abandoned the mission, I say to Stranger and he starts bussin up. The sell is one woman called Debbie. She comes into the living room holding some p's and says let me get three light and two dark. She's not yet finished by the habit. She still has this big yard, which isn't ghetto or anything, and she obviously buys her yout loads of toys. But she's on her way. Blonde hair, little black dress with a wrinkled cleavage pushed up in it and bare gold Argos jewellery hanging between her breasts. She's wearing black thigh-length stockings and as she counts out the p's, one of them rolls down to her calf and I can see blue veins running under the pale skin. She says something about how she's gonna get a jacuzzi built in the garden. Before we leave, a little girl walks into the room, picks her way through the toys and goes over to a chest which she opens, revealing a pillow and some blankets, almost like a little bed. She picks up one of the broken toys, a Buzz Lightyear figure with his wings missing, smiles at us and climbs into the chest before closing the lid on herself.

During the day I sit on a bench by the seafront with a copy of *For Esmé with Love and Squalor* – my favourite short stories by J. D. Salinger – and a bag of Skittles. Between pages of the book I've put thirty pebbles of work and I've eaten most of the Skittles and put a whole load of b into the packet. When a nitty comes up to me, I tell them to have a Skittle and shake

275

out however many wraps of buj they want, or I open the book on a certain page which has the work tucked in and tell them to take what they paid for. Whenever I run out, I go back to the hotel room where Stranger is jamming and reload. Then back to the bench to wait for the next sell while the sun shatters into thousands of pieces that dance all over the sea into the distance.

Later I give a nitty and his girlfriend two rocks in exchange for driving me to hit sells in another part of town. We park up on one bruckdown-looking street and one brer with no top on comes running up to the driver's window, which is open, shouts you fucking owe me you cunt and bangs my driver in the face. Blood hits the windscreen. Then he takes the keys out of the ignition and runs into a yard. My driver's got a broken nose and his girlfriend is shouting that fucking dickhead he's got no right, but they're moving so scatty they can't even explain what any of it was about. I get out of the car. Fuck it, I'm gonna have to go into that yard and get the car keys back. The door isn't closed. The brer is sitting at a table in the living room with his top off, holding the car keys and smoking a roll-up. He fucking nicked me brown the cunt, he says as I walk in. Yeah well that's got nuttin to do with me bruv, I say. I'm tryna do business. You taking the keys is gonna fuck up my business. So unless you want it to get real sticky, you need to let off with the keys. He doesn't look at me. Then a brainwave. I say I'll give you two dark for your trouble. He looks up at me and says you can't make it three? I take two wraps of buj out and say no I can't. He gives me the keys, I give him the b and walk out of the yard and get into the whip. Later, my driver parks up on a quiet residential street and starts piping up work with his chick. I leave them as thick white smoke unravels through the car.

By Sunday morning everything is finished, so Stranger and I jump on a train back to London. When we get to the block in Hackney we give the big man his p's and the line and he says rah you did the ting proper still. I heard how you dealt with getting the car keys back as well, you done your ting. He gives me my cut and says so what, you ready to do this ting on Monday yeah? I say nah g I got uni work to do, I'm already behind with that shit as well. Skitzo says what? You're tryna say you got better plans than making three bills a day? He licks his gold tooth as he looks at me and I say listen, I got way more important tings to do than this shit. I've got a fucking 10,000 word dissertation to write and I ain't compromising that shit for no one. The big man laughs and says nah he's a real one, respect my g, and he spuds me while Skitzo screwfaces the floor. Then the big man says anytime you wanna work with man again, just holla at me. It's five in the afternoon so I go Westfield and buy myself a pair of patent leather Pradas before the shop closes.

It's Monday morning. I've got exactly five days before I have to hand in my dissertation. Sitting at the dinner table in Plaistow, I force the words out. I write everything by hand before typing it up. Papers spread around me like dead leaves covered in snail trails of black ink. Every 2,000 words I reward myself with a zoot. Sometimes I lose track of what I'm tryna say. Sometimes I gotta stop myself from going off on one. There's this next book I've decided to use as a reference: *On Murder Considered as One of the Fine Arts*. True though. If you think about all them gangster films, Tarantino and Scorsese and so on, people love to be entertained by murder. The right combination of coldheartedness, the character's drive for revenge – and don't forget the lighting. Special effects. The right balance of shadows. Watch it from your sofa or a seat in a cinema with some popcorn to munch on. But see the real thing on the news, fuck it, see it in real life and your insides will tremble and you'll cover your face as if you could rub what you just saw out of your eyes. And then you'll want to look again, fascinated by the ugly reality.

Thoughts spiralling out coz I'm bunning zoots, drinking Boost and not getting enough sleep while I write and write. And then, suddenly I've got only 2,000 words to go and I'm basically already there, just need to write a conclusion. In the end I manage to hand in my dissertation typed and ready, just in time for the deadline. I feel like it's drained me of words and ideas, left me with only breath and movement. I need to sleep. Fuck it I need to throw away all my notes.

Rex gets out of pen just as I'm finishing it all.

I go to check him in Finsbury Park because he's out on licence and the prison service put him in a bail hostel there, full of mandem who've just been released. I see him walking down the road towards me and something inside me flies up to the sky and I start grinning teeth. I go to spud him and he says come on brudda give me a hug, wa'um to you? We hug in the street while the sun polishes the sky and I look up and the world feels new for a second. I can feel all the bulk of muscle under his hoodie and I'm like rah brudda, you got some size on you and he's like truss me Snoopz, man's strong now, I can curl you like a dumbbell. I laugh and say whatever man and he picks me up like it's nuttin, right there in the middle of the street, cars going past, lays all six foot of me across his arms and starts doing curls like a madman. I start bussin up and he says I told you brudda, they're not ready for Rex, I'm back.

Then I start to wish that I'd done all the moves with Rex and not with Gotti and the sadness comes back so I say come we go bun a zoot brudda.

The bail hostel is straight fuckery. Full of nittys. I can smell work and buj and sweat as soon as we go downstairs to his room. Rex says I swear down Snoopz, I can't wait to leave this place and not have to sign myself in at the front desk and just be able to open my own door with my own key whenever I want. We start bunning, but he frasses out and goes to sleep after like five draws coz all he's used to are them skinny jail zoots, not these fat cones full of loud that I'm always billing. I throw a blanket over him and leave the hostel.

The first thing he does once he's settled into freedom is to go on a move with one crazy Tottenham yout called Demon who was his co-d in Rochester. They go and rob some traphouse in Manor House and when Rex comes back from it he gives me a watch that has a white gold spider covered in black diamonds set into the face and the bezel has bare tiny white diamonds around it and I'm like brudda you can't give me this, you've just got out, you should keep it or shot it or suttin. Rex says nah Snoopz, that's for you, you never forgot about man when I was locked up, you're my brudda for life. He tells me how there were three man in the trap. How him and Demon kicked off the door and ran in there bally'd up with straps. How one of the youts jumped right out of the bathroom window before they could grab him. How they made the other two youts lie face down before taking their phones and watches and food and any p's they could find. How before they left, Demon turned around, cocked his strap and aimed it slowly at the head of one of the youts who was lying on the floor and Rex had to grab his arm and say what's wrong with you fam, why you so eager to kill, we've just got outta the bin. I say brudda you shoulda phoned me, I woulda been on it, and Rex says I did, but you said you was working on your dissertation when you answered the phone so I thought no point telling you coz you gotta focus on dat.

And then I graduate. After all the madness. BA in English. Imagine. I just missed out on a First in my dissertation as well. Rex comes to the graduation ceremony. He has P.O.M.E. freshly tattooed on his neck. Product Of My Environment. He stands around talking with my parents and Danny and then we take photos with me in my gown and mortar board. Everyone is smiling, grinning pure teeth.

AFTER CHRISTMAS

A YEAR AFTER getting my degree I start trapping. So does Capo.
How else am I gonna pay for my pilot's licence? he says.

It is Boxing Day evening and my mother and Danny are
playing chess in the living room, warmed by a fire in the fireplace that my father hacked out of the wall. He'd worked out
where the chimney flue was – it wasn't his idea, my mother
always wanted one – and over the course of a week, he hammered
the wall away to reveal the original fireplace. My mother often
comes home with pieces of wood salvaged from skips, old chairs
and planks to feed the fireplace.

Capo put me onto the cro ting, so I've built up a punk line
selling big bits. But it's when Rex hooks me up with Chizzle
that it really pops off for me. I say obviously I'll sort you out
brudda, what do you want for it? And Rex says don't be dumb
Snoopz, I don't want nuttin, I just wanna see you up – you're
my brother. Chizzle has a traphouse in Hounslow and he's got
the whole block on lock – a small building, about six flats in
total – and he's patterned it so that everyone living in there

works for him in some shape or form. I've been dropping Chiz a box of punk every two weeks. Whenever I link him I can tell if he's been bagging up coz he's got hay fever and the dust from the punk makes him sneeze and his eyes puff up. He breaks the box down into draws and moves it all like that. A whole box – that's 1,000 grams, broken down into 1.8-gram draws, shotting them for a score each and moving the whole ting in under two weeks. That's pretty fucking impressive fam I said to him and Chiz said dun know my broski, man's in the trap day and night, I don't sleep.

I've been staying more often at my parents' flat, spending a night or two each week and when they start asking too many questions, or I just want the space to do whatever I want, I go and stay at one of my bredrins' yards. Things are going well, I bought everyone Christmas presents and the rest of my p's are piling up at the back of the sock drawer in my old bedroom.

My father is in the kitchen reading something. Everyone's belly is full. The flat smells of pine needles and cooked goose fat. I've never had goose before but Mama said she wanted something special this Christmas.

I leave the flat without anyone noticing and go downstairs. Chizzle's brought back a ninebar I gave him last week. Actually I gave him half a box, but he's bringing back the other half for me to get rid of. The cro isn't what he wanted. It's cheese not ammi for starters, the buds are wet, tight and heavy, and there's a lot of sticks in the pack. Not the usual quality that I drop on him and he says it's made his line slow down coz the sells don't want it. Not gonna lie, I blatantly fucked up. There's a lesson in this. Never take shit food just coz you're hungry innit.

I meet him at the bottom of the building. He leaves the cab waiting outside. You look stressed fam, I say as we buck up in the hallway. Chizzle is short and solid, a judo prodigy in his younger days, but his mum never registered him for citizenship when he came from Ghana at the age of four. She fucked man up, said Chizzle one time when I asked him why he wasn't tryna get into the Olympic judo team for Great Britain. So instead of being a judoka – he told me that's what you call it – he's a shotter. He starts telling me how the shit punk fucked up his line. I wave my hand down down down for him to talk quieter coz I don't want the neighbours to hear us. He smells of the cheese I dropped on him. Rah it smells kinda loud still, I say as he gives me the ninebar wrapped in plastic bags and he says yeah the smell's decent but trust Snoopz, the food's really not all dat. I stuff it under my hoodie and then I let him out of the front door. Shout me as soon as you got suttin better, he says as he gets in the cab.

I go upstairs, hoping that the cheese is still in the original smelly proof that I gave it to Chizzle in. Back in the flat I slip my creps off, then head straight up to my room. Sit down on my bed and get the foodsaver out so I can split the cheese into ounces and reseal them in plastic. I'll take them to Uncle T's later. He can get rid of pretty much anything I give him.

As I open it, I realise it's not in the smelly proof. It's loosely wrapped in plastic bags and my room fills with the smell, mad loud, as if the dark green buds were oozing sap all over the walls, bursting the room's seams. I get onto my bed quicktime and open the windows. Downstairs I hear my brother saying oh my God what is that smell, it's as if someone brought dog food into the flat and I start laughing as I'm standing on my bed. I hear my mother say it's a terrible smell, what is it? Then the sound of windows opening downstairs.

My brother comes upstairs, straight into my room and I say don't bate me off Danny, shit.

He says I know, that's why I said it smells like dog food. But it's unbearable, I thought you stopped smoking.

I did, it's just my boy brought me a big bit of punk to resell and I had to bring it into the flat.

Gabriel the whole flat stinks, and he whispers it again with wide eyes, then smiles.

I can't really tell what he thinks about it all. He goes downstairs. I wrap everything back up, thinking why am I moving loose like this?

My father steps into the room, hovers by the doorway, wrinkles his forehead and says Gabri whole house is smelling of marewana, and I try not to laugh at how he says it. When I was a child I used to always find those wrinkles worrying. Deep creases running one above the other. I thought they must be there because he's sad and I'd rub my hand down his forehead, thinking if I can smooth them out then all his worries will go away.

I say I'm sorry Tata, seriously I haven't smoked anything I swear, it's just my friend came and dropped me off a jacket that I left at his house and coz he smokes it stinks of weed now.

He walks out of my room and says all right all right, I'm just telling you whole flat smelling now and is very hard to get rid, and he goes back downstairs. I just keep saying sorry sorry as his steps creak.

I go downstairs, enter the kitchen and repeat the story I came up with to my father again. I'm not sure what I'm tryna do. I think I want him to feel better. It's been a good Christmas so far. It's the smell that bothers him but he's back to reading the newspaper again. I go into the living room and repeat myself for the benefit of my mother. It doesn't work. She is on her feet, the chess game abandoned, eyes all glassy and severe.

Where is this jacket? she says. I want to see this jacket, where is it?

I say it's upstairs Mama, I've put it in my wardrobe.

Later, when I tell Rex about this he says I shoulda gone upstairs at this point, grabbed a handful of punk out of the bag and rubbed it all over one of the jackets in my wardrobe. Brudda, what were you thinking? Come on, you're not dumb Snoopz, you know you was flopping the ting. I say to him but brudda, she followed me and wasn't gonna take no for an answer.

Show me this jacket Gabriel, I want to see the jacket. She carries on.

I say I'm not showing you the jacket Mama and I start going back upstairs, but she follows right behind me and says show me this jacket, I want to smell it.

I stop halfway up the stairs and say whatdafuck is this abnormal behaviour? I'm not showing you the jacket, stop following me. My father comes out of the kitchen and asks her what she's doing in Polish and Danny says come downstairs and stop this weird behaviour. Why can't she just chill the fuck out? Just for once. But my mother is covered in spikes. Maybe that's how she survives the world. Maybe that's how she survives me. I don't fucking know.

Back in my room Danny comes in again and says you do realise you don't have the right to get pissed off like that since it's blatantly a lie what you're saying and it's your fault there's this smell in the flat? I say what do you want me to do then, tell them the truth? He says yeah, maybe? I don't know. But it's you who fucked up, it's not Mama's fault.

I pack the foodsaver and the ninebar into a travel bag. I call Uncle T and explain the situation and he says come through whenever you're ready my son, I'll get rid of it for you no

285

problem. I pick up the bag and go downstairs. I walk into the kitchen and announce to my parents that the reason the house stinks now is because my friend came and dropped off nine ounces of weed and I brought it into the flat thinking it wouldn't smell. Yeah that's right I sell weed, that's how I make my money, I mean how do you think I could afford to live in a flat on my own before Christmas? You know I haven't got a job, how do you think I afford all these new clothes and Christmas presents for everyone? I let it all out without breathing once.

My mother flinches but her face is still frozen, staring at me in such a way that I don't feel fuck all about what I've just told her. My father just looks annoyed that my mother forced me to tell the truth. My mother calls for a family meeting in the living room.

It goes like this: Daniel and I sinking into the scratched leather sofa in front of the little table with the abandoned chessboard. Across from us my mother asking interrogation-style questions. My brother telling her this kind of question is irrelevant and that I don't have to answer. My father sitting in silence next to her, looking away from us all, at the wall, closed lips moving silently as if he's chewing words. I point out that if we were living in Holland, we wouldn't be having this conversation coz legally I'd be considered an entrepreneur and not a drug dealer.

Where did you get it from? Who are you going to sell it to? Where are you going to sell it? She presses ahead; questions that I'm never gonna answer. My brother points this out as she asks each one. It reminds me of when we were little and we had all these secret jokes and ways of making each other laugh at things when our mother was punishing us for whatever we'd done that had pissed her off.

At a certain point she tells me I ruin people's lives with this. What people? I ask. Young people, she replies and Danny and I start bussin up. Eventually, I get tired of the whole thing, my mother annoying me in the way that only an old mother full of love and misplaced beliefs can annoy you. I interrupt her and say sorry but what's the point of this?

My mother turns to my father and says I find it very upsetting and wrong that I'm having to do this on my own. Don't you have anything to say to your son? She says it in her usual aggressive manner, totally missing the point that it's her who wanted this dramatic circus.

My father turns to look at me. I am very upsetting, he begins and my mother interrupts him. Upset or upsetting? Danny and me are like why are you doing that? She says but I don't understand what he means. I say Tata please continue. I cannot accept that anyone in my family is involved in criminal things, especially my son who is most talented person I know, who can do so many artistic things, for you to choose to selling drugs. I know how is hard for you to get job – to get *a* job, says my mother and then she starts explaining to him in Polish what's wrong with his grammar.

When he finishes, his voice goes light and friendly, he looks at me and says now finish, you have to go somewhere yes? I nod and get up. It's getting late, nighttime is filling its belly with streets and rooftops, my mother's face is jagged stone and I don't want to be here any more.

I go into the hallway, put my Nike creps and jacket on and pick up the sports bag with the foodsaver and nine zeds of cheese inside. As I start down the stairs to leave the flat, my father comes out of the kitchen stopping me quickly, Gabri, and I turn. He holds out a box of mince pies to me. For you and your friends, he says with a smile on his face, eyes like drops of silver taking cover beneath his eyebrows which he styles in this way so that they go up into little points like some evil wizard in a cartoon. Thank you Tata, I say and smile. I unzip my bag and fit the mince pies in, on top of the foodsaver, pressing right next to the wrapped-up cro.

As I leave the flat I start crying silently, tightening up my face with my eyes all blurry, but I can't work out if I'm sad or if it's just the way I'd clocked my father's love for me has no limits, even while it pushes against something terrible. It doesn't stop until I get to the bus stop and my breath shudders inside my mouth as I breathe out slow, wiping my face with my sleeve, getting vexed with myself like stop being a fucking pussy, wa'um to you, fix up – because the bus is coming and I have to go SK and get rid of this food.

When I get to Blake Court I see these new purple lights going all the way up the length of the block, looking like some tripped-out nightmare, all that grim concrete flooded in purple and heavy shadows. Whatdafuck is this I think as I buzz Uncle T and he lets me in.

The door is on the latch and I lock it behind me, shouting yo yo yo as I come up the stairs. Wagwan Snoopz, shouts Uncle T and I enter the kitchen. Uncle T's long time bredrin Sparky General is there. They're sat around the glass kitchen table, Uncle T in that old black office chair he'd found dumped outside the block that he uses to roll around the kitchen when he can't be bothered to stand up and go to the sink or fridge – arthritis in both knees from years of working as a plasterer without protective equipment – and Sparky is sitting at the other end beneath a faded Bob Marley poster, which is drained of colour by days of sun pouring through the kitchen window. They're

288

bunning big spliffs with no roaches, kingsize Rizla rolled up proper yardie style. Thick gold sovereign rings on Sparky's fingers, tiny bits of ash from his zoot floating up, clinging to the night in the thickness of his locks.

You're a lifesaver, I say to Uncle T as I start unpacking my bag. Snoopz, anytime you need to get rid of some food just come to me, says Uncle T. I give him the box of mince pies and he says for me? I say yeah pops, merry Christmas and he says thank you son, I'm gonna have one right now, and he opens the box. I take the ninebar out of my bag and start unwrapping it.

The *Kilburn Times* is spread out on the kitchen table with bits of ash scattered across the page and Sparky is saying it's fucking bollocks mate, see this Jackie Sadek woman and Uncle T says who? I just read it to you, says Sparky, she's the head of a council project in Brent, which was supposed to clean this place up. Listen to what she says: 'South Kilburn is a wonderful place to be, terribly well connected to central London, really leafy – it's got everything going for it' and Sparky starts laughing hahaha and the laugh turns into a throaty cough. Uncle T says South Kilburn? She's talking about South Kilburn? Ah lie she ah tell. I say yeah, coz if somewhere's leafy you can't get gunshots and man getting poked up and nittys everywhere right? Listen to this though, says Sparky. When she gets asked what happened to the 50 million pound which the government gave the council to sort the estate out – Uncle T shouts 50 million? 50 million? Sparky continues – when she gets asked what happened to the money, she says she's unsure but she now feels 'the only way is up'. Whataload of bollocks, says Sparky as he finishes reading. Well they're gonna have to show something for it, no true dat? says Uncle T. That's probably why they put those bloodclart lights on the block. I say yeah I saw those when I was coming up, dafuck is that about? I hear the council's taking them down again next week, says Uncle T.

I spud Uncle T and Sparky – I'm off. See you later Snoopz. Outside it is raining and as I come out of the block I see purple light swimming in black puddles. I pull my hood up and start walking home.

THE WORLD'S MOST

I'M IN THE trap with Capo and we're counting money. Capo's fingers move mechanically over and over again, as if he's glitching and this one moment is stuck on a loop. Focused. He says make sure that each note has the Queen's face on top, line them all up the same way. You gotta have standards, he says. Most of the p's are going right back to the plug anyway, since Capo got all this food on tick. I guess he's tryna make a good impression. We separate fifties and twenties and tens so that every thousand-pound stack is made of the same notes. We only drink bottled water because the kitchen is mad dutty, full of cockroaches, and every half an hour one of us goes and sprays Febreze in the hallway and on the front door. The boxes of ammi are vacuum packed so there's no smell, but we open some of them to make smaller orders – half boxes and ninebars – and pack them again with a foodsaver. Every time we buss one of the boxes open, the smell bursts into the room, hijacking the air around us. Plus we've been bunning zoots as well, towel rolled up and pressed against the bottom of the door, window cracked open – all the tricks – just in case. There's a samurai sword on the sofa that Capo's sitting on.

Since I started doing the cro ting, this has to be the most I've seen. Twelve boxes – twelve kilos – like hard plastic pillows full of dark green buds. It's the biggest order so far coz Capo's line is banging and the plug knows he'll get his p's. That's the thing about Capo. Everyone knows they can rely on him when it comes to this ting. When we finish counting the bread it comes to 125 bags. 125,000 pounds in cash. I wonder how many different places, how many different moments and hands these notes have existed in. Now they've ended up in stacks, held together by green, blue, yellow and red rubber bands, piled up inside a Selfridges shopping bag. The cro and the p's together comes to over 200 bags. My family has never known that kinda money. My head spins. When we picked up the food from the connec in East London, we passed a massive billboard on the side of one building just before Stratford. There was no advert on it, just big black letters on a white background that said *Sorry! The lifestyle you ordered is currently out of stock*. Capo says he wants to get a flat in Hackney to use as a traphouse, but Hackney's getting mad gentrified. I say Hackney mandem need to do more shootings to keep the house prices down and we laugh. But I mean it.

I go to the toilet and I'm so gassed about the p's and all the food that I bell Rex. I say brudda I've just finished counting out 125 bags with Capo and we've chopped up like twelve boxes of ammi. Rex says what? Where are you now? I'm gonna phone Shredder and tell him to come with the van and a burner and we're gonna run up on you now. I say what? No brudda. Not Capo. Capo's family. You're not robbing Capo. Rex says whatdafuck are you on Snoopz? That's a life-changing sum of money. All you have to do is hold a gunbuck, it's not like I'm gonna let off the mash in the yard. I promise I won't break your nose or knock any teeth out, I'm just gonna buss your forehead open to make it look realistic. Capo will never know. I say brudda, that's not the point, anyone else and I'd be on it, but Capo's family. I can't do some snaky shit like that. Rex starts switching – I'm supposed to be your brother, how can you not let your brother do that after everything – and I'm like you *are* my brother but I gotta have some principles, not this, not now. I'll ride out with you on anyone else. Rex's voice goes flat and he says cool and puts the phone down before I can say anything else.

He's over hungry right now coz his bredrin Jim Jones got murked a few weeks ago. Stabbed in his heart when some brers kidnapped him and tried to rob him. Jim Jones was Rex's connec for the buj. Rex was always telling me it's that ten out of ten which makes the cats keep coming back like clockwork. On a real though, Jim Jones was actually Rex's bredrin, not just a plug, but true it's easier to get upset about losing a connec for good buj than it is to get into your feelings about your bredrin getting duppied. What bunned Rex even more was that Jim Jones' mother didn't allow any of his bredrins to attend the funeral. Something about she wasn't gonna have any criminals at her son's graveside.

The next day I go to see Rex. Usually he calls me every morning, but this time I call him and when I say I'm gonna check you, he says yeah whatever, I'm in the trap, and then he puts the phone down. But I know how he stays. That's my brother innit. I go to check him in Stamford Hill. Orthodox Jews walk past in the street rocking long black coats and wide-brimmed hats. He uses one chick's yard as a traphouse. It's in a brown block that looks exactly like all the other buildings in the estate and no matter how many times I come to check him, I never remember which block it is. I call him and he looks out of a window and says buzz flat six.

The chick opens the door for me. She's wearing hot pants and a T-shirt, and she has a tattoo of a gun and the postcode N16 on her thigh. The flat is baking, heating turned all the way up. Rex is chopping up work on the table and wrapping it in clingfilm. A documentary called *Hitler's Henchmen* is on the TV. He loves documentaries about World War Two. Sometimes when we're bunning, he'll start lecturing me about some obscure shit that I've never heard, about resistance fighters or German military tactics or suttin. I sit down on the sofa next to him and bill a zoot. After a while I say it – you know I love you brudda but I just couldn't let you rob Capo. He laughs while he stares at a piece of work on the scales and says I love you too, that's why you pissed me off yesterday, I was just feeling a way Snoopz, I'm not actually gonna eat him, Capo's cool. And just like that it's settled. We bun zoots and watch a documentary about the SS.

When his sells start calling he says are you rolling? Course brudda. Come then. We get in his whip and he says this brer's gonna have a good bit of money for me coz his giro dropped last night. You know the dates yeah? I say. Yeah brudda come on, I know when all my shoots' giros drop, he says. Then he starts blasting Gucci Mane, non-stop trap lyrics, and I lean back in my seat as he drives us to Finsbury Park.

He parks up on one road outside a dusty white building full of broken windows and torn curtains. A sign over the entrance says Sunny Vale Hotel. We're going in there Snoopz, just watch how they move coz these are some proper scatty nittys. He takes me into the crackhouse. The nittys gather around him, holding crumpled notes in their hands – I want three light, no make it four – and some of them stare at me. Rex says this is my brother, if anything happens he'll come back and shoot all of you. I almost laugh, thinking really? Will I? I didn't know anything about this arrangement but I guess I will. Rex finishes serving the cats and we leave. Where you looking to go? he asks me. I need to be in Cricklewood I say. Gotta help Capo bag up some more cro. I can drop you off in Kilburn if you want, says Rex. Safe brudda.

Later I'm jamming with Capo in the traphouse in Cricklewood. We've just finished chopping up a box into four-and-a-halfs. I'm reading a *Daily Mail* article on my phone and every few lines I'm like whatdafuck, this is some bullshit. Capo says wagwan? What you reading?

I'll tell you what's wrong with this Capo, with this whole fucking society; it's the fakeness innit. Blood are you seeing this? Typical white journalists writing bullshit about the roads, which they know nothing about. Nah man, I swear down they chat so much shit and then they get published and people read their lies like it's legit. But then those same people don't fucking know that there are ends like South Killy and they don't believe that man are seeing people get licked down every day, hearing gunshots at night, seeing all sorts of crazy shit. Like see this dickhead, some white, blonde, English woman who writes for the *Daily Mail* and what does it say here? *One woman's terrifying account of why her middle-class neighbourhood suddenly doesn't feel so safe any more.* So what happens yeah, is this woman's walking home with her youts near SK and some bullshit pops off. Basically she writes how one gang of youts was chasing some chick from next ends and they're all throwing bottles and then the bottles are crashing next to the woman and her youts and she's got her fucking pram n dat so she's getting all shook and blood, do you know what this bitch writes? She writes, *as a journalist, I'd devoted years to infiltrating London's violent teenage gangs* . . . Infiltrating gangs? Are you fucking mad? You ain't infiltrating shit. Undercover feds infiltrate gangs, not some fucking white woman from the *Daily Mail*. Real g's ain't never gonna talk to you or tell you anything about their life. At best, all you've done is gone to some random estate in London and talked to some wasteman who wants some clout, so he chats some shit to you and you're like I can turn this into an article. Don't laugh brudda, this is serious. Like forreal, how did she infiltrate them? Did she pretend she's a fucking nitty, tryna smoke work or suttin? Did she pretend she's selling her pussy or suttin? Don't chat shit innit. Blood are you seeing her picture? Are you seeing this picture of her?

I hold the phone towards Capo who's just finished vacuum packing another four-and-a-half. He looks up, sees the picture and shakes his head. Then he stands, opens the window, grabs the Febreze and starts spraying it into the air around us.

Look at her outside her fucking countryside house, they're balling bruv, some fucking rich upper-class people blood. Any black yout from the hood they're gonna be shook of him and think he's in a gang or whatever. Fuckssake, this is what I can't stand Capo, this fakeness innit. You get these journalists writing this bullshit about the roads for a paper like the *Daily Mail* and everyone gets scared, everyone gets shook. And then blood, just to make it even worse, what does she say? Listen to this bullshit: *I ran, clutching my terrified children. It was the wrong thing to do of course. I'd drawn attention to my fleeing family and a splinter group gave chase to us calling out get the whiteys.* Are you fucking dumb blood?

Capo laughs, leans back against the sofa and sparks a cigarette.

Get the whiteys blood? Like you fucking know that no youts on road in London are gonna shout get the whiteys. Maybe they shouted oi rob that white woman innit, but no fucking youts on road are gonna run after a white woman and shout get the whiteys, get the whiteys. Typical *Daily Mail* racist bullshit, stirring shit up, creating fear, tryna make people shook of black youts, shook of road youts, shook of mandem who wear hoodies and Nike creps, like everyone's just doing the same cruddy shit you get me, like what *is* this bullshit? Can you believe it blood? Fucking get over it. Real life, you just bumped into real life innit, it burst the little bubble that you live in and that's what happens. I fucking hate shit like this you know, it gets me mad.

Capo says that's why I don't read newspapers fam. You should 'low it man, stressing yourself out when everyone knows it's full of lies.

But Capz, I've even seen this shit in books fam. These journalists, these observers who ain't from the roads, ain't spent a day in their lives doing dirt, writing about mandem who do dirt, inventing, imagining, creating all sorts of demons for their readers to believe in. But *we* know the truth. *We* know what's really going on and then you read this bullshit and there are people actually making money from writing these untruths. Imagine.

Fuckinell, that was a rant and a half, says Capo, you should bun a zoot, and he gives me a bud of amnesia.

WHO THEY WAS

I'M BACK AT home with my parents. The flat asleep, darkness drifting softly all around. I'm in the hallway. Breathe out and as I close my mouth, somehow the entire bottom row of my teeth slides over the top row and clamps my jaw shut. The pressure on my top row is immense. I panic because I can't open my mouth. The bottom row is pressing pressing pressing hard against the top and I know I'm gonna have to move my jaw into its natural position at some point. I give in to the pressure because I can't take it any more and there's no other way for me to open my mouth again. My jaw moves back into place and the force and pressure snaps the entire top row of teeth out of my gumline. Loose teeth crumble onto my tongue. I hold them in my mouth. A few are still attached to my gum, but barely. I can feel them move as my tongue slides over them.

It takes me half a minute of checking each individual tooth in my top row by trying to wobble it with my thumb, for me to realise I've had that dream again. Every time it's the same. Nothing strange happens to make me realise I'm having a dream.

No distortion of reality. Every time I feel the loose teeth in my mouth, I realise I'm never gonna have my natural teeth again and it's a terrible feeling of loss. When I check my teeth after waking up, the relief is so real that it stays with me for most of the morning. I don't know what the dream means but it's way more disturbing than any of the violent ones. At least with those, when I wake up I know I'm back in reality. With the broken teeth I just think it's the morning after I snapped my top row of teeth and I'm full of sadness, wishing that I'd never allowed it to happen, before I realise I was dreaming. It's like the only time that I truly feel regret and the feeling is unbearable.

I never used to have this dream. Not before all the moves and eats and all the madness. Before finding out that sticking a gun in the belly is mad scary, more scary than sticking it to a man's head even. Before the moves with the clamping and ripping ice and popping Rollys and Cartiers. Before all the kicking off doors and running up in yards you'd never seen the inside of. Before the outlaw tattoos and the diamond teeth. Before knowing to wash gunshot residue out of your ears with petrol. Before finding out that when someone gets shanked or shot in the belly, you might just smell shit if their intestine's been punctured. Before learning about true friends and snakes and the two being one and the same. Before knowing that Anyone Can Get It. Before a thick woollen bally for the winter and a thin cotton one for the summer. Before swimming down to the bottom and realising you've run out of breath. Before the dreams about broken teeth. Before all that was the first ever move, the first ever eat, the first time.

I was thirteen, it was half term and I'd gone to see this brer I'd made friends with at private school called Henry. His parents were mad rich, they had one of them big yards in Barnes where we could go upstairs to a room which he called the games room, with a big TV in it and a PlayStation, and we could get forgotten up there and play games all day long. There was a fridge downstairs stocked with cans of Dr Pepper and bottles of Snapple – the drinks fridge he called it, separate from the normal fridge full of food – and I'd never seen anything like that. To me it was some proper *MTV Cribs* shit where you'd see rappers showing off their kitchens and swimming pools and alladat. I made myself sick from drinking five cans of Dr Pepper back to back and eating a jar full of M&M's and packets of Monster Munch. Then we ordered Domino's and I stuffed myself with pizza and didn't want to go home.

It was late afternoon when I got back to Royal Oak station. I walked over the rusty green bridge, tagged up with spray paint, and as I crossed the road after the bridge, I saw a group of mandem about my age – six of them – walking towards me. I was only one street away from home. They blocked me as I was about to pass them, they'd all pulled their hoods up and they surrounded me against this wall on the corner of the road and said oi rudeboy, hear what. They pulled out shanks and one of them held his borer to my throat, the point pressing into my neck hard enough that I didn't want to move in case it cut me and he said you see this blade blood, you see this blade? This is gonna go into your throat if you try lying you get me. I tried to look at the blade without moving my head. They started asking me where you from blood? And when I hesitated they said run your p's, what you got on you? You got a phone? I didn't know what to say. I wanted to lie and say I've got nothing but I also didn't want to lie just to protect myself. I thought I don't wanna get poked up and I choked on my words.

I was vexed with myself coz my voice trembled and all I could say was allow me, as they tapped my pockets. I had about £12 which my father had given me because he knew I was going to spend the day with a friend from school and he didn't want me to feel left out if there was something for us to spend money on. I never got pocket money usually. So they took all the coins out of my pockets and just at that moment a group of primary school children with four teachers walked past. The teachers could see what was going on. The brers never even put their shanks down or tried to hide them. I looked at the teachers as they walked past. I wanted to say help but I thought that when they saw the knife getting held to my throat they'd step in and do something. But they didn't. They looked at me, then looked away and walked past, fussing over all the little children in fluorescent vests. The brers who were yacking me looked away for a second. I burst to the side and sprinted round the corner. I remember I was wearing white jeans and my legs felt long and thin like sticks that could snap at any second and I jumped over a wall into the front garden of some random house and just crouched in the bushes, heart beating like mad, hating myself for feeling shook, for having been a victim, for not banging that brer in the face.

When I got home, my father asked if I had any change from the money he'd given me. At first I said that I'd gone out to Pizza Hut and spent it. But later I told him and my mother that I'd just been robbed and had knives held to me and everything. My father clicked his tongue and said nothing and my mother said why didn't you run away? You must always run away, and that hurt me more than anything. It was the ultimate humiliation. As if they were telling me that I was from a family of victims, a family of people who run away. I realised that no one was gonna tell me how to stand up for myself and I'd have to work it out alone. Maybe it was because they'd come to this country for a better life. But the problem for me was that the only reality I had was this one. So I promised myself that I'd never be a victim ever again, that I'd never just allow someone to take my shit from me, that I'd never run away like a pussy, that I'd never allow anyone to make me feel like nothing, to make me feel frozen like I had no power. I felt that I understood something that no one was ever gonna tell me: that I was alone in this world and no one had my back and if I was ever gonna make it, I better start being ruthless. I better start being coldhearted. I better start rolling with a shank on me every day coz next time I'm gonna stab man up. I better start— I went to my room and then my father called upstairs, dinner will be ready in five minutes. I came downstairs and my mother said have you washed your hands and I said yes, all annoyed with her and when I sat down to eat I felt like we didn't even know each other properly and I didn't say anything for the whole meal.

Then came the first eat. I was fourteen. It was about one in the morning. The flat was asleep and I put on black jeans, a black Nike Athletic hoodie and tiptoed past my parents' bedroom, listening to the snores and praying to myself that they'd continue. When I got downstairs, I went into the kitchen and got a carving knife out of the drawer next to the sink. I remember the moon coming into the kitchen but it stayed there while I went into the hallway, slipped my trainers on and crept out of the flat. I left the door on the latch, went downstairs and waited outside the entrance to the building. I stuck some takeaway menus that I found in the entrance hall along the doorframe, so that it didn't close behind me. There was a high wall leading from the door to the street so anyone walking by wouldn't be able to see the doorstep until they walked right past. I was lurking.

A couple came past and I jumped out of the shadows with my hood pulled over my head and the kitchen knife pointed at them. Give me your fucking wallet now. The woman screamed and ran into the road and the man shouted help as he followed her. There was another man walking by on the other side of the road. He stopped and shouted you mother-fucker and then he crossed into the road where the couple were standing, the woman holding on to the man as if the wind might blow her away, and I stepped back into the shadows, pushed the door open, kicked the Chinese menus out of the doorframe and closed the door. I raced upstairs, shut the flat door, crept into the kitchen, replaced the knife and went back to my room. I opened the window quietly, climbed out onto the balcony and down below I saw two police cars and a bully van parked in the middle of the road, blue lights scattering all over buildings and cars, dancing with shadows. Some feds were standing in the road talking to the couple I'd jumped out on, while others were checking the basements of our building and the buildings next to us.

The next morning, I got dressed for school, took a smaller kitchen knife than the one I'd grabbed the previous night and went out. But I didn't turn left to go to the tube station, I turned right and went up the road. As I got to the corner I saw a woman coming towards me. I walked up to her, pulled the knife out of my pocket and put the point to her throat. It was a sunny morning, no one was around and she whispered please no and gave me her phone. I turned around and ran to the tube station, jumped on the train and went to school. It was a private school, I was only there thanks to financial assistance based on my academic and musical abilities, as well as the sacrifices of my parents, and most of the boys there were from mad rich families so they all had the latest phones. When I got there, one of my friends said oh you finally got a phone yeah?

I was thirteen when I saw my first stabbing. It was at Stowe Youth Club where I always went after school to MC. We'd just finished a set and these brers from Coldhearted Crew tried to rob the DJ for his records. When he didn't let off, they shanked him twice in his arse and leg and took his record bag. After the third stabbing I saw there, I stopped getting mad adrenaline rushes whenever it happened and I'd watch the youth workers pulling whoever was getting rushed to safety, leaving bloody smudges all down the floor.

In the end, I got expelled from the private school for too much fuckery before I even got round to doing my GCSEs. I ended up going to this special college for youts who'd all been expelled or excluded from school. First time I held a gun I hadn't even turned sixteen. I went to Hyde Park with my boy from the college who brought the strap for me coz I had beef with some next youts and we tested it out in one of those avenues lined with bushes and trees near the Albert Memorial. It wasn't a little bang like in the movies, but a mighty BAOWww that ripped through the air and made all these birds rush out of the trees into the sky. I had no idea that there were so many birds hidden in there.

In places like South Killy it starts off with the olders sending you out to get food. I mean food food to eat, not buj n work and all dat. They send you to Harlesden to pick up jerk chicken and rice n peas, taking the piss with you on some sendout ting.

But the youngers do it because what else is there to do? It's all pressures and expectations and the greed to get to the levels that you see the olders on. You can't escape it either. You come home from school and you walk past it all. And the more anyone tells you to avoid it, the more you're drawn to it. So the youngers do what the olders tell them and then they start delivering packages and holding a next man's strap under their bed and they feel important, they feel more than just the average person coz let's be real, who wants to be an average person? After a while, the olders send you out to go and do shootings and alladat and one day you wake up and decide that since you've already put in work for your older, the next time he tells you to go and do suttin for him, you're gonna say fuck dat. You've got the strap, you know how to buss it and on top of that you're sick of being used by others to do their dirt. And before you know it you've changed beyond your own recognition of your-self and you're ready to beat it off on anyone who tries to treat you like some eedyat lickle yout.

This is what my bredrin Smurf – Uncle T's nephew – tells me as we sit in Uncle T's living room bunning zoots, after I've just told him about the first ever eat I did when I was four-teen. He blows out smoke and some game show on the TV chatters away. That's £6,000 you can add to your total, says the host. Audience cheers. Do you want to stick with that or go for the higher offer?

Smurf continues slow and quiet, full of a seriousness that muffles the sound effects and the cheering crowd and presenter.

Then what happens is they get so deep in this ting that they don't even realise time is passing them by, and then you get these brers who do too much and they lose their mind. Like they can't keep taking the constant pressure of watching their backs every day, turning their mind to do wickedness every day, the only way they can sleep is to bun and juice till they frass out and hope they don't dream coz they don't know what's gonna come for them in their dreams. That's why bare killers end up smoking b. The only way they can stop seeing the face of the man they've licked down is to smoke buj fam. Or at least when they're on the buj, they don't feel afraid when they see the man they've killed asking them why did you do it? And before you know it, this brer who used to be a top badman in the ends – had all the gyaldem on his dick, loving him off, and no one could step to him, had all the ice and the Gucci and brand new whips – before you know it, that brer's turned into a nitty smoking food on the block. And when it comes to them olders, the youngers don't even remember who they was. No one even cares who they was. I'm telling you fam. That's why I say you cannot win.

I say but fam, I know couple man who won, certain man who made bare p's shotting and managed to escape it all and they're doing well now.

Brudda, you think they won but they ain't won. I'm telling you, he says. They *will* lose. Doesn't matter how. I always remember people saying fuck dat Smurf, what you talking bout? Look at myman. He come out the game, he's got his yard, he's got his business, he don't even touch food or straps no more. Cool. Myman was dead a year later. Then they might mention a next man. Similar. Had everyting sorted. Came out the game. Then he gets locked up for suttin else. Coz at the end of the day, you cannot fucking win. This is what I've come to realise fam. It's bad blessing.

I hear you, I say, and on top of dat everyone's disturbed by this shit. Bare man are seriously disturbed from living this road life.

306

Smurf nods and draws his zoot like he don't wanna pause to breathe. He is short and the sofa he's sitting on looks like it could do with another person. When he blows smoke out he does it slowly and watches it, eyes narrow, concentrating on its journey, as if he's sending a message to somewhere on its back.

Even me fam, I say and stop to catch a cough in my throat as the punk burns my lungs. Certain times I find it hard to do normal shit like going to family gatherings and being around people, coz it's like they don't have the same frame of reference to the world that I do, you know dem ones brudda? And then say I'm in Central or Sloane Square or suttin. I'll walk past some rich people's yard and look through the window and see a man and woman sitting on the edge of their bed, watching TV. And as I walk past, I see there's another room and the window's open and it's the next room along from where them people are jamming and I'm like rah, there's no camera right here, I could jump over these railings, go in through the window – obviously I'd have to bally up and put gloves on n dat – but I could run up in there, stick it on them, take their shit, get them to open the safe or whatever. Like that's a proper instinctive— I mean it's not like fantasising about it. Everyone can fantasise about shit. I could fantasise about being a millionaire and having some sick house of my own or being famous or some shit. Fuck it I could fantasise about flying if I wanted to. But with this I'm not fantasising, I'm actually working out how to do it. Going through all the steps. Like I'd make sure to gunbuck the man before I even tell them what I want, or if I ain't got a strap I'm thinking about where to shank him so he don't bleed to death but he knows I'm serious. It's like whenever I walk past jewellery shops I start thinking how thick is the glass? Where are the cameras? How many people are in the shop? How many security guards?

Smurf says that mentality's fucked fam. It's like you've been poisoned. And it's not just the mandem. You have these gyal who won't care that you're living on the edge, even when the shit you're doing is not normal. Like say you go on a move, these kinda chicks will say make sure you get me some jewellery or make sure you come back with suttin for me. But the worst ting about all this shit Snoopz, is that even after all that madness, a man won't feel satisfied. It's never good enough, like you still feel you ain't gone far enough. It don't matter if you've duppied man or you've robbed bare man or whatever. You always need to do more but you don't even realise how nuttin fulfills you coz you're empty all the time and there's this hole in you that can't be filled.

What Smurf and I don't talk about is the constant tensing up, body getting ready for beef to pop off, ready for a screwface from someone to turn into more than it is. Because if you try and get out of this life, that's when it gets worse. I mean just when you think it can't get more peak, the second you relax, you drop your guard and then say you're out shopping in Oxford Street with your girl or suttin and you run into some ops who recognise you coz you used to roll with so-and-so or you were in this gang or whatever, straight away it's on. Right there and then, in a crowd of shoppers and tourists, man are backing out the Rambo knives to soak you up. No one gives a shit if you've changed, if you're not about dat life any more, if you've left it all behind. And if you're dumb enough to say some shit like that when you run into enemies, the only thing it'll mean to them is that you've become weak now, that they've got nuttin to fear in terms of retaliation, and that just feeds them with more motivation to do you suttin right there and then. Easy stripes to earn.

Or sometimes, when you're on your own and you're in a part of the city where you don't feel totally secure, you'll see a bag of mandem coming down the road towards you or jamming on the corner ahead, and you can't turn around or cross the road coz that would just show that you're shook and you're not shook, you're not shook you tell yourself, you just have to walk through and be ready. And before you even walk past you've prepared for the worst, your body floods with adrenaline, the backs of your thighs feel like they're gonna melt, your belly floats into your chest and you start planning what you're gonna do. You start clocking if there's anything you can grab and use as a weapon – if you're not rolling with one already – you prepare yourself for sudden violence.

Imagine every day being full of these moments. Most of the time nothing happens, but your body and your mind keeps going through these extreme cycles of preparedness and it makes you feel mad exhausted, mad stressed, and you bun more and more cro to try and feel calm, but really it just makes you more and more parro and your imagination runs wild.

Time is a strange land to walk through. A few months of this mad life, a year, two years, can seem like forever. As if things will never change. Thinking we're the ones who won't be followed by a new generation that will eventually take over, as if nothing could ever come after us. As if we're final and the world will end with us. We've taken over from the previous generation of badman and now this moment is ours forever. But this moment is just a whisper in the dark that everyone forgets when the new day comes.

Sometimes I'm not sure who I am any more. There's all these masks we wear that confuse us. It's like looking in a mirror and if you've worn a mask for too long, you convince yourself that it's your real face you're looking at. And then you can't even recognise yourself no more. Even the truest parts of yourself can be hidden by lies. It's like morality and belief; imagining that it's this real natural thing that exists in you and always has, when in reality you've been programmed from day dot – from when you were born – to have this differentiation between good and bad.

I stumble out of my thoughts and look at Smurf who is staring at the TV without watching it. The screen shudders blue in the twilight of the front room. Indistinct quiz-show banter between host and contestant continues – Warner Brothers cartoons always ended with the phrase that's all what? Is it A: Folks, B: Friends, or C: Kids?

But it can't drown out the silence in the room, swelling up in the space between us, as if we've just gone too deep, revealing too much to each other – to ourselves even – forcing us to consider things we've tried to avoid. If you don't give it words it doesn't become a reality, but it's too late now. I look at Smurf. Rico was one of his tightest bredrins. The other day Smurf told me he seen the brer who duppied Rico on Harrow Road. We all know who done it but ain't no one snitching. Imagine that. Bumping into your bredrin's killer and not being able to do anything. I could see that Smurf was itching to go and do a madness.

He's recently started doing this personal trainer ting, even though he used to be one of those brers who never left his yard without a mash on him. Used to be a one-man army forreal. He wouldn't pet to buss his gun and do some dirt all on his ones like a real g. But now he's tryna be on a positive tip, tryna set an example for his youts and for the younger generation – whatever that means. But in this moment, all I can see are three gold chains hanging from his neck, and as he blows smoke out of his mouth I catch the glint of an iced-out tooth. I swear he's rocking more chains now than he used to when he was on road. He told me earlier that since he's started doing this personal trainer ting, whenever a client pays him by card, he goes to the ATM straight after the session, withdraws the money, takes it home and puts it in a shoebox. At least he's into his healthy eating ting though, buying fresh coconuts and kale and broccoli and making smoothies.

One morning I go with Dario to SK to get a draw from Chris on Princess Road coz Uncle T doesn't have anything and he's waiting to reload. A dirty mattress leans against a wall next to the street sign. I see couple mandem jamming on doorsteps who I don't know and who don't know me and I keep it moving. It feels like a lifetime ago since we all had Bimz's block on smash, spending our days in and out of his yard. I see one mixed-race brer up ahead, standing in the middle of the pavement as he talks to two women. He looks at me for a second and turns back to one of the women without making any space for me and Dario. The women are on either side of the pavement and he is in the middle. I'm thinking nah, this brer's tryna boy man off like we should step off the pavement or say excuse me like some dickheads. I walk past and his shoulder bounces into my shoulder, but I walk through him. As I go up the steps to Chris's door I turn and see him watching me, smiling. He doesn't look away.

When I get the draw inside I say to Dario, blood did you see how that brer was moving? Blatantly saw man and didn't even try make the slightest space for us to walk past?

Dario says I know Snoopz I know, he's some eedyat, just 'low him anyway.

We leave Chris's yard. The brer clocks me again and this time he turns around and plants himself in the middle of the pavement with his arms crossed and his legs apart. I'm thinking this dickhead. Man's tryna g check me forreal. I'm gonna have to see what he's really on. There's no space for me to walk past, so this time I proper barge him up and as we carry on down the street I hear him shout fucking prick.

I turn around. What? Dafuck are you saying blood?

He says whatdafuck is wrong with you? Why you barging me for? Can't you see man standing here or suttin?

I walk up to him and as I get close to him he starts smiling and he pushes me in my chest. The next thing I know, I can hear him screaming, my eyes are full of a red glow and nothing else, like when you look at the sun with your eyes closed, and I realise I've got his ear between my teeth. I'm about to rip it off. But when I hear the way he's screaming, I let go coz I know he ain't built for this. I don't remember getting my teeth round his ear in the first place. I grips him up and with one hand I dip into my pocket, get my keys in between my knuckles and start sparking him in the top of his head. He falls over one little wall in front of someone's yard and pulls me over with him. Dario comes round the wall and separates us and I get to my feet. He stands up, takes his T-shirt off and puts it to his head, little black rivers of blood coming down through his hair. He pants and stares at me. I swear he's still smiling.

I walk off with Dario and Dario says you didn't need to do dat Snoopz, there was no need.

I go did I fuck him up though?

Dario kisses his teeth and goes obviously bruv, but you didn't need to.

And I go but did I really fuck him up though?

I feel shit for the rest of the day coz I keep thinking how I didn't do enough damage to that brer.

REGENERATION

YEARS LATER, I go to South Kilburn to buy a draw from Uncle T and I see the blocks getting knocked down.

It is April. I moved to south London three years back and started shotting coke on weekends to support myself while trying to work out what to do with my life, so I haven't been to SK in time.

When I get to South Kilburn I see what's left of Bronte House and Fielding House, two of the eighteen-floor blocks that once towered over the estate, which are now getting demolished. They are fenced off with corrugated metal, advertising some construction company: New Homes Coming Soon in big black letters and lots of hopeful computer graphics of apartment complexes lined with trees and people holding their children's hands as they stroll through on a sunny day – always a sunny day in those computer projections – and behind the corrugated metal walls the shattered blocks with their entrails hanging out, hearts torn out, broken ribs. The sky pours in around them. The rest of the estate; corroded by time and silence, and sprouting up on its edges are new builds. Glass and metal, flat and clean with that boredom of newness; neat courtyards, newly planted trees and shrubbery looking plastic.

I stare up and see the bare interiors of flats as cranes demolish the blocks bit by bit, floor after floor. It makes me think how from now on, anything that happened in those blocks will only ever exist in the distance of memories and other people's stories. Soon there won't be anything physical left, like when you see somewhere you used to live or hang around and you say that's the block where so-and-so lived or where this and that happened, and because the building still stands, it's like those people and incidents are still alive in some way, there's still a physical trace, a memorial. But here it's like the traces of lives and moments are getting erased, turned into dust and broken concrete, removed and then disposed of. In the future no one will even know that there was a Bronte House and a Fielding House in South Kilburn. It will be as if these towers never existed and who will even care about the lives and stories that took place in the flats, corridors, lifts and stairwells?

Some time later I'm on the tube, reading the *Evening Standard* and I see this police appeal which says: *Police have released an image of a man thought to be responsible for an armed crime wave across south London. Betting shops and banks have been targeted in the last month, with officers believing the same man is behind all 13 raids. In each robbery he walks up to the counter and points what appears to be a black, semiautomatic pistol at cashiers before demanding money and in some cases he threatened to shoot staff. Anyone with information is asked to contact Crimestoppers anonymously.* Beneath this is an image of a CCTV still from one of the robberies. It is Gotti. He doesn't even look any different from all those years ago. Caught slipping by CCTV as he cut out of a bookie and pulled off the bandanna covering his face too early. He must have clocked as well, coz he's staring right into the camera, his eyes full of that faraway darkness you'd get lost in if you tried looking for something.

It's the first time I've seen him in seven years and I feel that pinch in my gut, missing our days of hunger, nights of eats. But seeing this now, it strikes me that while I've been tryna think of a way to claw my way out of this world, Gotti swam to the bottom and never went back up for breath, just stayed there. Maybe the deeper he got, the more he forgot about finding a way out. No one tells you that when you're known for being a certain way, there's not just the pressure to live up to your reputation, but you also absorb the power of it and act upon it, fuelled by it, reinforcing and furthering it, until what's really holding you back from getting out of this greazy life is yourself.

I put the paper down and look around the carriage thinking how mad it is that although we're all human beings sharing the same space, we know nothing about each other and we never will. We're just bodies, just muscle and blood, same way the blocks are just concrete and windows, and yet what we can't see is all the life, all the things that are going on, within. And when we look at another human whose life is unconnected to our own, we sense nothing of the soul inside them at all. Like these people sitting next to me; they'll never know how I used to eat people, shank people, do all this craziness, how I love listening to trap music and Chopin piano waltzes and I shot coke and write love letters to this girl I met calling her my whirlwind. For a moment I catch myself wishing I could put on the bally and gloves and get the strap and go and do some eats and feel my heart between my teeth beating so hard that

315

I have to bite into it so I can swallow. But there's no one to do it with now and I force the feeling back down like when you're on the verge of throwing up, but with all your body focused into the strain of the effort, you manage to force the vomit down while no one notices.

When I get off the tube at Kilburn Park, Mazey bells me and when I pick up he says blood have you seen the *Evening Standard* today and I say Gotti, and he says I know it's a mad ting innit. Thirteen moves fam, and then I say brudda I wish I'd been there, and Mazey laughs and says you man woulda been unstoppable.

Couple years later, I stop shotting coke when Capo gets shift. Capo's been dropping me some banging bits of white on the regs and I don't trust anyone else to be my plug. So when feds run up on him in his flat one evening and catch him while he's in the middle of bagging up the soft and then they find big bits of cro and a bag of bullets in the yard, I just know that it's time to stop. Or at least to take a break. Anyway, my mother recently found a whole bunch of capsules full of coke and stacks of tens and twenties in my sock drawer at home – I know what you're doing Gabriel, I went to put some socks that I'd washed in your sock drawer. Unblinking stare. But it's not as tense as it used to be. It's like my life has worn down her thresholds over the years, it doesn't shock her really, although I can see she's doing her best to be shocked. I say well I ain't got a job and I gotta eat somehow and she says so do something proper with your life before it's too late.

The thing is my life has brought her into certain realities that she can't change, that she's had to accept even though she might not want to. Just like it's become normal to me that most of my bredrins have been to pen and certainly everyone I'm friends with has been arrested at some point. And it's normal that we've all seen at least a couple of stabbings in real life, it's normal that everyone's known people who died way too young, who died violently. That's just how it is. Anyway, stupid of me to be stashing food and p's in my parents' yard. I'm not living in South for now coz I've been arguing with my girl – love ain't easy forreal – but at least she's burning sage and praying to her ancestral spirits. She always tells me she lives in hope. But I can't be living at my mum's like some wasteman, especially when I've stacked p's by trapping hard. Need to find somewhere else to stay and last time I checked, Uncle T's still got that spare room. Not long after Capo gets sentenced to five years, I arrange to move back into my old room in Blake Court.

I pack some garms, grab some books and then I have breakfast with Mama and Tata. When we finish breakfast, Mama is talking about how one of her friends thinks everything is a joke and how she can't stand people being like that and my father laughs and she says yes laugh, laugh, that's what you always do, I don't know what there is for you to laugh about and I say I don't know what there is for you to be so sour about. She says no one needs your comments, with her eyes all sharp. No one needs your comments either, I say. Don't talk to me until you've eaten your breakfast, she says. I'll talk to you whenever I want, I say and she says no you won't and I say yes I will, I'll say what I want and I'll do what I want, you can't control me. And she says one phone call, one phone call and I'll show you and I'm thinking here we go again, whatdafuck is she on about? The only phone call she could be talking about is calling the feds on me. I say whatever, you can't do anything, I'll do what I want just like I've always done and she says no you won't, there'll come a time when I show you how you can't and I say no, you won't ever show me fuck all, you've been tryna control me since I was a child and it never worked and it never will. She says are you threatening me? I say threatening you? How am I threatening you? I'm simply telling you that you won't ever stop me from doing whatever I want. She turns to my father and says he's threatening me and my father says to me just stop shouting.

I can't take how they act like if I shout it's unnatural, it's wild, it's crazy, as if people don't shout and get angry, as if it's not a normal human emotion. This is how I've always been — do they still not realise that there was nothing anyone could ever do to stop all of this, to stop everything that happened? Never in a million years could they have imagined having a son like me. But it happened.

Later, I've packed all my bags and I'm sitting at the kitchen table having a glass of water before I go. There's still that framed drawing on the wall of the crocodile approaching the rabbit and it's like we all know the crocodile's gonna eat the rabbit but no one's gonna stop it, the artist wouldn't draw it another way coz that's life — ah so it go as Uncle T would say — and my father comes into the kitchen and sits down at the table opposite me. He's survived a quadruple heart bypass and cancer in the last five years, he's not as big as he used to be and he moves more gentle now like he's carrying something fragile which he can't drop, coz if it breaks, no one will be able to fix it.

He leans forward and says I must tell you Gabriel. Real life it's only contact between people and we must find a way because life is not easy. You are angry with all your lovers, you are angry with all your friends, you are angry with your mother, with your brother, sisters — of course you haven't sisters but you are . . . anger is a part of humanity.

318

Yeah exactly, I say.

But to find a way not to shout, to be a more − of course this is need training. I am now clever man because I had five years of depression so I done generally nothing. No really, because I was out of life, I feel a bit like what this name of, you know this man whom Jesus Christ take him from his death?

Lazarus, I say.

Oh exactly, Lazarus. I am little bit like Lazarus, of course if you read Lazarus you know when Jesus Christ returning him to the life, Lazarus was little bit smelly, his body was start to decomposing, so I am in better situation, but you realise life is too short for all this anger, all the time these violent feelings. You know, life is brutal.

My mother comes downstairs. I don't say anything, I just hug her and she holds on to me, laughs a bit to herself, almost sad like, and says I know you want to be good.

I say I love you Mama.

She leans back to look at me and says oh that's a new one.

Then she hugs me back and tells me that when I was born I was so small I could fit in the palm of her hand. She walks over to the fridge and gets a box of Ferrero Rocher chocolates out and says do you like these?

I say yeah, why not.

She says so let me give you one, so that your last memory of your mother is something sweet, so you can't say I'm not a good mother.

I laugh and say you've always been a good mother. I take the chocolate from her and she gives me three more.

Less than a week before I moved back to South Kilburn, a twenty-year-old girl called Mohanna Abdhou got shot and killed right in front of Uncle T's block. She was standing with her bredrins in front of Dickens House right next to the playground, it was a warm Friday evening at the end of May and bare little youts were playing in the playground as summer crept in. Two brers on pedal bikes rode into the estate and the first thing everyone probably noticed was that they had ballys over their faces and hoods pulled up and black puffer jackets and gloves on, even though it was warm and everyone was out in sweatshirts and T-shirts. Maybe Mohanna was just catching jokes with her bredrins before going home to her family after a day of working at the shop where she had a job, or maybe she was chatting to some brer from SK who she liked – maybe some brer was even chirpsing her, tryna get her number, telling her friends oi your bredrin's kinda peng still, what's she saying? Laughter and sun and that freshness in the air when summer's coming and even the concrete towers look okay when sunlight spills gold all over them. But then the brers on bikes slowed down in front of the group jamming next to Dickens House and one of them pulled out a strap and fired a shot. The heat of the day shattered. Everyone scattered. He fired three more shots and then the two brers on bikes pedalled out of the estate, down Malvern Road, cameras catching them at every moment and Mohanna dropped to the ground at the foot of the block and the children in the playground screamed and ran and all the SK brers who were there with her and her friends ducked out long time, they started running as soon as they saw the brer in the bally pulling out a strap – the mandem who were blatantly the intended targets probably quicker to run coz they were prepared for some shit like this – and Mohanna lay on the ground, bleeding from her belly. Half an hour later she died, surrounded by paramedics and armed police and some of her bredrins who came back. It's mad coz it's basically exactly the same spot where Chicken got shot in the head by Bugz Bunny after jumping off his balcony.

When I move in to Uncle T's there's a small pile of withered flowers at the spot where Mohanna died, and stuck in the door of the shop, just across from Uncle T's block, a murder poster with her face on it. Because round here some things never change never change never change.

It was probably some Mozart youts or some KG youts, tryna score points by licking down some SK brers, because that beef just never stops, although it used to be much worse. There were way more shootings here back in the day and on a real level, when all the balconies were full of mandem posted up, those two youts could never have just rode their bikes into the estate without getting challenged. Mandem woulda been shooting back forreal. So although it's bad, it's nothing like it once was.

When I walk through now I don't see anyone I recognise and no one recognises me. Walking past people on Malvern Road, it's as if they barely notice my existence. On a real I barely see anyone at all. It's as if everyone is hiding indoors and the only sign of life is the constant accumulation of rubbish next to the rubbish chutes, right under the sign that says STRICTLY NO REFUSE TO BE LEFT IN THIS AREA. Black bin bags, bursting with rotten food and nappies and plastic wrappers and fuck knows what else, piled next to broken chairs, old TVs, metal poles and wooden boards; the driftwood of hidden lives in these blocks. The only other thing that tells you there are still people, families, heartbeats within these blocks, is when night yawns over the place, submerging the buildings in a gloom that only gets darker and darker, and then you see lights in windows. But the strange thing is that I've never seen a light go on, no matter how many times I've stared out of my window as night falls, it's like everything happens in secret. I've never seen anything as lonely as those windows, looking as if someone left the lights on before abandoning their home.

Sometimes I see some of the new mandem on one of the balconies, bunning zoots and chatting shit, but in general, silence runs the blocks now, silence is posted up on the balconies and lurking on the dirty staircases and in the pissy stairwells. The lift in Blake Court still breaks down and some of the lights on the stairs are still broken and the walls are even more stained and peeling. But I never bump into any nittys or mandem lurking on the stairwells with straps poking through their jeans, although one time I come down the stairs one morning and I see a machete stashed on a little ledge just above the rubbish chute like it was put there to be readily available at a moment's notice. The walls are scratched up, paint coming off in huge sections revealing pink concrete beneath, and often one of the lights on the staircase doesn't work so sections of stairs sit in darkness. Someone has written Fuck Da Feds in blue marker on the ceiling of a stairwell. And there's no one on D-block no more, no one posted up or anything, like all you ever see now at night are the empty balconies and rows of doors and low yellow lights soaking the concrete in loneliness. Some of the flats are even boarded up now coz soon, all the blocks are gonna get knocked down to make way for new homes.

So I'm back at Uncle T's, in the same room I lived in for two years when I was eighteen. There's still not enough hot water every day but there's one of those plastic shower hoses you attach to the taps on the bath, so instead of the bucket baths I used to have, it's showers. Uncle T rarely cooks now, rarely ever makes curry goat or stewed chicken and usually it's fried eggs and bacon that make the corridors smell of oil and burnt grease. He's always saying I'm just gonna lie down to rest me knee, and then I hear him snoring, coughing and choking in his sleep. When he gets up, he goes into the kitchen to sit on his dusty black office chair and he smokes cigarette after cigarette, shouting at the TV which never answers him back. Then it's night and he goes to lie down again, and soon he falls asleep. Sometimes I wake up at two or three in the morning and I can hear him in the kitchen, rolling about on that office chair with the TV bubbling away and the smell of cigarette smoke drifting into my room, turning the air bitter and harsh. The yard is never as noisy as it used to be. More times the only noise in the flat is the TV in the kitchen and the TV in Uncle T's bedroom and the TV downstairs in the music room. They're always on, even though the only person watching TV in the whole flat is Uncle T. At night he sleeps with his TV on, the whole night through, game shows chatting away, bursts of clapping, explosions and car chases, canned laughter from American sitcoms in the early hours. His buzzer doesn't go off like it used to. Business isn't popping like it used to. Sometimes his door knocks and it takes him a few minutes to get down the stairs coz he can barely walk now. Then he sits downstairs, tryna catch his breath, smoking a cigarette before coming upstairs. Sometimes his oldschool bredrins pass through, but they rarely play the sound system, most of them just sit in the kitchen with Uncle T and bun couple zoots before going back to wherever home is.

One night I wake up and I can feel bassline pumping from downstairs. It's one of the first times I've heard the sound system in ages. The walls are vibrating. I check the time on my phone and it says 1.45 a.m. I sit up in bed, listening to roots bouncing up the stairs and through the walls, hoping that none of the neighbours are gonna knock his door and ask whatdafuck he thinks he's doing on a weekday blasting music after one in the morning. I listen to the whole set. At 2.30 a.m. it stops and my ears are filled with the cooling breeze of silence. Then I hear Uncle T come shuffling up the stairs, breathing heavy as he walks past my door to go into his bedroom. He turns the TV on, voices chattering through the wall, and after a few minutes I can hear his snoring. But I don't feel tired at all and I only fall asleep when the light behind my curtains starts casting a pale shade of morning blue onto the ceiling.

Taz, his eldest son who I used to move with, is in a care home, stuck on a ventilator, completely paralysed after collapsing and falling into a coma one day, which no one can explain coz only he knows what he did. The only thing he can move are his eyelids to blink. Man can't even breathe on his own. One day they have to do a special operation on him coz he's having complications with his digestive tract, which is connected to a tube in his stomach, and using a system of blinks which the nurses have developed with him, he communicates to the doctors that he doesn't want to be resuscitated if his heart stops on the operating table. He survives the operation and I go to see him. His face is all puffed up and raw-looking and there's a tube going into his nose and a big tube sticking out of his throat and a white bib spread out beneath it and there are other tubes going into his stomach and legs and machines beeping and his mouth is hanging open all crooked and dry and his lips are crusty and his hair has grown long and it's kinda picky. I lean over him and put my arms around him and whisper into his ear it's all right Taz, everything is all right, just forget everything, forget it all

324

and I hear the rasping of his breath through the tube in his throat and when I stand back up I see his whole face has gone bright red and he's crying. I go out into the hallway and his half-sister Ayesha is there and Ayesha sighs and says it's just the same old Taz, with a smile like she's remembering something distant. I say no it's not, it's not the same old Taz. It's never gonna be the same old Taz, and then I turn round and walk out of the building and wait for Uncle T and the others to finish the visit because I know I never want to see Taz again.

Uncle T's other son, Reuben, has been locked up for ten years now, seven of those in Broadmoor, and no one knows when he'll be out. Silence stretches out its tired limbs through the flat and Uncle T sits in the kitchen bunning a zoot and playing a game on his iPad while the ten o'clock news flickers on the TV. The Father of the Year Award in the living room is still there, but years of sunlight have bleached away the signatures of his children and his own name, so now it looks like an empty certificate waiting to be filled in. It's as if the details have been erased by the sun working hand in hand with time, as if the father of the year has been defeated by the removal of his sons from this world, both of them lost in a twilight of existing without being seen.

One morning I decide to walk to the shop in Precinct, just opposite where Bimz used to live, the shop where Mazey used to buy Skittles and I used to get cans of KA Black Grape and where we all used to cop chip n Rizla. But when I get to the precinct, the whole place is boarded up. I mean literally every window in every block is boarded up and there are no shops. Where the shops used to be is surrounded by walls of corrugated metal and there's not a person in sight. I walk up to Bimz's block, looking for something, past the boarded-up flats, and I climb the stairs we all used to sit on ten years ago. On the first-floor landing I find it. Scratched into the wooden door of a storage space next to one of the flat entrances is the name SNOOPZ. I touch the letters and for a moment I feel like I want to rip the door off and take it with me. Then I'm like whatdafuck am I even doing and I go down the stairs and start walking back to Uncle T's.

There is scaffolding all over Blake Court now. A giant ribcage with decaying concrete lungs and collapsed electric veins in rubber skin, throbbing within it. Just ahead of me, walking up to the entrance is a brer in an orange hi-vis boiler suit with a little girl. He's telling her to wait as he digs in his pocket looking for keys. I pull mine out with the fob ready and shake them so he hears the jingle and he turns to looks at me, his face cracking into a smile which floats into his eyes. I lean over, tap the fob to the metal pad, the door does its high-pitched whine as it opens while we stare at each other and I smile back but I can't place the face.

Wagwan my don, long time no see, he says and spuds me. I remember his face. For a second I can see a darkness that's buried much deeper in his eyes than the smile of recognition. I've seen it before. In Gotti. In others. It's one of the faces from the balcony back in the day. Wagwan my g, I say. We step into the block and wait for the lift. He's carrying a plastic bag heavy with shopping and the top of his boiler suit is tied around his waist; one of them orange boiler suits worn by people who work on the train tracks at night. The little girl next to him stares up at the red LED numbers counting down as the lift descends and she presses the lift button as if she might be able to make it come quicker. He says I knew I recognised you, where you been fam, I ain't seen you in years. Yeah I've been living out of ends still, I say, tryna remember a name, a conversation, something. Maybe he thinks I'm someone else but I

326

carry on anyway. Where you been staying? he asks. Fucking Brixton, I say and it's like I try and swallow my words back down as I look at the little girl who's bouncing her rucksack on her back, acting like she ain't noticing us. But at the same time I remember being a child, remember having adults talking around me thinking I wouldn't pick things up, when really my ears would do their best to tune into snatches of conversation that I could grab onto and find something to intrigue me, some mystery that I didn't quite understand, something new to learn like a bad word or an event that I wasn't supposed to know about. The brer says rahtid, Bricky yeah? So what you back now? I say yeah fam, I'm just doing my ting, I'm writing a book and living in SK but I'm not sure how long I'm gonna be here for. Swear down? he says. That's good to hear my don. I say do you remember Mazey and them man? He says fam, not gonna lie, my memory's kinda fucked you know. After I went on the run and they put me on *Crimewatch*, and then I done four years behind the door, I just started getting bare memory loss. I forgot bare names of mandem I used to know, it's kinda fucked still. I say I hear you brudda, while I try and remember who it actually is that I'm talking to and I look down at the little girl. She has a beautiful golden face like a riddle and her canerows are neat and perfect.

The lift doors open. We get in the lift and the little girl swats her father's hand away saying no I'm pressing it, and she presses 4. So what you been dealing wid? I say and he says I'm just working now, I'm not trapping no more and he grabs one of the orange sleeves of the boiler suit wrapped around his waist as if to show me. You need to give me your number still, he says. I hand him my phone and say put your digits in, I'm gonna WhatsApp you so you have my number. He puts the number in and saves it under Pimp SK. I still can't remember who he is. I say save my number and he says you're – and I say Snoopz – and he says oh yeah forreal, man like Snoopz and his smile grows, warm, unexpected, and he spuds me again.

We get out of the lift on the top floor, go through the magnetic doors to the landing and he says you gonna see Uncle T yeah? And I say that's where I live g. Swear down? I live right next door to you then, he says as we continue down the walkway and the black wires are still hanging from the ceiling and some of the lights on the balcony are still broken, flickering, horror film like. I say so you've been living here since you got outta pen? And he says nah g I was banned from South Killy for three years when I got out. Feds put me on raasclart ASBO innit, but now I'm living here at my mum's with my daughter and the twins. When they put me on *Crimewatch* for the straps I went on the run for like six months, it was mad still. As he's talking it's like I've dived into the deep end of a pool and everything outside is a muffled hum and I realise who he is. It's one of them FAC man who sold straps to the undercovers. He's one of the mandem they didn't get in the raid. I remember seeing him on *Crimewatch* when he was named as a fugitive and I keep thinking to myself how does he know me though – and then I can hear him saying but I'm done with all dat now, just working and tryna look after my kids. I say do you remember Gotti? And he says yeah I remember Gotti, he shot Curtis in the head innit and I'm like what, swear down? And he says yeah g, Gotti shot Curtis in the head couple years ago, but he didn't even killim and Curtis was looking for him for time. That brer was active still, and I say yeah I know, we used to do moves together and now myman's doing a ten for bare armed robberies on bookies and banks in South, and he says rah and his voice trails off.

He pulls his door keys out and I notice faded tattoos crawling down his bicep. Then he says if you're writing a book man could tell you some serious stories like you won't believe them you know. I had to get my twin sons off heroin when they were born coz their mother was smoking b all through her pregnancy and I had to take her to raasclart court to get them off her. She was crazy, fucking bare next man, sniffing coke, smoking b, fucking her sister's husband for four years – and every time he says fucking, he kind of rolls it under his lip, quieter than the rest of the words coming out his mouth, as if he thinks he can hide the word from his daughter. As if she won't catch it like that. She's turned away from us, looking across from the balcony at the little park that sits in the centre of the estate, overshadowed on either side by the two huge blocks that are still standing, and I say that's mad stress you got fam, I feel it for you. He says truss me fam, I got stories you won't even believe. Anyway shout me g, he says as he unlocks his door and I spud him and say good to see you after all these years g, even though I don't remember the last time we spoke to each other and I turn and go to Uncle T's door.

Yo yo yo I hear behind me, urgent, and I turn around and my neighbour says yo she's saying goodbye to you, and he's pointing towards his daughter and I see the little girl halfway through the door, sticking her head out and I see her smile for the first time, couple baby teeth missing in the bottom row, eyes full of brightness like pieces of the sun and she's waving at me. I hesitate, taken aback, and then I say bye-bye and wave back at her before turning around and unlocking the door to Uncle T's. I step in and an incredible sadness fills my stomach and I go upstairs and say to Uncle T yo pops I need to bill a zoot.

Night unfolds itself in the sky. I go to the shop to get a packet of M&M's and a bottle of Magnum. When I walk back, I look up and see the moon all big and white, spilling over Blake Court like it's washing the concrete down and for a second I think about how this is the same moon our ancestors have looked at, the same moon that's always been there, that every human has ever looked at while thinking about life and the world around them. As I get to the block I see silhouettes on the balcony as if there's mandem jamming there like back in the day and now the moon looks swollen and heavy like it's weighing down the net of clouds holding it up in the sky and I feel sick of this place. But when I get onto the balcony there's no one there, just one of the neighbours smoking a cigarette before going to bed.

Walking down the balcony I see a moth hovering beneath a light, not moving crazy, bouncing off the light like how I normally see them, just hovering beneath it. There's this thing I once heard about moths, how in reality they're tryna to get to the moon and how electric light always fools them so they end up crashing themselves against lightbulbs, burning their wings, tiring themselves out until they go into some confused sleep, attached to a wall or ceiling near the light, or until they die. But this one is different. It's as if the moth has realised it's never gonna make it to the moon and that this light, right here on the balcony of Blake Court, is good enough for it – as long as there's some light it will be good enough. As I open the door to let myself in I hear an argument breaking out somewhere between the blocks and as I close the door, I can hear one voice shouting loud and clear across the emptiness of the estate, shutuppussygogetyourgun. I go upstairs, feeling like something heavy is pressing down on my shoulders,

like the ghosts of all my memories and everyone who used to
be here left behind a scream and

Acknowledgements

To Mama and Tata, I hope it hurts less now.

To my brothers who've been down for me from day dot: Craig Narcisse, Sebastian Bennett, Tyrown Walker-Dawkins, Dario Carter, Travis Carter, Sahr Kaimakiende, Abimbola Mahoney, Ileki Scarlett, Elliott Balogun, Benjamin Oluonye, Khalid Alleyne, Ahmed Elfatih Elmardi. Our stories will live forever.

To Richard Adams for believing from the beginning. My big brother Kola Krauze, my twin Daniel Pióro. My cousins Daniel Slavinsky and Michael Slavinsky. My godfathers Adam Low and Patrick Wright. Janet and Cliff. To JB, W&N.

To Joel Golby for giving me the first eyes for my short stories. To Jacob Press, Claire Sparks, Jamilea Wisdom-Baako and Shani Gordon for all the discussions. To Nicholas Kaye for everything. To Harry Grayson, bussin cases.

Mad love to Anthony Bryan and Yassmin Foster. Family tree.

To my editor Helen Garnons-Williams and publicist Michelle Kane at 4th Estate, and my agent Jo Unwin for not being afraid.

To South Killy and all the ghosts. This is the echo, trapped on the page before it fades.

RIP Zeus, Tank, Jim Jones, Antoni Krauze, Mateusz Krauze. Free Rayla. Free the mandem.